Acclaim for
Flood

"Bold, compassionate, exhilarating, wrenching stuff."
—Niall Harrison, Internet Review of Science Fiction

"[*Flood*] shows flashes of the brilliance that continues to guarantee Baxter's place as one of the most inventive writers that science fiction has ever produced."   —SF Site

"A gripping near-future allegory of global warming. At times Baxter's narrative is as relentless as the inexorable waters, but that, you suspect, is his idea."   —*BBC Focus*

"*Flood* has an increasing sense of gravitas and even, by the end, a genuine weight of mourning. It's actually a novel that gains in power as it goes along, and as it becomes increasingly apparent that no miracle technofixes are in sight. A largely old-fashioned disaster tale presented with spectacle and efficient pacing."   —*Locus*

"A central narrative that's as relentless as a Panzer sweeping across lowland France in 1940. Amid huge events, the author still finds time for the intimate, the human-sized."
—*SFX Magazine*

"Covering events from the UK to the US, from Australia to Tibet, this is a comprehensive disaster novel that has a very global feel . . . an homage to human survivability . . . deserves to sit high on the blockbuster shelves."

—*SFFWorld*

continued . . .

FLOOD

Stephen Baxter

A ROC BOOK

ROC
Published by New American Library, a division of
Penguin Group (USA) Inc., 375 Hudson Street,
New York, New York 10014, USA
Penguin Group (Canada), 90 Eglinton Avenue East, Suite 700, Toronto,
Ontario M4P 2Y3, Canada (a division of Pearson Penguin Canada Inc.)
Penguin Books Ltd., 80 Strand, London WC2R 0RL, England
Penguin Ireland, 25 St. Stephen's Green, Dublin 2,
Ireland (a division of Penguin Books Ltd.)
Penguin Group (Australia), 250 Camberwell Road, Camberwell, Victoria 3124,
Australia (a division of Pearson Australia Group Pty. Ltd.)
Penguin Books India Pvt. Ltd., 11 Community Center, Panchsheel Park,
New Delhi - 110 017, India
Penguin Group (NZ), 67 Apollo Drive, Rosedale, North Shore 0632,
New Zealand (a division of Pearson New Zealand Ltd.)
Penguin Books (South Africa) (Pty.) Ltd., 24 Sturdee Avenue,
Rosebank, Johannesburg 2196, South Africa

Penguin Books Ltd., Registered Offices:
80 Strand, London WC2R 0RL, England

Published by Roc, an imprint of New American Library, a division of Penguin
Group (USA) Inc. Originally published in a Gollancz hardcover edition. For
information contact Gollancz, an imprint of the Orion Pubishing Group, Orion
House, 5 Upper St. Martin's Lane, London WC2H 9EA. Also previously published in a Roc hardcover edition.

First Roc Mass Market Printing, May 2010
10   9   8   7   6   5   4

For Mary Jane Shepherd née Ramsey
1930–2007

One

2016
Mean sea-level rise above 2010 datum: 1–5m

1

Every pothole and every crevice in the road was flooded. As the truck swerved through the streets of Barcelona the water sprayed up over Lily in her pallet under the chassis, stinking, oily stuff that worked its way under the parcel tape that covered her eyes and mouth. It was raining, too, a hard persistent rain that hammered on the truck's metal roof, adding to the engine's roar and the distant rattle of gunfire.

Another jolt slammed her body into the metal surface above. Grunting, her lips working against the tape over her mouth, she tried to wriggle, to relieve the pain in her shoulders and neck, from arms pulled behind her back. But each twist only shifted the ache somewhere else.

There was one other hostage under here with her, trussed up with tape and stuffed under the body of the truck, the pair of them head to foot like sardines. Lily thought it was Helen. Lily straightened her legs a bit, as gently as she could given the jolting. Her shoes had been taken away, and her bare toes touched hair. But Helen didn't respond. Lily had taken these rides seven or eight or nine times, and she'd learned that each of the others, Helen, Gary, John and Piers, had their own way of dealing with the experience. Helen's way was to just take whatever came. All that mattered to her was getting her baby back again at the end.

The truck juddered to a halt, its engine idling. Lily heard rapid speech, a jabbering in the Spanish she knew a little and the Catalan she understood not at all. One of the voices was Jaume's, the fat, sweating young man who grew nervous easily. He was probably negotiating their way through a toll barrier erected by some militia or other. Still the rain rattled on the truck walls and hissed on the tarmac, and spattered noisily on the clothes of the talking men.

Lily heard Jaume clamber hastily back into the truck. Gunfire spat. A round thudded into the body of the truck. The driver hit the gas and the truck shot away, jolting her shoulders again.

Wrenched around, the fleeing road surface just centimeters below, Lily wriggled like a fish in the silver tape, barely able to move, struggling against the pain and the rising panic. Helen didn't make a sound.

Lily was one of the longest held of the hostages.

Spain had already been collapsing five years ago, when Lily had first come here on assignment to the American embassy. The country was riven by its own unique separatist and ethnic tensions, spanning hundreds of years from the legacy of the Muslim invasion of the eighth century to the toxic divisions of the twentieth-century Civil War. Now all this was exacerbated by an influx of migrants from a desiccating Africa. The tipping point into disintegration was a right-wing coup against the monarchic government.

As the peacekeepers and aid charities labored, the great shapers of the global scene had moved in, aggressive corporations and financial institutions seeking profit in the remaking of a crumbling state, and on the other hand sponsors of grassroots anger stirring up revolt and terrorism. The splits fissured and overlapped, and Spain became a shattered, fractal state, a Lebanon of the west. By now, it seemed, even great cities like Barcelona had been taken over by armed factions.

If you were in the middle of it, the kaleidoscope of conflict and fragile alliances was bewildering and fast-moving. Lily had in fact been taken by a fundamentalist Muslim group, all those years ago, when her Chinook had been shot down. Now she was held by Christian extremists. She had been passed from hand to hand over the years like a parcel in a children's game. And still it went on. Here she was bundled up in tape and shoved under a truck, once again.

After a few more minutes the truck stopped again. Doors banged. Lily heard Jaume and the other guards moving around the truck, talking rapidly and softly.

Then she was grabbed by the ankles and hauled out from under the truck. She was dumped on her back on a hard, wet, lumpy surface—cobbles? It *hurt*. Rain battered down at her, soaking her belly through her T-shirt and her bare legs between the strips of tape. She could see nothing; she had no idea what was happening to Helen.

Then she was picked up by rough hands at her feet and armpits. She was lifted like a child, turned upside down and thrown over a shoulder, and an arm clamped over her bare legs. She was carried at a half-run. Whoever it was must be strong, Lupo or Severo. But the running jolted her again, yanking at arms still bound tightly behind her back, and her head lolled. The rain beat down on her back. Her feet were cold. She felt old, older than her forty years, weak in the grip of the man's strong youthfulness.

She was brought into an enclosed space, out of the rain. The texture of sounds changed, the running footsteps echoing. Somewhere big, roomy, empty? The guard tripped over something, jerking Lily, and he cursed in Catalan. He hurried on. Down steps now, into another echoing space, a cellar maybe. The steps were solid, like stone. Her head brushed some kind of lintel; she was lucky not to get hurt.

The guard, breathing hard, leaned forward and tipped her off. She braced, expecting to fall to the floor, but she clattered onto a chair, hard, wooden. A knife worked its way up her body, slitting the tape over her legs and torso, then behind her back to release her arms. She felt the blade's hard tip, but she wasn't cut. There was hot breath before her face, and she smelled the tang of cheap fatty food. It was Lupo, then; he liked his hamburgers.

When her arms were free she longed to stretch, to massage the aches out of her muscles. But she knew the routine. She held up her right arm and extended her right leg. The shackles closed tightly over her wrist and ankle, the metal cold and constricting. She gave an experimental tug. A chain rattled, only a short length of it, firmly anchored.

She was still blinded, her mouth still covered. But the guard moved away, and she heard the others elsewhere in the room, the guards' muttering conversation, grunts from the manhandled captives. She lifted her hands and pulled the tape down, freeing her mouth, and gasped at the air. Then she fiddled until she found the strip ends and pulled the tape away from the rest of her head. She kept her eyes clamped tight closed in case the tape dragged at her eyelids. The back of her head stung, but her shaved scalp didn't allow the tape much purchase. She dropped the bits of tape at her feet.

She was exhausted, every muscle aching. She looked around.

This wasn't the usual basement. It was like a vault, stone-walled, grimy, very old, cut in two by a row of twelve arches. The only light came from a dry-cell electric lantern sitting on the floor. There were carvings on the walls, images of some wretched woman suffering torments, and she glimpsed sarcophagi. A crypt? There was a smell of damp. Lily saw water stains on the walls, and a slow seeping from beneath the arches, and dusty puddles on the floor.

She was sitting on a hard, upright wooden chair, and was shackled to an antique-looking radiator. Three guards stood in the middle of the vault, Jaume and Lupo and Severo, their Armalites slung over their shoulders, smoking anxiously. Even in the dark Severo wore his sunglasses—in fact they were Lily's USAF-issue sunglasses, taken from her on the day her Chinook was downed, when everything she possessed was stripped from her.

And on more chairs, in a ring around the walls, sat the hostages in their T-shirts and shorts, their feet bare, strips of silver packing tape still clinging to them. Four of them besides herself: everybody was here, then; they were still together.

Helen Gray sat cradling Grace, her baby, returned to her after the transfer, the focus of her whole world. Twenty-five years old, tall, she was very pale under her freckles, very English-looking, fragile. Gary Boyle, the even younger American research scientist, sat bewildered, as if stunned. His fear and distress were always beguiling to the guards' bullying streak, and his arms and legs were purple from the bruises of his beatings.

Piers sat slumped in his chair, a grimy towel over his face. Piers Michaelmas was the senior British military officer who had been Lily's principal passenger in her Chinook. He had been working for a Western alliance trying to prop up the then-new military government. It was long months since he had retreated behind his towels and his blindfolds, and he rarely spoke.

And John Foreshaw, American civil contractor, tested

his shackles, as always edgy and impatient, at his most dangerous at moments of flux like this.

They all looked so similar, Lily thought, male and female, British and American, military and civilian, young and not so young, in their grimy underwear, pasty pale from the lack of daylight, their eyes hollow, their scalps and faces shaved bare. But they were all white, and all British or American, the categories that made them valuable as hostages.

There was nothing else here, none of the usual equipment of their long captivity, the foam mattresses and grimy blankets, the plastic bags they had to shit in, the old Coke bottles that held their drinking water and their piss: this time, nothing but themselves.

It was John who spoke first. "So where the fuck are we now?"

Jaume plucked his cigarette from his mouth and blew out a mouthful of barely inhaled smoke. Like the rest of these "Fathers of the Elect" he was no more than twenty, twenty-one years old, only half the age of John, Piers, Lily. "La Seu," Jaume said.

"Where? What did you say? Why can't you fuckers talk straight?" Once John had been fat; now his jowls hung from his cheeks and under his chin, as if emptied out.

Gary Boyle spoke up. "La Seu. That's the cathedral. Dedicated to Saint Eulalia. A thirteen-year-old martyr. I came here as a tourist, when I was a kid . . ." He glanced around. "My God. This is the crypt. We're chained up in a cathedral crypt!"

"It's just another shithole, is what it is," John said. "There's water pouring down the walls. We'll fucking drown, if we don't die of pneumonia first."

"Holy place," Jaume said easily, in his heavily accented English. "You with God here." He started walking toward a shadowed staircase, followed by the others.

John called after them, "Hey! Where are you going? Where are our mattresses? There's no food here. Not even a bag to shit in."

"God provide," said Jaume. "Has looked after saint since ninth century, will look after you."

John started dragging at his chains; they rattled noisily in the enclosed space. "You're leaving us here to die, is that it?"

Lily instantly wondered if he might be right. There was nothing to suggest they were here for a long stay. She tried out the thought, the idea of dying. She wasn't afraid, she found. She had been in the arbitrary care of frightened, ignorant young men for five years; even without the cruel games and the mock executions, she had grown used to the idea that her life could be terminated on a whim at any second. But she didn't want to die stuck in this hole in the ground. She felt a deep, intense longing to see the sky.

The guards continued to retreat up the stairs, and John yanked at his chains. "You fucking kids, you grab a handful of hostages and you think you can control the whole world."

"John, take it easy," Lily said.

John was raging now, his face purple. "You're fucking cowards is what you are. You can't even finish the job properly, you're not men enough for that—"

Severo turned and fired his Armalite. The burst was loud in the enclosed space. John's body shuddered as the bullets hit. One shot got him in the face, which imploded in a bloody mess.

Gary screamed, "John. Oh God, oh God!"

"No coward," said Severo, cigarette in mouth. He followed the others up the stairs and out of Lily's sight.

John was splayed over his chair. Blood pooled thickly on the floor. Helen hunched down over her baby, grasping her close, rocking, as if nothing else existed in the world. Piers turned his hooded head away, his body slumped.

Gary was crying, hunched over, weeping with shock. Chained up meters away from him, Lily couldn't reach him.

John had been an asshole in some ways, but Lily had known him for four years. Now he was gone, gone in an instant—killed before their eyes. Worse than that, *discarded*. Of no value to their captors, not anymore. And the implication was, neither were the rest of them.

"It's over," Helen said. It was the first time she had spoken since they had been brought here. She held her baby on her chest, her chin resting on Grace's head. "I'm right, aren't I?" Her accent was crisp northern English, her vowels flat. She had been a language teacher.

"You don't know that," Lily insisted. "Maybe some other group is late for the handover, that's all."

"They killed John," Gary said heavily.

Helen said, "And that bloody lantern is going out. Look at it! Bastards couldn't even give us a fresh battery. We're going to be left in the dark, with a stinking corpse. Left to die."

"Oh, Jesus," Gary whimpered. And Lily heard him groan softly; she knew that meant his bladder had released.

"It's not going to happen," Lily snapped. "Let's get out of these chains." She tugged experimentally. The radiator was bolted massively to a stone wall. "Look around before the light goes. There must be something down here, something we can use—"

"How about bolt cutters?"

2

The new voice was a man's, English, coming from the stairs. They all leaned over to look. Even Piers turned his hooded face.

Torchlight flashed. Lily raised her unchained hand to shield her eyes. She made out two, three, four people coming down the crypt stair. "Who's there? Who are you? *¿Como se llama usted? ¿Me puede ayudar, por favor? Me llamo—*"

"You're Lily Brooke. Yes? USAF captain, serial number—"

"Tell me who you are."

He lifted his torch to illuminate his face. He was black, maybe forty; tall, square, he wore what looked like battle dress with a purple beret, and a shoulder-flash logo: the Earth cradled in a cupped hand. "My name is George Camden."

"You're English. Military?"

"A private security force. I work for AxysCorp." He tapped his shoulder logo. "I've come to get you out of here. You're safe now." He smiled.

Nothing changed inside Lily; there was no feeling of relief. She couldn't believe it. She remained tense, wary, waiting for the trap to spring.

"AxysCorp," Gary said. "Who John worked for."

Camden shone his torch. "You're Gary Boyle, of NASA? Yes, John Foreshaw works for us. We're operating in conjunction with the coalition peacekeepers, the government forces. But at AxysCorp we look after our own." He flashed his torch around. Piers flinched from the light. "So where's John?"

"You just missed him," Helen said bitterly.

"Missed him?" Camden's torch found John. "Oh. *Damn* it."

Lily lifted her shackled arm. "You said something about bolt cutters?"

Camden waved forward his men. "Let's get on with it."

Released, they were helped up the crypt stairs.

The cathedral's interior was a sandstone cavern, looted and burned. They stumbled out through a massive door called the Portal of San Ivo, and onto the street. The cathedral was a squat Gothic pile, the labor of centuries. Its carefully worked face had been cratered by shellfire. The rain fell, hard and steady, and the water stood in spreading puddles on the street, making every surface glisten.

A small helicopter stood by, resting on its rails in the rubble-strewn wreck of some building. When the hostages emerged, a couple more AxysCorp operatives who stood by the bird came running. Lily, a pilot five years out of the game, didn't recognize the model; it bore the bold cradled-world logo of AxysCorp.

As the AxysCorp people got themselves organized, the four hostages stood together, Helen cradling her baby, Gary blinking in the light with a grin like a kid at Christmas. Unbearably, Piers Michaelmas still wouldn't remove the dirty towel that hid his face. Lily peered up longingly. At least she had got to see the sky again. But the cloud was solid, and the rain quickly soaked her bare scalp and thin clothes. It was July; at least it was warm. But, surrounded by the men in their dull green battle dress, she felt oddly diminished, all but naked in her T-shirt and shorts.

An AxysCorp man with a Red Cross flash on his arm took a quick look at the four of them, and then, with apologies, lifted Helen's baby from her arms. "Just for a bit—just until we're out of here. I've a cradle for her. She'll be safer that way." Helen protested, but could do nothing about it as he walked away with the baby, jiggling her in his arms. Lily thought she could feel the bond between mother and daughter stretch like steel under tension.

George Camden murmured to Lily, "I'm surprised she's so close to the child. It was the product of a rape—"

"She's Helen's," Lily shot back. "The father doesn't matter. Said's gone anyhow. His comrades chased him out."

"We know about him," Camden said gently. "Look, it's all right, take it easy. You really are safe now."

"None of this seems real." It was true: the helicopter, the battered cathedral, the leaden sky, were all like elements of the hallucinations she had suffered when in solitary.

"I knew John, you know." Camden smiled. His teeth were clean, cleaner than Lily's had been for five years. "I still can't believe we came so close to saving him, after all this time. If he was standing here he'd be complaining about the rain."

"That was John," she conceded. "But it's been raining a long time. We heard it in our last holding cell, out in the suburbs somewhere. I don't remember this kind of weather in Barcelona."

"Things have changed in the five years you've been gone, Captain Brooke." There was distant gunfire, a hollow crump. Camden listened to something, though he wore no earpiece. "I think we're set to get out of here." He walked toward the chopper.

Just for a moment, the four of them were left alone again.

"I guess this is it," Gary said certainly. "After all the months and years."

Lily looked at them, hopeful young Gary, bruised mother Helen, brittle Piers. "We shared something, didn't we?"

"That we did," Helen said. "Which nobody else is ever going to understand."

And now here they were released into a world evidently transformed. Lily said impulsively, "Listen. Let's make a vow. We'll stay in contact, the four of us. We'll look out for each other. If one's in trouble, the others come looking. That includes Grace, by the way."

Gary nodded. "If something good comes out of this shit, I'm in." He held out his hand, palm up. Lily put her hand in his. Then Helen laid hers on top of Lily's. Even Piers reached out blindly. Lily had to help him take hold of the others' hands.

"For life," Lily said. "And for Grace."

"For life," Helen and Gary murmured.

George Camden came bustling back. "Let's go. We've a C-130 waiting at the airport."

They hurried after him.

They clambered aboard the chopper and strapped into canvas bucket seats. Even here Piers kept the towel over his face. Helen wasn't allowed to hold her baby, though Grace was only a couple of meters away, strapped into a bucket seat in a cradle beside the medic.

The chopper lifted with a surge. Lily, professionally, thought the pilot's handling was a little rough.

The bird rose up past the face of the cathedral. Sprawling and shapeless, it was more like a natural sandstone outcropping than anything man-made. Lily could see the scars of war, shell pocks and shattered spires and gaping holes in a burned-out roof.

Then she was lifted higher, and she peered out curiously at the cityscape. In the five years she had been cooped up she had seen little but the inside of suburban cellars and warehouses. Barcelona was a blanket of development bounded by the Mediterranean coast to the southeast and mountains to the northwest, and on either flank by rivers, the Llobregat to the south and the Besos to the north. Neighborhoods clustered around low hills. The newer districts inland were a neat quilt of rectangular blocks, and glass-needle skyscrapers studded the business district and the coast.

There were obvious signs of the conflict, the burned-out buildings and rubble-strewn streets where only armored vehicles moved, a glass tower block with a blown-in frontage, one district burning apparently uncontrolled. But amid the damage there were signs of prosperity, whole suburbs walled off and made green and white by lawns and golf courses and bright new buildings. Even from the air you could see that Barcelona, distorted by violence and the invasion of international agencies, had become a city of fortresslike gated suburbs for the rich, surrounded by older neighborhoods that were crumbling into shantytowns.

And water lay everywhere. It pooled in the streets, lay at the feet of the tall buildings in the business district, glimmered on the flat roofs of the houses and in gullies and drains, mirrored surfaces reflecting the gray sky like pools of melted glass. Those bounding rivers seemed to have spread over their flood plains. She had thought Spain was supposed to be drying out. That was why Gary had been here in the first place: to map a climate evolving toward aridity.

To the southeast a surging Mediterranean broke against

sea walls, with no sign of the sandy stretches she remembered. She tapped Camden on the shoulder. "Where's the
beach?"

He grinned at her. "I told you," he shouted back. "Things
have changed. Just as well for you, actually. All this flooding has been driving the extremist types out of their cellars
like rats out of drains. They had nowhere left to hold you.
As to the rest—well, you'll see."

The chopper surged and swept away, heading inland.
Lily felt dizzy, her empty stomach growling.

3

When they walked out of the Savoy, Lily and Gary had to negotiate a chest-high maze of sandbags that blocked off the short access road to the Strand, where their car was to meet them. A uniformed footman showed them the way through. He carried a big monogrammed umbrella that kept off most of the steady, hissing rain, and he wore Wellington boots that shone as if polished.

Gary pointed at the sandbags, which were made of some silky-looking fabric and marked with the hotel's logo. "They even do their sandbags in style. You Brits are amazing."

"Thanks."

Out in the street, waiting for the car, Lily was in the open, if only for a few seconds. After days of choppers and planes and cars and trucks, military bases and embassies and hotels, she still felt as if she hadn't yet been released from her confinement. But the sky was all cloud, and the London air, though it tasted cleaner than she remembered, was hot and wet.

She glanced along the length of the Strand, at the shop fronts and the grand hotel entrances. So much was the same, so much had changed. London buses were now long snaking vehicles like trains, their carriages bright red, hissing through the sheets of water on the road when they got a chance to move forward in the jams. Every surface, including the taxi doors and bus panels, was covered with animated commercials for West End shows and TV events and Coke and Pepsi, and ads for "AxysCorp durables" like clothes and white goods, and for various competing brands of electronic gadgets whose nature she didn't even recognize: what was an "Angel"? Football was bigger business than ever, judging by the ads for the FA Cup Final, moved from May to July and to be played between Liverpool and Newcastle United in Mumbai. And everywhere she saw slogans for the World Cup: "England 2018—Two Years To Go." All this animation was a shimmering layer spray-painted over the world, reflected in the oily sheets of water on the road.

And yet the people hurrying by seemed oblivious to the shifting light, the unending dull roar of the traffic. Many of them had a dreamy look on their faces, some of them talking into the air, laughing, gesturing, unperturbed when they clattered into each other. Lily had grown up in Fulham, an inner suburb—she was on the way to her mother's home there today—and she had never felt at home here in the heart of the city. Now, while she had been away, a whole new generation of confident, blank-eyed young people had grown up, believing that London and all its marvels had only been invented yesterday, and that this, their own moment in the urban light, would last forever.

The car drew up to the curb, gleaming silver, big articulated wipers keeping back the rain. It was a Ford but Lily didn't recognize the model. Gary pointed out that it didn't have an exhaust. There was a US Embassy pass tucked behind the windscreen, and a soggy Stars and Stripes hung limply from a half-meter pole. The footman opened the doors for them, still expertly handling his umbrella. Lily and Gary scrambled into the back. The interior was plush and clean and smelled of new carpets.

The car pulled out, forcing its way into the stop-start stream of traffic. The driver said the direct route was pretty much impassable. So he turned off the Strand as soon as he could, heading into the maze of side streets. Here they were able to make a bit more progress, before coming to a halt at a queue before a burst drain.

The driver glanced in the mirror and grinned at them. He was maybe thirty-five, with a mass of tightly curled blond hair. "You're the hostages, aren't you? My dispatcher said something about it." *Sahm-fing a-baht it.* He had the kind of accent that used to be called estuary, when Lily had been taken.

"We *were* hostages," Gary corrected him mildly. "We're us now."

"Yeah. Fair enough. Good for you. You both American, are you?"

"Not me," Lily said. "Half-English, half-American. Born and raised in Fulham."

"OK. Well, do you mind if I do this?" He pressed a button. The little Stars and Stripes furled itself around the flagpole, which slid into the hull of the car and out of sight. "Most of the work we get is for the Embassy. But we don't like to tell 'em that their flag attracts potshots."

Gary shrugged. "Fine by me."

The jam lurched forward another couple of meters, and the driver took the opportunity to nip up another side road. They got to the end of this before hitting the next queue.

"So they let you out into the wild, did they? Must be a relief."

"I'll say," Gary said.

It was, Lily thought. They still had some engagements, notably a reception by Nathan Lammockson, owner and chief exec of AxysCorp, the company which had prized them loose from the grip of the Fathers of the Elect. And then Lily would have to attend a briefing with senior USAF officers at Mildenhall in Suffolk to see if there was still a career for her in the Air Force. But in the meantime they were both glad to be free of the medics and counselors—and in Lily's case some emergency dental work—and a little freedom was welcome.

The driver shook his head. "Five years chained to a radiator. Can't imagine what it was like. Amazing you didn't kill each other. Or yourselves. Although I've been stuck in this car for four years, sometimes it feels like that. And married for six, and that's the same, hah!" He glanced at Lily. "So, a London girl. Nothing's changed much since you've been gone, has it? Nothing changes much, not really."

"I don't remember it being so damn wet. It was wet in Spain too. You know, where we were kept."

The driver pulled a face. "Nah. Just funny weather. Mind you they couldn't complete the regular league season this year. I mean the football. First time since 1939, too many matches washed out. And Wimbledon hasn't finished in its two weeks for the last three years. There's a bloke down the cab shelter who reckons it's all down to the Chinese."

Gary asked, "What is?"

"The rain, the floods. China's drying out, isn't it? Stands to reason they'd want more rain, and hang the rest of us."

Lily couldn't tell if he was being serious or not.

Again the traffic lurched forward, again the car shot through another gap and turned off. Lily tried to follow the journey. They headed roughly west and south, pushing through the maze of Mayfair streets north of Green Park. Then they turned down through Knightsbridge, heading for the Brompton Road.

The driver saw her peering at street signs. "Don't worry, love, I'll get you there." He sounded defensive.

"I don't doubt it," she said.

"Used to be a cabbie—a black cab. This pays better. But I took the Knowledge. Of course a lot of the regular routes don't work anymore what with the road closures and the floods. You just do your best. Half the punters don't see that, they think you're ripping them off." He put on a vaguely Middle Eastern accent. " 'Are you sure this is the correct route, Mister Driver?' That's why I packed it in. The agency work is less stressful. Oh, you fucking arse—"

He pulled his wheel violently to the right, to avoid an expensive-looking car that aquaplaned in a slick of filthy water and ran into a wall. They avoided a collision, but endured another five minutes of motionlessness before the police cleared the crash.

A bit further on and some major building work was obstructing the carriageway. The driver said a lot of London's older buildings were being made flood-resilient—having their foundations reinforced, their lower floors lined with sandbags. They didn't get much further on past that before they ran into a crowd of angry-looking business types and shoppers and school parties, spilling onto the roads. The driver flicked on his radio. A Flying Eye report said that the Knightsbridge tube station had had to be evacuated because of flooding. The report went on to talk about a gathering North Sea storm that was expected to bring problems to the east coast.

The driver turned the radio off, and they waited for the blockage to clear. Lily peered out at the lines of traffic, the stalled cars and blocked roads, the miserable, sodden people splashing along the pavements, everybody trying to pursue their business. Their own fractious, short-tempered journey seemed a lot longer than just a few kilometers.

*   *   *

It was a relief to reach her mother's home, and get out of the car. Lily wasn't sure whether to tip the driver, or how much; there seemed to have been a pulse of inflation while she'd been away. She handed him twenty pounds. He looked neither disappointed nor surprised, and drove away.

Lily took a breath, and got her bearings. They were in Fulham, in Arneson Road, a kilometer or so north of the river. The house was one of a row of late-Victorian terraces, all heavily renovated and plastered with satellite dishes. Sandbags slumped in the small front garden, and the cellar, which had a window half-hidden by the pavement, was boarded up, evidently abandoned. Lily felt odd to be back here, after so long away. Everything seemed smaller than she remembered. She felt peculiarly glad she'd thought to bring Gary with her today, a kind of emblem of her other life.

Gary peered up doubtfully at the house's three floors, the PVC frames that had replaced the original sash windows. "Kind of a skinny house," he said.

"Skinny but deep," Lily replied, trying to be bright. "More room than you'd think. Come on." They walked through a low gate. A path had been cleared through sticky mud that smelled faintly of sewage. "Anyhow my mother makes the best chocolate cake in west London."

But it wasn't Lily's mother who opened the door, but her sister Amanda. And Lily learned her mother was dead.

Amanda walked them through the house to the kitchen. It was open-plan from the front door, and had been that way since the internal walls had been knocked down in a 1970s conversion.

Lily glanced curiously around at the living space. Her mother's books were gone, her slumped antique furniture vanished. The tattered old carpet Lily remembered from her childhood had been lifted too, to be replaced by cheap-looking ceramic tiles. The lower walls were bare of paint or paper, and Lily could see channels crudely cut in the plasterwork where power points had been raised to a meter or so off the ground. The fireplace, which had been blocked off in the seventies renovation, was now open again, and blackened by soot, evidently recently used.

The small kitchen had been much less modified than the living room, and was just as cluttered as Lily remembered, though now with Amanda's characteristic kipple, principally masses of spice bottles and jars to support her passion for Indian cooking. Amanda sat the two of them on high stools, and handed them mugs of hot chamomile tea. On a shelf over the table stood a row of photographs, of Lily's mother, Amanda's kids, and one big portrait of Lily herself, her official USAF image, a younger self smart in a crisp uniform. Lily was touched to see it there.

Lily tried to take in the fact that everything about her life had changed while she had been absent from it—that her mother had died a whole two years before, that her sister had moved from her old flat in Hammersmith into what had been the family home. Maybe she had been detached for too long. She just felt numb.

And she could tell that Gary, who she'd only brought

home on a whim, felt awkward to have walked in on a family tragedy.

Gary knew all about Lily's family from their endless conversations in Barcelona. Lily's mum had been a GI bride, of sorts, who had met and married a USAF airman stationed in Suffolk. He had given her two daughters before being killed in a friendly-fire incident while working on logistical support during the first Gulf war. Lily had never lived in the States, but she had dual citizenship. With her dad dead when she was fourteen, Lily's mother had been her anchor.

Amanda said, "I didn't want to tell you on the phone, when you called ahead earlier about visiting." She was edgy.

Lily said, "I appreciate that."

At thirty-five Amanda was five years younger than Lily. She was, in fact, about the age Lily had been when she was taken. Always taller and thinner than Lily, she had her black hair pulled back into a knot behind her head, and she wore a black dress that looked practical, if maybe a size too small for her. Though there was no evidence of smoking in the house, Lily thought she saw traces of the old habit about Amanda, a cigarette-shaped hole in the way she held the fingers of her right hand. "What gets me is why the government didn't tell you. You've been out of Spain for five days already."

"I think they're treating us as possible trauma cases." That was because of Piers Michaelmas, who had been so obviously damaged by his captivity. "They've been feeding us news bit by bit. Selectively."

Looking around, Gary said, "Looks like you've had a trauma here of your own."

"Well, we got flooded out in the spring. It's all been so bloody complicated, you wouldn't believe it. The insurance, you know. You have to wait an age for a loss adjuster to come out, and in the meantime you're not supposed to touch anything. Not even clear the mud out. It stank, Lily, you wouldn't believe it, street muck and sewage all over the floor. Carpets ruined, of course. No electric or water or gas, buckled floorboards, the water stink seeping out of the plaster for weeks afterward—it was just a nightmare.

We were lucky we didn't get any of the toxic fungi growing out of the walls. Old Mrs. Lucas got some of that—do you remember her? And even when the adjuster has been, you only get a payout if you commit to climate-proofing. Mind you I do admit I much prefer floor tiles to carpet, don't you? So much easier to keep clean. Of course we were lucky, you know, Lily. Some of the properties around here were condemned altogether."

Gary said, "I guess these old barns weren't built to withstand a flooding. What happened? River burst its banks?"

"No. A flash flood . . ."

A sudden deluge had followed days of steady rain that had left Victorian-age drains and sewers choked. With nowhere to go, sheets of water ran over the ground, seeking a way down to the river, pouring through streets and into houses and schools.

"The kids got home just before the level started rising in the street; we were lucky about that. It poured in under the door. We went upstairs and just huddled. We saw a car get washed away, washed down the street, can you believe it? Then it started pouring up from the sink and even out of the toilet, black mud that stank of sewage. That freaked out the kids, I can tell you. It's just as well Mum didn't live to see it."

Lily said, "It's hard to believe, all this happened to you and I didn't even know about it."

"Or about your mom," Gary said. "I'm glad I spoke to my own family, my mother. I'm looking forward to seeing her real soon."

Amanda poured him more tea. "When will they be sending you home?"

"A couple more days. I hear flights out of the civilian airports are problematic."

"Tell me about it. Heathrow is nothing but flooded runways and power-outs."

"I'm pretty sure I'll blag a seat on a military flight soon enough."

"You're not in the military, though?"

"No, but I do a lot of work with them. I'm a climate scientist." When he was taken he had been fresh out of a NASA institution called the Goddard Institute for Space Studies. "That's why I was in Spain. It's a climate-change hot spot. The interior is desiccating, turning into kind of like North Africa—or it was. All that rain wasn't in the old models and I've not caught up with the latest data. I was on my way to run some ground-truth studies of geosat observations on sand-dune formations outside Madrid, when, wham, a car pulled off the road in front of me."

"I can't imagine how that must have felt."

Gary said, "The first thing I thought was, how am I going to finish my job?"

Lily remembered she had felt much the same about her own abduction. It wasn't fear that struck her at first, more irritation at being plucked out of her life, her own concerns—that and some residual shock from the Chinook crash, even though she, the crew and the passengers had all walked away from it. At first she had been sure she would be released in two weeks, or three, or four. It was some time after that that the long reality of her imprisonment had cut into her consciousness, and other, stronger reactions had started to take over. Looking back, she wondered if she would have stayed sane if she had known from the start it was going to be all of five years before she was free again.

Amanda was watching her silently.

"Sorry," Lily said. "Woolgathering."

"There's things we need to talk about, Lil," Amanda said awkwardly. "The will, for one thing."

"Oh." Lily hadn't got that far, in the rather shocked halfhour since they'd arrived.

Gary stood, setting down his cup. "You know, you two need time."

"You don't have to go."

He smiled. He had a broad face that could be prone to fat, a mouth that smiled easily, a freckled forehead under a receding tangle of red-brown hair. Now he covered Lily's hand with his. "Babe, you just had some seriously bad news. Look, I'll be fine, I'll take a walk. It's for the best."

Amanda also stood. "It's good of you, though I feel like a dreadful hostess. If you want to walk, just head down to the Fulham Road—that way." She pointed. "You'll reach the High Street and then the river, near Putney Bridge. There are parks, a riverside path."

"Sounds good to me. I'll feed the ducks. And I'll be back here in, what, a couple of hours?"

"You'll get soaked," Lily said.

"Not if the pubs are open. Um, can you loan me an umbrella?"

Amanda showed him out.

The sisters sat on the tall kitchen stools, sharing a box of tissues, talking of their mother, the house, Amanda's kids, and how Amanda hadn't been able to get her mother buried close by; in London even the cemeteries were overcrowded.

"Mum left everything to the two of us equally. After she died it was all held up for a year; there was no news if you were alive or dead. Eventually the lawyers agreed to execute the will and release Mum's estate. We got the keys and sold up and moved in. I mean, if we hadn't I couldn't have afforded to pay for the upkeep of this place, the recovery after the flood damage and whatnot. That bastard Jerry is still paying maintenance for the kids, but the bare minimum, it wouldn't have helped with this . . ." Lily saw how distressed she was becoming, how guilty she felt. "Lil, I'm sorry. I thought you were dead. I had to sort things out."

Lily put a hand on her sister's arm. "Don't. You did what had to be done."

"You can move in here with us. Or we can sell the house and split the money, whatever you want. Although house prices have been flatlining in Fulham since the flooding."

"We don't have to decide that today."

They had got some of it out of their systems by the time the front door opened and the kids came barreling in.

5

ily hadn't seen her nephew and niece for a year or more before her abduction, a gap she had had five years to regret. Now here they were, grown like sunflowers, and let out of school early to see their aunt.

Kristie was still young enough to give her long-lost aunt a hug as instructed. Suddenly eleven years old, she grinned at Lily with a mouthful of steel brace. "You missed the Olympics," she said.

Benj, thirteen, with Day-Glo yellow hair, was more diffident, and he had a dreamy expression on his face, as if he didn't quite see what was going on around him. They both wore brilliantly colored clothes. Kristie had a bright pink backpack on her back, and chunky amber beads around her neck. The children looked like exotic birds, Lily thought, fragile creatures that didn't belong in the grimy adult world of flood damage and rain.

"You're home early from school," she said. So they were; it wasn't yet three o'clock.

Kristie shrugged. "Wet play."

Amanda raised an eyebrow. "It's the rain, the floods. They don't let them out at break times, or for games. They come home fizzing with energy. Pain in the bum."

"The Olympics, though," Kristie said. "The Olympics were right here in London and you were stuck in Spain! Did you see it?"

"Well, no," Lily admitted. Although the captives had thought about the London games. They marked the passing of time by such milestones, grand dates they remembered from the outside world—*this* must be happening about now, in some other place. "We didn't have TV. Was it good?"

"I was there every day of the last week," Kristie said proudly.

"That must have cost a lot."

"Not really," said Amanda. "It didn't go too well. The weather, the drug scandals, the terrorists. In the end they were giving the tickets away to kids and OAPs, anything to fill the stadia. After all these kids will be paying for it for the rest of their lives."

Lily asked, "So did you go, Benj?"

Benj shrugged. "For a couple of days. Wasn't much. It was *years* ago."

Amanda glared at him. "Are you on that damn Angel? What have I told you about using that thing when we have guests?"

"Oh, Mum—"

"I've heard of these things," Lily said. "Why don't you show me, Benj?"

He fished in his jacket pocket and produced a gadget as slim as a cigarette. It was heavy in her hand, seamless, warm from his body heat. Benj set it with unconscious skill, Lily couldn't follow what he did, and a bright, brassy pop tune erupted inside her head: "I love you more than my phone / You're my Angel, you're my TV / I love you more than my phone / Put you in my pocket and you sing to me . . ." The Angel beamed its music directly into her sensorium, some-how stimulating the hearing centers remotely, without the need for wires and earpieces.

"Cor."

"That's 'Phone,'" Benj said. "This year's big hit."

"I never heard it. Well, I wouldn't have."

Amanda said, "Of course everybody *has* to have one of these things. It's a fashion statement, you know? And it's a pain to be zapped in the street by some kid who thinks you need a headful of drums and bass."

Benj nodded wisely. "That's why they get taken off you at school."

"They're working on a video version. Imagine that!"

Lily said, "It's amazing how much is new since I've been away."

"Nothing useful," Amanda said. "Not really. Just distractions. What we need is big engineering to keep the flood waters out. The Thames Barrier ought to have been just the start. But that's not the fashion nowadays."

"We did the floods at school," Kristie said. She dumped

her plastic backpack on the table and began rummaging in it. "Green studies. Like how the Fens are below sea level. When it floods there the water *ponds*. They used to pump it away or drain it, but it's harder now the sea level has risen by a meter."

"A meter? Really?"

Kristie looked vaguely offended, as if Lily didn't believe her. "We did it at school," she repeated. "They told us we should keep a scrapbook of all the changes."

"What sort of changes?"

"Funny things that happen with the floods. Look." She dug a handheld out of her backpack, set it on the table and tabbed through entries. Lily peered to see the tiny font.

The first entry was a short video clip about an old man who had been to every Crystal Palace away game for sixty years, he claimed. "Man and boy, rain and shine, I support the Palace." His accent was broad, old-fashioned south London. "Rain and shine since I was ten year old, but I'd have had to swim to get to Peterborough this week. Never missed a game before, not one, what's it coming to . . ." As a contrast Kristie had added a clip about the Cup Final being played in Mumbai; the football was either a world away, or if you followed a local team you couldn't even get to it anymore.

Another piece was from America. A black woman was describing how she had had to abandon her home in Bay St. Louis, east of New Orleans. The Army Corps of Engineers had run a vast project of relocation back from the Gulf coast, abandoning swaths of shoreline to wetlands as a natural barrier against post-Katrina storms. This woman had had her old home bought out by the federal government, and was relocated. But she had then been forced out of her new inland home in turn by the threat of a fresh, even more drastic flooding event. "I never wanted come here, the Bay my home, my momma's home, but Governor says, woman, you gotta go. So I pack up my kids and my dog and I go. And now look, the damn sea's in my parlor again, and what I want to know is, what's the point of moving if that ol' sea he just follow you anyhow? . . ."

A snip from a children's news program outlined the effects of the flooding on the wildlife in your garden. There were striking images of river weed stuck in the branches of trees. The rain washed insect eggs off the leaves where they had been laid, so later there was no food for the birds in their breeding seasons. In Kristie's garden, and across England, there had been a crash in the populations of blue tits.

"These pieces are good," Lily said to Kristie. "I mean, well selected. You have an eye. Maybe you should be a journalist."

"I want to be a writer," Kristie said. "Stories instead of news though."

"The floods ruin the farmland." Benj muscled in, evidently not getting enough attention. "That's what we learned about, what's going on in Yorkshire. You get salt water on the grass so the cows won't eat it, and the leaves on the trees shrivel, and hawthorns turn black, and that. It's causing a crisis in the agri-insurance industry."

Amanda snapped, "Never mind the crisis in the agri-insurance industry. Go and have a wash before you eat anything."

There was a shrill beeping. Lily produced the phone that the Embassy had given her. It was another flat, sleek product, like a pebble, smooth to the touch. She raised the phone to her ear. It was Helen Gray, angry and distressed.

6

Lily had no idea how to use this newfangled phone to contact Gary Boyle. Indeed, she didn't even know his number. So she took herself off out of the house to find him, huddled up in a heavy waterproof coat she borrowed from Amanda.

Dodging the spray from the cars, she found her way down to the Fulham Road, well remembered from her childhood, but much altered, change upon change, much of it very recent. The grand old villas had mostly been converted to flats, or demolished altogether to be replaced by shops and restaurants and gas stations and estate agents. And you could see the scars of flooding everywhere, tide marks on low walls, slick mud in front gardens, a lingering scent of sewage. Many of the properties were boarded up, in fact, condemned because of flood damage.

She cut down Fulham High Street, heading for Putney Bridge Road. A ticket outlet advertised discounted seats at all the West End shows. Amanda had told her it was so difficult traveling now that it was easy to get tickets for the opera, the shows, even the big football matches. Always free tables in the restaurants too, but the menus were restricted because the international food distribution business was so badly hit.

Before she reached the river she cut down some steps to reach Bishop's Park, a leafy garden over which the slim tower of Fulham Palace thrust to the sky. The rain, not too heavy, hissed from the thick summer leaves of very old trees. The lawns were flooded, and ducks and moorhens swam complacently on ponds that bristled with long grass and stranded trees.

She found Gary sitting on a bench on the footpath by the riverbank, before a green railing from which hung an orange lifebelt. Lily sat down with him. Gary was humming softly, and tapping his feet. Evidently he'd discovered Angels. He had always talked about how he missed music, down in the cellars; Lily guessed he was catching up.

The Thames was high and fast-moving, it seemed to her, an angry gray beast that forced its way under the pale sandstone arches of Putney Bridge. On the far bank boathouses glistened in the rain; nobody was out rowing today.

Gary said, "I counted seven joggers since I've been sitting here. And four people with dogs."

"Somewhere in this park," Lily said, "is a memorial to the International Brigade. Who fought for the republic in the Spanish Civil War."

"Small world," he said. "Your sister's hospitable. Made me welcome."

"Well, that's her job, sort of. She's an events coordinator. She's been having time off since she found out I was released. She says she's taking the kids out of school and to the Dome in Greenwich tomorrow, end-of-term educational treat stuff . . ."

"That river looks high to me."

"And to me."

"Is it still tidal, as far as this?"

"I think so."

"Look at this." He produced a handheld, a gift from AxysCorp, on which he'd been watching news and recording clips; he shielded it from the rain with his hand.

It wasn't just London. Much of the country was in the grip of chronic flooding, which seemed to have become a regular event. Britain's great rivers were all swollen, all had broken their banks somewhere, and there were refugee camps, parks of caravans and tents, on higher ground near the Trent, the Clyde, the Severn as far as Shrewsbury. There was a particular crisis unfolding this summer in Liverpool. Lily was shocked by a satellite image of East Anglia. The sea had pushed deeply beyond its old bounds across the Fens, lapping toward Wisbech and Spalding, and there were freestanding lakes everywhere, dark blue in the processed image.

The images seemed unreal. Lily was surprised everybody wasn't talking constantly about what seemed to her an immense transformation. But she supposed that over the years you got used to it. It was just that she had been fast-forwarded to an unfamiliar future.

Gary said, "Some of these incidents are fluvial—exceptional rain, flooding rivers. The coastal events come from the sea, obviously . . . I guess you got the call from Helen."

"Yes. I never knew that bastard Said was the son of a Saudi prince. We were privileged to be abused by him."

"Yeah, so we were," he said sourly.

Most of their guards had been Spanish. But when they were in the hands of Muslim factions some had come from further afield. Some Muslim radicals dreamed of retaking every piece of Waqf, the territory claimed under the first eighth-century Islamic expansion, from Spain to Iraq. And so combatants were drawn to the conflict in Spain from other parts of the Islamic world.

The prisoners had cared nothing, really, about their guards' provenance. All that mattered about the guards was how they behaved. Christian and Muslim alike, they were almost all very young men, almost all radicalized by the fiery words of preachers—almost all poorly educated, and obsessed with sex. Some were stable, almost normal-seeming; they could be friendly with their captives, and some even seemed to crave their captives' affection.

But some guards harmed them, even though the prisoners were supposed to have value as hostages. There could be punishment beatings, belt-whippings. Usually there was at least some such excuse for the violence, for instance when Lily had gone on a hunger strike. But some had gone further than any possible justification. These were mixed-up young men taking out their own frustration and confusion; it didn't really matter who you were or what you had done. Lily's own worst experience had been an amateurish *bastinado*: to be trussed up, hands behind her back and shackled to her own ankles while the soles of her feet were beaten with an iron rod, an unbelievably painful experience. That had not been Said but a man like him.

She had come to believe that part of the motive for such assaults was always sexual, even if the attack itself wasn't sexual in nature. You could feel the excitement in the man standing over you, smell the salty spice of his breath at your neck, hear the rapid pumping of his lungs.

As for sex itself, Lily had been groped and pummeled

by foolish boys, but she seemed to have had a manner that embarrassed rather than excited them. Helen Gray, fifteen years younger, hadn't been so lucky. After two rapes by Said, or three—Helen had been taken away each time and wouldn't talk about her experiences, though the blood and bruising made it obvious—the other guards had put a stop to it. After a time Said went away, perhaps posted to some other front of the great battlefield.

But not before he left Helen with his child. Her pregnancy in captivity, aided by her fellow captives with their bits of first aid and field medicine, and then a delivery by a scared drafted-in medical student, had been terrifying. But at the end of it there was a baby, Grace, whom Helen had loved immediately, and cherished every day of her imprisonment.

"And Helen never knew she'd given birth to a Saudi royal," said Gary. "A princess!"

Helen had become convinced this was why her baby hadn't been returned to her, since the first moment of their rescue five days ago under La Seu. The baby must be at the center of some enormous diplomatic row.

Gary said, "So you think that's why Helen called us, why she's so adamant we should go to the AxysCorp reception?"

"I guess so. If Lammockson can get us out of Barcelona, maybe he can get the baby back from Riyadh, or wherever the hell she is. So we go, I guess."

"Sure," Gary said. "We said we'd stick by each other, didn't we, the four of us? But, Lily, your mom—"

"There's nothing I can do for Mum," Lily said firmly, "but Helen and the baby I can help. In the meantime we're going to my sister's for dinner. You'll love the kids. Come on."

They set off back, plodding out of the park and over sodden pavements.

At the roundabout where the High Street joined the Fulham Road a drain had blocked, and a lake had formed. The cars were pushing through it, raising great rooster-tails of water, and Lily and Gary had to detour. By the time they made it to the Fulham Road they both had wet feet. This was life in London now, it seemed, rain and wet shoes and road blockages.

But by now the schools were emptying, and the roads

filled up with yellow school buses, American style, another innovation since Lily had been away. On the Fulham Road they merged into a growing crowd of parents and children, noisy, laughing, hurrying along the pavement between gushing gutters and lines of sandbags. Lily wondered how many of the world's nations were represented in the exhilarating rainbow of faces around her. This was an old village long overwhelmed by the growth of London, a place you just drove through, but people still lived here just as they had when Lily was a kid, still worked and went shopping and took their kids to school, still were born and grew old and died in this place.

And then the rain lightened, and a shaft of sunlight broke through the scattering clouds and glimmered from the water that stood on the roads and in the gutters, on lawns and playgrounds. Unaccountably, on this day she had learned her mother had died, Lily felt optimistic. She was free, and here was the sun trying to shine. On impulse she grabbed Gary's hand, and he squeezed back.

7

The next day George Camden phoned Lily early at her hotel. Camden was the smooth ex-military oppo who had retrieved them from Barcelona. Camden said that the summons to lunch with Nathan Lammockson that day was confirmed. Lammockson's "hydrometropole," as Camden put it, was in Southend, some fifty kilometers east of central London at the mouth of the Thames Estuary. A chopper would pick up Lily and Gary from London City Airport at eleven that morning.

Gary met Lily outside the hotel, in the rain. He was gazing into his handheld. "You followed the news? Remember that North Sea storm on the car radio? Well, it's on its way south."

The rain was already lashing down, and now a storm was on the way. "Great."

"Overnight flooding all down the east coast . . ."

He showed her the handheld. The BBC news was all about the weather, with images of the Tyne breaking its banks and forcing its way into the fancy restaurants along Newcastle's Quayside. The island of Lindisfarne, only ever connected to the mainland by a tidal causeway, was cut off, stranding pissed-off holidaymakers. Beaches in Lincolnshire had been damaged. There were flood alerts out for East Anglia, for Boston and King's Lynn, where the sea was challenging new flood barriers around the Wash. And so on. The weather girl's animated map showed the storm as a milky swirl of cloud that was still heading south.

Lily asked, "Is this unusually bad? If it keeps coming south, is London threatened?"

"They haven't said so. I don't think this is even a particularly powerful storm. If it combines with all the fluvial

runoff or a high tide it could become a difficult event. But I
don't know. Things seem to have changed."

"Kristie, my niece, you know, said sea levels have risen
by a meter."

His eyebrows rose. "A *meter*? Where the hell did that
come from? A meter rise wasn't in the old climate-change
forecast models until the end of the century, even in the
worst case."

"I wouldn't believe everything Kristie says. She's quite
liable to have mixed up her meters with her centimeters."

"Well, if she's right it would make a mess of everything . . . I just don't know, Lily. I'm three years out of the
loop, and Britain's not my area anyhow." He glanced at her.
"Kind of stressy, your sis."

"Always was. She's not dumb, though. She took a law
degree. But she ended up in events, handling people rather
than dealing with cases. She has that kind of personality,
I guess. Bright, bubbly, engaging. A bit fragile. But on the
other hand, neither you or I are raising two kids."

"That's true enough," he conceded.

After their years together he knew the rest: that Lily
had never married, and it was many years since she had
had a relationship that lasted much beyond six months. At
one point she had sworn off men entirely. A base commander had hit on her, and when she didn't come over he
threatened to put her on sentry duty: a pilot qualified on
three different birds, stuck on the wire. The guy was later
drummed out of the service for "command rape," in the
jargon. But the damage to Lily's capacity for relationships
was permanent. She'd never *meant* to end up alone at age
forty, but that was the way it worked out.

The handheld flashed up a new projection by the BBC,
showing how the storm might curve into the Thames Estuary later in the day.

And then the news channel cut away to a breaking story
from Sydney, Australia. Picture-postcard images of the land-
marks, the Harbour Bridge and the Opera House, were in-
terspersed with scenes of rising waters in Darling Harbour
and Sydney Cove and Farm Cove. The water was already
splashing over the bank walls around the Opera House and
spilling onto the curving cobbled pedestrian footway. For
now it was a novelty; tourists filmed the incident with their

phones and leapt back squealing from the water, an adventure that made their holiday memorable. But in the Royal Botanic Gardens to the south of the Opera House water was gushing from broken drains and ponding over the grass. And out of town at Bondi, would-be surfers looked down on a beach entirely hidden by breaking waves.

Lily found it hard to take in this news, as if it was crowded out by the images she'd seen of Britain. Flooding in Sydney? How was that possible?

Gary looked thoughtful, puzzled.

Another headline flashed for their attention. The Test match at the Oval, between England and India, had been abandoned for another day.

The car arrived.

8

City Airport was east of Greenwich and the Isle of Dogs. They endured another slow jerking ride, driving north of the river along the A13. They peered out at the towers around Canary Wharf, glimpsed through the rain. By the time they reached the airport, according to the news on Gary's handheld, people had died in the flooding at King's Lynn and Hunstanton, around the Wash, and the storm had pushed down the east coast as far as Great Yarmouth and Lowestoft.

The airport was small, the runways sheeted by rainwater and battered by winds, but planes were taking off and landing, leaping up like salmon from alarmingly short runs.

The AxysCorp chopper was the same lightweight new model that had picked them up from Barcelona. They boarded quickly and the chopper soared into the air. The pilot seemed to have total confidence in his machine, despite the buffeting wind. Lily felt confident, too, now that she was in the bird, more so than in a car squeezing its way through the crammed and troubled streets of London, for here she was in her element.

East London opened up beneath her. The Thames was a band of ugly gray. The neat line of the Thames Barrier, just a kilometer from the airport, was stitched across the water, its steel cowls shining in the rain. Gary pointed out that the Barrier was closed, the massive yellow rocking beams lifted beside each pier, and foam was thrown up as white-crested waves slammed against the raised gates.

The bird rose higher, dipped its nose, and soared east down the Thames Estuary and over lorry parks and storage sites and defunct factories, the gray-brown industrial zone that surrounded London. Lily was struck by how heavily developed the flood plain was, with new housing

estates and shopping precincts in Barking, Woolwich and
Thamesmead sparkling in the rain like architects' models.
She made out the soaring bridge at Dartford where the
M25 orbital motorway crossed the river, the last crossing
before the sea. Streams of cars and freight from the docks
at Tilbury and Grays queued at the toll gates for the bridge
and the tunnels. A little further east both riverbanks were
more or less walled with glass, huge retail developments
summoned into existence by the motorway.

Further east yet, as the estuary slowly widened, she
saw the sprawling docks of Tilbury to the north, and to the
south the matching development of Gravesend, beyond
river-lashed mud flats. All this was downstream of the Barrier, outside its putative protection. The Barrier was designed to protect central London from tidal surges heading
upstream. Further on and the river swung around to the
north, widening rapidly. Even out here there was extensive
development, with acres of refineries and oil stores and
gas tanks at Coryton and Canvey Island, an ugly industrial
sprawl. And then the estuary opened out to embrace the
sea.

Southend-on-Sea was a tangled old town that hugged the
coast inside the line of an A-road to the north, a trace
across the landscape. Lily made out a remarkably long pier,
a narrow, delicate-looking line scratched across the surface of the sea. Waves broke against the town's sea wall,
sending up silent sprays of white, and water pooled on the
promenades.

The chopper took them over Southend itself to a small
helipad a little further to the east, close to Shoeburyness.
A pier roofed by Plexiglas led off over a stretch of sandy
beach to what looked like a small marina, a row of blocky
buildings with boats tethered alongside. But the "buildings" were afloat, Lily saw, sitting on fat pontoons.

Despite the gathering wind, the pilot dropped them
down with scarcely a bump. A couple of AxysCorp flunkies in blue coveralls, hoods up, came running out to the
chopper towing a kind of extensible tunnel. Lily and Gary
were barely exposed to the wind and rain before hurrying
through the tunnel and into the pier. Looking along the
covered pier, with the rain pouring down the glass walls,

Lily saw a party in full swing, laughter and lights and glittering people.

Another flunky took their outer coats, and they were given towels to wipe the rain off their faces; there was even a small bathroom. In a discreet black suit, the man was perhaps twenty-five, unreasonably good-looking, and spoke a soft Sean Connery well-educated Scottish.

When they were ready the flunky led them onward. At the end of the passageway they were met by a waiter with a tray of champagne, and they took a glass each. Then they walked into a cavern of a room, with square walls and a high ceiling. A tremendous chandelier, a stalactite of glass and light, was suspended over a wide doughnut-shaped table on which drink and food were stacked up. The walls, painted in pastel colors, were underlit, and expensive-looking works of art hung in rows. The paintings seemed oddly dark, glowering, relics of antiquity in this modern opulence.

People moved through this space, easy and confident, the men mostly suited, the women in long dresses. Their brittle conversation was crashingly loud as they ate the food and drank the drink, marveled at the chandelier and inspected the artwork. News crews followed them, teams of cameramen and interviewers with microphones. In one corner a string quartet played, their music inaudible under the babble of talk.

And all this was afloat. Lily could feel the sea surge, just gently, and that great chandelier tinkled and glittered. The rocking wasn't unpleasant, in fact; it went with the buzz of the champagne—but Lily reminded herself she had had five years of detox, and wasn't yet used to drink.

"This," said Gary thickly, "is the fucking *Titanic*."

George Camden approached them, looking dapper in a tuxedo and bow tie. "Ah, Mr. Boyle," he said. "I've missed your wit these last couple of days. This isn't a ship at all— I think Mr. Lammockson would be offended to hear you say that—it's part of a hydrometropole, a floating city. If a small one."

"It's a what-now?"

"And Captain Brooke." Camden smiled at Lily. "You're very welcome. You are the guests of honor this afternoon, the four of you."

She glanced around. "Helen and Piers are here?"

"Oh, yes. Mr. Lammockson apologizes he's not here to greet you in person; he has some calls to make."

"That doesn't surprise me," Gary said. He had drained his champagne and was reaching for another. "Guys like that always have calls to make." He pointed at the left-hand wall. "Isn't that a Gauguin?"

"Never had you down as an art lover, Boyle." A couple approached them. It was Piers Michaelmas, in a crisp new British army uniform, with Helen Gray on his arm. "But of course you're quite right. And Gauguin is exactly the sort of obvious choice this gang of hedgies and market players would splash their money on. Hello, you two." Piers stood straight. His dark hair was cut short, military style. Only the lines around his eyes might have been a clue that here was a man who had spent much of the last few years in utter silence, his face hidden under a filthy towel from captors he could not bear to have look at him.

They compared notes. Their lives the last few days had been similar, a round of medical checks and debriefings and family visits and media events.

Only Piers seemed itching to get back to work. "All this ruddy climate stuff," he confided to Lily. "It's really kicked off while we've been banged up, quicker than the boffins ever expected. Something new going on, so I've heard, though nobody knows quite what . . ." He didn't have a word to say about their captivity or its aftermath.

Behind his back, Gary mouthed to Lily: "Denial. That guy is a walking case conference."

"Hush," she hissed back. She turned to Helen, who wore a simple black dress; she was beautiful, Lily thought, her blond hair cut short and expensively teased. But the dress, the hairstyle, just brought out her thinness and pallor, and a haunted look in her blue eyes. "So any news about Grace?"

"Nothing but dead ends," Helen said. "He was an Axys-Corp employee, that doctor who took hold of Grace in the first place. But since then they've passed her around like a live grenade. A US Army medic took her from AxysCorp, and then the British army took her from them, and then the Foreign Office got hold of her, and then . . . When I call any of them they put me on hold or refer me to a counselor."

Gary said, "I'm sure she's safe. They wouldn't harm her—"

"That's not the point," she snarled at him. "She's not with *me*. I don't care if she's the bastard child of a Saudi prince or not, I'm her mother."

"We're all as baffled as you are," George Camden said. "And we sympathize, Helen. We really do. And we intend to do everything we can to help."

"That's true, that's very true, I endorse everything George has said on AxysCorp's behalf." The new voice was booming, commanding; they turned as one, on a reflex.

Nathan Lammockson walked toward them.

9

Lammockson was a short man, hefty, his suit jacket a fraction on the small side so that his belly pushed out his shirt. He wore his gray-flecked black hair cut short to the scalp, and his double chin and fleshy nose were moist with sweat. He came trailed by a school of news crews. Murmuring inconsequential words, Lammockson shook hands with each of the four of them, the four he had saved from the clutches of the Spanish extremists. Lights glared and mike booms hovered. This encounter was clearly the centerpiece of the occasion, for him.

Lily had researched their rescuer in her free time since returning to England. Forty-five years old, Lammockson was a third-generation immigrant from Uganda. His grandparents had fled Idi Amin. He looked vaguely eastern Mediterranean; he claimed not to know or care what his ethnic origins were. By forty he had become one of the richest men in Britain. As far as Lily understood he had got that way mostly by buying up huge companies, using their own assets to secure the loans he needed to do so, and then selling them on for immense profits.

When the cameras were done with them Piers Michaelmas stepped away politely, inspecting what looked to Lily like a futuristic pager. "They're starting to issue flood warnings in London," he said to Lily.

"That North Sea storm?"

"Yes. The Barrier is already raised, but— Hello? Yes, this is Michaelmas . . ." He wandered away, speaking into the air.

"So," Lammockson said expansively. "You're enjoying the party?"

Gary, slightly drunk, said, "I always enjoy learning new words."

"Such as?"

" 'Hedgie.' "

Lammockson boomed laughter. "A hedge-fund manager. Probably describes twenty percent of the people here."

"But not you," Lily guessed.

"The *Financial Times* once called me a 'private equity magnate.' I like that word, don't you? 'Magnate.' Sounds like a wealthy Byzantine. Of course there is a whole class of us these days. London, thank God I was born here! It's so liberal it's like a tax haven for people like me."

Gary asked, "And, 'hydrometropole'?"

"Ah. Now that's more interesting." Bizarrely, Lammockson jumped up and down, his massive weight thumping into the floor. "We're afloat," he said. "The whole of this mansion is. I'm sure you saw that from the air. Afloat, even though I've got a swimming pool and a cinema and a gym and kitchens like you wouldn't believe. I've even got a floating greenhouse. I'm the amphibious man! The ultimate floodproofing, yes? You just ride it out.

"This is a floating city, a Dutch design. Now the Dutch have been fighting the sea for centuries—hell, their ancestors have been at it for two thousand years. Let me tell you something. The levees in New Orleans that failed when Katrina hit, they were designed for a once in thirty years extreme event. The Thames Barrier was designed for once in a thousand years. But in the Netherlands they plan for every *ten* thousand years. You want to guard against a flood, my friend, hire a Dutchman."

"And this is what you spend your money on," Gary said, flushed. "This raft."

Lammockson stared at him. "You're enjoying the champagne, aren't you?"

"We're none of us used to alcohol," Lily said hastily.

Lammockson laughed. "That's fine, you deserve it, drink what you like, say what you like. Look—what *should* I spend my money on? My son Hammond attends the best private school in London. Everything I do, I do for him." He pointed to a plump, sour-looking boy of about ten, wearing a tuxedo, who hovered near a waiter with a tray of wine. Lammockson said, "Father of my grandchildren someday. But there's only so much money you can spend on a kid. What else? I've climbed in rainforests, and flown around the moon in a Russian Soyuz ship. Look at my watch." He brandished his arm before Gary and pulled back his sleeve to expose a heavy bit of jewelry. "You know what this is? A Richard Mille RM004-V7. Cost me a cool quarter million. And I don't just own a watch. I have a watch *wardrobe*."

Gary grinned. "Well, that's class."

"But I can only wear one watch at a time, right?" He glanced around at the shining throng drinking his champagne. "You know, most of these guys don't get it. Even the ones who've actually made far more than me, they just don't get it. But I have a feeling you people do. You who've seen the other side of life."

"Get what?" Lily asked.

"That all this, the way we've been living, the way we've made our money, is under threat. Everything's changing."

"Climate change," Gary guessed.

"Yeah. Especially this fast new sort, the sea-level rise, climate change on speed. But that's not to say there isn't still money to be made. A time of change is a time of opportunity. When Rome fell, you know, there were guys who got richer than ever before. They'd already owned half of Europe. You just got to know when to move out, and how. You have to be a realist."

"And you're a realist, are you, Mr. Lammockson?" Lily asked.

"I try to be. Call me Nathan. Listen to me. The old way, the hyper-capitalism behind the private equity game, it was always a bubble and it's going to burst as soon as the stresses set in. The housing market in London is already going to hell, for example, everybody buying up the high ground, Hampstead and the Chilterns, and that's distorting the whole of the UK economy.

"But I got out of housing long ago. Now I'm making a fortune from disaster recovery projects. You know the idea? When the computers in some bank's basement go on the fritz because the floods come, I can switch over their operation straightaway to a dedicated backup suite in Aberdeen. The insurance industry, that's another open goal right now, the traditional firms are crashing from a new rush of claims."

"And 'AxysCorp durables,'" Lily said. "I saw the posters."

"Right," he said energetically. "People sense we're moving out of the old throwaway age. So now they want clothes that will last a decade, washing machines and cars that will run forever without maintenance, like that. And that new niche is precisely what I'm selling to."

"So while the world goes to hell you get even richer," Gary said.

"That's the general idea. But I want to do more than make money. I feel it's time for somebody to show some leadership, to show we can cope with this fucked-up world of ours."

"Somebody like you," Gary said.

Lammockson grinned. "You're being ironic, my drunken friend, but you're correct. That's why I'm going public—it's a conscious decision and a concerted strategy. Of course a high public profile needs big strokes. Stunts."

Gary said, "Our rescue was a stunt, was it?"

"It got you out, didn't it? I don't see anything wrong in doing good for you while getting something out of it myself. See those guys in the corner?" He pointed to a group of middle-aged men happily feeding on vol-au-vents beneath the great chandelier; dark-skinned, short, they wore their lounge suits with a kind of indifference. "Elders from Tuvalu."

Lily asked, "Where?"

"Island nation. Threatened by sea-level rise," Gary said.

"You're out of date, my friend," Lammockson said. "No longer threatened—swamped, drowned, vanished. It was abandoned long before the end, when the salt water ruined the crops and killed the coconuts. Oh, nobody died, though a nation did; all ten thousand people were evacuated to New Zealand and elsewhere. And the very last choppers to rescue the weeping elders from the rising waves—"

"Were AxysCorp?" Gary guessed.

"Damn right," Lammockson said. "Doing good in a public way. Showing leadership in a troubled world. That's my angle. *That's* what I'm doing with my money. And it's going to be essential in the future, believe me. I mean, as regards flooding, in this country you've got an Environment Agency that shows about as much leadership as a drowning kitten, and a government that keeps paring back investment in flood defenses. But if this fucking sea-level rise continues, we're going to see some major events."

Lily began to feel alarmed. "Surely it won't go that far."

Gary frowned. "I'm far out of the loop—I really need to find out about all this."

"You know, I'm serious about keeping in touch with you guys," Lammockson said heavily. "You have a unique perspective, a fresh look after years away at a world going crazy. And I—"

An alarm chimed, a subtle gong. The string quartet stopped playing.

George Camden listened absently into the air. "It's the storm, sir. It's coming this way, heading for the estuary. We're in no danger. But the guests should be informed."

"See to it," Lammockson snapped. Camden nodded and hurried away. Lammockson turned to the hostages. "Look, I hate to break this up but I should be elsewhere—"

"No." Helen had said nothing during Lammockson's monologue. Now she laid a hand on his arm. "Wait. I need to talk to you about my baby."

He refocused on her. "Miss Gray."

"It was one of your men, your doctors, who took her away from me. Wherever she is now, that makes you responsible."

"I fully accept that. We're doing all we can—"

"It's not enough," Helen said, a little wildly. She waved a hand. "Look at all these cameras, the microphones. Why don't I stand up and tell them that Nathan Lammockson, savior of the world, stole my baby?"

Lily touched her arm. "Helen, come on—"

"Why don't I go to the papers? Why don't I write a bloody book?"

"Miss Gray," Lammockson said. He faced her squarely, his full, formidable attention fixed on her. "*Miss Gray*. I hear what you say. And you know what? I fully accept it. You're absolutely right, morally. My men took custody of the child, and we took our eyes off the ball, and we're responsible. I'm responsible. I give you my word, solemnly, that I will find your baby and get him back to you."

"Her," Helen said bitterly.

"Her. I'm sorry. Look at this place. Do you doubt I have the resources to do it? No. Do you doubt I have the commitment to see it through? No. I got you out of Barcelona, didn't I? Go public if you want, Miss Gray, that's your right. All I'm asking is for a little time to deal with this, to resolve it."

Lily saw Helen was confused, trying to resist the force of his personality. Lily took her hand. "Helen, that sounds like the best bet to me right now."

Lammockson nodded, apparently satisfied. "Are we good? Yes?" He held Helen's shoulders. "We'll see this through, you and I. But for now, I've a room full of rich folk to comfort." He turned and walked away, staff clustering around him like ducklings following their mother.

Piers hurried back to Lily. "It's all kicking off. There's an alert out all along the estuary. I'm in contact with Gold Command. They're mobilizing everything they've got. AxysCorp are putting their choppers in the air too, to be assigned to rescue operations. There's work we can do—will you come with me? Lammockson's staff are organizing a chopper for us. We can beat the storm if we move fast."

"It's a long time since I flew."

"You're not expected to pilot anything. But you know your way around choppers. You could be a big help."

Lily suddenly thought of her sister and the kids, who were supposed to be in the Dome this afternoon. Transport out of there was always a bottleneck. "Can you get me to Greenwich?"

"I'm sure we can." Piers turned to Gary and Helen. "You two may be safest here."

Gary said, "No thanks. Listen. Piers, could you arrange to get me to the Barrier? I'm in touch with some colleagues there. I want to try to find out what's going on."

Lily said, "Gary, you're drunk. You're in no fit state—"

"Not drunk for long." Grinning, he held up a card of pills. "These days they have sober-up pills, Lil. You should check your mini-bar."

Piers said, "The Barrier it is. But we need to move."

Lammockson's deep voice boomed over a PA. The party was being spiced up by a flood warning, he announced, but there was no need for alarm, the hydrometropole was fully flood resilient, and everybody wise enough to have booked up for a disaster vacation would be whisked right out of here and catered for.

And the floor tilted beneath Lily's feet. The whole of the floating building was rising like a vast elevator car, carrying Lily with it. Some of Lammockson's guests stumbled; there was excited laughter.

Gary said, "Holy cow."

The room began to settle.

Lily said, "How high do you think that was?"

Piers shrugged. "Hard to say. A meter? Two?"

Lily knew nothing about the Thames Barrier, and London's flood defenses in general. "Surely the Barrier will be able to handle a wave that size?"

"I don't know," Gary said honestly. "The estuary will funnel the storm—the riverbed will be shallow. The surge will be higher by the time it reaches the Barrier."

"How much higher?"

He had no answer.

Piers snapped, "Come on, let's get our stuff."

They hurried after him, grabbed their coats, and ran out through the glass-walled pier to the helipad.

Lily checked her watch. It was just after three in the afternoon.

10

Fifteen minutes later an AxysCorp chopper was rushing west, heading back up the Thames, carrying Gary Boyle to the Barrier.

The storm system was already funneling vigorously into the estuary, but it would take an hour to travel from Southend to the Barrier. The chopper easily outran it, though the winds and driving rain were ferocious. And, below, the river raged, turbid and frothing, pushing against the banks that contained it. Already the mud flats opposite Canvey and Tilbury were submerged, and floodwater glistened at South Benfleet, East Tilbury, Northfleet and on Rainham Marshes.

Gary was dropped off at the control tower for the Thames Barrier, on the south bank at a place called Woolwich Reach. The chopper lifted again immediately, reassigned to help out with evacuation operations.

Gary, left alone for a moment, walked to the riverbank. He had to lean into the wind, and the rain lashed his face. It was a July afternoon and the air wasn't cold, but the low scudding clouds made it as dark as a fall day.

The Barrier piers strode across the river, steel sails each five stories high, glistening in the rain. The gates between the piers had already been raised, hollow slabs of plated steel each twenty meters tall, rotated up on tremendous wheels to turn the Barrier into a solid wall that rose seven meters above the regular water level. Bright red lights shone on the piers to warn any shipping that the river was closed. Gary had never seen the Barrier up close before, and the scale of it struck him. Each of the four central navigable channels was as wide as the central span of Tower Bridge, and each gate weighed four thousand tons. The Barrier was a monument to man's attempts to control nature.

But the natural was testing the human today. The river on the downstream side, pushing in from the ocean, was already significantly higher than that upstream; spray leapt over the clean lines of the gates.

And through the howl of the wind, Gary could hear sirens wail all along the estuary.

Two figures approached him, both swathed in luminescent orange coats. "Gary! Is that you? You asshole, you'll get yourself washed away. Have to put you on a lead, like those nutty Christians did in Barcelona."

"Nice to see you too, Thandie."

She wrapped him in her thickly sleeved arms. Thandie Jones was an oceanographer. When Gary had been captured she had been employed on weather-system modeling and climate-change studies for NOAA, America's National Oceanic and Atmospheric Administration. A black, strong-featured Chicagoan, she was taller than Gary but wiry, always stronger.

The man beside Thandie had his hood closed up over his mouth, so only his nose and bespectacled eyes showed.

Thandie said, "Gary Boyle, meet Sanjay McDonald. Another climate modeler, poor sap."

Sanjay exposed a bearded face and grabbed Gary's hand. "I work at Hadley—that is, the Met Office's Hadley Center for Climate Prediction. I heard all about you. Good to meet you, Gary. And I'm sure you're glad you've come back to find some real weather going on."

"Yeah," Thandie said. "Speaking of which, let's get out of it."

She led them both into the control tower. She took Gary down to a kind of cloakroom, where she fitted him out with protective gear: a wetsuit, boots, a thermal jacket, a hard hat, even a life jacket. Gary had never been shy before Thandie. He stripped down and began to prize himself into a wetsuit that didn't quite fit.

"You did me a favor phoning ahead to meet me here," Thandie said. "You've got a teeny tiny grain of celebrity, Boyle." She held her thumb and forefinger invisibly apart. "But it was enough to requisition me a chopper. We're goin' storm chasin'."

He grinned back. "I knew it was a good idea calling you."

Sanjay McDonald said, "I take it you two know each other well."

Gary said, "We were at MIT together. I studied under Thandie, actually. I went off to work at Goddard, and Thandie drew the short straw and moved to NOAA."

"Yeah, yeah," she shot back.

"But we worked in the same area, climate modeling, with Thandie focusing on the interaction of the ocean and atmosphere—well, I guess you must know that. We worked together on some predictive modeling to aid the post-Katrina levee reconstruction project at New Orleans."

"Our world, the world of climate modelers, is small," Sanjay said solemnly. He looked Asian to Gary, but his accent was as Scottish as his surname.

"We missed you," Thandie said to Gary. "I kept in touch with your mom. We signed the petitions, kept up the Web sites, nailed up the posters, tied the yellow ribbons on the trees on your birthday. Kept you in the public eye."

This sort of thing touched Gary deeply. During his captivity he had had no idea that people were making such a sustained effort on his behalf. "I appreciate that. I mean it. It must have played a part in getting me out of there. And I know Mom needed the support. I haven't seen her yet, though we've spoken . . ."

A few of the Barrier staff came through, all British, mostly men, looking harassed but excited.

Thandie said dryly, "Today's the kind of day that makes it worthwhile for the guys who work here. Validation Tuesday. We're trying to keep out of the way. Officially we're guests of the Met Office's Storm Tide Forecasting Service. They have a big modeling center up in Liverpool—"

"But the production models don't work so well anymore," Sanjay said.

"So," Thandie said, "here we are at the front line with our experimental models trying to patch together new solutions."

Gary said, "If the models don't work, I guess the Met Office can't say how this storm is going to play out."

"That's about the size of it," Sanjay said. "And that's why no warnings were issued about this storm until just recently. Ideally they like twelve or twenty-four hours' notice, so they can order the schools to stay closed in the morning, and keep the commuters out of the city, that sort of thing."

Thandie said, "And the models don't work because the world is going awry. You've been missing all the fun, Gary Boyle."

A deep mechanical groan reverberated through the concrete structure. Gary imagined the tremendous weight of the rising river water, pressing against the Barrier gates.

"So, you ready?" Thandie asked.

11

The chopper, run by the Environment Agency, was a modified Puma. It was fitted out with an instrument pod with temperature, pressure and windspeed gauges, and a neat little unit with radar and infrared monitors to measure the depth of the river water and other properties such as speed, surface roughness and temperature. A camera was mounted beneath the hull. There was even a sonde, a fish-shaped gadget attached to a winched cable that could be lowered into the water, though Sanjay insisted the sonde wouldn't be used today; the water was too turbulent, the risk of snagging on some bit of flotsam too great.

As Sanjay checked the gear, Thandie grinned at Gary with a glint in her eye, a look he recognized well. She had always had a streak of recklessness about her, a willingness to go chasing hurricanes and tsunamis, all in the name of science, always willing to go that bit further than anybody else. Disaster hunting, she called it, surfing the extreme weather.

And it scared him to his bones when they got into the chopper and Thandie herself took the pilot's seat. She pulled a radio cap over her head and started snapping switches. An engine roared into life and the rotors overhead turned.

Sanjay opened up a laptop on his knees to make connections to the chopper's instrument suite. He had a kind of harness that strapped the machine to his thighs. As it booted up he observed Gary's expression. "You didn't know she was the pilot, I'm guessing."

"You guess right."

"Well, nobody else was available. All the regular pilots have emergency duties. Lucky us—"

Thandie called back, "Hold onto your lunches, guys, this elevator car is going *up*."

The chopper surged into the air, rising over the control tower. For a few seconds while Thandie checked her handling they hovered in the air, buffeted by the wind; the chopper felt as fragile as a leaf.

Gary looked down. The Barrier was once more revealed, those steel cowls lined up stoutly, and the Thames raged more violently than he remembered from only a few minutes ago. On the shore, at a fence protecting the Barrier tower, he saw a crowd of protesters, all soggy banners and waterproofs, faced by a line of police in riot gear.

"What's their beef?" he asked.

Sanjay looked over his shoulder. "Rich versus poor. Protesting about the billions spent to protect London while the rest of England floods, and so on."

Thandie snapped, "Would they *prefer* it if London was drowned? Let's get to work."

The bird surged forward, heading east into the oncoming storm, and Thandie whooped.

The rain splashed against the cockpit glass, coming in so hard Gary could barely see out. The small cabin, crowded by the three of them and the science gear, juddered and clattered as it was thrown to and fro, harnesses rattling and the hull creaking. This wasn't like the smooth professional ride Gary had been given by the AxysCorp pilot earlier. Thandie seemed to challenge the storm, just barreling straight through the turbulence. Sanjay was trying to work his laptop. Now Gary could see why he had strapped the sleek pad to his knees.

Gary leaned forward. "So what have I missed in your branch of the soap opera, Thand?" He had to shout above the noise.

"Not much," she yelled back. "It's the same old same old in the academic world. Write your papers, scramble for citations, put together proposals for grants for a couple more years, fend off the wandering hands of eminent professors. Climate science has been booming the last few years, especially since all our modeling started going awry, but it's just as hard to make a living."

"Thus the life of the junior research scientist."

"Yeah. Oh, I got myself thrown out of the Royal Society, in London. Got in an argument with an old boy who called me a climate-change denier."

"You're kidding."

"Nope. But I came up with data on sea-level rise that didn't fit the paradigm."

"So you weren't denying anything."

"Just pointing out that something *different* seems to be happening. Something new, not explicable by the usual mechanisms, ice-cap melt and ocean-water thermal expansion. Those old guys have been arguing their case too long, Gary, and against too much below-the-belt opposition. They take any questioning, any at all, as attempts at refutation. But on the other hand, there are plenty of commentators taking these exceptional events as *proof* that global warming is a reality, even though there's no immediate causal link, and all the old deniers of global warming are getting worked up in response. It's a mess."

"Your data was lousy," Sanjay said. "At the Royal Society. Your conclusions were leaps in the dark. *I* would have thrown you out, even if you hadn't told Isaac Keegan he had his head up his arse."

"I regret nothing," Thandie yelled back. "The first reports of anything new in the world are always shouted down. You knew Hansen at Goddard, Gary, you know what it's like for mavericks." She sang, " 'They all laughed at Christopher Columbus . . .' "

"But you're still working," Gary said.

"Somehow, yeah."

"So what else don't I know? You got a man in your life these days, Thandie? Is there a Mister Jones?"

Thandie hesitated. Sanjay glanced over at him, then looked down at his displays.

Thandie said, "I guess you didn't hear about that."

"About what?"

"I met this guy. Dot-com entrepreneur who was interested in marketing personalized weather forecasting. Not the dumbest idea in the world. You'd base it on public-domain wide-area models, supplemented by a sensor suite that would track the micro-climate in the customer's vicinity and anticipated route—"

"Thandie. The guy?"

"Yeah. To cut a long story, we got married. Your mother was there—your ambassador, I guess. I got pregnant. Lost the kid. Then lost the guy, or we lost each other."

He was shocked by the suddenness of the telling. "Oh. I'm sorry. You didn't want to try again?"

"That turned out not to be an option," she said crisply. "Not for me. The doctors—hell, it doesn't matter now."

"Christ, Thandie, what a terrible thing."

"It's just life. We all go through these changes. Births, deaths, whatever. It was just a road not taken." She sat rigid amid the buffeting of the flight.

Sanjay tapped Gary on the shoulder. "Myself, I have two children, by two marriages. One child in Glasgow is mostly Scottish. The other in Middlesex is mostly Bengali. Life is always complicated, my friend."

"So it is. But—" But Gary had known a different Thandie before, a wild, reckless, exuberant, imaginative Thandie. He wondered if he would ever be able to get to know this new, damaged person. "It's a tragedy that I've been away so long."

Sanjay said, "A tragedy for you, your family and your friends. You must resent what was done to you."

"Hell, yes." More and more as the days went by, in fact. Maybe he'd got too used to his captors, or even fond of them, or some damn Stockholm-syndrome thing. Domesticated by his long captivity. Now he was out and going through some other process; now he hated them.

But the chopper dipped, and he was reminded that the world was going through its own novel processes, which had no patience for the revolutions in his head.

The chopper swooped over a peninsula that jutted out from the north bank of the river, incised by a deep brook. Industrial facilities sprawled across both sides of the brook, oil storage tanks and refineries and chimney stacks and big gas storage vessels, all embedded in a web of walkways and pipelines. One big line strode overhead across the brook itself.

Gary asked, "Where are we? What is that?"

"Canvey Island," Thandie called. "And to the west of the creek, that's Coryton. Petrochemical installations."

The terminals were serviced from the river. One immense supertanker huddled against a jetty, with the compact shapes of tugs nearby. Brightly lit, a carpet of sodium light, this landscape looked as if it went on for kilometers, and Gary could see it had some protection from the water in the shape of a stout concrete sea wall that had to be meters high. But the land wasn't entirely given over to industry. There were estates of houses down there, clusters of brick red like scrubby flowers huddling in the rain, some of them only a half-kilometer, less, from the industrial plant.

And there was clearly an evacuation underway. Gary saw cars streaming out of the housing estates, crowding the roads that fed into the big arterial routes to the north. It was so dark now, though it wasn't yet four in the afternoon, that most of the cars had their lights on. The traffic, however, was all but motionless, and helicopters, bright yellow search-and-rescue machines, prowled along the riverbank. Gary saw all this in glimpses through sheeting rain, from a chopper that bucked and rolled in the wind. He heard Thandie talking to some kind of air traffic control.

And now there was a spark of lightning, a crackle of thunder.

"The storm front's only a couple kilometers thataway," Thandie called, pointing east. "Sanj, how's the data? You got GPS?"

"I got that," said Sanjay, staring at his screen. "Climate sensors nominal, though that wind gauge is going to rip clean off at this rate. And the pressure's dropping. Nine seventy. Nine sixty-five . . . The radar's working, the sonar not so well, you'd expect that. It would help if this tub wasn't bucking like a fairground ride."

"Doing what I can, brainbox."

Gary had had no idea that all this industry was out here. "It's like a city in itself. And kind of vulnerable, isn't it?"

"When it comes to fuel London's a big and thirsty monster, Gary. But they're prepared for floods, they drill for them." She snapped a switch, and the radio cut into a feed from a refinery crew going through shut-down procedures, working through checklists of pumps, furnaces, compressors, valves, catalytic crackers.

"Leaving it late," Gary said. "The storm's been tracked since Scotland."

"A flood warning itself is an expensive event," Thandie said. "With more than a million people living on the Thames flood plain, you don't raise the alarm unless you have to. The river traffic is a problem too. The Barrier seems to be raised more often than it's lowered nowadays. And shutting down those refineries is no joke, you don't just throw a switch. It *costs* to abandon the processes they put their materials through. False alarms are unpopular. People are terrified of liability, legal claims."

"And in this case," Sanjay said, "the error bars around the storm's probable track and effects were just too wide to be sure. I told you, our modeling is breaking down. What's worse is that the interfaces between different models aren't working so well either . . ."

Gary understood the principle. Mathematical models of the weather were generally based on dividing up land, air and sea into discrete elements and tracing the progress of variables like pressure, temperature and wind speed through from one element to the next. You might run a coarse model for the whole of the North Sea, and as a storm passed the Wash or the Thames Estuary you would feed predicted conditions from the ocean model to finer-grained models to see what happened in there. But if all the models were suffering because of some underlying change in the physical condition in the planet's weather systems, it would be at the edges and interfaces that errors would particularly multiply.

Sanjay said, "The last great London flood was back in 1953. That event led to the construction of the Barrier, eventually. Much of Canvey is below sea level; people died here. But that flood was a convergence of high tide with a big storm surge."

The low-pressure air at the heart of a storm could lift the level of the sea below it, physically sucking it up into a hump that could be hundreds of kilometers across. And then the winds could drive the high water against the coast or into a river estuary. That was a storm surge.

"So is this a surge? Are we hitting a high tide?"

Sanjay said, "The storm is driving waves ahead of itself, but I wouldn't call it a significant surge. And as for the tide, the predictions now are all over the place."

Gary said, "So this event doesn't have those key features that characterized the 1953 event. And yet we're getting a flood even so."

"Looks like it," Sanjay said. "It's not even a particularly severe storm." He sounded unhappy, as if the real world were a bit of grit in the oyster-shell of his science.

And Thandie called, "Oh shit. Here it comes." The chopper dipped and bucked as she hauled them back out over the river for a better view.

Gary, peering through a rain-streaked window, saw the wave coming, water raised and driven by the North Sea storm and bottled up in the narrowing, shallowing estuary. As it advanced it spilled almost casually over flood barriers and walls, and on either bank a dark stain spread over the roads and gardens and parks.

Thandie called back, "You getting this, Sanj?"

Sanjay was using a joystick to control the camera slung beneath the chopper's body. "Pretty good," he reported.

"We're feeding the rolling news channels . . ."

The flood reached the petrochemical refineries and storage tanks. The water spread around the feet of the huge structures, looking as black and viscous as the oil that was processed there. Some lights failed, and a few abandoned cars were quickly submerged. The depth of the water must be increasing rapidly.

And now the flood started to spill over the housing estates. Thandie swooped lower so they could see. The rushing waters poured onto access roads still crowded with cars. Vehicles were overwhelmed, their lights flickering and dying. People scrambled out of their cars through windows and doors, and climbed onto the cars' roofs, or tried to wade through the rising water. The current shoved the cars themselves, piling them into the fleeing people like logs.

All this Gary saw from above, from the warmth and comfort of his helicopter cabin. There was no human noise, no screams or cries; it was all drowned by the storm's roar and the thrum of the chopper's engine. Suddenly this was no longer just a stunt weather event, a puzzle for climate modelers. "Christ," he said, "there's a disaster going on down there."

"The whole damn day is already a disaster," Thandie said. "Let's just do our job."

The chopper roared up into the air and headed west. The flooded estate was reduced to an abstraction, a mélange of water and land.

12

Pursuing the storm front up the river toward central London, the chopper flew over Tilbury, ten or twelve kilometers west of Canvey Island. There was a much more massive evacuation project going on from this heavily populated area, with traffic edging out of Tilbury to the north of the Thames and Gravesend to the south. Electricity substations were overwhelmed. The lighting in whole districts started to blank out. In the river itself a container ship had been caught, apparently as it tried to turn, and had pitched over, spilling containers into the water like matchsticks. That alone was a major rescue operation, Gary saw, with helicopters and what looked like lifeboats clustering around the stricken ship.

The chopper flew on.

"We need to understand this," Thandie murmured. "Understand it, and do something about it."

"Mean sea levels are up by a meter," Gary said.

Thandie turned. "Who told you that?"

"It came from an eleven-year-old."

Thandie grunted. "Well, she might be right."

"It *was* a she, actually."

"Of course it was."

"Nobody knows for sure," Sanjay said. "Trends are hard to establish. What we've actually seen are exceptional fluvial events, and exceptional incidences of tidal flooding, like this event. All over the planet. Ocean temperatures are rising too. The additional heat is fueling storms."

"Like this one."

"Possibly. The data's patchy."

Gary asked Thandie, "What do you think?"

"That the oceans *are* rising. The data might be patchy,

Sanjay, but everything points that way. The secular trend
will become apparent with time."

"So how is this happening? A meter is a hell of a lot.
When I was abducted that was an upper limit for the sea-
level rise quoted for the end of the century, not for 2016."

"I remember it well," Thandie said dryly. "The good old
days of global warming."

"So what's the cause? You say it's not just glacier melting, the ice caps, or the heat expansion of the water itself."

"All that's going on, as it has been for decades," Thandie
said. "But this is something else."

Sanjay said, "It's an argument that's been raging for
a couple of years. And Thandie has some hypotheses—
haven't you, my dear?"

"Don't patronize me, you smug Brit loser. Yes, I got
some ideas. All I need is a way to validate them."

"And then you can write your book and go on TV and
scare everybody to death, while making a fortune in the
process."

Thandie lifted one gloved hand with a middle finger
raised. Then she slowed the chopper to a hover. "Jesus
Christ, look at that."

Gary looked down at a six-lane road bridge that boldly
spanned the river, fed by complex junctions to north and
south. The north bank was lined by industrial developments, with wharves and jetties jutting into the river. Behind the industrial site was a broad splash of concrete and
glass, brightly lit from within, from the air like a series of
immense greenhouses. To the south he glimpsed an even
more spectacular city of glass, set in what looked like a
chalk quarry, with acres of manicured parkland.

"Where are we?"

"The Dartford Crossing," Sanjay said. "That, my American friend, is the M25, the London orbital motorway. Even
on a good day it's a doughnut-shaped car park. And this is
where it crosses the river."

"And those retail developments?"

"Lakeside Thurrock to the north, Bluewater Park to the
south. Shoppers' paradises . . ."

Today these developments were having a very bad day
indeed. Helicopters hovered, some of them big USAF Chi-

nooks, their spotlights shining down on river water that lapped ever higher around the abutments and approaches of the big motorway bridge. The water had forced its way behind the industrial areas around Lakeside, isolating them, and was pushing its way into the retail development. By the crossing itself Gary saw an immense bowl where the roads snaked through toll booths, a bowl filling steadily with water. Car lights failed as they were submerged, and people swarmed like ants.

"The motorway's jammed up," Thandie called. "I'm listening to the police reports. The tunnel was closed already because of the threat of flooding, so the bridge and its feeder roads are clogged. Plus you have a lot of extra refugee traffic pouring in."

As Gary watched, the lights in the northern shopping complex, Lakeside, went out. "Jesus."

"The storm front is approaching the Barrier," Sanjay said, peering into his laptop. "I guess this is the moment of truth."

Gary asked, "So will the water overtop the Barrier?"

"Ah," said Sanjay. "That's the forty-billion-dollar question. It's a 1960s design based on 1960s assumptions about future flood event probabilities. Even before this new sea-level rise phenomenon, the revised projections based on global warming were ringing alarm bells—"

"The police are asking us for help," Thandie said, listening to her radio feed. "They're organizing pickup zones. Kids, women with babies, the sick and injured. We can take some out to higher ground. Keep running until our fuel gives out."

"Here it comes," Sanjay said, staring at his screen. "I think the water's overtopping the Barrier gates. My word."

Gary looked at Thandie. "Let's help."

"Yeah." The helicopter dropped out of the sky toward the darkened carcass of Lakeside.

13

Inside the Dome at Greenwich, Amanda was almost relieved when the arena show was cut short by the evacuation announcements.

Everybody stood up and streamed into the aisles, excited despite the distant ringing of fire alarms. It was nearly the end of a long day anyhow, Amanda supposed, and she knew kids; most of the audience here would be ready for the bright lights of the tube station or the warmth of their buses, ready for home. As for Amanda herself, whiskery boy bands singing Elizabethan madrigals for "educational" purposes, as mandated by the national curriculum, wasn't her idea of a fun way to spend the afternoon.

But Amanda and Benj sat on either side of an empty seat. Kristie had gone off to the loo. Uncertain, Amanda glanced across at Benj. "She'll have the sense to come back here, won't she?"

But Benj didn't reply. He sat back in his chair, a dreamy, absent look on his face. She had put an embargo on his Angel during the show, but he had snapped it on as soon as the evacuation order came over the PA.

Amanda worried vaguely. She didn't even know what the alarm was about. She'd heard people muttering about terrorist scares, but she was willing to bet that the filthy weather had something to do with it. A flood on the Jubilee Line, the underground route that had brought her here with the kids; that was more likely it. But she fretted about what it would mean for her if the tube was flooded. The underground was the main way you got off the peninsula. There must be buses, but they would be packed. They faced hours waiting around, maybe in the rain, and the kids would be fractious.

She glanced around. Most people had gone already, this

two-thousand-seat "Indigo2" arena draining remarkably quickly, only a few stragglers remaining. No sign of Kristie. Amanda wondered if she should go to the toilets to find her.

It occurred to her to try her phone. When she called Kristie she got a "no signal" message.

She paged around news services, trying to find out what was happening. There was no reception from the local services, even the BBC. She got a CNN feed, but that didn't feature whatever was going on in London but the latest problems in Sydney, Australia, where the flooding had worsened markedly. Amanda stared at pictures taken from the air, of water spilling from the harbors deep into central Sydney, and a panicky evacuation from the glass needles of the CBD, Sydney's central business district. The highways out of the city were jammed, and there was a crush at the main rail station, though reports said that the trains had already been stopped. Even now the cameras lingered on the postcard icons. The Opera House stood on a kind of island of its own, cut off from the mainland. It was like looking at movie special effects.

She shut her phone down and glanced around. No Kristie.

A Dome staff member walked up the aisle toward them. He was a young man with vertical red hair. He was chewing gum. "Sorry, Miss. You have to go. We need to clear the venue."

Miss. Amanda smiled; he was only a few years older than Benj. "I'm waiting for my daughter. She's in the lavatory."

"I'm sorry but you have to go now. It's my job to get the venue clear."

"I'm waiting for my daughter."

The boy backed off, nervously, but he seemed distracted; he must be getting instructions from an Angel of his own. "Please. I'll have to call security. I have to clear the venue. It's the evacuation plan."

Benj stood up. "Oh, come on, Mum, there's no point winding him up. She's probably hanging around outside the toilets anyhow. You know what's she's like."

She felt oddly reluctant to stand up, to leave the seat without Kristie. It meant a definitive break with her normal day. But she supposed this boy was telling the truth about security; she had no choice. "All right." She stood and followed Benj out of the row of seats.

They made their way to the main entrance area. This was a cavernous plaza facing a row of glass doors, lined to either side by ticket offices and shops, a deserted Starbucks. The Dome roof itself loomed over her, a faintly grimy tent that trapped hot, moist, stale air. She could hear the drumming of the rain on the canvas panels high above. It was always gloomy in here, enclosed.

There was no sign of Kristie outside the loo. Another staff member, a hefty woman this time, wouldn't allow her to go and look inside. "The toilets are clear, ma'am."

"But that's where my daughter went."

"The toilets are clear. She can't be in there."

"Look, she's eleven years old!"

"I'm sure you'll find her waiting for you at your party's emergency assembly point."

That threw Amanda from anger to a feeling of inadequacy, of helplessness. "What assembly point? I don't know anything about an assembly point."

"I do, Mum," Benj said. "It was on our tickets. Car Park Four."

The woman pointed. "It's signposted, very easy to find." Her walkie-talkie squawked, and with an apologetic glance at Amanda she turned away.

Benj took the lead again. "I know the way, Mum. Come on."

"Let's try calling her again."

Benj lifted his own phone. The screen flashed red: no signal. "I've been trying. I can't even leave a message. Look, she's not completely thick. She knows where to go."

"Well, I hope so." She followed him, reluctantly, but she knew there was no choice.

They were among the last to leave the Dome; the crowds had streamed out quickly. As they crossed the floor of the entrance plaza they were joined by the last stragglers emerging from Entertainment Avenue, the big circular shopping mall that curved around the arena at the Dome's core, a corridor of shops and restaurants, fancy lampposts, even trees flourishing in the tented gloom.

They emerged into rain driven almost horizontally by

the wind. Amanda glanced back at the Dome. The rain ricocheted off its dirty fabric roof. She could see only a little of it; it looked oddly unimpressive, for its curve created a horizon so close to her eye it hid its own true scale. Bad design, she thought. And when she looked away from the Dome, toward the car park, she saw massed, chaotic crowds. She had no way of judging numbers. There might have been tens of thousands here, a mob like a football crowd. Her heart went cold as the scale of what was happening began to press on her.

Benj took her hand, holding his hood closed around his face. "This way to the car park." They made their way forward, splashing through water that puddled on the concrete and tarmac and gradually formed more extensive ponds. People milled everywhere, shuffling along in their raincoats. But nobody seemed alarmed. The younger children were excited. Nobody seemed upset except Amanda. Benj and Amanda tried their mobiles again, but there was still no signal.

There was some kind of emergency going on around the tube station. The station itself had been fenced off by a barrier, manned by bedraggled police. Amanda stared at a steady stream of soaked, frightened-looking passengers, emerging on foot from the deep tube line. Paramedics in Day-Glo coats, working in pairs, forced their way in through the emerging crowd, and came out again carrying stretchers.

The sight of the drenched people, the bodies on the stretchers, horrified Amanda. She found it impossible to believe that only half an hour ago, less, she had been sitting in an arena, warm and relaxed with her kids beside her, listening to a boy band murder madrigals. And now, this. Had people *died*?

And if the Jubilee Line was flooded, the tube network was probably shut down entirely. Travel was going to be a nightmare, even once they got off in Greenwich. Bit by bit the day continued to unravel.

Benj pulled her hand. "Come on, Mum, I'm getting cold."

"Yes. I'm sorry." They hurried on.

14

Lily and Piers had to wait for a chopper to take them from Shoeburyness to Greenwich. The hydrometropole's limited landing facilities were clogged by craft whisking parties off to their "disaster vacations." This was a kind of insurance policy offered by Nathan's AxysCorp, where in the event of a calamity like a flood you were just taken away to a luxury hotel, somewhere safe, to ride it out, and let somebody else deal with the mess. Lily was bemused to see how accustomed the world had become to disaster. Some of these fleeing plutocrats didn't even pause in their drinking as they were escorted smoothly from party venue to vacation transport.

At last Lily and Piers got their chopper, and lifted. The wind was rising all the time, and even this pilot's consummate skill couldn't save the bird from shuddering as it rose, the hull groaning, the engine roaring as the rotors bit into the turbulent air.

The delay hadn't been long, but enough that by the time they flew over greater London, heading west, the flooding was already extensive. The river had breached the flood defenses on both banks, and buildings and lampposts and trees protruded from the water like toys in puddles. Evacuations continued frantically all along the line of the rising water, the roads crammed with chains of slow-moving cars, trucks, buses, fire engines and ambulances, their lights gleaming like jewels, and with a denser, porridgelike mass that had to be people fleeing on foot, too many of them and too far away to distinguish, human beings reduced to particles.

Piers looked down at the inundation, his gaze frank and intelligent, listening in to the police feeds. A situation like this should bring out the best in him, Lily thought, his training and instinct for command. But he was pale, and he had lost weight like the rest of the hostages. Their captivity was only six days past, and they all had finite reserves. But the world evidently wasn't going to wait for their recovery.

When they passed over the Thames Barrier the pilot dipped to give them a view. The Barrier, a line that cut across the river, was overtopped all along its length, and a kind of waterfall thundered down on the upstream side, throwing up spray and churning up the river water.

"That," Piers murmured, "is a sight to tell your grandchildren about. A once in a thousand years event, supposedly. Actually the Barrier is itself now the subject of a rescue operation. Chaps trapped in the control towers, and in some kind of connecting tunnel under the river. The city's defenders now need defending themselves. Well." He turned away.

The chopper dipped and surged onward again, heading steadily west.

At last they swept over Greenwich. The pilot stayed high, keeping out of the way of the rescue operations already underway.

Here the river described a fat S-shape in a great double meander, creating two peninsulas, one dangling from the north bank and the other from the south, from Lily's vantage pressed up against each other like yin and yang twins. The fatter, pendulous peninsula on the left was the Isle of Dogs, a tongue of lowland incised by dock developments, some centuries old; to the north, at its neck, the huge new office developments around Canary Wharf sprawled, acres of glass glistening. The slimmer peninsula to the right, pushing up from the south, was Greenwich. Lily could clearly see at its tip the spiky dirty-gray disc that was the Dome—once the Millennium Dome, now called "The O2." Somewhere down there were her sister and the kids.

All this was only a few kilometers west of the breached Barrier. And already the waters were breaking over the land to north and south, drowning wharves and jetties and flooding jammed roads, and choppers hovered over the landscape, angels of despair.

"Unbelievable, you know," Piers Michaelmas said.

"Thirty years ago, forty, hardly any of this was here. Just the docks, the old housing stock. Derelict, basically. Now look at it. The police are saying there are somewhere over half a million people down there right now, in the office blocks and the leisure developments. It's a blister, a huge concentration of people."

"All on the flood plain."

"Hindsight is a marvelous thing." He listened again. "I know you want to get to the Dome and find your sister, yes? But I'm being called to the Isle of Dogs, Millwall, a major evacuation there."

"We'll split up, then."

"Yes." He leaned forward. "Pilot, did you get that?"

The pilot nodded, distracted, listening to his own feed. "My computer's asking for clearance. Having to talk to two different Silver Command stations . . . I can take you to Millwall first, sir. Put you down in Mudchute Park, they've given me clearance for that. Then I'll hop over to Greenwich with Captain Brooke."

"That'll do," Michaelmas said.

The chopper slid north over the river and dipped down toward the Isle of Dogs. Detail coalesced, housing, a park, streets already running with filthy water, and Lily made out the line of the DLR, the Docklands Light Railway, striding on its elevated track toward the north. A group of police and military trucks had been drawn up in the park, evidently some kind of field command post. The water lapped around the vehicles' wheels.

The pilot set down gently on sodden grass. The door slid open, allowing in a buffeting wind and a spray of cold rain.

Piers pulled up his hood, grabbed an emergency pack, released his harness and clambered out of his bucket seat. He twisted back and grabbed Lily's hand. "Good luck," he yelled.

"You too. Now piss off and close the ruddy door."

He grinned and stepped out. The door slid closed, and the chopper lifted immediately. Piers watched the bird rise, his hand sheltering his eyes from the rain.

Piers made his way straight to the field command center in the park.

His rank, and recognition by some of the officers, got

him into a meeting in a briefing room full of laptops, TV screens and whiteboards, into the center of things. Here the local chief constable hosted a rolling conference with representatives of the ambulance and fire services, the local authority, the utilities, the Environment Agency, transport, health, and the media, a couple of local reporters. The British system was to have the police at the heart of the management of civil emergencies. Most of the attendees here had mobiles clamped to their heads. Piers knew the mobile networks had been co-opted for the emergency services' use, a shutout that would be giving civilians problems by now, even if the power hadn't failed to the phone masts.

Piers listened for a while. The centerpiece of the planning seemed to be the evacuation of the most flood-prone areas, which was in fact most of Millwall. With the roads already clogged, the plan was to get the public out using the Docklands Light Railway, north and to the mainland. It was only a few kilometers; nowhere in London was far from anywhere else, geographically. The DLR ran on an elevated rail, above the anticipated flooding, and even when the power went it could conceivably be used as a walkway.

Of course what would become of the refugees after that was anybody's guess. City Airport was flooded. Traffic was clogged all over London, and there was a solid jam on the M25 rippling back from the flooding at the Dartford Crossing. And there were other problems. Aside from the pressure on the mobile networks, Docklands hosted some major internet service providers and international landline telephone exchanges; communications were fritzing all over the place as the area was flooded, building by building.

Piers knew about the wider disaster management strategy. The efforts of dozens of groups like this across London would be fed up to a "Gold Coordinating Group" chaired by a senior police officer, which would in turn report to the Cabinet's crisis committee. And even beyond that, he was sure, given an emergency on such a scale there would be contacts among the international community. He had already seen Chinooks over the river, the Americans putting military assets into play from their bases in the UK, and the Europeans must be planning recovery and support packages. There was huge tension in the room, a clamor of voices, phones ringing constantly, heavy lines scrawled across maps and then scrawled again, as the group tried to handle the many facets of this multiple, unfolding disaster. Piers imagined being drawn into these frantic discussions, his advice sought, a new role defined, new responsibilities assigned. He was trained for command-level roles; in theory there was much he could contribute here.

But he felt oddly brittle, his head somehow full. He began to avoid eye contact, as if he could not bear to be engaged. He had an odd flashback to the cellars under Barcelona, the times the guards would maliciously whip away his towels or blindfolds and try to catch him with his eyes open, to break through to his soul.

He needed to get out of here, he realized suddenly. He slipped out and back into the storm, pulling his hood over his head, and walked off into the streets.

Car Park Four was on the far side of the square. All the car parks had been full when Amanda and the kids had arrived this morning, but now most of the cars had already gone or were packing the exits, their taillights crowding red, leaving behind a surface of pale pink gravel slick with water.

Benj pointed to the left, toward the river side. "I think that's our point over there." Amanda saw a huddle of fifty or so adults and children, one of a number of such groups gathered under signposts all across the plain of car parks. Benj's eyes were sharper than hers, and he was good at remembering instructions; she was sure he was right.

They hurried that way, through the rain, splashing through puddles. They had to make their way through barriers of blue railings, and she could hear the rain hammering down on the double roof of the Beckham football academy. They were nearly run over by a big four-by-four that came bearing down on them out of nowhere, screeching across the parking spaces, driven by a frightened-looking young woman with a tiny scrap of a toddler strapped into a car seat behind her.

Benj was alert, and he looked around curiously. For once the world was more interesting than his Angel. "Look at that boat, Mum. It looks awful high." It was one of the fancy high-speed Thames Clippers, tied up at the spindly, modernistic Queen Elizabeth Pier. The boat was riding up in the water and heaving as waves passed. The river must be high, then.

They reached the group. A policewoman stood with them, hands behind her back, smiling, an image of calm competence. Looking around, Amanda saw more police scattered through the crowds, gathering groups together.

But she couldn't see Kristie. Benj went off to try to find her. Amanda waited, hanging back from the group. Everybody else seemed calm, everyone but her. She felt embarrassed to have turned up in such a panic, without one of her kids, in such an incompetent mess.

Benj came hurrying back. His hair was plastered down by the rain. "Mum, she isn't here."

She couldn't take it in. "What do you mean? Then where is she?"

"I don't know," he said, his voice small.

She stood there staring, almost angry at him for coming back with the wrong answer. Kristie *had* to be here. She glanced around at the calm policewoman speaking into her radio, the children subdued but not frightened, the dismal, soggy car park, the Dome with its crown of spiky pylons thrusting into the air. Racked by fear and inadequacy, she longed not to be here, to be safe in her office in Hammersmith, surrounded by her files and her laptop and with a phone that *worked*, safe in a world she knew and could handle. Not this rainy desolation.

The policewoman stood on a low wall and clapped her hands. "Can I have your attention?" The kids' chatter fell silent. "I've had fresh instructions. Look, you can see how things are. The tube is out because it's flooded. The buses are all full up, and have mostly gone anyhow. I'm afraid we're going to have to walk out." There was a groan, but the policewoman smiled brightly. "Don't worry, this is the standard evacuation plan and it's been rehearsed. It's not far." She pointed south. "We'll go that way, following East Parkside, and then along the southern approach to the Blackwall Tunnel. It's a flyover, so you'll be safe from the flooding." *What flooding?* "Now, the roads are already clogged up with cars, but we've kept the hard shoulder open and we're looking to open up another lane too, so it should be easy enough. There'll be lots of other people walking too. It's only"—she hesitated, looking at the younger children—"let's say half an hour to the stations, Westcombe Park or Charlton, and they'll be laying on special trains to take you off." Off where? Amanda wondered. How do we get home? "That's all. If you'd like to form up into a column, I'll follow at the rear . . ."

As the people gathered obediently into a crocodile, Amanda pushed her way through to the policewoman. "My daughter. Kristie Caistor. She's got lost."

"I'll put a call out," the policewoman said. "We've a contact system in place, Mrs. Caistor. I'm sure—"

"I'll wait," Amanda said desperately. "She might come here. She's bound to be frightened."

"It's much better if you move on. We have to get the whole site cleared."

Amanda snarled, "That's what they've been saying to me since I was kicked out of that stupid arena by a fucking kid."

The WPC blanched, wet, tense. She fingered the radio button at her lapel.

Benj plucked at Amanda's sleeve, horribly embarrassed. "Mum, please."

Somebody screamed, one of the kids. "My feet are wet!"

And suddenly Amanda was aware that her feet were colder, too, and her ankles, her shins. She glanced down. Water, cold and full of muck, was washing over her shoes. She looked to her left, toward the pier. Water gushed over the retaining wall, a steady stream of it, pouring out over the flat surface of the car park. For a heartbeat or two, the people just watched the water rising around their shins, pelted by the rain.

Then there was a surge, and a wave topped the wall and rushed down toward them. Children screamed, and parents broke and ran, dragging their kids away from the water. Amanda reached for Benj.

Then it was on them like a tide coming in, a wave of water that reached Amanda's knees, and then another pulse came that soaked her to her waist and made her stagger.

The policewoman was yelling, "Go that way, the way I told you! Go on toward the flyover! Keep together!"

The party struggled in that direction. But the water continued to pour over the bank wall, spreading eagerly over

the car park. The current was surprisingly strong for such
shallow water, and it was difficult to walk through it. One
little girl went under. The policewoman and her mother
helped her up; she surfaced, coughing, soaked to the skin.
And still the water poured over the wall.

Amanda tried to stay standing, staring wildly about.
"Kristie. Kristie!"

"She's safe!" It was Lily, running up out of nowhere, in a
wetsuit and heavy orange coat, splashing toward her. And
Kristie was with her, holding Lily's hand, her pink backpack bright.

Amanda grabbed her daughter gratefully. Even Benj let
Kristie bury her face in his coat.

Amanda said, "Lily, where the hell did you come from?—
Never mind. Where did you find her?"

"She couldn't get back to you, and she couldn't make it
here, so she went to a police missing-persons point. They're
all over the peninsula. Smart kid. They logged her in, I
found her there, came for you—"

A fresh wave came over the wall, and they all jumped.

Lily grabbed Kristie's hand. "Come on, we need to get
out of here. The chopper's waiting."

"What chopper?"

"AxysCorp."

Benj said, "What about everybody else?"

"We can't take everybody," Lily said grimly. "I'm sorry,
Benj."

Amanda asked, "Lily, how can all this be happening?"

"I don't know," Lily said. "For now I just want to get us
out of here. Now come on. Hang onto me . . ."

Clinging to each other, they struggled through the increasingly powerful currents that swept across the car park,
heading for the chopper.

15

So this was Millwall, heart of the east end, a tough old community that stretched around the western shore of the Isle of Dogs, with the dock cut through its heart. Piers had never been here before.

The boom that had brought such glamorous developments to Canary Wharf and Greenwich had evidently passed this place by. But there were signs of redevelopment, industrial parks and commercial buildings and estates of flimsy-looking new housing that crowded out the older stock, what Piers's mother would have called "two-up two-down." None of it was being spared by the river water that pulsed along the streets, black and stinking of rot and sewage, lapping at front doors lined with sandbags and rolling over scraps of front gardens.

No cars were moving. The streets were lined with parked vehicles, and a few were abandoned in the middle of the road, their electrics soaked. There was hardly anybody on the streets. Through open windows Piers heard the chatter of battery radios, but there were no lights, no TV sets glowing; maybe the power was already off. The residents seemed willing, for now, to accept the official advice to stay put. Inside the houses he saw homeowners wearily hauling TV sets and bits of furniture up the stairs. But some of the houses already had blankets hanging out of upstairs windows, a sign that rescue was needed, blankets soaked by the continuing rain and flapping in the breeze.

He turned down a terraced street, and he heard rushing water. He looked back. A wave that must have been a half-meter high pushed down the narrow street toward him, black and oily and crusted with rubbish, plastic bins and milk bottles and bits of paper, and a dead bird, a rook, gruesomely spinning in the water.

He turned off the road and through a garden gate, instinctively trying to get away from the water. He climbed a step to a sandbagged front door. But the water came lapping over his legs anyhow, reaching to his knees, the sudden drag making him stagger.

The front door behind him opened. "Here, watch out for my gate." An old woman, in purple cardigan and slacks, stood at the door with a crutchlike metal walking stick. The flood pushed over her heap of sandbags and spilled into her hall, and made her stumble back. "Ooh, oh my Lord."

"Here." Piers hurried forward. He managed to catch her by the elbows before she fell. He set her right as the water pooled past them on into the house. "Are you all right?"

"Oh, look at my carpets, what you want to go and do that for?"

"I'm sorry," Piers said.

She looked up at him doubtfully. With a wisp of gray hair, she might have been eighty. She must once have been pretty. "I thought you was the nurse. You're not the district nurse, are you?"

"No."

"Today's not my day. But I've packed my bag for the hospital." She pointed to a small leather case that sat on a polished table in the hall. "It's got all my bits. I've got my pills, and I put in my spare teeth, like Kevin said. But you aren't Kevin, are you? My eyes aren't so good."

"The nurse? No, I'm sorry. My name's Piers."

"Piers! Well I never. My name's Molly."

"Nice to meet you, Molly."

"You're not a copper, are you? So what you doing standing in my drive, then?"

"I'm a soldier."

"Oh," she said, if that explained everything. "Well, help me on with my coat, dear."

He hesitated for one second. Then he stepped inside the house to get her case and her coat. The hall was cramped, the walls crowded with photographs and bits of embroidery in frames, and there was a smell of rarely washed woolens, rapidly being overwhelmed by a sewagelike river stink. He found a heavy overcoat on a rack, and held it up for her.

"Got your car, have you?"

"A car? No."

"An ambulance then. Well, how are you going to get me to the hospital?" She looked down at the filthy, steadily rising water. "I mean I can't stay here, and I can't walk with my knees."

"No, I don't suppose so." He glanced out at the street. A policeman in waders and a bright yellow jacket worked his way down the road, hammering on front doors. An evacuation order, and coming late enough too. Doors were opening, and people were reluctantly emerging from their houses, bearing kids, suitcases, bundles of possessions.

Piers looked at Molly, and down at the swirling water. This is something I can do, he thought.

He put his hands on Molly's shoulders and looked her in the eye. "Are you sure you've got everything you need? Your bank book, your NHS card—"

"Oh, yes, all packed, Kevin gave me a list. Large print too, he's really very good."

"This is a bit awkward—but do you need the lavatory for a bit? I'm not sure when we'll get to a toilet."

She laughed at that. "I'm all right, dear, let's get on with it." She peered past him. "Still can't see your car."

"Well, I don't have a car, I'm afraid. Let's see how we're fixed." He dug under his jacket, and took the belt from his trousers. He looped this through the suitcase handle and buckled it, and then hung the case around his neck so it dangled behind his back, over his slimmer emergency pack. It wasn't terribly heavy. Then he reached for Molly. "Now then, madam—"

When he picked her up she laughed again. "Oh my word, what a day this is turning out to be." But she put her arms around his neck, and settled easily.

He stood in the hall, balancing her weight. She was a solid woman, and heavy, but if he stood straight the case on his back acted as a kind of counterweight. He knew he was thin from his captivity, his muscles wasted; he wouldn't last for ever. But he was confident he could make it for maybe a kilometer, which might be enough. "Off we go, Molly." Carefully he stepped over the sandbags, and out onto the path.

He let her fumble for a key so she could lock the door. "Last time I was carried over this threshold it was by my Benny, and that was going the other way, oh I'll remember today all right."

"So will my back," Piers said ruefully. He splashed down the path.

"And these sandbags go back to the war. Really they do. I was a little girl then but I remember it clear as day. My dad dug the sand into his garden but he always kept the sacks, never know when they might start up again, he said, and he was right wasn't he, in a way . . ."

Letting her talk, he bent his head away from the rain and walked slowly, carefully. He headed east, roughly, toward the line of the DLR. The current of the flood water was fast, and though the water was still below his knees it tugged at him surprisingly strongly. One step, another, in the swirling, increasingly fetid water. He was determined not to get knocked over or trip.

"Oh, I'll remember this day I will, are you sure I'm not too heavy? I've got some mints somewhere, do you want a mint? . . ."

The AxysCorp chopper lifted Lily and the others from a soggy sports ground in the lee of the flyover. The helicopter dipped its nose and they flew north, panning over a peninsula that was becoming an archipelago. The water lapped all the way around the Dome now, and the car parks had vanished. Soaked to the skin, Amanda sat with her kids at her sides, holding them both close, shuddering.

The pilot glanced back. "Thought you might like to see this, Captain Brooke. Seeing as you missed the Games and all . . ."

The chopper sped across the swollen river, and surged further north. Here, spreading up across Tower Hamlets and Newham as far as Hackney, was the Olympic Park. This was in fact the valley of a tributary river, the Lea; it too had burst its banks. Lily recognized a velodrome, and what looked like a complex for hockey or soccer, and a bowl of a stadium, all of it abandoned, desolate, rusting, even vandalized. The filthy water spread across the valley and swirled around the Olympic facilities, as if coloring in a map.

The chopper dipped again and soared away to the west, toward central London.

People in Millwall knew Molly Murdoch. One old man a couple of streets from Molly's home, who was determined

himself to stay put, offered Piers the use of the wheelbarrow he used on his allotment. The water was still shallow
enough for that to work, and Piers lowered in his passenger, carefully, trying not to splash her, apologizing for the
muck.

"That's the ticket," said Molly as she settled into the barrow, and Piers wearily put her suitcase on her lap. "Home
James!"

So they trudged on.

They joined a gradually merging crowd, all walking or
limping, some pushing baby buggies and barrows and
wheelchairs. The crowd converged on a DLR station called
Mudchute, on the edge of the park where Piers had been
set down. The railway itself ran along a brick viaduct a few
meters above the ground. A team of police and DLR employees organized the queuing, and supervised access to
the platform.

Molly got priority from the police for her disability. Piers
needed a hand getting her in her barrow lifted up to the
platform. They didn't have long to wait for a train, though
it arrived packed. Piers was relieved the trains were still
running at all. Again Piers and Molly were given priority
treatment, though they had to dump the wheelbarrow to
make space.

With Piers sitting beside Molly on a soaked seat, the
train set off. Outside Mudchute the track was tree-lined,
but he glimpsed residential streets. Over an Asda super-
store whose car park was steadily filling with water, they
were joined by more refugees pushing supermarket trol-
leys laden with children and possessions. Past Crossharbor
Station a train was stranded on the other line, its smart red
livery gleaming in the rain, its doors gaping open. A line of
refugees straggled past awkwardly.

They crossed the water to South Quay Station, and entered the office district, thirty glass buildings all jammed
in, mostly lit up. This was a city in itself, Piers thought, like
an American downtown planted alongside the much older
community just a few hundred meters to the south, insu-
lated from it with its fast tube links and enclosed rail routes.
It felt very eerie to be traveling along this curving rail track
surrounded by these gigantic developments; it was like
a trail through a mountain range. But the old docks that

stood at the feet of the buildings had overspilled, and the buildings were glass cliffs looming up from a shallow sea, through which people struggled, sodden lumps.

At Canary Wharf the line ran beneath the great tower itself, One Canada Square. It was like riding through a tunnel cut into a huge sequoia, Piers thought idly. But the tower, fifty floors of it, was surrounded by a moat of water, and its underground mall must already have been flooded. All over the face of the great monolith above him lights blazed in the gathering evening. He could see office workers at their windows, in shirts and ties or colorful blouses, drinking coffee, peering out at storm-lashed London. Some had binoculars, and others took snaps with their mobile phones; you could see the flashes. Piers knew that the flood wasn't necessarily bad news for some of these spectators. A disaster was an erasing, an opportunity to rebuild and make a profit in doing so, and perhaps establish a bit of financial control you hadn't had before. The corporate barons of Canary had never much cared for the old communities like Millwall they had to share the Isle of Dogs with. Now was their chance to change the balance, perhaps. Some of the office workers were laughing at the dispossessed refugees at the foot of their tower, and raising their glasses in salute.

16

Helen Gray was driven into central London. The jam was solid for kilometers.

On East Smithfield the AxysCorp driver muttered an apology and swung the car off the road. Helen, riding in the back, was thrown against her seatbelt, and then jarred as the passenger-side wheels jolted up onto the curb. Sirens were wailing. A police officer in a Day-Glo yellow coat worked his way down the road, gesturing at the drivers to clear the roadway. All the way up the road ahead, Helen saw, with the twin spires of Tower Bridge looming into the gray sky beyond, the traffic had squeezed itself off the road, parting as if for Moses. Even the enormous new bendy buses found a way to shove themselves out of the way.

The rain fell steadily, streaking Helen's window. But she could see pedestrians pushing past, in waterproofs or just in City suits, under umbrellas or holding briefcases over their heads like shields, stepping through the murky, spreading puddles. Many of them had mobile phones clamped to their ears, or they spoke into the air, gesturing; even more glared at phones that stubbornly refused to find a signal. Talk, talk, talk; she imagined a mist of words rising up like steam from the soaked streets.

But the car was warm and dry, and so was Helen, isolated from the chaos outside, comfortable in her blue AxysCorp all-weather, ten-year-durable jumpsuit. The only sounds were the soft hum of the idling engine, the hammering of the rain on the roof. Nothing outside the car seemed real.

She still wasn't moving. She tried to set aside her mounting tension. She had insisted on being brought back into London because she had a contact in the Foreign Office, a man called Michael Thurley who, nominally in charge of the case of her baby, had promised to meet her at the end of the working day and update her with progress. To Helen the whole jaunt out to Southend had turned out to be a distraction, irrelevant to her main purpose. Now she was determined to keep her appointment in Whitehall, whether London cooperated or not. But every time the car was brought to a halt like this, anxiety squeezed her. How bad was this flooding going to get? She had the sense of everything falling apart bit by bit.

The reason for the road clearance became apparent. With a blare of sirens and a flash of blue lights a fire engine came barreling down the road, heading the wrong way down the lane. The engine rushed past Helen, a wall of red-painted metal. It led a convoy of police cars and vans, ambulances and paramedic vehicles, even a few camouflage-green Army trucks. The heavy vehicles threw up spray in great fountains.

The AxysCorp driver was a solid-framed woman, aged maybe forty, her face square, her chin strong. She'd discarded her peaked cap some kilometers back to reveal close-cropped gray hair. "We've got it easy," she said, listening to the murmur of her radio controller. "They're using bulldozers to clear the North Circular and let the emergency vehicles through. What a mess, I hope they're all insured."

The last of the convoy, a couple of police motorcycles, roared past. "Right, they're through," said the driver. She dragged at the steering wheel, gunned the engine, and pulled the car out into the lane that the police had cleared. She was among the first to react, and she pushed the car hard past walls of stationary cars.

Just for a few minutes, before the traffic pulled back out onto the empty road, they made good progress. They overtook cars and yellow buses full of evacuated schoolkids, and ambulances and paramedic vehicles coming from the emptying hospitals. They hurried over the junction with Tower Bridge Approach. Then, with the brooding mass of the Tower itself to their left, they passed the big tube station with its open plaza. Helen saw thousands of people swarming up from the underground ticket halls, some of them looking shocked, many soaked even before they came out into the rain. Maybe the tube network was flooding, then. If so, she wondered where all these thousands spilling into the heart of the city were supposed to go.

On a bit further they went, down Byward Street and along Lower Thames Street, the traffic slowing and clogging all the time. There were roadworks everywhere, great pits dug into the surface; London was always in the process of being rebuilt, and today the holes and ditches brimmed with water. Helen glimpsed the river itself, high and raging, looking as dense as some molten metal, like mercury, not like mere water at all, rising high beneath the functional concrete arches of London Bridge.

The traffic congealed further as the driver maneuvered the car around the approaches to London Bridge. To her right Helen glimpsed the City's spindly new skyscrapers, extraordinary sculptures of glass erected since her capture. Helicopters slid past their impassive faces. Still they kept moving, past Cannon Street and Southwark Bridge. But now their luck ran out, the road clogging like a furred-up artery. Worse, she could see pedestrians streaming over the spindly Millennium Bridge from the South Bank, adding to the congestion.

The driver shrugged. "I guess this is it. Sorry. You want I should turn around? The worst problems are going to be in the West End, up ahead. We could go north and—"

"No. I've got to get to Whitehall. There or the RAF Memorial on the Embankment. That's where I said I'd meet my contact if I couldn't get to Whitehall."

The driver glanced at her, not unsympathetic. "Whitehall? Look, it's not my place to give you advice. You're the one who's trying to find out about her kiddie, aren't you?"

"That's my business," Helen snapped.

"It's just that Whitehall's practically on the river. If anywhere's going to flood it will be there." She showed Helen a kind of sat-nav screen, a bit more advanced than the technology Helen remembered. It showed flickering high-resolution map panels, Westminster and the West End, whole areas marked by a gray overlay. "Mr. Lammockson trained us up in flood scenarios. They're probably evacuating the government buildings, if they haven't already."

"I don't have a choice," Helen said miserably.

"Are you sure? I can still get you out of here, you know."

"I know. Thank you. I have to do this . . . What will you do now?"

"Don't you worry about me."

"Do you have family?"

The driver turned away. "Two boys. Their dad pissed off back to Greece with them five years ago. At least they won't get flooded out there, hey. You see, we're in the same boat, you and me. Although today I wish I had a bloody boat, ha-ha. You don't know London, do you?"

Helen shrugged. "Only as a tourist."

"Well, it's not a good day to be sightseeing. Listen. If you get stuck, head for the Strand. Off Trafalgar Square. You can't miss the Strand."

"Why there?"

"Because that's where the old shore used to be, the docks, before they concreted over the river. 'Strand' means 'shore.' And even if the river's bursting its banks it's not going to go higher than that, is it? Stands to reason."

"I'll remember. Thanks."

"You take care."

Helen lifted her hood over her head, and pulled it tight at her neck and around her face. She checked her coverall was zipped up. Then she braced herself and opened the door.

17

She had to push against the wind. Gusts of rain soaked her face immediately, and stuck lanks of hair to her forehead.

She moved away from the car, shoving through panicky crowds, working her way westward, toward the Blackfriars bridges and the West End beyond. There wasn't much difference between the road and the pavement now, with people working their way around the stationary traffic. Drivers were abandoning their cars too, the doors opening like shells cracking, people emerging wincing into the rain. Above the babble of shouted conversations she heard car alarms and the wail of sirens, the flap of helicopter rotors somewhere overhead, and everywhere the hiss of the rain, from the roofs of the cars, the tarmac, the clothes and umbrellas of the pedestrians. The world was cold, windy, wet, noisy.

And under it all she thought she heard a deeper growl, coming from the east, from downstream, like the shuddering snarl of an approaching animal.

It was slow going. It was barely possible for Helen to get ahead a meter or two before being brought to a halt by the anxious directionlessness of the crowd. There were people with kids, tourists. She saw a huddle of Japanese or Koreans in see-through plastic ponchos, their eyes wide with shock, shouting into mobile phones. The men wore shorts and sandals, their legs black from the murky water.

After a time, pissed off and already tiring, Helen stopped at a Coke machine, dug out some money and bought a bottle. A soldiers' trick she'd picked up in her time in Barcelona: you drank the soda for the sugar rush and the caffeine. She drained the bottle quickly, and just dumped it and walked on. It wasn't a day to be too concerned about litter.

Past Blackfriars she rounded the curve of the Victoria Embankment. The road here was lined by trees and lampposts, and monuments stood in memory of Britain's grander past. The river side had a protective wall at about waist height, with steps where you could climb over to get down to a jetty or a pleasure boat. Today the river raged high, splashing just below the lip of the wall, sending showers of spray into the road. She hurried on toward Waterloo Bridge. The south bank opposite was crowded by the IBM building and the National Theater, with a huge new block of flats behind the theater, yet another newcomer dominating the view.

And then a tremendous sheet of water rose up above the embankment wall, towering into the air and splashing down over the hurrying crowds. The water was filthy, muddy. People screamed and cowered back. But others lifted their cameras and phones to capture the show. Helen pushed on, booted feet splashing through muddy water that ran down the camber of the road to the drains. But the drains themselves were full, backing up, spilling more water than they swallowed.

Passing under Waterloo Bridge, with the Eye a fine circle on the opposite bank, she could see the pale sandstone of the Palace of Westminster, far down the curve of the river. Still the river roared, its uneven surface flecked with white-capped waves. Helen got past the Cleopatra obelisk and under the Hungerford railway bridge. No trains were running, and people were fleeing over the bridge on foot, fleeing in both directions, spilling onto the road. Everywhere people were staring into their phones, pressing the keyboards, shouting into them. Others, desperate for news, crowded around the stationary cars, many of which had radios working, powered by their batteries. Cars and phones and running people, and the surging river, and the endless rain.

At last she reached the RAF Memorial. She stopped here, staring helplessly. The memorial was a bronze strip-cartoon plaque that illustrated the exploits of pilots and ground crews during the Second World War. She had been brought here to see it six or seven years ago; she couldn't have been much more than eighteen. Her parents had sneered at it as poor art, but Helen had been rather affected by its directness and emotional engagement. Lashed by rain, muddy water pooling around its base, it seemed entirely irrelevant now.

And here came Michael Thurley, walking toward her from behind the memorial.

About forty, he was dressed reasonably sensibly, compared to most around him; he wore a serge suit with Wellington boots, and a robust-looking bright red parka. But the rain obscured his glasses and he wiped the lenses compulsively.

"Mr. Thurley." She was so overwhelmingly glad to see him she felt like kissing him, but you didn't kiss Foreign Office officials. "You got my message."

"Yes, I did," he said ruefully, "but I rather wish I hadn't. Bloody silly rendezvous point in the circumstances, Ms. Gray, if you don't mind my saying so." His voice was clipped, brisk, his accent containing a trace of a public-school-and-Oxbridge background.

"I couldn't think of anywhere better—I don't know London. You came, anyway."

"I couldn't very well leave you standing, could I?" He pulled his parka hood forward to shield his face better; he had to shout over the noise of the rain, the river's raging. "We do have a sense of responsibility in the FO. And your friend Nathan Lammockson has been pulling various strings to make sure we act. But I have to tell you Whitehall's mostly been evacuated already. Actually in the emergency I've been assigned as a liaison to New Scotland Yard—the police, you know, I'm working on protocols regarding getting various foreign dignitaries out of London. But even Scotland Yard's been evacuated now, relocating to Hendon, the police college, and that's really where I ought to be . . ."

"I appreciate your staying for me."

"Yes. But it's all such a mess, isn't it? Look, you can see how we're fixed; today is not a good day to be pursuing your case, I'm afraid. But we do have assurances from the Saudi government and the Spanish police that no harm has come to your baby—"

"You told me that yesterday." She dropped her head, suddenly oblivious to the rain, the pushing people, the water around her feet. After the efforts it had taken her to get here, to know that she was no further forward was crushing.

Thurley stepped a bit closer. "There's no more we could have done in the circs, I'm afraid. I understand. Well, actually I don't suppose I do understand, or ever can. No kids myself. What I mean is, I sympathize."

"You're trying to help. I know that. It's just I never expected my life to turn out like this."

He forced a smile. "You're what, twenty-five, six? Your whole life's ahead of you, believe me."

"But my whole life is defined by the baby. By a *rape*. Like my feet have been nailed to the floor, and I'm never going anywhere ever again."

"I'm sure it's not like that . . ."

She heard screams. She looked up. Suddenly the water was rising all along the street, as if it were a vast bathtub filling up. People were splashing in their summer shoes and sandals through the water, climbing steps, some even climbing onto the river wall. As the water rose around their wheel arches, the stranded cars' alarms started to sound.

Thurley pointed. "Look. It's coming out of the drains." Manhole covers had been forced up by the sheer pressure of the water, which was bubbling out of the ground. "Good God, I think that's a rat!"

Now that distant thunder deepened. She looked along the river, facing downstream. And she saw the storm coming. A vast wave spanned the river, white-topped, scouring toward the Hungerford Bridge. Where it passed fountains of spray leapt up over the river walls. People were standing on the walls photographing it; she saw the speckle of flashes. But water was pouring down the Embankment itself now, a river on the road surface, paralleling the surge. It was still a long way off, but she saw people being knocked off their feet, stationary cars pushed aside like toys before a hosepipe.

Suddenly this day of flooding was more than an inconvenience, more than just something in her way. People must be dying, right here in her field of view.

She tried to focus, to think. She grabbed Thurley's arm. "Come on. We need to get away from here."

He seemed hypnotized. "Ah . . . Quite. But which way?"

"The Strand," Helen said immediately, remembering her driver. "This way."

Pushing through the crowds, they hurried back along the Embankment. They had almost reached their left turn into Horseguards when the water reached them, a knee-deep wash. There was garbage in the water, bits of paper and plastic bags and fast-food wrappers, slicks of oil and sewage. People clung to the wall, to lampposts, to the stranded cars; others were knocked off their feet, to come up drenched and sputtering. Even now people held onto their phones rather than use both their hands to support themselves; Helen saw the little screens glowing everywhere. She found herself leaning into the current, pushing to make her way forward, like walking into a tide, but she and Thurley kept their feet.

And now the river reached a new height and poured over the river wall in a torrent. The cars jostled forward, like boulders in a fast-flowing stream. People screamed for help.

Helen and Thurley made it to Horseguards. There was no respite here; the black, muddy, oil-streaked water surged after them as they struggled through the crowd. Helen was tiring by the time they reached Whitehall, and Thurley was wheezing, out of condition, exhausted.

But Whitehall itself was already flooded. They stared at another river that gushed down the street toward them, immersing people up to their thighs, pouring away from the higher ground to the north. It ran down past the pale sandstone frontages of the grand government buildings and flooded eagerly into roadwork trenches.

Thurley looked south, the way the water was running. "Look at that." He pointed at a rubber police launch fighting its way against the current. "That's Downing Street. They're evacuating."

"Yeah." She turned and looked north. She could see Trafalgar Square at the end of the street, the steps and pillars of the National Gallery rising like a cliff. "We can get out that way. But we have to fight the current . . ."

They started to slog upstream. All around them a crowd of people had the same idea. They pushed up the street, or climbed along rows of railings. But the current was growing more powerful.

Thurley slipped. Grabbing for him, Helen fell herself, face down. She felt the turbid stuff pushing into her hood, soaking her hair, and seeping inside her coverall. She kept her mouth closed, remembering the water that had come bubbling out of the sewers. She nearly made it up, but then somebody fell into her and pushed her down again, and she couldn't get her feet underneath herself. She felt herself slide backward, along the tarmac of Whitehall. She panicked, she wouldn't be able to get up, she would drown in a meter of dirty water.

But then a strong hand grabbed her by the scruff of her neck and hauled her to her feet. She stood there dripping before a mountain of a man, T-shirt and shorts and tattooed arms, like a rugby player gone to seed. Soaked to the skin, he actually had a can of lager in his left hand. He leered at her, and with his right hand he squeezed her breast through the coverall's soaked fabric. She recoiled, disgusted, and he laughed and stomped away.

Here was Thurley, drenched. "Not much of a hero," he shouted.

"Prick," she snarled. "Hope he drowns on his own vomit. Come on, let's get out of here."

They pushed on. She was soaked now, her face and hair wet, river water inside her suit, and it was much harder going.

But they reached Trafalgar Square. On the north side the National Gallery and the old church of Saint Martin in the Fields were above the water, and people stood or sat on the gallery's steps. But in the square itself the gushing river water was forming a lake, lapping around the famous old fountains. There had to be thousands of people in this view alone, swarming around the square and climbing the gallery steps. She saw no sign of police, no evidence of attempts at orderly evacuation. She glanced up at the column on which Nelson stood, imperturbably surveying the latest shocks to be inflicted on his city.

Thurley touched her shoulder. "Look up there." He was pointing to the roof of the National Gallery, which was carpeted by gray. Pigeons, thousands upon thousands of them. "You mentioned the Strand, Ms. Gray."

"Yes."

He pointed right. "Thataway."

They splashed through the deepening water, staggering across a road, past dead traffic lights and cars like boulders in a stream, and people everywhere, struggling to get to safety.

18

Another descent for the chopper dipping down toward the carcass of London, another rescue routinely handled by the AxysCorp crew, this time of a mother, child and grandmother stranded in Wapping, an area of old dockland converted to river view flats. Lily helped strap the refugees into their bucket seats.

The rotors growled as they bit into the air, and the chopper pushed on further upstream to her next job. The bird was already nearly full of old folk and women and kids wrapped in silvery emergency blankets, but she was going to keep flying until she ran out of fuel or reached her capacity; she could hold as many as a hundred refugees packed in tightly.

Glancing through the open door, Lily saw water black as oil soaking down the streets of London, and across the squares and parks, the river exploring the contours of the floodplain that had long been denied it. Choppers flew everywhere like busy insects, both yellow search-and-rescue vehicles and military machines—even Sikorskys that must have been flying out of American bases. Boats of all kinds, small private powerboats and inflatables and police launches and lifeboats, buzzed around houses and office blocks where blankets dangled limply from upper windows. Away from the central flooded areas Lily could see thin lines of traffic barely moving on the blocked arterial roads, and emergency vehicles moving against the flow in toward the disaster area, blue lights flashing. It was a July evening and still bright, but you could see the areas where the power had failed where streetlights failed to shine, and ad hoardings stood mute and blank. She had an AxysCorp handheld, and the little screen showed her frantic images of soldiers racing to save key installations, Royal Engi-

neers and the Royal Logistical Corps building levees and
laboring with pumps to try to keep the water out of substations and water-treatment plants. London's floodplain was
crowded not just with office blocks, shops and houses, but
with the city's core infrastructure, even hospitals and police
stations.

The handheld bleeped, flashing a headline from outside
London. The news was from Sydney. There the flooding
had struck deep into the heart of the city. The state government was trying to organize a managed evacuation west
along the route of Highway Four, toward the higher ground
beyond the Nepean River some thirty kilometers west of
the city. Reception centers were being set up further west
yet, in the higher ground of the Blue Mountains. The Aussie
government was struggling, the commentators opined. The
country had never been hit by such a calamity. Floods in
Sydney and in London, Lily thought, floods on both sides
of the world. How strange.

The pilot murmured, "Wow, look at that." The chopper
banked again.

Lily put down the handheld and looked out.

They flew past the Eye, a circular necklace of glass
beads, stationary now, its base in the water. People were
clearly visible, trapped in the cars, tiny stick figures like flies
in amber. And on the far side of the water Lily saw boats
crowding around the Palace of Westminster, like explorers
cautiously approaching sandstone cliffs.

Suddenly Lily was overwhelmed by the sheer scale of
it all. She looked away and wiped her face with a gloved
hand, pressed her eyes.

The old lady she'd just strapped in reached over to pat
her hand. "There, ducks. It'll sort itself out, you see."

The chopper surged and banked again, buffeted by the
continuing storm.

19

From Kristie Caistor's scrapbook:

    Three days after the flooding hit, Kristie snipped a report from BBC News about the efforts in flooded London to rescue thousands of people who had been trapped for days by power failures in electronically locked hotel rooms. This in itself would have been a major incident at any other time. It struck Kristie as funny.

20

Kristie was on spotter duty that morning. "There's the water man!" She came bundling down the stairs, her wooden-soled clogs noisy on the bare floorboards. It was not quite seven in the morning.

Amanda was just about ready for work, in a crumpled suit that could have done with a dry-clean. She wore sturdy walking boots and waterproof gaiters, and had work shoes shoved into her backpack handbag. She clutched a coffee in one hand, the last dregs of last night's thermos. She winced as Kristie came flying downstairs. "God, Kris, do you have to make so much *noise*?"

Kristie, eleven years old, was too full of life to care. She rummaged through the heap of buckets and plastic bottles they kept by the door. "Come on, Auntie Lily, it's you and me again."

Lily shoved a last bit of bread into her mouth and got up from the table, making for the door. Her bare feet felt cold on the swollen floorboards. She kicked her feet into her slip-on rubber boots, and began to collect bottles for the string bags. Kristie was fixing their improvised yoke over her shoulders, a broomhandle padded with an old blanket and bearing two plastic buckets. Lily said, "I thought it was Benj's turn this morning."

Amanda snorted, primping at her hair, using the TV's blank screen as a mirror. The power was off, as usual. "That slug's still in his bed. I swear he'd spend the whole school holiday in that pit if I didn't kick him out of it."

Lily ruffled Kristie's tight mop of curls. "Oh, it's just his age. Just as well you've got a willing worker in this one."

Amanda, stressed as ever, softened a bit. "Well, I know that. And I'm glad you're here, Lil. I don't know how we'd be coping if not. God knows how we'll get on if things are in the same sort of mess when the schools go back."

"Just earning my keep." She grabbed Amanda's gardening gloves. "Come on, then, kid, let's get this over." Kristie opened the front door.

Amanda called, "I'll be gone when you get back. I'll get Benj out of bed to open the door—"

"I've got my key," Kristie called back. "See you tonight, Mum, love you lots."

"Lots. Bye!"

Kristie let Lily pull the door closed. It had swollen in the flood four weeks ago, and had never quite fit into its frame again. They plodded down the short front garden path, lined with grimy sandbags, and set off along the street.

They walked roughly southwest, away from the low morning sun, heading toward the river. They mostly stuck to the pavement, but there were places where the water had lifted flagstones and you had to step aside. The roads themselves had generally been cleared, but there were still a few abandoned cars lying around, shoved roughly off the road, their interiors ruined, their windows smashed, their hubcaps and wheels generally stripped, their petrol siphoned off. Water stood everywhere, in the gutters and parks and gardens, and on the flat roofs of the petrol stations. But everybody knew not to drink it, not even if you managed to filter and boil it; the standing water was full of the filth of a city whose water-treatment works and sewage plants had been comprehensively drowned.

As it had been for days the sky was without a shred of cloud, and though there was the usual rising scent of mud and sewage from the water, a deep freshness in the air told of a hot English summer's day to come. The air was cleaner than it used to be, actually, since there was so little traffic on the roads.

Kristie said nothing as they walked. She put on a pensive sort of expression, as if she was trying to be moody, to look older. But in the sunlight she skipped, and splashed in the grimy puddles. Eleven was a complicated age, Lily thought.

They came to the bowser. Lily and Kristie weren't the first here; they never were. A patient line had formed, residents with buckets and bottles and plastic bowls, watched over by a young, bored-looking auxiliary copper. The bowser was a big blue plastic tank with an inlet valve and a single brass tap, dumped unceremoniously at the corner of the street. It was supposed to be filled by the big army tankers several times a day, but the residents had learned the hard way that you could only rely on morning and evening deliveries, and even they came at random times.

So they joined the line. Save for the bright primary colors of the plastic buckets this was a medieval scene, Lily sometimes thought, grimy people in shabby clothes queuing at the well. But at least the disorderliness and panic of the early days had gone. A rough-and-ready rule had grown up, that each household was allowed as much water as two people could carry away. The neighbors had quickly learned who to make exceptions for, and who needed help.

Lily had even got to know the faces in the queues, though she knew few of their names. Here were the Nurses, two retired ladies in their sixties or early seventies, perhaps lovers grown old. Here was Single Dad, thin, careworn, heavily tattooed, no more than twenty-five, with the battered Tesco trolley full of Coke bottles he filled up for his three toddlers. Here were the Yuppies, a stressed-looking young couple with hollow eyes who had seen their City jobs vanish, and had been reduced from their high-flying, caffeine-fueled lifestyle to soggy handout lines like this. This morning they were moaning about the difficulty of obtaining money, with ATMs down most of the time and credit card terminals rarely working in any of the shops and stores.

Nobody looked down the street. Nobody paid any attention to the lake that glimmered there, wide and placid, even though, Lily thought, it was a sight that would have astonished them a few weeks ago. This wasn't the river; it was technically the "Hammersmith embayment," a wide area of lowland where the flood water had been trapped behind a higher bank. At its edge the road surface just slid into the water, the pavement and road signs and traffic lights submerging, and small waves lapped against the front doors of abandoned houses and shops.

The line moved painfully slowly. It always did; that single tap was niggardly. It struck Lily that it was remarkable how much *time* you spent on the basics of life now, on hauling water home or queuing at Tesco for whatever food was available that day, or walking to work as Amanda did every morning, making a journey that had once taken minutes and could now stretch to hours.

But Lily was able to endure it. She seemed to have evolved a mental discipline during those long empty days in Barcelona, especially the times she had been held in solitary. She was able to wait through emptiness, through hours, whole days, with the constructive sections of her mind shut down—she could close down her flight reflex, one post-release psychologist had said to her.

Anyhow today wasn't so bad. It was remarkable how much more cheerful everybody felt when the sun shone. The Londoners queuing in this English street, grimy and stolid, were jolly enough. Many of them looked hopefully at mobile phones that still remained without a signal for most of each day. But some whistled or chatted, others gazed around vacantly as their Angels whispered in their heads, and around them the red tiles of the roofs of their crammed-in suburban houses shone in the sunlight.

Kristie hummed to herself, and adopted the glazed expression of an Angel-user—even though it was fake, for Lily happened to know her Angel wasn't working this morning; she'd forgotten to plug it into its charger when the power came up last night. Lily felt a stab of affection. Kristie was of a generation that was having to learn to live a life reduced to basics, a generation for whom words like "bowser" and "sewage" and "triage" were becoming far more important than "email" and "phone" and "Angel." The flood and all its implications had inundated a myriad lives like Kristie's, she thought, a cosmic intervention into the already tangled stories of parents and children, lovers and enemies. Just as, she supposed, her own sudden resurrection from limbo had dumped her into the lap of Amanda and her kids. Lily considered ruffling Kristie's hair again, then rejected it as too childish.

At last they reached the head of the queue, and bent to fill up their bottles and buckets. When they were done they plodded back home. Water was always unreasonably heavy, but they had worked out their system, with the yoke to spread the weight over shoulders and the gardening gloves to protect hands that held the string bags, and they toiled up the slight rise.

A light plane buzzed over. They both stopped and looked up. It was a novelty, you usually heard helicopters. The plane's chassis was bright red, a jewellike toy in the blue morning sky, and it trailed a ragged banner.

"It's a Flying Eye," said Kristie.

Maybe. But it wasn't here to spot traffic. Squinting, Lily could just make out the words on the banner: WATCH THE COCKNEYS SWIM DOT COM. Lily had heard of this, a band of provincial London-haters who hacked into CCTV and phone footage of the ongoing disaster, and re-broadcast choice selections.

Kristie didn't react, and Lily hoped she hadn't been able to read the message.

When they got back to the locked-up house it turned out, entirely predictably, that Kristie didn't have her door key after all. That was eleven-year-olds for you. Kristie hammered on the door, yelling for Benj. Lily was relieved when it only took a few minutes for Benj to shamble down from his room.

"Telly's on," he said without preamble. Kristie dumped her water and hurried in.

Lily shoved the water inside so she could shut the door, and put down her own yoke. In the house, the big screen was illuminated, the sound turned up high. It sounded like a news channel.

So the TV was on. More to the point, that must mean the power was on—unusual, for an early morning. Lily made for the kitchen. She filled the kettle and turned it on, and began opening cans and hunting for the rice in its plastic packet. With luck she could get lunch cooked before the power failed again.

From here she could just make out the screen. The news was local, with more details from the flooding. The effects on wildlife were being shown, with burrowing creatures like moles and voles forced up from the saturated soil, and ground-nesting birds like sand martins and oyster catchers driven off. A groundsman was shown scooping fish from a lake on the flooded Oval cricket ground; it was thought they had been put in there as a prank.

And then the story changed, and the image flicked over to an aerial view of a flooded landscape. This was the Bay of Bengal, the captions said, the coast of Bangladesh, a complex delta where the Brahmaputra and Ganges rivers reached the sea, and most of the population of a poor country scraped for a living on the coast or offshore islands. Little of this landscape was more than two meters above sea level. Now flooding had come, and whole islands were submerged. Lily saw before-and-after images, lagoons with shrimp pools and coconut palms transformed to drowned places where a few survivors clung to trees and the roofs of ruined mud-and-thatch houses.

A camera viewpoint pulled back to reveal long lines of refugees, their clothes the color of mud, plodding through knee-high water in search of dry land. There were enormous numbers of them, adults and children, in this one shaky shot. More advanced areas were not spared: a failed embankment had turned an airport into a lake, with helicopters and military aircraft piled on top of each other. Lily couldn't tell from the commentary if some kind of storm had hit, a typhoon; it sounded as if the sea had simply risen, relentlessly, to do this damage.

And now, as if the viewpoint pulled back further still, the news program switched to a summary map of the world that showed the shapes of the continents outlined in bright blue, all around the shorelines and in the major river estuaries. The blue was a graphic showing how flooding emergencies were cropping up everywhere, in the Americas, north and south Europe, India, Asia, Africa, Australia. Whole low-lying regions were threatened too, like Bangladesh, Florida, Louisiana, the Netherlands, and river deltas, many densely populated. In great cities like New York, Vancouver, Tokyo and Shanghai, populations who had watched the travails of London and Sydney now made frantic preparations of their own.

Ten percent of humanity lived within ten meters of sea level, hundreds of millions of people. Now the risen sea, or the fear of it, was driving them away from their homes, a tremendous flight of population gathering all over the planet. But the images blurred after a time, one desolate stream of rain-soaked refugees looking much like another.

A tagline reported the plight of the Newcastle football

team, trapped in Mumbai after losing the Cup Final. And the news flicked out as Benj cycled through the channels. At last he settled on a kids' channel, showing a gory cartoon.

Lily had just got the rice boiled when the power failed again. Both the kids groaned in frustration as the TV died. Lily hastily poured the last of the boiling water into another thermos, and shoveled in instant coffee after it.

21

Early that afternoon Piers Michaelmas came calling for Lily. He knocked on the door, standing there in battle dress. He refused a coffee from the thermoses.

He was here, he said, to take her on a boat ride into the heart of London. "Sorry I couldn't call. Blessed phones, you know what it's like. Here." He handed her a mil-issue satellite phone. "For future contingencies."

"So what's this trip about?"

"Call it old times' sake."

So she lodged the kids with a neighbor, and put on her blue AxysCorp coverall. They walked briskly down the street, past the bowser, to the shoreline where the road was submerged. Here a Marine waited for them in an inflatable orange boat tied up to a lamppost. The Marine helped Lily and Michaelmas into the boat, and made her put on a life jacket and a light face mask.

Then he pushed the boat away and started a small motor, and the boat drilled straight down the line of the drowned street toward the old riverbank. Lily found the face mask confining; it was like a surgeon's theater mask, but given the rising stink of the river and the unidentifiable lumps that floated in the water, she was glad of it.

She watched the Marine check his position on a GPS sleeve patch. He had a kind of miniaturized sounder set up in the boat at his side, and he peered suspiciously at every shadow in the water as they passed. "Tricky navigation," she said.

"It is that, miss," he said ruefully. He was grizzled, his skin leathery, though he looked no older than forty. His accent was robust Scottish.

"Don't be modest," Piers said. "Harry's always been a bit of a sailor, is what I hear."

"Aye, that's true. I grew up on Skye, you know. But this is different. After all, nobody's sailed down the Fulham Road before, that I know of. It's full of obstacles, traffic cones and cars and rubbish. I can't see a thing in this murk, so thank Jim for this sounding stuff." The safest course, it seemed, was to make your way down the center of the submerged roads, or better yet to seek out the old river itself, where you could be reasonably sure of clear water beneath your keel.

They reached the Thames a little way upstream from Putney Bridge. There was low clearance under the bridge's arches, enough for this dinghy but not for anything much more substantial. Indeed one expensive-looking cabin cruiser was stuck fast. The current was quite strong, the murky water turbulent and smelling faintly of rot and sewage. Lily saw a cloud of mosquitoes, a new arrival in a transformed city.

From the river the old banks were quite invisible. The river had become broad, the flooding spreading as much as a kilometer inland. Houses, schools, churches, industrial developments all poked out of the muddy water, isthmuses of brick and concrete and steel and glass. An elevated section of road soared, a bridge going nowhere, cars stranded motionless on their backs. The remaining population clung to bits of higher ground, islands rising out of the water. Lily saw kids waving from one, and a helicopter perched in a school playing field on another. The Thames valley was turning into an archipelago.

Piers showed her a sketch map based on satellite imagery of the latest version of the river's course. "You can see the floodwaters have gathered in these 'embayments.' Independent hydrological units, I'm being trained to call them." The embayments were lagoons, sudden, spectacular features in themselves, some kilometers long, bearing the names of the areas they covered: Hammersmith, Westminster, Bermondsey, Isle of Dogs, Greenwich. "They're virtually cut off from each other by necks of high land, though there are tunnels and sewers and so forth that connect them. The good news is that flooding in one area doesn't necessarily imply flooding elsewhere. The bad news is you have to pump them all dry, they won't drain naturally . . ."

Under Wandsworth Bridge, they saw a copper restraining a bunch of youths from going for a swim. The Marine tutted and shook his head. "Soon as the sun's out people want to go paddling, even with the floating corpses and the turds and that."

"Civilians, eh, Harry?" Piers said. "But you can't blame them. A lot of people are playing around. You know, you can take a motorboat ride into Westminster Hall. I'm told *that's* been flooding since the thirteenth century. Or a gondola trip around Soho. And in the City the whizz-kid types are waterskiing around the skyscrapers."

Lily studied him. "You seem very sanguine, Piers. I don't want to pick at old wounds, but you weren't a particularly relaxed character back in Barcelona."

He stiffened a bit, but smiled. "Well, so the shrinks keep telling me whenever they get their hands on me. But it's just so good to be *out*, isn't it? That's what's starting to sink in, I think. Even though we've been plunged into crisis the moment we stepped out of the wretched AxysCorp chopper."

She knew he was divorced, without children, and had no family to visit, no real home to go back to. Before his abduction he had been a senior figure in military and diplomatic circles; that was why he had been attempting his peace-brokering in Spain in the first place. Now, after his strange, brave, demon-exorcising adventure on the Isle of Dogs, which he had told her all about, he seemed ready to engage with his own world again, and she was glad to see him functioning.

"As regards the flooding," he said now, "we're moving into a different phase. The long term. Tough decisions have to be made, and followed through. And that's what I'm beginning to wrap my puny brain around. Rather therapeutic, I'm finding it."

As they talked they passed beneath more of the bridges of London. As they neared the Chelsea Bridge she could already see the towers of Battersea Power Station looming defiantly above the water.

She asked, "What tough decisions?"

He glanced around, as if they might be overheard. "The worst is yet to come, believe it or not. The services are working flat out to recover the power stations, and get the water-treatment works running again, and so on. We're continuing with the immediate recovery operations—there are twenty hospitals in the flooded regions to be evacuated, for example. We've also got far too many temporary holding centers not yet cleared, old folk and mums and babies who've been stuck in schools and church halls for weeks.

"But a few more days of these conditions and you're looking at epidemics. Typhoid, cholera. The water's full of toxins from the industrial areas too. That's not to mention the deaths we're already seeing through starvation and thirst. All this even if the flooding doesn't recur."

That last sentence, with its *if*, chilled her.

"We want to do everything we can to avoid a full-scale evacuation of London. That really is a last resort. We're preparing for it, of course. We're bringing in assault craft and inflatable boats, battlefield ambulances and field hospital units, heavy gear from across the country. It's like another D-Day! Away from the city we're assembling new caravan parks and tent cities on the high ground, the Chilterns and the South Downs and so forth. We're even looking as far north as Birmingham. We're using military police to keep open the routes out of London.

"But the thought of doing it for real, of moving *millions*, is an horrific one. I mean we have no way of shifting most of them save just walking them out. Not to mention the fact that the citizens in the reception areas aren't altogether happy about the idea of accommodating so many drowned-out Londoners. I suspect a lot of pie-eating flat-cap types in the north are rather enjoying seeing London dished!

"But the fact is we have a capital city whose infrastructure is ruined—water, transport, communications, power. Millions homeless. Insurance claims alone could bring the financial sector down. The international banks and so forth have already relocated to their disaster recovery centers—our friend Lammockson has no doubt made plenty of money out of that—but what's to induce them to come back? It will take London years to recover from this, if ever. And so there are limits to what the country can afford . . ."

"But we must try," Lily said. "I think you're looking forward to the challenge, actually, Piers, for all you're a doom merchant."

"Well, perhaps. I admit it is nice to get up in the morning

with something to *do*. I think I'm a realist, however. Things won't be as they were before. But we will recover, one way or another, if the waters go down."

And she noted that word again. *If*.

They sailed under Lambeth and Westminster bridges. The Palace of Westminster, lapped by water, was lit from within, a rump of the government machine defiantly functioning inside its walls.

Harry nosed the craft cautiously toward the shore, away from the course of the river, just before Hungerford Bridge. "I'm aiming for the centerline of Northumberland Avenue," he murmured, concentrating, watching his sensors and the lampposts and building fronts that protruded from the water around him. "Have to be careful not to snag . . ."

Trafalgar Square came into sight. Lily saw that a Chinook sat proudly before the steps of the National Gallery.

Harry killed the engine, and jumped out into water that rose up to the crotch of his waders. He tied up to a lamppost before the ruined shopping parade on the south side of the square, and helped Piers and Lily down into the water. Then he went back to wait with the boat.

They waded the few meters to the square itself. The water was grimy here, even worse than upstream in Fulham, littered with floating garbage, splitting bin bags, the corpses of pigeons. In the square itself the water was only centimeters deep, but they had to pass through a military cordon to get to it. Aside from more squaddies around the square's perimeter, and what looked like gallery staff coming and going laden with packages, the square was empty. Lily looked back the way they had come, down Northumberland Avenue. The buildings of London stood proud of water that stretched to the horizon, flat and calm and gleaming in the sun.

"I can't help thinking of those elders from Tuvalu," Piers said. "You remember, at Lammockson's party."

"What about them?"

"I wonder if they're gloating."

"Hm. So why the Chinook? Why the perimeter?"

"Can't you tell? They're stripping the National Gallery. The water didn't quite breach the steps, but it did make a mess of some of the cellars. We've got squaddies helping the staff move their treasures to upper stories, or shipping them out altogether to the higher ground. I just thought you'd like to see what's a pretty unusual sight—a Chinook at the feet of Nelson."

"You're showing off, is what it is, Piers."

Gary Boyle came strolling up, grinning. Lily hadn't seen him since Lammockson's party on the afternoon of the flood. And here came Helen Gray, walking arm in arm with an older man Lily didn't recognize. Lily felt inordinately glad to see them all, islands of familiarity in a world full of strangeness. They embraced each other.

Piers said, "We did promise to keep in touch, back in Barcelona. I thought we should get together again before the winds of fortune scatter us. Oh—lest I forget." He handed the others mil-spec radio phones of the type he'd given Lily.

Helen introduced her companion. He turned out to be with the Foreign Office; he was called Michael Thurley. "Mike was assigned to help me sort out the issues around baby Grace. And no," she said with a forced smile, "I haven't got her back yet. Don't even know where she is."

Gary said grimly, "I can guess what your future plans are, then."

"Well, I don't have a choice, do I?"

Thurley said, "And I'm intending to help her." He said he had got a kind of sabbatical leave to travel with Helen full time. Their first destination was to be Saudi Arabia, home of the baby's father. "It's become something of a cause for me, I'm afraid. We of the FO didn't achieve a great deal for Helen—and she did pretty much save my life on the day of the flood."

He sounded tweedy, self-mocking in a very English way that reminded Lily of Piers. His mannerisms seemed exaggerated, and he linked arms with Helen like an older brother. Maybe he was gay. Lily sensed a strength in him, under the public-school bullshit. She did wonder if there was something else he was really after, if he was glomming onto Helen to serve some need of his own. But the flood had been a great trauma for a lot of people. Maybe Michael was simply as he said he was, his motives uncomplicated.

Gary said, "So what about you, Lily? You going to stay with your sister?"

Since coming out of the hole in Barcelona she'd been living from day to day, without thinking much further. Her USAF pay was coming in for now; she supposed she'd be pulled back into the fold eventually. But ahead of that she'd made no plans. "I haven't decided."

Gary said immediately, "Then come with me."

That took her aback. "Where?"

"Iceland."

"Say what?"

He told her of his encounter with an old friend at the Barrier, a ragged-sounding American oceanographer called Thandie Jones.

"There's more to what's going on than they're releasing to the public." He waved south over the square, at the placid water. "This wasn't a freak event, a one-off storm. Thandie thinks there's a global sea-level rise going on. And that's why there's been flooding all over the country, all over the damn world—"

Piers said, "Now hold on. Much of the flooding has come from flash flooding, freak rainstorms—"

"Caused," Gary said, "by an exceptional loading of water vapor into the atmosphere, driven in turn by heat energy in the rising ocean. The science, the modeling is there, Piers. I grant you it's patchy, and there's no consensus. But Thandie thinks her data is good, and she's going out to collect more. We're talking about sea-bottom exploration, Lil. How cool is *that*? Thandie's reporting this up through her own hierarchy, to the National Science Foundation in the US. But no government, no intergovernmental agency, will back her—in particular the IPCC, the climate change panel—because, she says, if they did it would be a tacit admission that there's a real problem."

Piers snorted. "Well, she would say that, wouldn't she? As opposed to the possibility that her 'science' is a whole lot of nonsense."

Gary said, "Well, now she's got funding—thanks to me."

Helen saw it. "Nathan Lammockson. She's tapped him up."

Gary grinned. "Old Nathan likes to splash the cash where it will do some good, especially if it's visible. What could be more visible than saving the world? Anyhow this new program of exploration is being run out of Iceland, and that's where I'm going. And I want you with me, Lily. I don't know what we're going to face out there. I'd like to have somebody with me I could trust."

She smiled. "And I'm the best you could come up with?"

"You'll do," he said earnestly. "And besides you'll help keep Nathan on board."

Helen was frowning. She pointed to the south. "Isn't that water level a little higher than it was before? That bin over there is almost submerged now—the shop fronts—I'm sure it wasn't like that before."

Harry the Marine was waving from the boat, in water that was waist deep.

"My God, you're right," Piers said. "We have to go. That's that, then."

For one last moment they stood together, the four hostages, Thurley. Helen said wistfully, "Don't forget me. Or Grace."

"We won't," Lily promised.

"Come on, Lily," Piers snapped, "let's get you home." He grabbed her arm and hurried her down the steps, splashing in ever-deepening water toward the boat.

By the time they got back to Fulham the river had already pushed out dramatically, a small rise in level translating to a major wash inland over the shallow streets. This time there was no storm, nothing but a clear blue sky. Without apparent cause, the water just rose.

From the boat Lily hurried toward Amanda's home. She glimpsed a police van splashing up the Fulham Road, heard an amplified voice ordering an evacuation. Residents were piling stuff in the street, carrycots and water bottles, suitcases, bundles of gear wrapped in blankets. Others, evidently intent on staying put even now, were feverishly sandbagging their drives and doors. The bowser was standing in a pool. Residents were queuing even so, in rubber boots and waterproof trousers, the Yuppies and Single Dad; water still poured from the brass tap. But there would be no more deliveries here, Lily saw.

Amanda's front door was open. Lily hurried in. Filthy

water poured down the stairs, black and reeking. Lily saw
the two kids sitting before the TV, which was, by some miracle, working, the power still on. The kids looked subdued,
unwilling to move.

Amanda came stamping down in her rubber boots, carrying rucksacks and clothes. She still wore her work suit.
"Lily, thank God you're back. Can you give me a hand with
this lot? It's started pouring out of the toilet again like last
time. You're supposed to drop a sandbag down there, but
that didn't work last time either. Well, this is it, isn't it?"

Lily grabbed bundles. "I heard them calling for
evacuation."

"It's on the news." Amanda glanced around at the filth
on the stairs, the damp, moldy patches on the walls. "Just
when you think it's over, when you've had enough, it starts
up again." She seemed more angry than stressed, grim
rather than panicking. Lily wondered if she was in some
way relieved that the worst was here at last. Amanda called
to the kids, "You'd better get up there and sort out what
you want, you two."

But Benj said, "I don't think we'll be going anywhere,
Mum." He pointed at the TV screen. It was showing a live
news broadcast, a helicopter view of cracked tarmac, fallen
flyovers, crushed and burning cars.

Lily stepped closer, trying to read fallen signs. "That's
the M25. Junction with the M40."

"That's all we need," Amanda said. "Is it something to
do with the flooding?"

"Maybe." But now postcard-sized cutaways showed
more devastated junctions. All the major junctions around
London's orbital motorway had been blown up: the M1 and
M11 to the north, the M40 and M4 to the west and Wales,
the M3 toward Hampshire, the M23 south to Sussex.

"They've smashed up the roads," Benj said simply. "The
trains too. Nobody wants us."

Kristie said flatly, "Watch the Cockneys swim dot com."

The picture froze, broke up, and died.

Two

2017–2020
Mean sea-level rise above 2010 datum: 5–80m

22

May 2017

Piers Michaelmas sent an oil company jet to pick Lily up from Denver, where she'd flown in from England, and bring her to Texas.

Houston from the air was utterly flat, a grid-plan cityscape set down in a country of low hills, pine forests, swamps and bayous. The only topography was man-made; the glass blocks of downtown looked like a huge sculpture set up on the plain. To the east was the bay, with the lines of the Ship Channel clearly visible and more industrial sprawl beyond. This was the area colonized by the petrochemical industry, domed storage tanks and spindly fractionating towers like a comic-book city of the future, spreading kilometers away toward the Gulf of Mexico. On the bay itself a tracery of levees and barriers gleamed, protection against the rising sea, huge constructions in themselves, brand new. But Lily saw that, despite the new defenses, the bay waters had already penetrated the old coastline, and pooled at the feet of the white storage tanks. All this under a pale smoggy sky, in heat so intense the air shimmered, a city under a grill.

Lily looked along the sweeping curve of the Gulf Freeway, hoping to glimpse the blocky architecture of the Johnson Space Center where tomorrow she was due to meet Gordon James Alonzo, a real-life astronaut. But it was lost in the detail.

On landing she took a call from Piers, advising her on where to meet him.

The airport terminal building was a glass block so aircon-cold she considered digging a sweater out of her carry-on bag. Then she had to walk a few meters under the open Houston sky to a waiting limousine, and it was like step-

ping into a sauna. When she got into Piers's car it was so
cold it made her shiver again.

Piers wore an open-necked, short-sleeved white shirt,
and black shorts that looked like cut-down suit trousers.
It was nine months since Lily had last seen Piers, back in
London; she'd suggested meeting up when she found out
they were both going to be in the Houston area. He patted
her shoulder brusquely, and took her bag and lodged it on
the floor. The car pulled out. The driver was all but hidden
behind a screen of smoky glass.

"You still travel light," Piers said.

"I live light," Lily said as she buckled up. It was true;
what she owned wouldn't have filled more than two or
three backpacks. "I've never felt the need to acquire much
stuff. Certainly not since Barcelona."

"Quite. It's not really a time to put down roots, is it? Not
unless you're a banyan tree." There was that mordant wit,
the infrequent flashes of which had always made her feel
warm. "So was the flight OK? How do you feel?"

"Like I just jumped into a plunge pool."

He laughed. "Ah, that's Houston for you. Always been
a tough environment, as hot as Calcutta, barely a human
place at all. And, I must say, when I started working here
I came down with a string of colds. My doctor said my immune system was weakened by the temperature swings.
And how are Amanda and the kids?"

"Fine. Still in their caravan park outside Aylesbury. They
still haven't been allowed to go home to Fulham. The kids
swim to school. I'm kidding! My own work's going OK."

"On this diving project, I suppose."

"Just background stuff for now, mostly in England."

They were driving toward downtown; the central skyscrapers loomed ahead. Houston seemed to be a mash-up
of residential, industrial and retail developments. It looked
rather dated, Lily thought, very 1960s. She saw sprinklers
working away at lawns of tough-looking thick-bladed
grass.

Piers's manner and accent hadn't changed at all, despite
his immersion in Texas for so many months; he was still
cool, ironic, officer-class British. But his eyes occasionally
unfocused. He must have an Angel, or the latest mil-spec
equivalent, speaking in his head; even in her company he

remained separated, alone. But, clear-eyed, clean-shaven, his hair neatly cropped, he looked healthier than she'd ever known him.

"I can see you adapted, Piers. Nice shorts, by the way."

He raised his eyebrows. "My shorts are serviceable and neat, thank you."

"You're enjoying life here, aren't you?"

"Well, Americans are always welcoming. Houston's a pretty diverse place, I think. There's even an Iranian district now, quite remarkable. But the main thing I like is the *room*. Only an hour to the Gulf coast, only a day's drive the other way to desert, or hills ... The work is the thing, of course. Having something meaningful to do makes a big difference to one's morale, doesn't it?"

"That it does. I saw the levees from the air."

"They're talking about a tidal barrier further out, a series of gates that would dwarf the Thames Barrier. Typical bloody Texans. But they do have a lot to protect. Most of the detailed work I've been doing has concerned Houston's petroscape."

The protection of the Gulf was a public and private project, a shared task of governments, oil companies and other multinationals. Piers was the leader of an exchange party from Britain, who were applying the lessons learned safing British oil facilities like Canvey Island to the much larger-scale problems here.

"You wouldn't believe the size of it, Lily. This is the largest concentration of petrochemical refinery and storage facilities in the world. A hundred kilometers of tanks and cracking towers, stretching from Houston all the way to the coast."

"And all of it threatened by the sea."

"Quite," he said mildly. "Galveston Island, for instance, rises only three meters or so above sea level—I mean above the old datum. Houston is even worse off. It was built on marshland in the first place, and there's been subsidence because of the oil and water they've been pumping out of the ground here for so long. In some places the city is actually *below* the old sea level. Well, we know that the average global rise is already up to five meters. If the sea did break through—well.

"But immense as it is, this project is an incident in the

bigger picture. You have to see that this is a global crisis, impacting a world already afflicted by climate change, energy shortages and ideological tensions. We are trying to save the hubs."

"The hubs?"

"You'd be surprised how dependent our worldwide network of energy and material flows is on a few key nodes. Grain silos, power stations, oil sources and refineries."

"Like Houston."

"Like Houston. And of course an awful lot of these facilities are on the coasts, even on flood plains. So we're trying to sustain that network as far as possible. In the short term it's all about emergency measures. For instance we're trying to make sure all the tanker fleets are kept at sea. Any manufacturing or processing facility we believe might be lost is being worked as hard as possible to produce durables for the transition period—that is, the transition until everything's been moved inland or uphill, and is made safe against the floods. Bronze, stainless steel, plastic, that sort of thing, age-resistant. You should see the Goodyear plant."

"Goodyear? The tires people?"

"They've been here for decades. Now they're churning out mountains of the damn things."

"Why do we need tires?"

"Rafts," he said.

That simple word took her aback. She had had the sense with Piers since they had come out of Barcelona that he was much closer to the center than she was, that he knew far more than she did, that he looked that much further into the future.

The car slowed. They were southwest of downtown at an intersection of two major avenues, Montrose Street with Westheimer Road. She glimpsed galleries, cafés, restaurants, bars, shops. It was a lively area that Amanda would probably have called "counter-cultural."

"This is the Montrose District," Piers said. "One of the few walkable neighborhoods in the city. I thought you'd appreciate being here. Your hotel is just around the corner—there, you see? Look, I have to go back to work for a few hours. Sorry to abandon you for now." He handed over her bag.

On impulse, she kissed him on the cheek. "Later then."

"Sure."

The car door opened, and Lily jumped out. Again she was struck by the sheer physical intensity of the sunlight that bounced off the sidewalk flags. There were few people around in the heat of the day.

Piers called from the car, "Oh, Lily—make sure you're in your room at about midnight. I'm fixing up a conference call with some old friends. Call it my treat."

"It's a date."

The car closed itself up and slid away. She hurried up the steps and through sliding doors into the hotel's cool, dark interior.

23

Helen Gray and Michael Thurley took a late breakfast in the IAEA trailer they shared.

Then, still early in the morning, they prepared to take Piers's conference call. They installed themselves in a bar close to the waterfront of Bushehr's old port, and set up their laptops on a plastic table. The computers were battered relics of the noughties, all the International Atomic Energy Agency could afford. The heat was already gathering. But the open-fronted bar was used to western visitors, and was equipped with fans and plenty of iced water, and would be bearable for an hour or more yet.

While they waited for Lily to log on Helen sipped orange juice, and looked out at the Persian Gulf.

Bushehr was at the end of a long, flat island, once joined to the Iranian mainland by a tidal marsh; now it was cut off by the rising sea, and you got here by boat or aircraft. A battered cargo ship made its way toward the deep outer anchorage, probably stuffed with the dried fruits and raw cotton that were the principal exports of the region. Its gray form passed between rows of buildings. Looking inland Helen could make out the industrial hinterland of the old city, the food-processing and engineering facilities attracted here to serve the regional oil distribution center that was the town's main function. There was a smell of spices, of oil, of hot metal, of thick coffee from inside the bar, and a muezzin call floated on the hot morning air.

And there, like a pale mushroom rising above the old port, was the containment dome of the nuclear power plant, the reason they had come here.

The laptop screens lit up. There was Lily sitting in what looked like a hotel room, and Amanda, her sister, in the cramped confines of a caravan or a mobile home. These were just still images. They had to wait a few more seconds for the links to be fully established; bandwidth wasn't what it used to be. Helen and Michael had never met Amanda, but had got to know her online through Lily, like a member of an extended family.

Helen murmured to Michael Thurley, "So this is it. No Gary, no Piers—even though Piers is supposed to have set up this online reunion in the first place."

Michael said, "Well, Gary's at the bottom of the bloody sea somewhere, so you can't blame him. But as you say, Piers set it up. You'd think he could find half an hour to speak to us."

"He did it for Lily. That's what he says."

"Surely for himself too." Michael rubbed an unshaven chin. "I was brought up a Catholic, you know." Actually she hadn't known that about him. "We were quite a tight community, we Hampshire Catholics. Not many of us, for one thing. I lapsed at a young age, seventeen or so." He smiled. "Not everybody in the church was as tolerant of my homosexuality, my 'sin,' as they might have been. But my mother continued to practice.

"A few years later my father died suddenly, and my mother said she had lost her faith. She stopped attending Mass. I found it rather upsetting. Although I had no intention of going back myself, I found it somehow comforting that *she* continued to practice. As if I had a route back. Well, she did go back for my sake, she made her confession and that was that. A good thing too. I think she found the church a comfort in the years before she died."

"So maybe Piers is the same, you think. He won't meet us, but it's comforting for him to know that the rest of us still do."

"Perhaps. But do any of us really understand each other? Why, I don't even understand *us*."

And nor did Helen, though she had had to try to explain her relationship with Michael to the IAEA inspectors and nuclear engineers, western, Russian and Iranian, who regularly hit on her. She was a single mother, Michael a homosexual in early middle age, and they were locked in a peculiar relationship: sexless, passionless—but not really platonic, it was more than that. They had come together in the trauma of the London flood, of course. Maybe they had found in each other something they needed, something each had lacked separately.

Or maybe, on some deeper, more cynical level, all she really cared about Michael was that he still represented the best chance she had of getting her child back.

Lily's image jerked to life. "Are we on? Howdy from Texas."

Amanda smiled, her face lighting up, and blew kisses. "Hello Bushehr, here are the votes from the Luxembourg jury."

Helen and Michael waved back, feeling foolish, sitting in this empty bar waving at aging laptop screens.

They quickly established where and when they were: Lily in her hotel room in Houston at midnight; Amanda in a caravan in the Chilterns, not far from Aylesbury, where it was very early morning, "sitting on a hillside with a bunch of sheep and half the population of Chiswick"; and here were Helen and Michael outside an Iranian nuclear plant, some thousand kilometers south of Tehran.

Amanda said, "I don't really understand why you're there. Aren't you looking for your baby, Helen? His father was Saudi, not Iranian. And I don't know what you have to do with nuclear reactors . . ."

It was a complicated story. This reactor, built under contract by Russian engineers, was not long ago a pricking-point of world tension as a pivotal point of Iran's uranium enrichment program. But Bushehr sat right on the Persian Gulf, and, like more than four hundred of the world's nuclear facilities, was threatened by the rising sea. Not only that it was a lousy piece of engineering, full of design flaws eradicated from most plants since Three Mile Island. The IAEA team were rushing to work with the Iranians to decommission it before the sea had a chance to overwhelm it.

"Naturally HMG is supporting that effort," Michael said. "I managed to get myself assigned to our small diplomatic team. All an excuse to stay close to the trail of baby Grace, you see."

Grace had disappeared into the complicated clutches of Said's branch of the Saudi royal family. One patriarchal figure in that branch, however, a distant cousin of the Saudi king, was more of a realist than the rest, and had appeared to offer compromises. This man had been swept up by the global crisis, as had everybody else, and had been sent to Iran as part of a Saudi inspection party. The Saudis needed a presence here because any fallout from Bushehr would have threatened the whole of the Gulf downwind, including Kuwait, Dubai and Saudi itself.

Michael had got himself attached to this mission in the hope of making contact with this helpful Saudi prince. "But progress is slow," he admitted.

Helen thought that was an understatement.

Amanda shifted in her chair. "Well, *we* couldn't get much further from the coast, and just as well. There's something I want to show you." She tapped at an out-of-shot keyboard. "I'll see if I can download it. It's a map they published yesterday. I wish Benj was up, he's the one who's good at this stuff, but he won't be awake for another six hours minimum . . . Here we are."

Down came an image of Great Britain, as the country had been transformed by the flooding, a composite of hundreds of satellite photographs. Helen quickly found that it was interactive; you could touch the screen and it would allow you to zoom and pan, and overlay town names and roads. They played with this for a while, discussing what they saw.

The map was strikingly different. The Thames Estuary had broadened to a bay that swamped the marshes of Essex and North Kent. The beaches of the south coast resorts had vanished. In Somerset the sea had swamped the marshes and peat moors, and lapped around Glastonbury Tor. In East Anglia the Fens' ancient drainage systems had been overwhelmed, and the sea had pushed inland for sixty kilometers or more, through Peterborough to form a new shore at Cambridge. In the north the Humber Estuary now snaked into an inland sea that covered what had been low-lying Yorkshire farmland. In the west the Lancashire coastline from Liverpool up to Lancaster was submerged; the city of Liverpool itself had been all but abandoned.

Helen felt oddly dislocated. Her years in Barcelona had jolted her out of her lifelong habit of taking in information through screens. She had to remind herself that this was real, that the sea really was taking these big bites out of

Britain, that this was the changing country Grace would come home to, someday.

Amanda was talking of her life in the caravan park. Even now, though the worst of last year's storm-driven London floods had receded, the resources hadn't been found to repair the abandoned housing stock in Fulham and Chiswick and Hammersmith and elsewhere. "These caravans are putting down roots. We've got mains, electricity and water! But it drives me crazy, it's so small, I don't have three quarters of my stuff..." Helen sensed that under her sparky talk Amanda found the thought that she might *never* be allowed back home, never able to rebuild and repair, disturbing on some fundamental level.

In the meantime life in Britain was changing in more subtle ways. Transport was more difficult, with washed-out road and rail links and the steadily increasing cost of fuel, and this was forcing a profound adjustment on everybody. Amanda's kids were going to local Buckinghamshire schools, crowded with London refugees who were picked on by the locals. Amanda still commuted daily into her job in London, but she made the last leg on a riverboat that sailed past drowned riverfront flats. She did her shopping in a Waitrose or a Tesco's in Aylesbury, going in and out by bus, but what you could buy in the supermarkets changed daily as their supply and distribution chains broke down. Small independent stores were making a comeback, in fact, boasting fresh local sources.

"Everything is sort of stretched out of shape," Amanda said stoically. "I sometimes think it's as if we're regressing to the past. Local schools, jobs, food. But things are still working, just."

Lily sympathized about the caravan. "I can imagine you and the kids crammed in there. I expect I'll have more room in Gary's submarine."

The talk turned to that, the nature of the dive, the dangers, its purposes.

Lily said, "Gary, Thandie and their crew simply don't believe the UN's assurances about the limits to the sea-level rise."

Amanda snorted. "Never mind the scientists. Just ask Benj and Kristie. There's endless online chatter about it all. You have Aussie kids who watched Bondi Beach disappear,

Inuit kids watching the permafrost drown in the Arctic—
and a lot of them measuring what's going on in some way,
even if it's only chalk marks on a pier. Kristie's keeping up
her scrapbook of this stuff—do you remember that project,
Lily? I mean they're all just kids, but kids aren't necessarily stupid, my kids certainly aren't, and they're telling each
other what they see. And *they* all agree that the rise is real,
and in fact it's accelerating. So, Lily, you don't need to go
diving at all. Not unless it's just an excuse to get up close
and personal with that astronaut."

"Gordo, you mean—"

"That's what I've been telling her too," came a new
voice.

In her screen image, Lily looked up, startled. "Oh, hi,
Piers." Helen saw Lily shove sideways to let him sit beside
her; they seemed to be on the edge of her hotel room bed.

Helen and Michael exchanged a glance. So Piers had
made it after all.

"Looking good, Piers," Helen said. "Texas cooking
agrees with you."

Piers smiled, but it was a strained expression, and his
eyes looked dark. Helen remembered it was past midnight
for him, and he'd clearly been working hard. He turned to
Lily. "'Gordo.' You name-dropper."

"He's taking me on a personal tour of Johnson tomorrow. How cool is that?"

"Well, it's good that you should see the space center before it becomes a museum."

Piers's tone startled Helen. He was right, of course.
Despite heroic efforts Cape Canaveral was under severe
threat; from space Florida looked as if it had been cut in
half by the ocean. But the remark was cynical for Piers,
and personal, even cruel. One of the many secrets they had
learned about Lily in Barcelona was that Lily had joined
the USAF, despite being raised in Britain, in the faint hope
of making it into NASA; this was an old dream for her,
now flung back at her by Piers. Perhaps he was tired. Or,
just maybe, there was some small grain of jealousy lodged
in his soul.

Lily, however, didn't react.

Piers said now, "Just a minute." He reached forward and
tapped at an invisible keyboard.

The laptop images blinked, then recovered, but the picture quality was poorer, the sound scratchier.

Amanda asked, "What was that? Something on the fritz?"

"No. I put us through a military encryption filter; we're reasonably secure now. Look, I overheard the last bit of your talk. I want to give you some advice, all of you. This theorizing about the sea-level rise is actually irrelevant. Whatever happens to the ocean, in future things are likely to get a good deal more difficult."

" 'Difficult,' " said Michael.

"Yes, difficult. I talked over some of the bigger picture with Lily earlier. We're already seeing petty wars triggered by refugee flows and shortages of fresh water and dry land, new pressures exacerbating old tensions. At present it's the usual flashpoints that are kicking off, India versus Pakistan for instance—though that conflict's largely overwhelmed by the sheer scale of the humanitarian crisis unfolding in the deltas. But nowhere will be immune, ultimately."

His dry, laconic way of speaking was oddly chilling. Helen wondered what briefings might lie behind his words. "So what's your advice, Piers?"

"To go home. Back to Britain, as soon as you can. Look—Britain is under pressure, from the loss of farmland, the flooding of London and the other cities. And we're still heavily reliant on imported food and energy sources. But the fact is Britain is an island, and that gives us a certain natural security. It always has. The government is beginning a crash program of resilience, of securing food and energy supplies without a reliance on foreign imports—I mean, we have coal, North Sea gas and oil, nuclear. Even in some of the worst-case climate change scenarios Britain fares reasonably well. A Gulf Stream collapse, a cooling of the north Atlantic, might be balanced by a general warming of the Arctic."

"We should retreat to Fortress Britain," Lily said. "While the rest of the world drowns."

"Well, just think about it. You did want us to stick together, Lily. What else can I do but give you my best advice?"

Lily said, "I appreciate it, Piers, but you're not going to put me off my dives. There's no scientific consensus about the sea-level rise. Don't you think it's worth a few submarine jaunts to try and find out?"

"The correct question is, is it worth losing your life?" He looked at her steadily. "I'm actually concerned for your safety, Lily, believe it or not."

She reached across and grabbed his hand. "I know. But I have to go. Because if I don't, who's going to look after Gary?"

He laughed. Then he pulled his hand away, withdrawing into himself again. He stood up. "I need to get back to work."

Helen frowned. "You can't be serious. You're exhausted."

Piers smiled, ducking so the others could see his face in their screens. "I'm fine. Good night, all."

"Good night and good morning, Piers," Amanda said.

When he'd gone, Michael shook his head. "He's wearing shorts and no tie, but nothing has changed about him. I've said it since the first time I met him. One of these days that man is going to snap like a dried twig."

Lily snorted, and stretched. "Well, he's not talking me out of my submarine trip. And I'm not done chatting yet, the night is young. What say we have a coffee break? I'll see if I can get this lousy military filter off the link."

They agreed, and broke up. Lily filled the screens with a silly saver image, some relic of her childhood perhaps, a puppet aqua-girl with long blond hair and webbed feet who swam past to a soppy crooning song.

But Helen's phone sounded with a news flash. A nuclear warhead being hastily moved from a flood-threatened missile facility on the north German plain had been involved in a high-speed vehicle pileup. The warhead had partially detonated; Hamburg had been declared a disaster zone, and the German government was appealing for aid.

24

From Kristie Caistor's scrapbook:

Mrs. Reese Shelby of Belle Glade, Florida, used her blog to protest the state's use of school buses to ship low-category prisoners from flood-threatened correctional facilities to safer institutions upstate.

"It's not just that my kids have to tramp their way to school through the pouring rain, that's not what I object to. And it's not even that the governor has put the safety of thieves, murderers and rapists ahead of the safety of decent people. No, what I object to is the state these convicts leave the buses in. The seats are vandalized, they scrawl the most obscene graffiti, and there are bodily fluids *everywhere* . . ."

Mrs. Shelby went on to protest about the government decision to open up selected national parks to refugees from flooded areas.

25

October 2017

Nathan Lammockson had Lily flown into Keflavik Airport, thirty kilometers west of Reykjavik.

An AxysCorp car met her there and drove her, not into the city itself, but inland, across desolate country. She glimpsed mountains, ice-crested. She was curious about this strange island; it was the first time she had visited. But she had no time to explore. Now that Lammockson had got hold of his bathyscaphe it was full speed ahead with his ocean survey project, and Lily was suddenly pitched into a whole new phase of her life. Lily Brooke, submarine pilot: who'd have thought it?

They arrived at what looked like a staid hotel. It turned out to be Bessastadhir, the residence of the president of Iceland.

The next morning Lily waited outside the residence for the car to return. The air was fresh and cold, with a bite in the wind from the sea, but there was no frost on the ground, no snow. Her usual AxysCorp coverall kept her warm enough, but she pulled the hood up around her face.

The car showed up, flying an AxysCorp cradled-Earth flag. This time Lammockson himself was in the back. And up front, Gordon James Alonzo was driving. Lily buckled up fast. Gordo drove like an astronaut; she'd learned that from the time she'd spent with him in the States. She hung on to the door grip as the car was thrown down the drive and out onto the road.

Lammockson offered her coffee in a lidded plastic cup. She refused, but he took a deep draft from his own cup, and there was a strong aroma. Lammockson wore a heavy overcoat of what looked like fake fur, finely tailored, very expensive; he used up most of the room on this seat. Before her the back of Gordo's head was like a warhead, solid, stubbled with silver-gray hair; a stocky man, big for an astronaut, he was around forty-five.

"So," Lammockson grinned at her. "Enjoying your trip so far, Lily? How do you like staying at the White House of Iceland?"

"Yes, how did you swing that with the president?"

"Well, the old girl owes me. I've brought enough investment and employment to this godforsaken rock in the last few months, while every other 'entrepreneur' around the world is filling sandbags and lying low. Besides, half the hotels in Reykjavik are flooded out, you'll see, same as everywhere else. And now you're being chauffeured by a genu-wine astronaut. Of course if not for me he'd be flying old ladies and puppy dogs out of the Mississippi floods, not piloting mysterious voyages to the bottom of the sea. I've got his balls in my pocket, and he knows it. Right, space boy?"

"You're a funny guy."

Gordo spoke in his usual Californian drawl, but Lily could hear the tension in his voice. In Houston, she'd got to know this stranded astronaut well enough to understand that his sudden grounding when the space program died was an open wound the size of the Mid-Atlantic Ridge itself. But this was Lammockson's way, she'd learned that too. If you worked for him, he never missed an opportunity to exert his power over you in the most brutal way, all delivered with that hustler's grin.

They were driving into the city now. Suburban Reykjavik looked a clean place, neat, modern in a European way, pretty little houses with brightly colored roofs, lots of concrete and glass. Occasionally she glimpsed the flat, steel-gray surface of the sea, with ice-capped mountains shouldering above the horizon. But out here the only sign of the flooding that must be afflicting this coastal port was the heavy traffic; traffic was bad all over the world, it seemed, everybody inching around the floods.

Gordo turned his head. He was good-looking in a big-boned surfer kind of way, but his neck was thick, and lines gathered around his eyes and mouth. He exuded competence. "You ever been here before, Lily? To Iceland?"

"No."

"We're sat right on the Mid-Atlantic Ridge. In fact Iceland is one of the ridge mountains, strictly speaking. So it's a good place for Thandie Jones to be running her sea-floor-spreading surveys."

"But it's not just that." Lammockson pointed out of the window to a large blocky building that sat on a low rise, topped by a glass dome from which light glimmered. "See that? I asked Gordo to bring us this way. It's a remarkable sight in my humble, and I try to make sure everybody who comes out here takes a look. They call it 'the Pearl.' Geothermal water distribution tanks. Since 1930 this whole city's taken nearly all its central heating from the heat of the Earth, the steam that just bubbles up out of the ground."

Lily thought she saw his point. "So the city is independent of external energy sources. Oil supplies, coal."

"Not entirely, but it could be made so," Lammockson said. "An inexhaustible supply. Not only that, we're sitting on an island. Defensible, see? Quite a thought, isn't it? This is a stable point, a refuge from the flooding, a place the post-flood recovery could begin . . ."

He said this briskly, businesslike, as if he was planning no more than a disaster recovery option for one of Axys-Corp's computer centers. But she had learned that this was the way he thought, as he acted: decisive, far-seeing, brutal. This Iceland operation was typical of Lammockson's way of thinking in that it achieved multiple goals, the ocean survey work and the establishment of a possible refuge for a dismal future.

They drove back through the anonymous suburbs and headed inland once more.

"Where to now?" Lily was here to be trained to pilot Lammockson's deep-submergence vehicle, and she'd imagined she'd be taken to the coast.

Gordo said, "We've established a DSV sim facility inland. Right now I'm the only pilot we've got; you'll be the second, though some of the scientists can double as pilots also. We're hoping to train up a slew more. Nathan and Thandie want to run their survey dives around the clock. It's a two-person boat, in the current configuration, one scientist, one pilot, so we need the cover."

"And you don't want to tie up the one operational boat while you're training novices."

"That's the idea. The sim is fairly crude, you'll see, but it's as good as it needs to be. Compared to flying Shuttle or Orion, the *Trieste* is a simple bird. More like piloting a dirigible. You'll have no problems with it."

"You said the *Trieste*?"

Nathan Lammockson looked at her, his eyebrows raised. "Name rings a bell?"

When Gary had made his invitation to join him, back in London, she had known nothing about deep diving. Since then she had done some Googling. "*Trieste* was the tub that explored the Marianas Trench in the 1960s."

Gordo said, "The boat was designed by the Swiss, bought by the US Navy in 1958, and in 1960 she reached the Challenger Deep in the Marianas, eleven thousand meters down, the deepest part of any ocean on Earth. No vessel has ever revisited the Deep. In fact no vessel constructed since has been capable of reaching such depths, manned or unmanned."

Lily said to Lammockson, "So this *Trieste* is named as a tribute to that pioneer."

"Not exactly," Lammockson said. "Lily, she *is* the *Trieste*, the original. Or what's become of her, in the years since."

After her jaunt into the Challenger Deep the *Trieste* was retired, but her pressure sphere, the most advanced bit of engineering, was incorporated into a new DSV called the *Trieste II*. The new boat was used as a test vehicle for the Navy's deep-submergence program, and qualified four "hydronauts." *Trieste* kept working until 1980, when she was made obsolescent by the Alvin-class subs.

"Which everybody's heard of, because Alvin went to the *Titanic*," Lammockson said. "While they stuck the *Trieste* in a naval museum at Keyport, Washington."

"And that's about where the engineering development stopped," Gordo said. "Last decade there was talk of replacing Alvin with a new breed of DSVs but it came to nothing."

"And the Navy won't even release Alvin for this project," Lammockson said bitterly. "Nor will Woods Hole."

Gordo said, "Woods Hole is a major oceanographic institute in Massachusetts. They operate Alvin."

"More like 'Arse Hole' if you ask me," Lammockson said. "The Russians have deep-diving submarines too, that they call Mir. Two of them touched bottom of the North Polar Ocean a few years back. But I can't get hold of those either. I blame the Shirshov Oceanology Institute in Moscow for *that*."

Lily nodded. "So you liberated the *Trieste* from her museum."

Lammockson snorted. "What choice was there? There's no time to redevelop a whole technology from scratch. The Iceland Glaciological Society is formally sponsoring us here, and God bless them. But I've had nothing but minimal cooperation, if you can call it cooperation at all, from agencies who should know better." He railed about other organizations and eminent individuals who, he claimed, had done their best to impede his project. There was a widespread denial of the reality of the ocean rise, because it didn't fit any of the old models of likely climate change, which themselves were still at the center of intense disputes. "But you just have to deal with them all," Nathan said.

"Well, that's what you're good at, Nathan," Gordo murmured.

"Yeah, I spend my life sucking off bureaucrats, lucky me. Anyhow I think we ended up with the right tub for Thandie's work. I'm happy with the *Trieste*. But of course it's not me who's got to fly the thing. Just think," he said, goading, "you're getting to see the deep ocean bed, Gordo. Exploring landscapes nobody's ever seen before. A consolation for not walking on Mars, hey?"

"You take what you can get," Gordo said. "For sure I'd rather be doing this than working with the rest of the guys, mothballing Johnson and Canaveral, or working on the panic launches." This was NASA-speak for a series of rapid-turnaround launches in which the inventory of vehicles at Canaveral was being fired off to Earth orbit, delivering whatever useful payload could be placed up there, mostly weather satellites and Comsats, before the launch facilities were finally lost to the flooding.

Lammockson laughed at him. "Shooting off those antiquated old birds before you turn into a museum piece yourself, eh, Gordo?"

Gordo shrugged. "You can't change your luck."

They were leaving the Reykjavik suburbs behind now, and the traffic was clearing. Lily saw that the road ran over fields of hard black rock, sheets of it, all but free of vegetation. It was like bulldozed tarmac. This was lava, she supposed, frozen in the air, some of the youngest rock on the planet—the stuff that built seabeds and pushed continents aside. But the lava soon gave way to a landscape that was very European, farmland and grass, save for the lack of trees. Sheep watched incuriously as they sped by, a released hostage, a stranded astronaut, and one of the richest men in the world.

26

The *Endurance* was a modern European research vessel, constructed in Italy and fitted out in dockyards in northeast England and Scotland. Her superstructure was studded with sensors, radar dishes and comms domes, and an ungainly drill derrick that towered over the hull. She was solid, sleek, streamlined, as gray and anonymous as the sea itself. Now she was serving as a support ship for the *Trieste*, which would be strapped to the deck during the cruise like a geeky toy submarine in a theme-park exhibit.

Endurance sailed roughly south from Iceland, following the line of the Mid-Atlantic Ridge—which, once Iceland was out of sight, would be invisible until they reached the next Ridge islands to protrude from the ocean, the Azores. The crew, many of them recruited by AxysCorp from the oil companies, kept working throughout the cruise. The purpose of the expedition was to explore the deep subsurface of the ocean, the layers beneath the seabed. So they had sonar and radar which probed at subsediment layers, and periodically they launched overboard a device like a mechanical porpoise packed with more sonar gear.

The most interesting work was the drilling. The ship would halt, held in place against the current by a computer-controlled array of propellers, and the oilmen all turned into roughnecks, adopting roles like "tool pusher" and "drill superintendent." They used their drilling derrick to sample the deep subsurface directly, hauling up meter after meter of mud, cores replete with data for the sedimentologists. They got on with this work on a sea that surged constantly, restless, its turbid gray flecked with mud drawn up from the deep ooze below, a sea that was troubled even when the weather was calm.

And down in the science lab, under the foredeck, the

sedimentologists swore as they sleeved their layered cores in Mylar, sliced them in two, used electromagnetic wands to test water concentrations, and picked out minute samples of rock types and living things, fine, unrepeatable work performed in conditions like a funfair ride.

Lily had crossed the Channel a few times, caught ferries to the Isle of Wight, Arran. She was no sailor, save for some dinghy work during her survival training with the USAF. The surging North Atlantic was a shock to her. None of the five "hydronauts"—Lily and Gordo, Thandie, Gary Boyle and a thirty-year-old meteorologist pal of Thandie's called Sanjay McDonald—was ever at ease, even Thandie who was the specialized oceanographer among them. You couldn't rest, you slept badly, and when you ate you couldn't always keep it down. Mostly they used up their time helping out the roughnecks with their drilling.

In fact, Gordo told Lily, it would be a relief to take the *Trieste* down into the depths; at least beneath the waves you could get a little peace for a few hours.

Once they were away from Reykjavik and out of Nathan Lammockson's direct control, Gordo took it on himself to draw up a manning rota for *Trieste* to reflect the science priorities and the need to rotate the crews to give them a break. Thandie and Gary were actually both capable of driving the *Trieste* themselves, so there were overlapping pools of four pilots and three scientists to make up each dive crew's complement of two, a pilot plus a scientist. As a result it wasn't until the fourth dive that Lily was to pilot the *Trieste*, and Gordo paired her with Thandie; tactfully he didn't explain his reasoning, but as Thandie was the most experienced of the scientist-pilots it made sense.

On her designated day, Lily went up on deck. It was a warm, blustery morning, under a blanket of rolled-up gray cloud; in fact they had arrived not too far north of the Azores, at around forty degrees north. But Lily, like Thandie, was bundled up warm in her AxysCorp-issue thermal underwear, coverall and parka, with a Mae West over the top; she had a Russian fur hat and gloves tucked in her pockets. Where she was going, she was assured, it was cold.

She watched as cables were attached to the *Trieste*, and

a derrick raised her into the air to swing her out over the ocean. Roughnecks working in pairs hauled on cables fore and aft to steady the boat. And Lily got her first good look at the ship that was about to become hers.

Around fifteen meters long, the *Trieste* had a stubby, roughly streamlined shape something like a conventional submarine. At either end were air-filled ballast tanks. But most of her hull was filled with flotation tanks full of gasoline, a hundred thousand liters of it, and Lily could see the release outlets of the heavy iron-ballast hoppers protruding from her keel. Her propellers were fixed to her upper deck.

And under the main hull hung the observation gondola, the pressurized sphere within which Lily and Thandie would be descending kilometers into the ocean.

Thandie approached Lily, waddling in her own Mae West. She was grinning. "So, virgin, you OK with this?"

"Ready to do it right."

"Christ, you sound like the space cadet. You'll love it, believe me."

Awkward in their life jackets, they clambered down a steel ladder to an orange inflatable, manned by a single crewman, waiting for them on the ocean surface. The crewman gunned his engine to take them the few meters to the bathyscaphe.

When they reached the *Trieste* she was rolling alarmingly, and the boat bobbed just as vigorously. Thandie showed off. She just stood up, got her balance, and stepped over the half-meter or so to the bathyscaphe. Lily, sooner safe than spectacular, was happy to grab hold of the crewman's hand, then Thandie's, as she made her own way across.

And then, as the mooring arm was released and the ship bobbed free, they gave a last wave to the watching crew and scientists on the deck of the *Endurance*. Gordo gave them a crisp salute. Gary stood beside him, watching silently. It struck Lily how odd it was to see that familiar face here, in circumstances that could hardly be more different from their long confinement in Barcelona.

Lily and Thandie climbed down through the access tunnel to the gondola. The tunnel ran vertically through the body of the bathyscaphe, cutting between two of the gasoline tanks. Lily had gone through this during her training with Gordo, and knew the drill. At the bottom of the tunnel she had to lower herself feet-first through a hatch into the gondola itself. The hatch more than any other component showed the bathyscaphe's age, its handles rubbed smooth by decades of wear.

Once they were both in, Thandie pulled the hatch closed. "Christ," she said. "This tub always stinks of gasoline. Let's get it done."

They shucked off their Mae Wests, settled at their stations and ran through a quick checklist of their essential systems. They would be kept alive by oxygen cylinders and a modern carbon dioxide scrubbing system, cylinders, fans, pumps, filters, derived from similar technology used on the Space Station. When the scrubbing system started up there was a wheezing noise, like the hum of the fan on an old-fashioned desktop computer. Lily confirmed that the propulsion system, the steerable propellers set on the upper hull, was functional. And Thandie checked that the external sensors were working, the TV cameras, a sample-collection pump system, a pod of down-pointing sonar and radar to explore the deep subsurface. There was a kind of robot arm which could be used to manipulate objects outside the hull.

As they worked, the gondola, fixed to the keel of the rolling hull, swung sharply back and forth. The bucket seats had harnesses, and Lily strapped herself in. But the rolling made it hard to work the controls, even to read the display screens, and her stomach churned. But she was most definitely not going to throw up in here. Thandie whistled as she checked over her equipment, deliberately nonchalant.

The gondola was a sphere only about two meters across, equipped with a couple of bucket seats, a small chemical toilet and a provisions bag. Opposite the hatch, looking downwards, was the single window, a solid block of Plexiglas set into the ten-centimeter-thick steel walls. There was actually a lot more useful room in here than there had been back in the 1950s. The interior had been stripped out and remodeled with modern instruments and controls; the scuffed walls were plastered with foldable screens.

But still the gondola felt very cramped to Lily. She could see why Gordo had taken to the work so easily; spacecraft like the Soyuz were just as confining. Lily was a flier, used to small cabins maybe but usually surrounded by infinite space. She wondered how well she was going to cope with the containment inside this steel coffin with kilometers of ocean piling up above her, and absolutely no way out.

Finally Lily tested the comms system. Gordo was acting as what he called "capcom" today; it was reassuring to hear his voice. They had a long-wavelength radio link, and also a backup hydrophone link, although at the depths they would reach it would take several seconds for a sound wave to pass through the water to the support ship on the surface above.

All was confirmed ready, by Lily, Thandie, Gordo and the *Endurance* crew. Lily tapped a screen.

The ballast tanks fore and aft flooded, and the *Trieste* dropped. Just for a moment there was a surge, like a fast elevator descending. But that soon smoothed out, and so did the rolling; already they had left the surface waves behind them. Lily glanced through the window. Looking down she saw nothing but a bluish glow, and random particles of murk.

27

Thandie looked over Lily's shoulder at the pilot's display. It was centered on a schematic of the ship, the hull sliced up into the floats and ballast tanks, the blister of the gondola suspended beneath, the image covered with status numbers. "Looks nominal to me."

"Yes . . ."

The principle of the bathyscaphe was pretty simple. She was like a hot air balloon, laden with ballast. Gasoline was used as the float material, the "air" in the balloon, because it was lighter than water but incompressible even at extreme pressures, and so retained its buoyant properties. The ballast was heavy iron shot. Right now the *Trieste* was heavier than the sea water she displaced, just, and so she sank steadily. The descent would be a powered dive, with Lily directing their fall to points of interest with the steerable propellers.

When it was time to lift, the external pressure would be too high to allow them to blow ballast tanks with air in the usual way. So Lily would shut down an electromagnet to release the iron ballast from its hoppers, and the *Trieste* would instantly become lighter than the water, and up she would go like an air bubble. It was a fail-safe arrangement; if onboard power failed the shot would be released immediately.

The whole design was an advance on older bathyspheres, which were simple balls of steel lowered from ships on cables, like bait on a fishing line. The *Trieste* was a free-falling, self-directing super-bathysphere.

Thandie tapped a depth meter. "We're dropping at around sixty centimeters per second. Well, that's about right, two kilometers an hour. The Ridge summits are around two and a half kilometers below sea level, and the

flank of the mid-Atlantic rise is five kilometers deeper than
that. I'm hoping to make it down to around four klicks
today—about two hours down." She sat back and looked
at Lily. "So. Welcome to my world."

"Thanks."

"We may as well relax." Thandie rummaged in the
provisions bag and produced a thermos. "You want some
coffee? We have chocolate. You're supposed to save it
until we're down in the depths, when it gets pretty cold
in here, seven or eight degrees, and you need the sugar
rush. What I always say is, fuck it." She hauled out a slab
of chocolate, tore off the wrapper, cracked it and handed
Lily a piece.

The two of them sat there, eating their chocolate sociably
and drinking coffee, while the smooth descent continued.

"I'm glad we're doing this," Thandie said, munching.
"We haven't had a lot of time together, you and me, since
all this started. But I feel I know you already. I should tell
you the stories Gary has about you, from Barcelona."

"Go on," Lily said cautiously.

"Like the time you took on the guard who walked in
wearing the ring he stole from you."

"Yeah. They took stuff off each of us in the first minute,
as soon as we were captured. But to tell the truth I was just
as pissed at the way he wore my sunglasses all the time."

Thandie laughed. "And the time you cut off your own
hair, rather than let them do it to you."

"I always wore my hair short anyhow. But I couldn't
bear to have them do that, you know? It was all I had left,
of me. So I fought back when they tried to shave me."
Which had earned her beatings, and from Said a threat of
violation with a broken Coke bottle. "They gave up in the
end and let me do it myself."

"And," Thandie said, "the time Gary said you dug him
out of the worst pit he fell into. When he had diarrhea, and
wasn't allowed out to the john. It wasn't the illness, he said,
it was the shame in front of the others."

And so Lily had lifted her faded T-shirt, dropped her
shorts and shat in the corner, just as Gary had. "My finest
hour," she said.

"Well, it worked, you were a true friend," Thandie
murmured. "You know, I don't know if I could have stood

it. Not the captivity, but the fact of not being able to *do* anything."

Lily shut up, as she had developed a habit of doing when people pronounced how they would react in situations they could know nothing of.

Thandie said, "I have to do things. I'm an agent, you know? The frustration would drive me crazy."

"Everybody feels like that. We all missed our lives, our families, our careers—"

"Yeah, but I got it in spades," Thandie said ruefully. "Lucky for me I had the smarts to pursue an academic career, where you can be your own boss, though you're continually fighting for sponsors and contracts and equipment funding. But even so I always seem to spot that limb and head right out on it."

"Like your theories about the source of the floodwater."

"Yeah." Thandie grinned, but her eyes were unfocused as she thought about it.

Lily knew that Thandie was getting her share of fame, or notoriety, through her outlandish hypotheses about the true source of the flooding and its likely rise—and everyone knew she hoped to get a book deal out of it. That was her true dream, it seemed, to transcend her profession, even the science, and become famous: to be *the* Thandie Jones, a media figure, a modern Jacques Cousteau. But to do that, of course, she needed to validate her theories with some hard data. Which was why she was down here now, spending Nathan Lammockson's money.

However it seemed to Lily that Thandie hadn't thought it through much further than that. After all, if she was right, if the sea-level rise really was going to become much worse than the consensus of experts was predicting, what would it mean for the world? Thandie was clearly ferociously intelligent. But it was possible she lacked some deeper qualities of imagination. Empathy, perhaps.

Maybe Thandie detected Lily's reservations about her. They ran out of conversation, and much of the descent passed in silence.

So they dropped into the sea, the dive's events unfolding relentlessly, the light outside deepening through shades of blue to black. As the air grew steadily colder condensation formed on the walls, making Thandie fret over the effect on her computer screens. It turned out a dehumidifier was faulty. After a time Lily pulled on her Russian fur hat.

At a kilometer down there was an ominous creaking. Lily imagined the small, cramped gondola being crushed like a meringue in a clenched fist. Thandie told her not to worry; it was just the external instrument mounts settling into place as they contracted with the cold.

More than two kilometers down, Thandie's sonar revealed the shape of the submerged mountains of the Mid-Atlantic Ridge.

She had Lily direct the bathyscaphe toward the mountain slope. Powerful quartz arc-light lamps fixed to the gondola's exterior picked out the slope, and they studied the TV image and peered through the small, murky Plexiglas window. Lily saw a featureless surface covered in some kind of ooze, a mess of mud, sand and rock. She could see only a few meters in either direction; there was no sense of the scale of the undersea mountain they cautiously skirted. Thandie powered up her radar system, and tested it out on the mountain slope. It returned bright, clear echoes, embedded in which, Lily understood, there was a wealth of data on the deeper structure of the rocks.

When they got close enough a kind of handler arm implanted small charges in the mud. After the *Trieste* was safely away, these would be detonated to generate seismic signals, another way to probe the rock's deep interior. Fish and crabs and worms swam by, disturbed by the arm. They were ordinary-looking creatures, but pale, adapted for the dark and the thousand-atmosphere pressures of this deep. Thandie quoted names like *echiuroid worm* and *ethusa* and *bassogigas*. It was an unprepossessing sight, a deep-sea fauna unremarkable to nonspecialist eyes.

Thandie had Lily sail the *Trieste* away from the slope so she could direct the radar to peer down the mid-Atlantic rise to the deeper floor. As soon as she did so the radar stopped returning clean echoes. The data display was flickering, jumbled.

"Shit." Thandie ran through a quick diagnostic. "Everything seems OK." She bounced a quick test pulse off the mountain; the echo came back clean. "But when I send the pulse downwards . . ." She shook her head. "If I take the results seriously, the sea floor down there is shattered. Broken up. Some kind of subsidence maybe." The bathyscaphe shuddered. Thandie grabbed the arms of her chair. "Now what?"

Lily hurriedly checked through her own data displays, running through possible scenarios: an implosion of a flotation tank, a propeller failing. All her indicators were fine. "But we're rising," she said.

"What?" Thandie leaned over to see. "We're heavier than the water, we can't be."

Lily said nothing; she just pointed to the depth gauge, which had gone into reverse. And she had started to feel queasy. She quickly checked the craft's stability. *Trieste* was spinning. "Spinning, and rising," she said. "It's like we're caught in some kind of updraft." She glanced out of the thick window. By the boat's lights she saw turbulence, muddy swirls.

"I knew it," Thandie breathed.

"What?"

"It's a fountain. Straight from the mantle reservoirs, coming up through some kind of shattered terrain."

Lily said, "Tell me what we're seeing."

"Water, Lily. Water bubbling up from the interior of the Earth. I think this is the source of the flooding, the sea-level rise. My God, Lily. I've been down here a dozen times. We've found some direct evidence before, seeps, changes in salinity, but nothing as dramatic as this. You found it on your very first dive!"

"But what is it?"

"A subterranean sea . . ."

Lily sailed them clear of the updraft, into calmer water.

Thandie said she had come up with the idea of deep subsurface oceans through luck. She was in the right place at the right time.

"It started with a study I came across from back in the noughties, where a couple of guys from UC San Diego went through a heap of old seismic signals. You understand that earthquakes generate waves that travel right through the structure of the Earth; you can track them and see how they are diffracted by the different density layers down there, and so on. What they found was a consistent weakening of the waves around a thousand kilometers deep, that's in the Earth's mantle, somewhere under Beijing. They showed that the muffling had to be caused by water, immense quantities of it, as much as the Arctic Ocean maybe, trapped in porous mantle rock. And there are other theories about how there could be more water down there in other forms, whole oceans trapped a molecule at a time in the structure of certain minerals in the mantle rocks."

"Subterranean seas."

"Exactly."

"So how does the water get there?"

"Well, maybe it's a relic of Earth's formation. The planet was born from a cloud of rock and ice, mostly water ice. It's generally thought that most of the water and other volatiles were boiled off in the heat of formation, and the oceans we ended up with were delivered later by impacting comets. But planetary formation is a complex business. There's no reason water couldn't be trapped in the infall, as Earth coalesced.

"Or the water could be transported down there from the surface by tectonic processes. We know that happens in the present day. Here we are at a place where ocean-floor plates are created. There are corresponding places where they are destroyed—subduction zones, where the plates are dragged under one another, back down into the mantle. And when that happens, a lot of water and other material is hauled down with them."

"So you knew about these deep reservoirs already. And when you needed a theoretical source for a sea-level rise—"

"I just plugged it in," Thandie said with a grin. "The data fell into my lap. Then it was a case of finding the reservoirs. I figured that if the water is being released anywhere, why not here, at the mid-ocean ridges, where material is being dragged up from Earth's interior?"

"Which is why we're here."

"Yes. I've got other data, charts of salinity and temperature anomalies and concentrations of various impurities, all of which pointed to some kind of ocean-floor *event* going on right here, along the Atlantic Ridge—and, I believe, along the lines of the other mid-ocean ridges too, though I've no good data to back that up. But an actual injection of water into the abyss is the smoking gun."

"But why should this deep water be released now, after the Earth's been around millions of years?"

"Billions, actually. Well, I hope to figure that out. But it isn't that dramatic an event, on the planetary scale. Look—the Earth is like an egg, with the core the yolk, the mantle the white, and the crust the shell. To cover all the land surface would require an ocean three times the volume of the existing seas—but this would amount to less than *one percent* of Earth's total volume. It would be an immense event for us, but only a little weeping of the white out onto the shell."

"It sounds plausible to me," Lily said. "But then I'm no scientist."

"You've got more sense than most of the boneheads I've been duelling with on the IPCC."

"Why can't they accept what you say?"

"Because they're all still bound up in generations-old arguments about climate change, which the new sea rise has nothing to do with, and which their existing models can't predict. Because they're in denial," she snapped. "And that is not a pleasant state to be."

"OK," Lily said. "But I think I hope they're right, and you're wrong. No offense."

"None taken. But I am right. I mean, now I've got the evidence." Thandie was wide-eyed; as Lily had suspected, she hadn't been expecting what they'd found today, and the implications were starting to sink in, perhaps for the first time. "I'm right. Oh, shit."

The bathyscaphe shuddered and spun again, caught in the turbulence once more. "Time to go." Lily reached for a joystick on the console before her. There was another shudder as electromagnets released the heavy iron ballast. Suddenly the *Trieste* was rising rapidly, still spinning, but as they ascended from the fountain the spinning was slowed by friction, and the water grew calmer.

Bit by bit, as they rose up, the sunlight penetrated the water's murk.

28

December 2017

From Kristie Caistor's scrapbook:
 The director of Mississippi's marine resources department lamented the failure of his scheme to cultivate mangroves in coastal areas of the state rendered uninhabitable by the flooding.

"It looked like the perfect way to make a constructive use of the abandoned land. Mangroves are kind of botanical amphibians. They can tolerate salt water, to a degree. They're natural breakwaters that stabilize the land against erosion and flooding. They are a source of lumber, and pharmaceuticals. And they are refuges for wildlife—birds in the canopy, shellfish attached to the roots, alligators hunting at the water surface. They're even terrific carbon sequestrators.

"But the sea is rising just too fast. Our mangroves are being drowned before they can grow, or do any good.

"We haven't given up, we're falling back is all, replanting further inland. I can assure the public that Mississippi's mangrove dream is alive."

29

The flight into New York from Reykjavik was diverted. The pilot announced this was because of a storm system in the North Atlantic. They would fly north and swoop down over Canada as far as Montreal, and then track down the valley of the Hudson to the airport at Newburgh, which was as close to New York City as you could land now. Nathan had arranged further transportation to get them from there to Manhattan. Lily, in the window seat of the block of three she shared with Gary and Thandie, heard mutterings among the passengers that the "storm" was actually a hurricane gathering somewhere west of Iceland.

"But that's ridiculous, isn't it?" she asked. "You don't get hurricanes this far north. And you don't get hurricanes in February."

Gary, on the far side, just shrugged. "We live in strange times, Lil." He closed his eyes and rested his head back.

Thandie, in the center seat, didn't respond at all. She had her eyes fixed on a screen on the seat back ahead of her, which showed sketchy handheld images of the Istanbul tsunami.

Lily gazed out of the window at a lid of cloud. She might have expected straight answers from climatologists. But the truth was they were all tired, she supposed, too tired even for a weather geek to care about a freak storm.

Nathan Lammockson's call to Thandie to come to New York, to present her science conclusions to a subcommittee of the IPCC at the Freedom Tower, had been last-minute; that was the way things worked nowadays. The three of them had spent a frantic twenty-four hours packing up their material at Thingvellir, the inland Icelandic town the survey team had decamped to when the flooding at Reykjavik had become overwhelming. Thandie had been ready to go for a while with her presentation material, her graphics and analyses, her pages of mathematics; she had firmed up her conclusions months ago, it seemed to Lily. The grunt work had been preparing her confirmatory samples, slices of sea-bottom core preserved in Mylar sleeves and specialized refrigerated containers, and lots of tiny vials of sea water for the assembled boffins to pore over. They were weary even before they stepped on the plane.

The truth was everybody was worn out, Lily thought. The flooding continued, the relentless sea-level rise went on and on, patchy and uneven and punctuated by extreme events but relentless nonetheless. Piers had told her it had been a great psychological shock in government circles when the rise had soared easily up through the ten-meter line, a limit that had been informally adopted as a worst-case upper bound by the UN and various relief agencies, derived from old climate-change forecasting models that now looked alarmingly out of date. Woods Hole reported the average rise to be *thirteen meters* globally since the start of the event in 2012, and continuing at an accelerating rate of three centimeters a day—an increase of nearly twelve more meters a year.

At the level of ordinary human lives, everything kept being mucked about. The pilot on this Airbus flight, for instance, needn't have bothered telling his passengers they were being diverted; you expected it. With so many of the world's major airports flooded, including hubs like Heathrow and JFK, airline routes and schedules were all over the place. Before she flew Lily had spoken to Amanda in her caravan park in the Chilterns. Amanda was assailed by increasingly odd weather, working from home as commuting to a drowned London was no longer feasible, and spending most of her free time queuing for water or persuading Benj and Kristie to keep attending school classes in a marquee. It wore you out, even if you weren't in one of the disaster zones, like Karachi or Sydney or Florida or Louisiana or Sacramento, or, now, Istanbul.

Everybody on the planet was tired, Lily sometimes thought. And there was no end in sight.

The pilot announced they would fly south of Newburgh, bank over New York City itself, and then head north up the Hudson, so they would be making their final approach into the headwinds. As the plane made its turn over Long Island, heading west toward the city, Lily peered out of her window, picking out the distinctive shape of New York Bay. She wished she knew her geography a little better. She made out the inland sea that had developed out of Jamaica Bay; somewhere on its fringe was JFK Airport, drowned, as indeed was La Guardia. At the mouth of the bay, at Rockaway Point, she saw a pale white line spanning the narrows, glistening under a blue-gray sheet of water: that was the levee the city authorities had thrown up to try to protect the bay and the airport, a barrier already overwhelmed. As the plane banked to the north Lily made out a second levee, this one between Brooklyn and Staten Island. But it too was drowned.

No fewer than four of these great levees had been thrown up in less than two years. The other two were to the west, across the Arthur Kill between Staten Island and New Jersey, and further east between Queens and the Bronx, spanning the East River under the Whitestone Bridge. It was a mighty system intended to save the vulnerable metropolitan areas from the then-expected rise of less than ten meters, a monumental effort. There hadn't been time to compute the final cost before the rising sea had overwhelmed it all.

As the plane headed north Lily was able to glimpse the transformation of New York City itself. Great bites had been taken out of Jersey City and Brooklyn, the roofs of buildings sticking forlornly out of the water. Around the shore of Manhattan the flooding had made a more detailed, almost fractal nibbling. In general south Manhattan was lower than the north, and that was where the flooding was most extensive, but the pattern was lumpy, uneven; Manhattan was a hilly island. Whole swathes of the flooded areas showed fire damage. And even those buildings not damaged by fire would be mortally wounded, Lily knew from her own experience in London, their walls and floors rotten with fungi, their foundations undermined, their joints stressed. She was looking down at square kilometers of desolation, thousands of homes, factories, offices and shops that could never be made habitable again, even if the flood water receded tomorrow.

Leaving the city behind, the plane fled up the valley of the Hudson. The valley itself was flooded in places, and bore the scars of evacuation, small towns overwhelmed by shanties, the hillsides stripped of trees for firewood. A linear refugee camp had spread along both riverbanks, a litter of tents and cars that stretched almost as far as West Point. When the flooding began, the first instinct of many New Yorkers had been to head up the Hudson in search of higher ground. Some had made it as far as Connecticut and New Jersey before the military and city authorities had blockaded the freeways at West Point. All over the world it was like this, Lily knew, the governments bottling up populations in the threatened cities on the estuaries and coasts, trying to keep some kind of control, seeking solutions that would keep everybody fed and watered and sheltered.

And as the plane began its descent toward the hastily laid-down airstrip at Newburgh, a few kilometers north of West Point, Lily glimpsed the vast new development being opened up to the north, approaching the foothills of the Catskills. Acre upon acre of brown earth had been scraped clear of forest and foliage, and patterned with mosaics of blocky prefabricated housing and the uglier sprawl of industrial developments. Here was the city's final solution, the levees and sea walls having failed: yet another tremendous project executed at huge cost and at enormous speed. New York was evacuating its essential functions, its industry and itself from the doomed environs of the bay and up onto higher ground. It was a remarkable translocation of millions of people, with a tearing-down and rebuilding of factories and power plants, houses and schools and hospitals. This was how a rich nation coped with such disaster, by building again, by continuing.

But there was an unevenness to the development, visible even from the air. You could see sprawling gated townships with villas and lawns and even the sky-blue gleam of swimming pools, surrounded by walls beyond which meaner communities of tents and tin shacks spread. Lily was learning the jargon, adopted from war and disaster zones around the world and now brought home: Green Zones for the rich, FEMA-villes for the not so rich. And she thought she saw tiny sparks in the country beyond the new settlement:

gunfire, the sign of the ongoing war between residents and refugees, and government against survivalists.

Thandie still had her head down, staring into her screen.

"You ought to see this," Lily murmured to her. "It's amazing. A whole city on the move. A year ago, two, you'd never have dreamed you'd be seeing such a sight."

"It's all amazing," Thandie said, her voice toneless. "All over the world."

"You're still looking at Istanbul?"

Thandie tipped the screen. "Actually I have to keep flipping channels. Most of the US stations are showing what's going on in Sacramento. Or even Washington, DC, for Christ's sake."

At any other time, Lily thought, either of those incidents would have been a major story. Sacramento was an unfolding, unexpected disaster. Storm surges had forced Pacific waters tens of kilometers inland across the Sacramento river delta, wrecking the irrigation systems that fed farms that supplied fruit and vegetables to half the country. Then when flash floods overwhelmed the Folsom dam above Sacramento, the city found itself caught between river and sea water. Hastily reinforced levees failed. A quarter of a million people were in flight, in this one incident.

"But this, Istanbul, is bigger than that," Thandie said. "Because it's something new. The start of the next stage."

Lily frowned; that sounded ominous. She peered at the screen. She saw a cityscape sprawling over hills and ravines, domes and minarets protruding from grimy flood waters, a fallen bridge, whole districts burning; too-familiar pictures, images that could have come from anywhere. "What am I looking at?"

"A view from one of the city's tallest buildings. A bank tower. Itself disaster-proof, probably. Istanbul spans the Bosporus—yes? The strait where the Black Sea to the north connects with the Sea of Marmara to the south." She tapped the screen, brought up an aerial view and traced a path. "This is the line of the North Anatolian fault, the place where the African tectonic plate is pushing north into the Eurasian. You can see it parallels the north Turkish coast and then passes under the Sea of Marmara.

"They knew a quake was coming. There have been

eight Richter-seven-plus quakes in the last century, steadily marching along the fault line toward Istanbul. That's why the rich have been building modern quake-proof developments on the hard rock on the Asian side of the strait, and the poor, millions of them, have been throwing up shoddy illegal houses on the soft rock of the European side." She passed her finger over the screen. "The quake itself knocked down *ten thousand* houses. The older buildings survived better than the modern, generally. I guess anything that has lasted a few centuries in a region like this is going to last a lot longer. Even the dome of the Hagia Sophia is intact.

"But the quake came under the Sea of Marmara, and that generated the tsunami, seven or eight meters high, which did a lot more damage when it hit the city. So now there's yet another vast refugee flow—"

"Thandie—what 'next stage'?"

Thandie looked up. Her eyes were hollow, unfocused, tired from staring too long at the screen. "Lily, as the oceans rise we're going to see a shift of isostatic pressures. The sheer weight of the floodwater will depress the land it lies over—the way the glaciers of the Ice Age pushed the continental land down so hard it hasn't finished rebounding yet. And those shifting pressures are going to stress the faults, the weak points."

"Like the North Anatolian fault."

"Yes. And hence the Istanbul tsunami."

"But you can't be sure that's the cause." She'd been around scientists enough the last few months, and indeed before that with Gary in Barcelona, to get a sense of how their minds worked. "It could be just coincidence. You said yourself that this has been a quake waiting to happen for decades."

"Yes. It could be coincidence. Or the start of a new kind of response to the flooding, a tectonic response."

"Terrific. And do you feel confident enough to say this to the IPCC?"

Thandie glanced out of the window, at fields and farmhouses and a glimpse of river that shot by as the plane made its final approach. "You're right. I can't be definitive. The IPCC is conservative. When they make their final report to the UN and the governments they'll strike out anything that can't be proven seven ways up. That's what they did with the climate-change predictions, all those years. But I'll flag it up even so."

Lily felt moved to comfort her. "You must get sick of always being the one with the bad news."

"Yeah." Thandie forced a grin. "Especially since I can't get a book deal after all, as nobody's publishing books anymore."

Lily patted her hand. "Nathan will listen."

"Yes. And maybe that counts for more than anything else."

The plane bumped to a landing and braked hard, the tires throwing up sprays of water from a soaked runway.

30

An AxysCorp chopper was waiting for them at the Newburgh airstrip, with a heavyset company guard already on board.

The pilot brought them back down the Hudson valley, and they descended at last over Manhattan, heading for Central Park. They peered curiously out through the chopper's blister hull at an island encroached on all its flanks by the rising rivers. The city's great buildings were an orderly forest of concrete and steel and glass, but you could see gaps in the forest, sprawls of rubble where buildings had fallen, often taking others down with them. Yet the city lived; away from the directly flooded areas traffic still moved, even glistening mustard-colored beetles that must be yellow cabs, and boats prowled busily along the drowned streets, drawing long wakes behind them.

Despite the rumors of the approaching Atlantic storm, the sky was clear and blue, the sun still high; it was a brilliant winter's day. The city shone in the sunlight, millions of windows glittering like so many sequins, and even the water that ponded around the feet of the buildings looked blue and pretty. It was like a postcard view of Venice as it once was.

The chopper brought them down onto a helipad in Central Park, on the Great Lawn just south of the reservoir. The pilot said this was as far south on the island as it was safe to land right now. The three of them clambered out, Thandie, Gary and Lily, followed by the pilot and the AxysCorp guard.

While the pilot unloaded their shoulder packs, Lily walked to the edge of the helipad. When she stepped on the green grass the ground gave under her feet, marshy, full of water. She looked around, shielding her eyes. It was years since she had come to Manhattan, to Central Park, and then it had been as a tourist. Glancing around you wouldn't think that anything had changed; here she was in this remarkable green space in the heart of the world's greatest city, whose buildings shouldered above the tree line in every direction. But looking south she could see grubby tents and lean-tos and threads of smoke from fires. People living in Central Park, then. And there was a smell of rot and sewage, a stink she had become too familiar with in London.

The pilot called her back to the group. She was a beefy woman who might have been thirty. She said now, in a broad Bronx accent, dryly humorous, "So welcome to New York. Here's your orientation guide."

"That won't be necessary," Thandie snapped.

"Mr. Lammockson's standing orders, so please listen up. You might notice a few changes since your last visit. The city isn't in as bad a shape as you might think. It's still working. But transport ain't what it used to be. We can't fly you any further downtown than this. And the subways flooded on day one."

New York's subways had been built after the sewers that drained them, and so had to run *under* the sewers. Even in normal times there had been an heroic, unending operation to pump water from the tunnels up into the sewers and out to the Hudson. When the flooding came the tunnels had filled up fast, and when the power to the pumps failed, there was nothing to be done to save the subways.

"So," Thandie said, "how are we supposed to get to the Empire State Building?" That was where they were due to meet Piers Michaelmas, some twenty-five blocks below Central Park South: a typically imaginative choice of landmark by Piers, Lily thought dryly.

"You walk, or take a yellow cab or rickshaw, or in the flooded areas flag a water cab. Pick the cabs that are licensed by the city. If you're not sure, ask a cop. You have GPS?"

Thandie lifted her arm; a GPS map, updated hourly with flood data, was projected on a patch on her sleeve.

"Use your common sense," the guard said. "Stay out of wrecked buildings. Don't drink anything that doesn't come out of a sealed bottle. Don't go swimming. Don't talk to anybody that doesn't look like he's washed for a couple of days. If the smell gets too bad, use your face masks. There is said to be cholera in the Lower East Side, so watch for that, you'll see the police tapes keeping you out. I say goodbye here, I gotta take this chopper home. But you'll have John here with you at all times."

The guard, John, nodded, and took a step back. Lily suspected he would be tailing them all the way to Freedom Tower, whether they liked it or not.

The pilot said, "So that's that. Any questions?"

Gary pointed to the clusters of tents, the fires. "What about those guys?"

"Refugees from downtown. The city ships them out, mostly to the big camps they've set up around West Point where they can be processed appropriately. But there are always more. Central Park serves as a big holding tank. Kind of a shantytown."

"That was what used to be here, before the city bought the land and established the park," Gary murmured. "Back in the 1850s. Pig farms and rubbish tips. Most of what's around us now is landscaped."

"What goes around comes around, hey buddy? Anyhow I'd keep away," the pilot said. "Any other questions?"

They said their goodbyes, the chopper lifted into an empty sky, and the three of them hefted their packs and set off south across the park.

The ground was marshy, and they stuck to the paths. Lily didn't look back, but she was sure the wordless guard was following discreetly.

They found that much of the lower section of the park, softball fields and playgrounds, was now occupied by a row of emergency power generators, fed by a fleet of tankers and guarded by police. Here was the beating heart of Lower Manhattan, Lily thought—and a ripe target for terrorists, if any of them had the energy left to strike.

Once out of the park, they cut down Seventh Avenue. The Stars and Stripes hung from many of the buildings, from jutting flagpoles and in windows, bright and brave in the sunlight. There wasn't much traffic around. There were as many bicycle-rickshaws as yellow cabs. A lot of the police were on horseback—but many of the "cops" Lily saw weren't NYPD but Homeland Security officers, or agents of private security contractors. There were other signs of the emergency of the kind Lily had got used to in London: trash cans overflowing, and big plastic water tanks every block or two, each with a short queue of people waiting by its taps.

There weren't so many pedestrians either, and those few were bundled up against the cold and wore waterproof trousers and rubber boots. But people still worked here. A few well-dressed types yacked into their cellphones, or into midair, constantly talking regardless of the ferociously high tariffs on the surviving networks. Despite the flood New York remained a financial hub. Indeed since the waters had invaded, the city itself had become a frontier for capitalism, like other disaster zones. Massive investment was being mobilized in flood defenses and relief programs and the great translocation to the new model cities to the north, and there were substantial profits to be made by those who fed off the flow of public money.

Rich or poor, everybody carried a whistle around her neck. Lily had seen in London how water just knee-high could knock you off your feet in a moment. Rubber boots were advisable too. The sidewalks were all damp, the tarmac running with what looked like river water, dense and foul, and sometimes you saw it bubbling up out of the drains. In places the sidewalk had collapsed altogether, where a broken sewer or subway tunnel had washed away its footing, and you had to walk around the mess. But people just plodded through all this, surviving, getting on with their lives, here as in London and elsewhere.

And, under the blue winter sky, many of the shops were open. The food stores and drug stores and restaurants and even the bars bore notices that biometric ID and ration cards had to be produced by all customers. Lily couldn't tell how current the fashions were in the clothes stores. A lot of stuff on display, in fact, looked like AxysCorp gear, Nathan's famous lines of durables, sensible coveralls and all-weather coats and boots and hats, good for ten years or more. Nathan Lammockson was still selling to the world, still making money. But some of the other stores were piled high with random heaps of goods, from toys to cellphones to coffee percolators to Angels. Lily had learned from Nathan that this was another symptom of the global economic dislocation. Firms kept on trying to function as long as they could, until their suppliers and markets were disrupted or disappeared altogether, and when they failed they dumped their stock in fire sales.

Some newspaper dispensers worked. Out of curiosity Lily paid ten dollars for a copy of the *New York Post*. The edition was thin and printed smudgily on coarse, many-times-recycled paper. The headline was the final cancellation of the soccer World Cup in England scheduled for the summer, for which the US team had been among the favorites.

At the 45th Street junction Thandie consulted the map on her wrist. "This way." Abruptly she turned right, heading west.

They followed, but Gary protested, "The Empire State is south and east of here."

Thandie just kept walking, following her map.

Lily knew roughly where she was heading. This was the Garment District, the hub of the city's fashion industry, where, back on Seventh, the likes of Ralph Lauren and Calvin Klein were commemorated with granite plaques embedded in the sidewalk. She'd walked here once with Amanda, who cared a lot more about clothes than Lily ever had. Now it seemed largely abandoned.

They came to a place where a couple of fire appliances were working. Firemen were pumping out a gushing drain. They sent the water through thick yellow hoses along 45th, running west, parallel to Thandie's path. The appliances' engines roared, and the men didn't look up as the walkers passed.

Beyond Eighth there were no more pedestrians. And at the intersection with Ninth, Thandie, consulting her map, stopped and looked up. Here was the water, covering the sidewalk.

It was a strange urban shore of the kind Lily had seen in London. The water, murky gray-brown stuff slick with oil, lapped around the feet of the buildings and the hulks of long-abandoned cars. Those hoses from the fire appliances ran underwater here, and there was bubbling and turbulence as they dumped the noxious stuff they had pumped out of the drains. In the buildings themselves there were lights in some of the upper-story windows, but most windows were smashed, and pigeons roosted, their guano staining the brown brickwork.

"This is a major transgression," Thandie said, pointing. "Runs south as far as 19th Street, covering Clinton and Chelsea, and to the north of here for a dozen blocks or so. The waterfront developments are abandoned. The GPS flood mapping is very good, it has this shoreline to within a few meters. I used to go skating at Chelsea Piers," she said, suddenly surprisingly wistful. She stepped forward until she was paddling ankle-deep in the murky water. She dug in her pack and produced a knife, folded it out, and prized something loose from a wall. She brought it back to show Lily and Gary. It was a mussel, about the size of a postage stamp, and a smaller clam. *"Mytilaster lineatus,"* she said. "And this little clam is *Cardium edule.*"

"So what?" Lily asked.

"Ocean creatures. You see them, their shells, in the sediment record. Among the first species to colonize when the sea overwhelms the land. Just as it's doing here." She dropped the shells back in the water.

They stayed for a moment at the edge of the water. It lapped, grimy, full of floating rubbish, plastic bags and fast food trays and aluminum cans and condoms, the detritus of a time that already seemed remote. And the water approached Lily's booted toes a little more with each small wave, like a tide coming in.

"Let's get on with it," Thandie said. She turned and led them back along the street.

31

Back on Seventh, which was relatively busy with bundled-up shoppers, it was as if the river incursion just a couple of blocks away wasn't happening, as if the three of them had walked through some kind of portal from a parallel world of sinking and submergence.

They headed to Times Square, making for Broadway. The square's giant billboards were dead, great black windows into emptiness—all save a couple of small panels shining red and white with Coke advertising, which must somehow have got around the city's power restrictions, unless the display was for morale purposes. The square was eerie, a huge empty space, the traffic sparse and few people around. But music echoed out of loudspeakers suspended from posts, Ella Fitzgerald singing "Someone to Watch Over Me."

At the intersection with 34th Street they passed Macy's. The store was open, but blankets and towels hung drying out of the upper-story windows. A giant billboard proclaimed that the world's largest department store was proud to host displaced New Yorkers in a time of crisis.

Piers Michaelmas was waiting for them, as promised, at the foot of the Empire State Building. He was in his British army uniform. He looked relaxed, his arms folded. "I knew you'd be late," he said, eyeing Thandie. "Been skimming stones, have we?"

"Yeah, yeah."

Lily embraced him briefly. "You're looking good, Piers. You've got to be the only man in New York in his dress uniform. How are you keeping your cuffs clean? My God, you're even wearing polished shoes."

"Oh, I always step carefully. One must look the part if one is attending meetings at the UN on behalf of HMG."

Thandie glanced at her GPS map. "You're working at the UN building? But there's a flood from the UN Plaza to the river."

"So there is, the whole area is a lagoon. You have to take a boat. But the upper floors are habitable; the organization is still working, though most of its functions are being mirrored in Geneva. There is a sense that one shouldn't give up, you know. My father ran a small firm of quantity surveyors. Once he was blasted out of his premises, in Manchester, by an IRA bomb. The next morning he set up shop in a pub at the bottom of the road, and hung a sign outside the door saying 'Business as usual.'"

Lily shook her head. "I never knew that about you, Piers. And I thought we'd talked each other dry in Barcelona."

"How dull if that were true. Now then, I would recommend we cut east, actually, things get a bit trickier further downtown . . ."

Piers led the way now, striding between the puddles down Fifth until they got to the intersection with Broadway at the Flatiron Building. From there they continued down Broadway, heading southeast toward Union Square. Thandie peered into her map.

The three hostages, Gary, Piers and Lily, walked together. Impulsively Lily walked between the men and linked their arms.

Piers spoke of Helen. "I got word she's in the US. She and her friend from the FO."

"You're kidding," Lily said. "The last time I spoke to her they told me she was shuttling between Iran and Saudi."

"Well, there was a failed coup in Saudi. I'm afraid we're likely to see rather a lot of that sort of thing in the years to come. Said's branch of the family tried to depose the King. It didn't work, and when the whole thing threatened to unravel into all-out civil war the US military stepped in. They extracted Said and his colleagues, took them to the US compound in Baghdad, and then brought them here."

"As what? Prisoners? Refugees?"

Piers smiled thinly. "I think that remains to be seen. Said has been asking for safe passage for his family."

"Ah. Which might include Grace," Gary said.

"Yes. I wouldn't want to get hopes up. But I would have

thought Helen's chances of finding her child would be vastly increased if she and Grace are both in the US."

Lily longed for that to be true. She wondered if she might get to speak to Helen, even meet her and Michael, before she had to leave the US again.

"It's good of you to support this IPCC presentation of Thandie's, Piers," Gary said. "Nathan appreciates it."

Piers grunted. "I'm sure he does. And I'm glad to have been able to facilitate things a little. But I don't think my uniform is going to make much difference to the audience Thandie will face. Boffins! They're all the same—constitutionally incapable of accepting authority."

Gary laughed. "Actually that's a pretty precise definition of a scientist's core competence."

"Well, perhaps it is, but it doesn't make you buggers any easier to deal with, does it?"

"This is important, Piers," Lily said. "If Thandie's right—"

"If she's right she must be heard, of course. But from what I hear, I still believe the chances are she's *not* right, for all that Nathan Lammockson would like it to be so."

"What do you mean by that?"

"I owe him a huge debt; I owe him my life. But in my judgment Lammockson is the sort of chap who longs for the apocalypse—you know, for everything to be pulled down around him, so that he can save us and build it all up again. He longs to live in times that provide a challenge commensurate with the stature he sees in himself. That's not to say Thandie is wrong. It's just that a man like Lammockson is predisposed to believe her catastrophic predictions."

Gary nodded. "Maybe. I do sometimes wonder if Nathan would keep the money flowing if Thandie's results *didn't* indicate that things are getting worse. Anyhow none of that proves she's wrong."

"No indeed," Piers said. "But there is a danger that in dreaming of fantastic catastrophes, we could fall into the trap of ignoring what's real."

"Which is?"

He paused and glanced around; they were at the intersection with 4th Street. "Come this way and I'll show you." He cut west for three blocks, leading confidently, until they reached Washington Square Park.

It was another tent city, like Central Park. Smoke rose from fires, and every square meter as far as Lily could see was crammed with rows of grimy, mud-colored tents, broken up by the green monoliths of portaloos. There were hospital tents, food kitchens, shower blocks, water tankers; it looked like what it was, an exceptionally well-equipped refugee camp. But there was a strong police presence, with mounted cops patrolling the perimeter of the park, barbed-wire barriers everywhere. To the north a triumphal arch rose up above the huddled tents, a gesture from a more favored age. Flags flew from the arch, celebrating agencies such as Homeland Security, the New York City Department of Environmental Protection and the city's Office of Emergency Management. A poster proclaimed free classes in DNA genealogy, which demonstrated that most Americans had a heritage containing a whole rainbow of ethnicity. A choir of NYPD officers stood under the arch, singing mournful Irish ballads.

There wasn't a blade of grass to be seen; the whole park was churned to mud. The air was thick with the stench of smoke and sewage.

Thandie said slowly, consulting her GPS, "Just here we're at a kind of neck in the flooding. To the west you have a pretty extensive lake covering much of Greenwich Village, running as far as 14th Street. The riverside development over there is drowned too. And to the east there's another major incursion, where the East River has risen over East Village and Alphabet City, lapping in as far as Second Avenue, even Third." She looked up. "Right here we're squeezed in the middle."

Piers said, "And this is where the refugees have come, the shopkeepers and restaurateurs and artists and writers and poets and whatnot from Greenwich from one direction, and the Puerto Ricans from Alphabet City from the other, along with a few wealthy white folk who colonized the gentrified areas west of Avenue B. Here they all are, living under canvas in Washington Square."

Gary asked, "With the police keeping them apart?"

Piers said, "New York is a melting pot, they say. That's being put to the test this year, I suppose. You can see they are running tolerance programs. Anyhow, do you see what I mean? Lily, we've discussed Nathan Lammockson and his grand gestures before. In my view *this* is the real work of

the emergency, by doctors and nurses and firemen and police and immense numbers of volunteers, the endless task
of providing shelter and food and warmth and averting
disease—the task of preserving lives, one at a time. Why,
I'm told this tent city has already seen a hundred births
of its own, and more deaths, in the six weeks it's been established. That's what's *real*. But this sort of project would
never be glamorous enough for Nathan Lammockson to
take an interest in. Well. Let's walk on."

He led them back east, but walked them now across Broadway and through NoHo to the Bowery, and then cut south
again, through Little Italy and Chinatown.

Thandie said they were heading through another flooding bottleneck, with SoHo submerged to the west, and
much of the Lower East Side to the east. Here there were
no convenient green spaces to colonize and no obvious
refugee camps, but the neighborhoods were quiet, tense.
Piers said this had been the site of disorder when the river
levels had breached ten meters, one catastrophic night
before Christmas. Floods of East Side refugees, many of
them first-generation immigrants, had poured into an area
of a few blocks already crowded with an ethnically diverse
community. Most of them had now been evacuated to the
north.

Piers's group cut down Park Row, and came to the
Civic Center at the foot of the great ramp that led up to
the Brooklyn Bridge. And here they found another urban
shore, where the street dipped into the water.

"I guess that's it," Thandie said. She folded away the
screen on her sleeve. "Nothing but floodwater from here
on south."

The sun was low now, and Lily had to shield her eyes
to look at the crowding buildings of the Financial District,
from the Gothic pinnacle of the Woolworth Building a
few blocks away to the gleaming new World Trade Center
towers to the southeast, dominated by the extraordinary
wedge shape of the tallest of them all, the Freedom Tower.
But though water pooled in the shadowed canyons at the
feet of the tower blocks, lights showed in their faces, and
there was much activity on the water, boats skimming back
and forth between the buildings.

"So they're still working in Wall Street," Thandie said.

"Yes," Piers said. "Much of it is shutdown, mothballing and transfer of functions. But it's good for the corporate image to have a presence in the disaster zone you're making a profit out of."

Gary said, "And the Freedom Tower—"

"Is where Nathan has set up Thandie's presentation to the IPCC," Piers said. "Nathan is nothing if not a showman. Though the Memorial is flooded, of course."

Thandie shaded her eyes. "It's years since I was here. I'm sure that skyline looks different."

"Every so often a building falls," said Piers. "They're all built on good Manhattan schist. But their sub-basements are undermined, and their foundations aren't designed for continual immersion in saline water. And then a storm comes along, and— There are generally few casualties; there's plenty of notice. When they give way they explode, you know; the steel cables within the reinforced concrete structures are under tension."

Thandie asked, "So how do we get over there, swim?"

"There's an AxysCorp boat. I'll call for it." He walked away, speaking into the air. As he did so the guard who had shadowed them all the way from Central Park emerged from a shadowed street, nodding at Piers.

A breeze ruffled Lily's hair. She looked east, out toward the ocean. Clouds were scudding across the sky, a great dish of them spread along the horizon, and she remembered the storm that had diverted her plane.

32

From Kristie Caistor's scrapbook:

According to his precisely worded blog, Harrison Gelertner was born and raised in San Francisco. He'd spent all his working life in that city; he had been a lawyer, specializing in civil rights cases. He had traveled the world—but oddly, through his wife's taste for the exotic, mostly abroad, never much in his own country.

Age sixty-five Gelertner retired. And age sixty-eight he found himself left alone when his wife succumbed to cancer; it was quick, shocking. And age sixty-nine he observed that large swathes of America, the country he had never seen, were fast disappearing under floodwater.

He resolved to put right the gap in his experience, while he had the health and resources to do it—and while it was still possible. He decided to begin at the top: at Washington, DC.

Thus in February 2018 he caught an American Airlines flight into Washington National. As it happened this turned out to be one of the last civilian flights ever to reach that airport.

On the face of it Washington wasn't impressive. It struck Gelertner as just a small American city, and a shabby one at that, dirty and grimy and apparently unbearably hot in the summer, though the weather was pleasant enough on a crisp February day. The flooding was already apparent, the water bubbling out of the drains and sloshing over the sidewalks; it was difficult to walk. Sirens wailed, and traffic backed up everywhere. There was a sense of urgency, of things fraying, he recorded in his blog, everything grubby and falling apart.

But then he turned a corner and came on the White House, just like that, the planet's center of power practically in the middle of downtown. According to the news on the Angel radio his grandson had shown him how to use, the President and her administration had long fled to their refuge in Denver. But the protesters were still here, a ragged band of them opposite the gates, their banners complaining about taxes, foreign wars and inequities in flood relief. And there were headquarters of other tremendously important institutions only blocks away, like the FBI and NASA and the World Bank. It was a city that was somehow too small for its significance.

He walked to the grassy expanse of the Mall, where the Washington Monument stood tall and slim. Gelertner oriented himself; there was the Capitol building to the east, the Lincoln Memorial sitting grandly to the west. The grass was soggy, giving under his leather shoes. Though he could explore the Lincoln Memorial as much as he pleased, the Capitol building was closed to visitors. And he was disappointed to find that the various Smithsonian museums were closed too, although there was much activity around them as staff bundled up precious exhibits for moving.

He was vague about the progress of the flooding. That evening the TV news showed alarming images and maps of the threat to DC; the rising ocean had pushed into Chesapeake Bay, and was backing up the Potomac to the city. He wouldn't have thought that DC would be under such immediate threat, but there you go, he recorded in his blog.

He was woken in the night by a fire alarm. The hotel had to be evacuated.

Gelertner had his airline ticket, but quickly learned the airport was closed. Unsure what to do, he stayed put. By mid-morning he found himself in a crowd of families, mostly black, mostly poor, waiting for a requisitioned school bus to take them to higher ground. Stern-looking Homeland Security guards made sure they didn't try to get away from their allocated group, or compromise the convoys that were already underway, taking out the remaining federal government employees, major corporate players and the rich.

Gelertner was out of the city by noon.

That was pretty much all he saw of Washington, a city he happened to visit in the midst of its abandonment. He saw nothing significant of the flood itself. It struck him as strange that the very first visit he made to the capital, at the end of his own long life, might turn out to be one of the last made by any tourist, ever.

Gelertner was particularly disappointed not to have got to see Apollo XI in the National Air and Space Museum. He never learned if the heavy capsule had been evacuated successfully.

33

Nathan Lammockson met them in an anteroom to the lecture theater, deep within the Freedom Tower, where Thandie was to present her results to a sub-committee of the IPCC. Thandie went off to wash and set up, and Piers disappeared, having business of his own with the IPCC delegates. Gary was called away to talk to other climatologists in the building, from NOAA's hurricane center in Miami and elsewhere. They were being tapped up by local weather watchers who were growing concerned about that incoming ocean storm, now referred to as system Aaron.

So it was just Lily who sat beside Nathan Lammockson, on a balcony that overlooked the theater where Thandie would present. The room was sparsely populated, a dozen of the hundred or so seats occupied by middle-aged types with the eccentric dress sense, hair styles and facial fluff that seemed to mark out the professional scientist. They knew each other, it seemed, and held conversations leaning over the backs of their seats. They ignored Thandie, who was scrolling through her presentation. In the air before her was a big three-dimensional display that held a trans-lucent image of the whole Earth. It spun before Thandie's touch; Lily could see her earnest face through the planet's ghostly layers.

Lammockson sucked on a coffee, and leaned over to Lily. "Quite a view we've got here."

"Yes. I like Thandie's three-D projector."

He glanced at her. "I guess you haven't seen a crystal ball before?"

"I missed a lot of the new toys while I was stuck down those cellars in Barcelona."

"Yeah. The principle's simple, as I understand it. It's a

fool-the-eye thing." He lifted his hand upright and mimed rotation. "You have a translucent screen, upright like this, spinning a thousand times a minute. And you have three projectors firing light at it, through systems of lenses and mirrors. So at any instant you have a slice through the three-dimensional object you're looking at. Spin it up and those slices merge in the vision. Terrific tool in medicine, I'm told. Surgery, you know, scans of skulls with tumors in 'em, that kind of thing. Of course they're mostly used for porn."

That made her laugh. "Actually, looking down on Thandie like this, I feel like I'm about to watch surgery."

He grunted. "Well, so you are, in a way. These arseholes will do their very best to dissect whatever Thandie puts before them. You got to understand how the IPCC works, Lily, what it's for . . ."

The Intergovernmental Panel on Climate Change had been established by the governments back in the 1980s to provide authoritative assessments on information and predictions regarding climate change.

"You have working groups covering the physical science of climate change, impact on the world, and mitigation. Now, that word 'authoritative' is the key. Everything about the way the panel operates is designed to reinforce that. Every time they produce a report you have a lead author for each section, but typically you'll get hundreds of expert reviewers providing tens of thousands of comments. The rule of thumb is they only let through what there's absolute consensus on. Especially when it comes to the Summary for Policymakers, which is the only bit anybody ever reads."

"Wow. It's amazing anything gets through at all."

"That's the point. The IPCC is ferociously conservative. You can criticize it for being too slow to respond to the evidence for climate change, for instance. But when it does speak the governments listen."

"So do you think they'll accept any of Thandie's data and conclusions?"

"Maybe the data. Less so the conclusions. There's bound to be a debate. Even those who accept the reality of the sea-level rise see it as a symptom of climate change, and can't accept any justification of it that doesn't come from their old models—can't accept it as something entirely new. A lot will depend on Thandie's headline prediction, I think. Right now they're clinging to eighty meters, tops, as an outer limit. I mean that would be catastrophic enough, but—"

"Why eighty meters?"

"Because that's what you would get if all the ice caps on Greenland and Antarctica were to melt. And the melting ice is the only source generally accepted for the ocean rise."

Lily nodded. "So it's going to be hard for them to listen if Thandie tells them otherwise."

"Exactly."

"So what do you think is going to come out of today?"

"Nothing, immediately. It will take them months to come up with a report. Even then the governments probably won't accept it, until the oceans are lapping around their feet. However other players will be listening hard." He glanced down at the lecture theater. "I could point to five of those clown-haired characters down there who are in the pocket of members of the LaRei."

"The LaRei?"

He grinned. "An exclusive Manhattan society. Even more exclusive than the MetCircle. You need a net worth of a hundred million bucks just to get in the door. The rich are listening, believe me."

She nodded. "And the rich will take care of themselves."

He eyed her. "Rich arseholes like me, you mean?"

That made her uncomfortable. This man was, after all, her boss. "Nathan—"

"Oh, don't worry. Look, I know what you think of me, even though I saved your lives. In a supposedly capitalist society everybody despises the accumulation of wealth, save those who have it. Listen. Damn right I'm intending to act. I'm not going to wait around until the governments get over their collective denial, as Dr. Jones puts it. Damn right I'm intending to save myself, and my son Hammond, if I can—and save my wealth, whatever that means in the coming world. Who wouldn't? But remember this: I sponsored Thandie's survey, I recruited the arseholes she needed from Woods Hole and wherever else. I'm even sponsoring this meeting today. What more can I do than that?"

Lily said nothing. She didn't believe he was after her approval, as such, or her praise. With Nathan it was all about dominance. But Nathan was no monster just because he had made himself rich. She could see his foresight in operation, as he steadily converted his wealth into more tangible assets, land and equipment and people. And if Thandie's projections about the speed of events in the years to come were correct, the world might need figures like Nathan, with the decisiveness and resources to make things happen fast.

Gary Boyle hurried in, a laptop under his arm. "Hi," he whispered to Lily, settling beside her. "I'm not late, am I?"

"Just in time. How's Aaron?"

He opened the laptop, and showed her an image taken from a camera on the roof. The sky was dominated by an immense swirl of cloud. "Windspeed rising. Pressure dropping. They've flown in a HIRT. That's a Hurricane Intercept Research Team, running around in speedboats and SUVs with weather instruments and laptops. And they've sent up a plane to drop a meteorology sonde into the eye. But they still don't think Aaron's going to make landfall."

Nathan said, "They don't think so, huh?" He murmured into a cellphone, ordering a chopper to be readied on the Freedom Tower helipad.

In the lecture theater, Thandie stood beside her translucent three-dimensional Earth and began to speak.

34

Thandie began with the basics, a summary of the data on the global sea-level rise. By now the rise was being logged in detail, as alarmed oceanographers had planted a dense network of tide gauges across the planet, and specialized satellites probed the ocean with laser and radar altimeters.

And Lily watched, fascinated, as Thandie demonstrated the raising of ocean surfaces across the planet. A ghostly pink meniscus lifted up, indeed it accelerated with time, the vertical scale exaggerated, pulsing and rippling, evidently a signal of multiple sources feeding into the global rise. The graphic image was backed up by labels, data and equations annotating detail, and text was downloaded into screens set before the delegates.

Thandie talked about the changing nature of the ocean. As well as a global rise the scientists were witnessing a drop in salinity, an increase in ocean heat, and a change in distribution of that heat. The warmth of the ocean drove the climate, and thus the climate was also being reshaped, said Thandie. She ran through new climate models by NASA's Goddard Institute, the Hadley Center in England, NOAA's Geophysical Fluid Dynamics Laboratory, and other groups in Russia, Japan, Germany, elsewhere. She showed how specific incidents could be tied to the anomalous warming, such as last year's early monsoon across Asia.

Gary whispered to Lily, "Yeah. It's the heat of the ocean surface that is spawning that big storm outside right now. Ocean heat is the fuel for hurricanes."

Thandie outlined the effects on the biosphere. There had been blooms and diebacks in the living things in the oceans. Coral reefs, for instance, were being hit hard by the temperature shifts and increasing depths of coastal waters.

All of this was uncontroversial enough. It was when Thandie moved on to the fundamental causes of the flood, and her projections for its future, that the IPCC delegates started muttering.

The oceans were rising. There was a complication that as the oceans heated up the water expanded, which itself contributed to the rise. But the blunt truth was that to fill up the oceans, just like a brimming bathtub, you needed a running tap.

It didn't take Thandie long to dismiss the consensus theory that the source of the floodwater could be melting ice caps. The caps, north and south, were monitored as closely as any other aspect of the planet's climate system, and yes, they were melting—in fact the global ocean rise was accelerating the melting in Antarctica and Greenland, as it lifted sheets of ice away from the rock that anchored it. But there was no way the measured mass loss from the ice caps could be fueling the global expansion of the oceans; the numbers simply didn't add up.

So Thandie spoke of other sources—of water stored within the Earth, and now being released. She produced images taken from the *Trieste* and other probes of vast, turbulent, underwater fountains, places where it seemed clear that hot, mineral-laden water was forcing its way out of the rock substrate.

And she produced her most striking figure. It was a map of the subterranean seas she believed she and others had been able to detect, from the evidence of seismic waves and direct submersible exploration. They were long reservoirs beneath all the major mid-ocean ridges, under the Atlantic, around Africa, spanning the Antarctic Ocean and surrounding the vast Pacific plate. The Atlantic reservoir was the best mapped, directly from *Trieste*; the rest she had had to construct from coarser seismic data.

Thandie had boldly given these sunken seas names, like Ziosudra and Utnapishtin and Deucalion, the last for the great Atlantic reservoir. Thandie said the names were variants of Noah, for a legend of a global flood had arisen in many cultures. Ziosudra was Sumerian, and Utnapishtin featured in the Gilgamesh saga. Deucalion came from Greek mythology. When Zeus punished the men of Hellas with heavy rain, he instructed Deucalion to build a chest within which he floated for nine days, finally landing on Mount Parnassus . . .

The delegates were increasingly restless, Lily saw, shifting in their seats and glancing at each other.

"Big mistake," murmured Nathan. "You don't bring in Noah with these guys."

Thandie moved on to the question of why it should be just now that the subterranean reservoirs broke open. But here she was on shaky ground. She could only point to dramatic and abrupt changes in Earth's climatic state in the past. Earth didn't move smoothly through climatic changes; it seemed to have only a fixed number of stable states, between which it lurched, rapidly. For the last two million years the climate seemed to have been flickering between ice ages, glaciation, and warmer interglacials. The transitions could be rapid, taking only decades, even mere years. Maybe this was just another of those dramatic but natural transitions.

Or maybe it was humanity's fault, Thandie said cautiously. She produced familiar statistics that showed how, since the Industrial Revolution of the eighteenth century, humanity had become a planet-shaping species now overwhelming natural processes, making significant changes to cycles of oxygen and sulfur and nitrogen and moving ten times as much rock and dirt each year as the wind and the rain. Maybe the level of human intervention in the Earth's cycles had reached what the climate modelers called DAI, for Dangerous Anthropogenic Interference. Humans were kicking the complex, interwoven, nonlinear processes of Earth so hard that the whole system was flipping over to a new stable state . . .

It seemed to Lily that Thandie had already lost her audience. The IPCC delegates looked away, chatted to each other, and one was even talking into a phone.

Thandie produced her conclusions, in a stark set of bullet points. She recommended funding for a widening study of the sea-level rise and its sources. For instance she wanted the use of US Army Deep Digger bombs, meant for busting bunkers, which could burrow deep and fast into solid rock, to confirm what was down there under the ocean floors. She wanted the big spaceborne planet-finder telescopes to focus on the physics of other watery worlds: did those planets have a dry-wet cycle? She wanted more modeling of the impact on the changing ocean heat distribution on global climate systems. She wanted modeling of the changing isostatic loads: would there be any more Istanbuls?

And, most of all, she wanted the delegates to have their governments prepare for, not a cessation of the sea-level rise, but an acceleration. There was no foreseeable limit to the volume of water her subterranean seas could yet release. The trends were still uncertain, but a long-term exponential rise was emerging: exponential meaning the rise would double, and double again and again, beyond any limit Thandie could see.

That was it. She didn't get a round of applause. There were a couple of questions, neutral points about details of the science. Then the meeting broke up; people simply stood and walked out. Thandie, isolated, closed down her display. Lily saw Piers enter at the back of the room. He snagged delegates by the coffee machines; he seemed to be trying to talk to them.

Nathan Lammockson sat back in his chair and puffed out his cheeks. "Well. She blew it."

Gary was looking worriedly at the data on his laptop screen. "They're not so sure about the track of the storm as they were. The city's Office of Emergency Management has woken up. Telling people not to try to evacuate the island, the freeways and expressways are jammed, where they're not already flooded or otherwise blocked. They should go home and prepare a safe room."

"Nice advice if you're living in a tent in Central Park."

"I think I'd better go take another look outside." He stood and hurried away.

Lammockson paid no attention to him. "She should never ever in a million years have mentioned Noah. What a balls-up."

"Come on," Lily said, standing. "You can buy me a LaRei-class coffee, and we'll go speak to Piers."

35

"You're right, Nathan," Piers said grimly. "The religious allusions put them off. That was certainly the feedback I got."

They were standing in a circle, Piers, Nathan, Thandie and Lily, in the anteroom behind the lecture theater, cradling coffees. Far from being LaRei-class, to Lily the coffee tasted sour, overstrong.

"All I did was assign a few names. What's wrong with that?" Thandie spoke rapidly, her gestures jerky; she gulped at her hot coffee. She was still on an adrenaline high from her presentation.

"You're missing the point," Nathan said, exasperated. "Shit, Thandie. I personally know people who believe that nuclear war is predicted in the Book of Revelation. You were too damn clever. You should have stuck to the numbers. You pressed the wrong buttons. And you gave the delegates a reason not to listen to you that had nothing to do with your precious science."

Piers nodded. "Anyhow, it's done. At least the argument got aired. So what now?"

Nathan ticked the points off on his fingers. "One. We keep arguing this process through. We work on the IPCC delegates, we put pressure on the reviewers, we try to talk directly to governments. And we keep gathering data. But, two. We don't wait for the wheels to grind. We prepare options."

"Options for what?" Lily asked.

"The worst case," Nathan said. "Whatever that is."

Gary came running up, breathless. "Look at this." His laptop showed a radar image, a knotted-up swirl of colored light creeping toward an outline map of New York City. "Aaron's not behaving as modeled. They think a new center has formed, invalidating the old forecasts. And there's minimal shear, meaning the high-level winds which can lop the top off a developing hurricane aren't helping in this case."

Thandie whistled. With her finger she traced a dough-nut of orange red, right at the center of the storm swirl. "Is that the eye wall? Must be fifty kilometers across. That's a beauty."

"It's a beauty that's headed this way," Lily said practically.

"The chopper," Nathan said. "Now!"

They ran for the elevator to the roof.

The weather had changed utterly. They emerged into a bat-tering wind, and rain that lashed horizontally, rain tasting of salt, accompanied by sheets of white spray. Lily was soaked in a second, her clothes, her face, her hair, and deafened from the wind's howl.

The sky above was a sculpture of swirling creamy cloud, a vast rotating system, a special effect. Lily saw lightning crackle between the layers, illuminating the cloud from within, pink and purple. It was impossible to believe that all this was just air and water vapor and heat.

The chopper sat on its pad, bolted to the roof by clamps, its rotors turning. They had to get to the bird by edging their way around the shelter of a wall, working hand over hand along a metal rail; otherwise there was a danger of being blown clean off the roof. The pilot was the same bluff woman who had transported Lily and the others to Central Park earlier. She helped them climb aboard, hauling them in one by one with unreasonable strength. She yelled into Lammockson's face, "Thirty more seconds and I'd have gone without you."

"Just get us out of here."

The doors slammed shut and the chopper's engine roared. They scrambled for seats and belts. The pilot released the runner clamps, and the bird soared up. Looking down, Lily glimpsed the slim, graceful lines of the Freedom Tower rising from the turbulent water that covered the Memorial.

Then the chopper surged west, heading over the Hud-son and hurrying inland. It was buffeted; even Lily, used to tough chopper sorties, felt exposed.

Gary snapped open his laptop. "Damn it. They're saying Aaron's now a category four. Borderline five."

Piers asked, "What kind of damage will that do?"

Gary tapped at his keyboard. "New York hasn't been hit by a hurricane since . . . 1938. Preparedness, nil. And the city's already flayed open by the floods. The colder waters at this latitude should weaken the storm—you know hurricanes are fueled by ocean surface heat. But on the other hand you have the peculiar topography of Manhattan. All those concrete canyons. The winds will be amplified."

"Shit," Lammockson said. "Well, that's it for New York. Thank Christ I got my assets out in time."

"The rich believe they have choices," Piers said grimly. "While the poor must accept their fate."

"I don't notice you turning down a ride," Lammockson snarled at him.

"The eye wall's about to hit," Gary said.

They all twisted in their seats to look back.

The hurricane was a bowl of churning air, like a vast artifact suspended over the heart of the city. Lily could see a storm surge already roaring through the streets of the Financial District, gray walls of foam and spray and sheer muscular water pushing between the tall buildings. Debris rode the waves, massive to be visible from here, cars, uprooted trees perhaps. And, incredibly, she saw the prow of an oceangoing ship being forced down one of the avenues.

Then the storm itself broke over the town. Lesser buildings simply exploded, burst open from within by the primal force of the wind. The towering skyscrapers survived, huddled together against the lashing rain, reminding Lily of images of emperor penguins. But there was a kind of sparkling around them, like a mist of raindrops before the buildings' sheer walls. That was glass, Gary said, the glass of a million windows sucked out of their frames and shattered, a glass storm that must be rending any living flesh exposed to it.

The chopper dipped its nose and fled toward the sanctuary of the higher ground.

36

December 2018

From Kristie Caistor's scrapbook:
 In the final days Maria spent as much time as she could in her flat, in central Manchester just off Deansgate, alone with her virtual child. Whenever Maria logged on, Linda always abandoned her toys and the soulless avatars who shared this domain with her, the pets and companions and nannies, and came running to her mother's image with squeals of delight.

Little Linda, a HeadSpace baby, was four years old now. She lived in an apartment cut into the side of a cliff, overlooking a sparkling sea. Maria had designed the place herself. The location within the virtual world called HeadSpace was nonspecific, but Maria had vaguely modeled it on the Sorrento coast, where she had had some happy holidays as a kid with her own family. Of course the sea was a hateful thing now, and Maria had installed louvered blinds to close the big picture windows and shut out the view. But the little girl playing on the sunlit patio still made a beautiful image for Maria to gaze on, in her desktop screen, in her damp, darkened flat.

Linda was Maria's baby, entirely virtual, painlessly born and raised within the glowing domain of HeadSpace. Everything Linda knew Maria had taught her. Maria had gloves and a headset, and she could hear the child laugh, feel her when her avatar hugged her, a ghostly presence through the pads on her fingertips. She still couldn't be with the child, not fully. Her screen was a barrier between HeadSpace and the real world—Dullworld as Maria thought of it, this damp, breaking-down world where she was stuck, a drab, childless thirty-seven-year-old.

But that barrier was going to melt away someday soon. The transhumanists had promised. Technologies such as

AI, genetic engineering and nanotechnology would acceler-
ate human evolution; they would uplift Maria herself into
a union of flesh and technology. And beyond that would
come the singularity, the point at which human technologies
became smarter than humans themselves. It would all ex-
ponentiate away into a glittering transcendence, out of anybody's control, the opening up of a new realm of enhanced
existence. She had been reading about this for years, for half
her lifetime. When the singularity came she would be able
to live forever, if she chose. And she would be able to step
seamlessly between one world and another, between the dull
world of Manchester and the shining realm of HeadSpace.
She could be with her child, in the light, as real as Linda was.

But the singularity was slow in coming.

She rarely heard from her transhumanist contacts now.
As the floods bit away there were power-outs or, worse,
failures at the ISPs that linked her to Linda in HeadSpace.
And Maria herself was distracted from her time with
her child. Forever hungry, thirsty, cold, she found herself
spending hours in queues for food and medicines, even
fresh water.

The fact was, her access to HeadSpace was the product
of a complex and interconnected society, the capstone of a
pyramid grounded in very old technologies, in farming and
mining and manufacture and transport and energy production. It was only as that essential pyramid was crumbling
that Maria became fully aware of its existence. The singularity came to seem more and more out of reach—an ab-
surdity, actually. You couldn't have the capstone without
the pyramid to hold it up.

It was a Sunday morning when the HeadSpace website
finally crashed. She kept trying to access it through that
day, over and over, into the night. She didn't accept it had
gone for good for twenty-four hours, when her own internet connection failed.

Then the power went. She sat in her dark, cooling flat,
her open hand against the dead screen, longing to pass
through out of Dullworld to join Linda in the pixelated
sunlight.

At last she began to mourn.

37

May 2019

"**Y**ou have to leave Postbridge, Amanda. You and the kids. Now."

Amanda stared at her sister. Lily stood in the door of the caravan, her rucksack at her feet, wearing a scuffed blue coverall stitched with AxysCorp logos. Lily was deeply tanned, her graying hair shaved short. She looked fit, lean and intent.

Wayne sat at the caravan's single table, shaping a bit of leather for a harness. At thirty-one he was younger than either of the women. Amanda was aware of the way he appraised Lily's body, the curves flattened and hidden by the coverall. He was like that with every woman he met, even those close to him—including, uncomfortably, fourteen-year-old Kristie. It was a habit Amanda had learned to ignore.

Lily ignored him too. She kept her gaze fixed on Amanda's face.

Amanda said, "How long is it since I've seen you? More than a year . . . Where did you say you've been working?"

"Peru. A big AxysCorp project there."

"Peru? South America? I thought Nathan was going to hole up on Iceland."

"Change of plan."

"Peru, though, Jesus! Well, it's doing you good."

"You have to leave," Lily said again.

"Why?"

"I can't tell you," said Lily, strained. "Come with me to London. There's transport out of the country arranged from there. I've got a car. It got stopped by the roadblocks and I had to walk, but it will pick us up at Cheriton Bishop." That was on the A30, the main trunk road east out of Dartmoor.

"London's drowned," Wayne scoffed at Lily. His own London accent came out strongly. *Drah-ned*.

Lily said patiently to Amanda, "There's a boat at Marlow. Then, further downstream, a helicopter."

Amanda asked, "Why can't the helicopter just come here?"

"It's not safe."

Amanda knew what she meant. Everybody was a bit insular up here on Dartmoor, hostile to the Londoners and the Brummies who still came pouring from their flooded suburbs across Salisbury Plain or the Cotswolds. The roadblocks were one thing, but there had been a rumor that somebody had taken out a police chopper with a surface-to-air missile, like some terrorist in Beirut.

Lily said, "AxysCorp says—"

"AxysCorp this, AxysCorp that," Wayne said. "Big corporations. Journeys across the country. You're like a relic from the past, from the last century, you're irrelevant."

"She's my sister," Amanda said, keeping her voice level, trying not to provoke him. "And she's come all this way to talk to me. I ought to listen at least—"

"Bollocks." Wayne dumped the leather pieces on the table, tucked his knife into his belt and stood. He was a big-framed man, muscular, tanned after the outdoor work, though some of his "London fat," as he called it, still clung to his frame, even after eight or nine months up here on the moor. You'd call him handsome, Amanda thought, seeing him through Lily's eyes. His best features were his blue eyes. But those eyes were cold as he stared down at Lily, and his expression was blank.

"You're family," he said to Lily. "You can have bed and board for a night. Beyond that, if you want to stay here, you have to work. Everybody has to work. That's the way of things now. We don't have room for dossers."

"My business is with my sister," Lily said quietly.

He stepped closer and shouted down at her, "We're together now, me and Amanda and the kids. So it is my business, got that?"

Lily stood utterly still, her slight form dwarfed by his. She had changed so much, Amanda thought. She had noticed that habit of stillness about Lily after her captivity. She was also, of course, a USAF veteran. Amanda had no doubt that if Wayne kept on threatening her he would end up on his back with a broken arm.

She stepped between the two of them and took Lily's hand. "Look, we'll talk this over. That can't do any harm, can it?"

Wayne snorted, his eyes still fixed on Lily's face. But he backed off. He sat down again, pulled out his knife and went back to shaping the leather with hard, firm gestures.

"Come on," Amanda said to Lily. "Let's sit down and have a cup of tea."

"You still have tea?"

"Well, no," Amanda said ruefully. "Used up the last of my stash months ago. But you can make a reasonable brew out of nettles—"

"Can we walk?" Lily asked sharply.

Wayne looked up. "I'm not too subtle, me, darling. If you've got a problem with me then say it plain."

"I've nothing to say to you," Lily said.

There was no contempt in her voice, but Amanda knew that was the kind of remark likely to inflame Wayne, who didn't like to be disregarded. She grabbed her jacket from a hook behind the door and pushed her feet into her boots. "We'll walk," she said firmly. "I'll show you around . . ."

Lily picked up her pack and slung it over her shoulders, as if she had no intention of returning.

They walked through Postbridge, not speaking. Amanda sensed they needed time to let the tension from the scene in the caravan drain out.

Postbridge was a pretty little village, right in the middle of Dartmoor, not much more than a scattering of farms, an inn and a chapel. A stone bridge crossed the East Dart River, a medieval construction Amanda had learned to call a clapper bridge. The sun was low. It was a bright spring day. This was a characteristically English postcard scene, though studded with modernity, telephone poles and power pylons and a mobile-phone mast.

You'd never have known anything had changed, Amanda thought suddenly. They were a long way from the coast here. You'd never know that an immense flooding had disrupted the whole world and drowned Britain to thirty meters or more, turning much of southern England

into an archipelago. What was different? Kids out playing
on a school day, maybe, or even working in the fields like
her own two; the village school was reporting only fifty percent attendance. The utter lack of traffic, though she could
hear the throaty roar of farm vehicles working the fields.
No newspapers in the little post office; the *Daily Mail* board
stood empty, blank and weathered. The English flags that
fluttered from every rooftop and out of every window, even
from the aerials of the stationary cars, the cross of Saint
George everywhere. And there was the warmth, of course,
the unseasonable warmth that had persisted all winter, and
had got the grumbling farmers out working their fields
earlier than they had been used to. But this had suddenly
become a desirable place, as you could tell from the caravans and mobile homes and tents clustered around the old
core of the village, including Amanda's own caravan, for
Postbridge was more than three hundred meters above the
old sea level. This was the heart of Dartmoor, the highest
location in southern England.

She glanced down at herself, in a battered quilt jacket,
worn jeans, heavy walking boots. She looked like a farmer's
wife—which, effectively, she was, though she and Wayne
hadn't married. The Amanda of 2015 wouldn't have recognized what she had become.

Lily took in the sights of the village curiously. "In the
States you see the flag everywhere, the Stars and Stripes,
and yellow ribbons tied to the trees for the lost. But I don't
remember all these flags in England. Except when the
World Cup was on."

That made Amanda smile. "Actually they're still playing
football, a lot of the big stadiums in the north stayed open.
A kind of cut-down league based on who can turn up.
Wayne follows it on the radio. Bradford City are the league
champions, imagine that. At least they've given up staging
big matches abroad. Pity about the World Cup though . . ."

The sisters passed out of the village and followed a
footpath south. They didn't get far before they came to
the village's barbed-wire perimeter. The path was blocked
by a rough barrier of a cut-down telephone pole, manned
today by Bill Pulford, son of a local farmer. He nodded at
Amanda and let them through.

Amanda tried to break the ice. "We're not far from Bel-

lever Tor." The tors, massive granite outcrops pushing out
of peat moorland, were Dartmoor's most famous feature,
back in the days when it was a magnet for tourism. "There's
a wood. Only conifers, but you get a lot of bird life now.
They've come up from the flooded valleys, I guess. And
some archeology, hut circles—"

"Where are the kids?"

"Working," Amanda said, pointing. "A couple of kilometers that way. The new fields have been laid out but they need
clearing; the farmers always need muscle for that. I'd rather
they were at school, but what can you do? Benj is sixteen now,
and Kristie fourteen, they make their own minds up. Anyhow
the outdoor work is good for them, and they get paid."

"With what?"

"The local scrip." She dug in her pocket and showed Lily
a handful of money. It was old sterling or euro notes and
coins, marked or clipped to reflect a local barter rate. "We
do get stuff from outside, of course, but—"

"Can you call the kids? Do you have mobiles?"

"Of course we have mobiles." Reflexively Amanda took
her phone out of her jacket pocket. It was four years old,
elderly by former standards; it had actually come through
the flooding of London with her.

"Call them," Lily urged her. "Right now. Get them to
come meet us. Maybe at the tor you mentioned? Would
they know how to get to it?"

Amanda weighed the phone in her hand, frowning. "I
don't know if I should."

"Please, Amanda. I wouldn't ask if it wasn't important."

"And then what?"

"I told you. We get out, the four of us, to the car at
Cheriton Bishop."

"It must be twenty kilometers. More."

Lily glanced at the sun. "It's not late. I walked here
yesterday and this morning. I stayed over in a pub. Four,
five hours should do it. The car will wait until the sun goes
down, later if I call."

"And then we all just drive off, is that the idea?" Anger
flared in Amanda. "You know, you've got a nerve, Lily.
Without any warning you parachute back into the middle
of my life. *My* life, the life I've been building for myself
here, me and the kids. It hasn't been easy, you know."

"I don't mean to mess things up for you." Lily sounded strained, tired; she seemed drained behind her South American tan.

"You're doing your best to come between me and Wayne, aren't you?"

"I don't mean to do that either. Look, please, Amanda—you have to trust me."

"Why?"

"I promised I wouldn't say."

"Promised who? AxysCorp, the great Nathan Lammockson? Why won't you say?"

"Because it would cause panic."

That made Amanda pause. Panic? Amanda had seen panic, a frantic sort in Greenwich on the day the Thames Barrier fell, and later a more long-drawn-out miserable sort of panic when the river started rising again and west London had to be evacuated. But here she was in Dartmoor, far above any flooding. What could there possibly be to panic about? She felt resistant, angry, unwilling.

Lily saw this in her face. "Please, Amanda, the kids."

Amanda had to trust her; this was her sister. And besides she could always come back when the fuss was over, whatever it was. She hefted her phone. "Shall I have them call at the caravan first, pick up their stuff—"

"No," Lily said. "Forget the caravan, forget packing. Just get them to meet us."

"Wayne won't take kindly if he finds out you're having us sneak off, if that's the idea."

"So don't tell him." Lily closed her eyes, and a muscle in her cheek worked. "Look, I'll make a deal. Once I have you and the kids in the AxysCorp car you can call Wayne, or whoever you like. My priority isn't Wayne. It's not even your feelings. My priority is only you and the kids. Your safety."

"You're scaring me," said Amanda, though she was still more angry than frightened.

"Good," Lily said bluntly. "Make your calls. Please, Amanda."

So Amanda pressed the fast-key numbers, and called.

38

I t would take a while for the kids to catch up with them. Lily and Amanda walked slowly to the tor.

A farm vehicle buzzed in a field. "More fields being broken," Lily said.

"Yes. They're growing crops up here now, instead of raising sheep and cattle. You can thank the warmer weather for that. There are problems, though. Like bluetongue, and African horse sickness. New kinds of viruses nobody's dealt with here before. The government vets still come around sometimes." It was another result of the flood-induced warming, a spreading out of the old hot regions of diseases of animals and of humans, like chikungunya and Rift Valley fever.

Lily asked, "Where do you get your fuel from?"

"There's a tanker port at Taunton." The lowland of Somerset was all but drowned, but harbors and port facilities had hastily been improvised close to what had been an inland town. "It's rationed, of course; it's really just for the farm vehicles and the power stations. We use the cars for emergencies. We've a few bikes too, Wayne has one. They've had to rebuild the port once already, when the sea kept rising."

"It's the same story all over."

"Nobody seems to know how long the tankers will keep calling."

"Who controls the rationing?"

Amanda looked at her. "Well, the police. Who do you think?"

"It's just that you're kind of remote up here. All that barbed wire. The SAM missiles," Lily said frankly. "Is it true the locals 'nationalized' the Tesco's in Taunton?"

"Sort of," Amanda said. "There was a lot of objection to the profits they were taking out of the area."

"That wouldn't have happened in the old days, would it? A lot of England is disconnected from the center nowadays."

"Well, the government is hundreds of kilometers away, in Leeds. They don't worry about *us*. Wayne says we could be self-sufficient here on Dartmoor, if we don't get swamped."

" 'Swamped'?"

Amanda ignored that. "The climate's better than it used to be. It's because of the sea level. It's as if we've sunk by thirty meters, so what was highland becomes lowland. Wayne takes samples of the changing populations of flowers, the moths and butterflies and birds. He's keeping a kind of log on his laptop."

"So this toyboy of yours is some kind of biologist, is he?"

"Toyboy, oh shut up. He's a marine biologist. He's from London. But he worked at the Dove Marine Laboratory in Northumberland before the floods."

"You never told me much about him, in your mails. What did you do, glom onto the first strong man you could find?"

Amanda flared again. "Speak to me like that again and you can walk to bloody Cheriton Bishop by yourself."

"All right. I'm sorry. I didn't mean it."

"You fucking did." But Amanda walked on. "Look, Lil, he's not perfect, but he's a decent enough man. He's got a PhD. He specialized in coastal life, but now the coasts are gone. Sometimes we travel, you know, even as far as the Solent, just to see how the flooding's progressing. Wayne says it's a sort of extinction event. It will take a million years for nature to make a proper coast again, the rock pools and sea caves and mud flats with their plovers and their whooper swans. Even the sand dunes are drowned. It's all gone now, and we won't see the like again in our lifetimes. Isn't that sad?"

"So he has a soul," Lily said. "Go on, then. Tell me how you met him."

They had met in the holding camp at Aylesbury, in a queue for a water bowser.

When the flooding had started, Wayne had decamped down from Northumberland to Charlton in south London, to be with his family. They had managed to get out, and joined the flow to Aylesbury. After their chance meeting Wayne and Amanda had become close, sort of, spending time together in the refugee camp's "pubs," marquees stocked with beer salvaged from the abandoned suburbs.

But the flooding continued. The sea had pushed far into the great river estuaries. The Thames was now an inland sea as far as Buckinghamshire. The Severn had intruded through the Vale of Evesham as far as Warwick, and with Liverpool Bay extending inland as far as Chester, it looked as if Wales was becoming detached from England altogether—just as the estuaries of the Forth and the Clyde, drowning much of Edinburgh and Glasgow, were cutting Scotland adrift. And the Cornish peninsula, dominated by the great upland masses of Exmoor and Dartmoor, looked as if it too was soon to be severed from the mainland by tongues of the sea. As for the rest of England, you could draw a line south from Middlesborough down as far as Cambridge, to the east of which there was only a ragged peninsula formed by scraps of high land like the Yorkshire Moors. In the southeast the sea had pushed far into the vales of Kent and Sussex, leaving the bands of higher ground, the North and South Downs and the Weald, protruding like the fingers of a rocky hand.

In the camps in the Chilterns, among the London evacuees, it had been a scary time. Everyone knew that the rising flood was pushing more waves of people inland from the valleys of the Severn and the Trent and the Humber and all the sea coasts, some of them driven on from camps to which they'd already been evacuated once, millions on the move.

At last, under pressure to accommodate still more refugees from the Thames valley, the authorities had started to break up the Aylesbury camp and move people westward. Wayne had invited Amanda and the kids to throw in their lot with him, and come to a community he knew of being established on Dartmoor. Amanda hadn't been sure of Wayne, if she was honest. But she couldn't see she had much of an option.

"So how did he know about this place?"

Amanda took a breath. "OK. Here's the part Mum wouldn't have approved of. When he was a kid, Wayne

used to run with a gang of Charlton fans. The football,
you know? I won't pretend I like it. I mean, it was just lads
being lads, but they were rough. Wayne grew out of it. But
he kept in touch with the lads in his gang. And some of
them, in later life, formed links with, well, fringe groups."

Lily nodded. "Hence the flags. The far right. Like the
British National Party."

"Not the BNP . . . Similar, I suppose. Look, Wayne isn't
a thug or a neo-Nazi. But he says he found ideas being
floated among these people that he wasn't hearing discussed anywhere else."

"Such as?"

"Such as, how would the world cope when the oil ran
out? I suppose it's all moot now, we have other problems,
but back then people feared anarchy. There was talk of
bolt-holes. Wayne says one group looked at locations in
places like Croatia, close to the coast, where you could
use local rivers for fresh water and live off solar energy.
Some of them started planning seriously. Making caches of
stuff."

"Survivalists with swastikas."

"If you like," Amanda snapped. "Anyhow when the
flooding came they dug up all those old plans. Wayne got
in with a group that had considered setting themselves up
closer to home."

"Dartmoor."

"Yes. Devon and Cornwall were a peninsula even before the flooding; I think there were vague plans to block
the main roads and cut it off. It was more pub talk than
anything else. But they had the location in mind. So when
we got moved on from Aylesbury, at least we had a place to
go. Wayne got hold of a Land Rover and a caravan, and—
well, here we are."

"Um. Complete with barbed-wire barriers and surface-to-
air missiles."

"It's the same all over, and don't tell me it isn't. People
have lost so much they're frightened of losing even more.
But I think it will calm down. We're not going to live through
some survivalist horror show, Lily."

"We're not?"

"You've been away. It's not so bad." She believed that,
actually. And she believed she had found strength and

resilience in making a home for herself and her kids in a
situation she would once have found completely unaccept-
able, and she resented Lily coming along to demolish it all
with a word. "It might get better," she said defiantly. "They
say that if it gets any warmer we'll be like the Greek islands here. Remember when Mum took us to Cephalonia
when we were kids? Olive groves and seafood and that
flat, glittering blue sea." It was a fantasy she entertained
in her head, especially on dark winter nights or when the
storms shook their crowded little caravan, a fantasy of a
sun-drenched future in an archipelago England.

Lily said nothing. She looked extraordinarily sad.

Amanda said, "That isn't going to happen, is it?"

"No." Lily took her hands. "I'm sorry, sis. I really do have
to take you away from here."

There was a sudden roar of an engine. A motorbike
came bolting along the footpath. Benj was riding it, with
Kristie clinging to his waist. Neither of them wore helmets.

Benj brought the bike clumsily to a halt. Kristie clambered
off, tearful, and ran to her mother. She had her battered old
pink backpack on her back.

Amanda launched in on them. "That's Wayne's
bike! What the hell do you think you're doing? He'll be
furious!"

"He already is," Benj said. "Hi, Auntie Lily."

"Hello, Benj, Kris." Lily looked wistful.

Amanda saw her kids through Lily's eyes. They had
grown so much, filled out, *changed*. The pasty, fashion-
conscious, Angel-obsessed teenagers of the days before the
flood would have looked like peacocks beside these sturdy
rustic laborers.

But Kris was crying. "Mum, it's my fault. I know you said
not to go back, but I had this feeling we were going away
for good—"

"*I* had a feeling," Benj said, "when you said Auntie Lily
was here."

"I didn't want to go without my stuff." Kris tugged on
her backpack straps.

Amanda glanced at Lily, exasperated. "It's the last of
her London things. Accessories, you know, sparkly bits, her
string of amber beads. And her teddy!"

"It doesn't matter," Lily said quickly. "She can bring it, now she has it. The question is, why did you come on the bike?"

"Because of *him*," Benj said. "He saw us."

And Amanda realized she could hear another engine's growl.

Wayne came roaring down the track on a big Honda. It was Bill Pulford's, Amanda realized. Wayne pulled up, killed the engine, and let the bike drop to the ground. He came stalking over, fists bunched.

Amanda forced a laugh, trying to ease the mood. "You know, Bill's going to kick up a stink if he knows you handled his bike like that—"

Wayne pointed a grubby finger at her. "You shut up." His hair was wild from the ride; his AxysCorp-durable coveralls were gray with muck, his eyes bright blue. "What the hell do you think you're doing? Off somewhere, are you? I knew it when I saw these two little arseholes running off."

Benj faced him. "I may be an arsehole, but don't call me 'little.'"

Wayne raised a fist.

To her own surprise Amanda grabbed his arm. "If you hit him it's over. Don't—you—dare."

He glared at her. But he backed off, and shook her hand off his arm. "Isn't it over anyway? Aren't you all fucking off with GI Jane here?"

Lily said evenly, "I've come for my family. I've no quarrel with you."

"Well, I've got a quarrel with you, lady. I've got rights. It was me saved them when we got kicked out of Aylesbury. Ah, go on, fuck off," he said to Amanda. "I'm sick of your whining. You can all go. All but *you*." And he grabbed Kristie's arm. She screamed and tried to struggle, but he was overwhelmingly strong.

Benj made a lunge, but Lily held him back.

Amanda advanced on him. "What are you doing? Let her go!"

"No chance," he snarled. He pulled Kristie against him, his big hand holding her waist, her arm twisted behind her back. "I've got what I want, the rest of you can fuck off. Go on."

Amanda saw it now. "It's been about Kristie all along, hasn't it?"

"Of course it has. I've only stayed with you while I've been waiting for her. Did you think I wanted you, you ridiculous old bag? How many kids could you give me? Because that's what it's going to be about in the future. Kids, strong sons, fertile daughters." Kristie struggled again, but he twisted her arm tighter until she subsided. "Of course it was always about her. While I was shagging you, I thought about her. Couldn't get it up otherwise—"

There was a soft detonation, like somebody spitting out a seed. Wayne let go of Kristie and fell to the ground, howling. His right boot had exploded.

Benj hurried forward and grabbed his sister. Lily stepped up to Wayne, on the ground, her pistol in her hand.

He was clutching the bloodied mess of his boot. "You stupid bitch, you've shot my fucking toe off!"

"If you make another sound I'll shoot out a kneecap. What use will you be then to your survivalist buddies?"

He glared, his face a mask of pain and rage, the sweat making rivulets in the dirt on his brow. But he said no more.

Amanda, shaking, took a breath. "You do keep interfering in my life, Lil," she said.

Lily turned to the children. "You two OK?"

"Yes," Kristie said. "Auntie Lil, don't blow his kneecap off if he makes this sound."

"What sound?"

She ran up to Wayne, timing the run as if taking a penalty at soccer, and kicked him in the balls. He howled and writhed.

"*That* sound," she said. She yelled at him, "Creep!"

"Kris, I'm sorry," Amanda said sincerely.

"Don't sweat it," Kris said coolly, her tears gone now. "He never would have got near me."

"No, he wouldn't," Benj said firmly.

"My God," Amanda said. "I'm raising vigilantes."

Lily checked her watch. "Look, he doesn't matter now. None of this does. We need to get to Cheriton Bishop to meet the car." She eyed the bikes. "We could be there in fifteen minutes on these things, if we had two drivers."

"I can ride a bike," Benj said.

Amanda said, "I know—"

"And so can I," Kristie said brightly.

"That I didn't know," Amanda said sternly.

"Leave my fucking bike alone, you witches," Wayne said from the ground.

"Shut up," Lily said mildly. "Well, then. Kris, can I hitch a ride with you?"

Wayne cursed as they got the bikes started and, apparently unable to contain his rage, actually got to his feet and staggered forward. Lily kept her gun visible. Amanda was grateful to get out of his sight.

39

Once they were in the AxysCorp SUV the kids were quiet, to Amanda's relief. It was the first time they'd been driven any distance since Wayne had brought them from Aylesbury in his Land Rover. But they looked big, overmuscled, grimy in the car's smooth interior.

They had to stick to the high ground all the way, mostly following minor roads. It would take them the best part of twenty-four hours to travel by car from Postbridge to Marlow, where the AxysCorp boat waited for them, a journey that might have taken a few hours before the flooding. Lily fretted over the slowness of the journey. Evidently whatever she feared was imminent.

They headed northeast, descending from Dartmoor to the Blackdown Hills, where they glimpsed the oil terminal at Taunton and the sea beyond. Then they headed east through Dorset. They had to cross various boundaries, roadblocks and barbed wire, as they traveled from one of England's petty new fiefdoms to the next. But aboard the car was a police officer, attached to this expedition by Nathan Lammockson. There was generally still enough deference for the central authorities for the copper's presence to see them waved through. But the car also carried a stash to pay tolls and bribes: sterling, euros, dollars, even gold coins.

When they drove northeast across the Salisbury Plain they glimpsed Salisbury itself, where the cathedral's spire, truncated by a storm, stuck out of a placid pond like a broken bone. Further to the north Stonehenge stood untroubled by the world's latest problems, though a ragged band of would-be druids had made permanent encampment around it, and prayed daily for relief from the flood.

They stayed the night at Newbury, sleeping in their

seats in the parked-up SUV. Then, after crossing a swollen Thames, they continued northwest through the White
Horse Hills, bridged the Cherwell at Goring, and then
made their way across the Chilterns to High Wycombe and
descended into Marlow. Here, moored over the drowned
lawn of a riverside villa that had once been worth millions,
a small AxysCorp powerboat was waiting for them.

Even as far inland as Marlow, Amanda discovered when
she got out of the car, you could smell the salt in the air.

The boat's engine humming, they sailed through Maidenhead and Windsor. Benj and Kristie clung to the rails,
looking at the view, drinking coffee and eating sweet biscuits. The pilot used GPS to keep to the centerline of the
river's old course, to avoid buildings and trees and other
submerged hazards.

They stared as they passed Windsor Castle, standing
proud on its brooding keep, though their tame copper
was wary, saying he thought it had been occupied by a
breakaway military unit. Elsewhere, where the banks were
lower, the swollen waterway spread to the horizon on either side, its placid surface broken only by the occasional
church spire or tower block. They may as well have been
at sea, Amanda thought, and it was only the pilot's GPS
that kept them on the river's original course. But no sea
was as grubby as this, its surface covered by slicks of oil
and Sargasso masses of plastic bags and tree branches and
upended wheelie bins, garbage islands that were home to
squabbling seagulls. On they went, the pilot intoning the
names of the drowned suburbs below: Shepperton, Hampton, Kingston, Richmond, ancient places now lost tens of
meters beneath the boat's prow.

The kids got bored of the unchanging view, and started
playing card games with the copper. Amanda was pleased
about that; they didn't notice when they sailed over Fulham, their own abandoned home.

They passed on downstream, skirting the abutments of
drowned bridges. As they approached central London the
traffic on the river began to thicken, rowboats and yachts,
few powerboats. The kids perked up as there were more
monuments to see here, glass monoliths protruding from
the grimy water. Rafts constructed of ganged-together rub-

ber tires nosed cautiously between the cliff faces of the buildings, and Amanda saw that divers were descending into the swollen water, hauling down plastic tarpaulins and power lines.

"What's this?" she asked Lily. "Salvage?"

"Some of it. But also storage. It's amazing how much *stuff* there was in London the day the Barrier was over-topped, Amanda, just a normal day, and it's mostly still down there—tools, machinery, even bottled water and tinned food. There's too much to bring up all at once. What they can't retrieve quickly they're trying to make safe from the rising water. A store for the future."

They passed through Westminster. Most of the London Eye was still above the water, like an immense bicycle wheel. You could make out ropes dangling from broken-open viewing pods, relics of the last rescue operations. On the opposite bank, the Big Ben clock tower stood a brave sixty meters above the water line. But one of its clock faces was smashed, only fragments remaining. The copper knew about that. "Some little-Britain nutter with a rocket-propelled grenade . . ."

Lily's phone chimed. She dug it out of her pocket. It was a heavy mil-spec model, a radio phone.

The copper's radio crackled.

And the AxysCorp pilot's screen lit up.

Benj saw this. "What's happening?"

Lily looked saddened, but oddly relieved. "What I've been waiting for. The seismologists got it spot on."

Amanda snapped, "Got what spot on?"

"There's been a major ocean earthquake, southwest of Ireland."

That sounded ridiculous. Amanda found herself laughing. "Ireland? You don't have earthquakes in Ireland—"

"It's what this has been all about, Amanda," Lily said. She started talking patiently about "isostatic subsidence," about how drowned land could be forced by the weight of the water down into the softer rocks beneath the crust, by as much as a third of the depth of the water above it. But the semi-rigid crust didn't like being bent. And thus the flooding was causing huge seismic stresses all over the world.

Amanda cut her off. "You've been spending too much time with Gary Boyle. What's an earthquake off Ireland got to do with us?"

"This," the pilot said. He produced a laptop and opened it up before them. "This is a view from Exmoor, looking west."

It was an image of the sea, and a line of black on the horizon, a line that thickened as Amanda watched. And in the foreground you could see that the sea was retreating, exposing drowned towns, fields.

"Tsunami," Kristie said immediately.

"A tsunami, heading for England," Amanda said, still disbelieving.

"It's happened before," Lily said. "It's in the geological record, tsunamis hitting the Channel ports and the Severn Estuary and Scotland, because of quakes off Ireland and in the Channel and off the coast of Norway."

"How high?"

"We don't know, not yet," Lily said. "We should be safe here. But it's going to make a hell of a mess of the whole west coast."

Amanda recalled images of the 2004 tsunami in the Indian Ocean, and Istanbul just a year ago, and Macao and Hong Kong since. Bodies hanging from trees. "So Dartmoor's not safe after all."

"Amanda, you can see why I had to get you out. This is going to smash apart what's left of Britain, and there won't be the resources to recover."

Kristie was staring at the screen. "What about Molly and Linda, and Barry and George—?"

"Local kids in Postbridge," Amanda explained to Lily.

"Can we warn them?" Kristie asked.

Lily handed over her phone. "Call whoever you like, honey. There will have been an official warning by now anyhow." Kristie immediately began to make calls.

Benj was angry. "You knew this was coming, didn't you, Lily? It's just like Greenwich. We just ran off and left them to die, even though you knew this was going to happen."

"Yes. But if I'd shot my mouth off none of us would have got away. Look—you've got a conscience, Benj, and that's a good thing. But can you see what I had to do?" She glared at him until he subsided.

*   *   *

Much later, when they were in the air aboard the AxysCorp chopper, Lily's phone chimed with another urgent incoming call. Kristie was still making her calls to Postbridge; she handed the phone back.

The call was from AxysCorp, in fact from Nathan himself. Helen Gray had been staying with family in Chester. She had been lost when the great wave hit.

Amanda took Lily's hand. "I know what that means to you. The first of you gone."

"I promised to look after her kid," Lily said desolately. "How the hell am I supposed to do that?"

40

June 2019

From Kristie Caistor's scrapbook:

A patrol of river police searching for survivors in submerged districts of Paris came under automatic fire from an apartment building.

A raid was organized. A gang of teenagers was flushed out; one officer was lost. Half-starved, many of them ill from drinking polluted floodwater, the teenagers had plenty of alcohol, and weapons. All but one had carried Kalashnikov AK47s.

This was a global phenomenon. Even before the flood there had already been something like a hundred million Kalashnikovs, or close imitations, circulating in the world, so simple was the AK47 to manufacture, so reliable was it at doing its job. Even more had been churned out by factories around the world before they had drowned. Many guns had been stashed away by "*faux* Napoleons," the French police spokeswoman said, fueled by visions of future wars over the high ground. Nobody knew how many of these stashes might exist across the planet, or where they were, or how many AK47s existed.

The AK47 was said to be the most effective weapon ever invented, in terms of lives taken. Now it was emerging as a final bloodstained monument to the age of industry and mechanized killing that had spawned it, and was likely to be a shaping force in the age to come.

The Parisian teenagers were, all but one, killed with the weapons in their hands.

41

October 2019

Gary Boyle was working at the instrument reel on the aft deck of the *Links*. He saw Sanjay McDonald hurry aboard just as the ship was about to cast off. He called and waved.

Sanjay made his way aft. Laden with a bulging backpack, Sanjay was sweating from the heat of the day, and he wore a thin linen mask over his bearded mouth to keep out the smoke from the Istanbul fires. He dumped his bag with relief, and accepted a flask of cold water from Gary. He lifted his mask and took a deep slug of water; then he poured the rest over his head and face. "Do you mind?"

"The ship's got its own desalination plant," Gary said. "Fill your boots."

"Thanks."

It was time to leave. A boatswain lined up cast-off hawsers into neat parallel rows. Gary could see the captain on the bridge, standing alongside the Turkish pilot who would navigate the boat through the strait. The whole boat shuddered as the twin screws churned the waters of the Golden Horn. Some of the scientists came up from the main laboratory below decks to see the sights. Mostly young, mostly weather-beaten and shabby, they milled around the deck, peering at the murky water, the walls of the channel. But this was a working cruise, and in the small compartment above the bridge, which they called the top lab, a couple of researchers were already booting up the echo-sounding gear.

Sanjay leaned on the rail and looked out at the skyline of Istanbul, gliding slowly past the ship. Despite the flooding, despite the quakes, it was still a stunning sight. Eighteen months after the initial quakes the stubbornly unbroken dome of the Hagia Sophia had become an iconic image for a stressed world, and the low morning sun glinted from the minarets and gilded domes of the mosques that crowded the old city. But smoke rose up in lazy towers from the burning districts, and choppers flapped through the murk.

Gary was glad to see Sanjay, who was one of a loose network of climatologists and oceanographers Gary had kept bumping into in the last couple of years, as they traveled the planet monitoring its extraordinary changes. But he'd thought Sanjay had missed his chance today. "You cut it fine, don't you?"

Sanjay shrugged. "You know what travel is like nowadays."

"Yeah. Well, there are plenty of spare berths. I'd guess only about half the promised attendees turned up, despite all Woods Hole could do."

"But Thandie Jones is here?"

Gary grinned. "You couldn't keep her away."

"This is a Woods Hole ship, isn't it?"

"Yeah." Gary kicked a rusty deck plate. "Used to be a salvage ship during the Second World War. Shivers like a drying-out drunk. But I figure if she hasn't sunk in eighty years, she's not gonna sink under me now."

"Let's hope not."

One by one the scientists drifted off to begin work. Gary's laptop beeped for his attention, as data came in from the various teams aboard the vessel.

The narrow Bosporus strait was the only connection between the Black Sea and the Sea of Marmara, which in turn linked to the Mediterranean through the Dardanelles, and then the Med kissed the Atlantic at Gibraltar. So the Bosporus was the only way the rising global ocean could reach the Black Sea.

For millennia the Black Sea had been a freshwater ocean, fed by several major rivers and draining out into the Marmara. But under the Bosporus's freshwater outflow there had always been a deep countering saltwater current going north, from Marmara into the Black Sea. Since antiquity, navigators had made use of this; you could lower a basket full of stones into the deep water and have yourself pulled against the surface current. The saltwater flow was a relic of the post–Ice Age surge which had seen a dammed and half-dried-up Black Sea refilled catastrophically from the rising Marmara. Now the oceans were rising again, and that subsurface salt current was much stronger than it had been. Gary supposed that eventually it would overwhelm the surface flow altogether, and the Bosporus would become a saltwater aqueduct, filling up the Black Sea basin.

From there, however, from the Black Sea, the rising ocean water had nowhere to go—not for now. An anticipated change in this situation was the primary motive for this expedition.

Another alarm chimed on Gary's laptop. Time for him to go to work himself. He began to unreel the instrument chain, dropping it into the water; it would trail the boat's starboard flank, thus staying well away from the screws.

Sanjay inspected the instrument reel. It was a cable of chain links, with more than a hundred thermometers attached along its length. "For measuring the temperature variations across the thermocline?"

"You got it. The Bosporus has to be one of the most intensely studied waterways in the world. And yet so much has changed, we know scarcely anything about its condition now. Every time you make a measurement it's a discovery . . . So where have you come from?"

"Australia."

"How are they faring there?"

Sanjay shrugged, his expression hidden by his face mask. "The sea is covering the coasts, of course. The inhabitants of the great cities, especially on the east coast from Melbourne up to Brisbane, are fleeing inland. Tent cities on the Great Dividing Range. But the most interesting event has been the sea's forcing its way inland from the southeast, up the Spencer and Saint Vincent gulfs. The Murray River Basin is pretty much drowned, and the sea has broken through to a lake, called Lake Eyre, which was actually below the old sea level."

"So Australia has had its own refilling episode."

"Refugees from Bondi Beach tried to surf the incoming waves. Fools." Sanjay laughed. "Elsewhere it is as you would expect. Dry places become dryer, wet places wetter. To a first approximation agriculture has ended in Australia. Now they rely entirely on imported food, such as they can get, and the rationing is ferocious. But the native Australians have gone."

"The Aborigines? What do you mean, gone?"

"They always remembered how to live in the continent's red heart. Now they are leaving the white folk to their drowning cities."

Gary put the question that every climatologist kept asking. "And if the sea keeps rising?"

Sanjay shrugged again. "Then the Aborigines are fucked. But so are we all, in the end."

The ship had reached the narrows between the steep bluffs of Kandilli and Kanlica, which still stood high above the water.

Gary asked, "So what keeps you going, Sanj? How are your family? Your kids?"

"They and their mothers are with my sister, Narinder, and her own family. They are in a village in the Scottish Highlands, not far from Fort William. Safe up there. But they may have to move. After the tsunami the central British government all but collapsed, and is capable of organizing nothing but evacuations and emergency relief. In the highlands the old clans are forming again! Our father left us a family tree he mapped back to before the time of Bonnie Prince Charlie. So we have allegiances."

"You're not tempted to join them?"

"Maybe eventually, if things get bad enough. For now the science keeps me occupied. We must continue. What else is there to do?" Sanjay glanced at the sky, which was all but clear of smog. He slipped off his mask and sniffed the air.

42

Having passed through the strait, the *Links* tracked the coast of the Black Sea to the eastern shore. She landed close to the border between Russia and Georgia, over a drowned seaside resort called Sochi.

There was no functioning harbor here. Shallow-draft boats had to shuttle the scientists to a kind of pier that had been improvised on a main north-south road called the Kurortny Prospekt. There was nobody to help them disembark save the ship's crew, and they had to haul their own luggage and equipment. But there were trucks waiting, hired by Woods Hole. Gary wondered how much the fuel had cost the distant bursars of Woods Hole.

Much of the town of Sochi, where it survived above the waterline, seemed abandoned, the shops and bars closed up or burned out, and there were few people about. A Russian girl called Elena Artemova, seconded from the Shirshov Oceanology Institute in Moscow, pointed gloomily to the mountains that loomed over the coast. "Everybody sensible has gone to the high villages," she said. "And so must we, for the night."

The trucks took the scientists and their gear up into the mountains to a village called Krasnaya Polyana—once a favorite of President Putin, a leathery, tobacco-chewing driver somberly informed them. The drive was spectacular but somewhat scary, the road snaking along ledges cut into steep mountain gorges. As they climbed Gary could clearly see how the coastal resorts had been flooded, their beaches drowned, and how the ocean had pushed deep into river valleys lined with conifers.

This was the Caucasus, the fat peninsula that stretched across the south of the Russian Federation, bounded by the Black Sea and the Sea of Azov to the west, and the Caspian

Sea to the east. Gary had studied the local topography. It was varied country, with the north dominated by steppe and to the south mountains, until very recently still snow-capped. What was most interesting to the climatologists was that northern band of steppe, stretching from Rostov to Groznyy, much of it a meadow carpeted with wild flowers and rush-filled river valleys. This was the lowest stretch of this neck of land that separated the Black Sea from the landlocked Caspian. And when the rising Black Sea broke its bounds, across the steppe was the way the water would flow.

At Krasnaya Polyana they were taken to what had once apparently been quite a grand dacha, a scatter of single-story buildings under a canopy of spruce. The trucks parked for the night, and the drivers disappeared to their own dwellings in the main village. The scientists explored the dacha, calling to each other. The only tall building was a grand limestone block covered with stucco and peeling paint. The long entrance hall had a decorated ceiling, the images obscured by damp, and iron spiral stairs led to rooms off the upper balconies.

There were staff here, locals, mostly elderly, who spoke no English, and Elena Artemova and other Russian-speakers had to interpret. They seemed disappointed the scientists were so few, and that they would need little space. Elena seemed embarrassed to be drawn into negotiating over fees with an elderly woman.

Sanjay said, "You wonder what use money is to people like this."

"Just as well this old crone hasn't figured that out," Thandie murmured. "While her sons have pissed off to the hills to grow corn and fight over the girls, she's stayed on, accumulating a stash of rubles against the day things get back to normal. Good plan."

"Perhaps she has no choice," Elena said harshly. "Did you think of that?" Aged twenty-eight, she was a gloomy woman, but beautiful. Her face was long, with pale, luminous skin, large eyes, a downturned mouth; she wore her hair pulled back, which emphasized the boniness of her forehead. "Perhaps her sons would not take her to 'the hills.' Perhaps she cannot work up there. This is all she has. Each of us is under pressure in a changing world, Thandie

Jones. And we don't all have rich western institutions backing our adventures."

Thandie snorted. "Don't give me that, Mother Russia. You're taking the Woods Hole dollar just like the rest of us."

"If not for us and the 'Woods Hole dollar,'" Sanjay said, "this old woman and those who work with her would go hungry. So everybody wins, yes? Let's leave it like that."

Neither Thandie nor Elena was satisfied, but they had been rubbing each other up the wrong way since Istanbul. Their ongoing argument, oddly, brought out the stereotypes in both of them, Gary thought, the dour moralistic Russian versus the cut-the-crap American.

Nobody chose to stay in the main house, though they would use its facilities, like the showers and laundry room. Instead the dozen of them settled for a cluster of the little single-story chalets under the shelter of the spruce trees. They were close enough together that in the shared yard outside they could build their evening hearth, an important ritual.

Gary doubled up with Sanjay. Sanjay, exhausted from his traveling, dumped his rucksack, kicked off his boots, threw himself on a bunk, and slept. Some of the Americans, stiff from the drive, started an improvised game of softball in the shade of the pines.

Gary went to find Thandie and, on a mischievous whim, Elena, and suggested exploring the village. The women eyed each other warily, but went along.

Surrounded by forest-clad peaks, Krasnaya Polyana was a pretty place, and at six hundred meters above the old sea-level datum was much too high to have been touched by the floods. It was good to walk briskly, and to breathe in air unpolluted by smoke or sewage. Gary could see why Putin had liked it—a man with taste, he thought. In fact it was probably better for the casual traveler now that twenty-first-century tourism had receded, so long as you didn't get shot by some Russian brand of survivalist.

They found paths that led to an arboretum, and to the remains of a hunting lodge that had to predate Putin, and indeed modern Russia; maybe it belonged to the tsars. And beyond that they came to a river valley, where a threadlike waterfall tumbled into a plunge pool.

Thandie glanced around. There was nobody in sight. "Fuck it." She ran toward the water, whooping, stripping off her clothes as she ran. She hopped as she got her jeans off. She was naked by the time she got to the water, her brown body lithe and muscular, and she splashed into the pool.

"Watch your feet on the rocks!" Elena called after her. "And the water will be cold—"

"Elena." Gary touched her arm. "Lighten up. Come on." He unzipped his own coverall.

"Very well. But no peeking."

Gary stripped bare. Elena kept her underwear on, sensible stuff, heavy pants and a kind of sports bra. She was bustier than she had looked with her blouse on.

By now Thandie was splashing about under the waterfall. Her crisp hair sparkled with water droplets. The water was cold enough to make Gary hop and squeal as he went in centimeter by centimeter. Thandie kicked spray at him. "You classic wimp."

"Oh, shut up. Christ, Thandie, you must have rubber skin."

Elena slid uncomplaining into the water. It was just about deep enough to swim, to float your body off the rocks. Elena took a few solemn breaststrokes, her unsmiling face staring straight ahead.

The three of them gathered in a circle. Once you got used to the water the cold wasn't so bad, and the contrast with the warmth of the air was refreshing. Gary did his best to keep his eyes away from Thandie's bare body, and from Elena, whose underwear, soaked, didn't conceal much.

As for the women, Gary knew he was no hunk, but he had thought they'd peek. But they seemed to be working harder at not looking at each other than not looking at him. Aha, he thought. Maybe that was why there was so much tension between them.

Elena said to Gary, "I suppose you must have dreamed of places like this, during your captivity."

"You bet."

"Forgive me for asking. I have known you for some time, but I do not know you well. We have not spoken of your captivity before."

"That's OK. Most people are embarrassed to mention it, I think."

"How long were you kept?"

"In all, three years."

"I am shocked."

"The others got me through. The worst times weren't the rough stuff, the humiliations and the beatings. Or a habit they had in one of our holding centers where they would throw us our food and make us scrabble for it, like apes. The worst time was when I was kept alone."

Elena nodded. "We are social creatures. We are defined by our relationships with others. Without that—"

"We're nothing." He splashed water into his face. "I always knew there were good times like this ahead of me. That kept me going."

Thandie said, "But there are no more good times for Helen Gray."

"No. Poor Helen. I don't suppose Lily has made any progress in finding out what became of her kid?"

"No. Though the child is still supposed to be in the continental US somewhere. Lily thinks she's become a pawn in the latest complicated diplomatic games regarding the various factions in Saudi, and what's going to become of their oil. Lily's sticking at it. Actually I got to see Lily when I was sent to South America. She's mostly working with AxysCorp in Peru. Something called Project City."

"What the hell's that?"

Thandie shrugged. "Who knows? Just another dumb idea of Nathan Lammockson's."

Elena turned to her. "You were in South America recently? How are things there?"

Gary said, "Maybe we should wait for the hearth . . ."

As the global flood event unfolded, the international band of climatologists, oceanographers, geologists, seismologists, hurricane-chasers and ecologists who traveled the globe gathering data and cooking up hypotheses had formed a community of their own. There weren't all that many of them to begin with, they were broadly of a similar age and from similar academic backgrounds, and they kept bumping into each other.

With time the data-gathering and the face-to-face sharing of news added up to a kind of ongoing global workshop that came to seem increasingly important. The civilian population was too concerned with just getting through the challenges of the next twenty-four hours, and the governments with providing the essentials of life to a stressed population—and, perhaps, hanging onto their own power. It was only in the endless conversation of the itinerant scientists that a planetary consciousness of what was going on was maintained.

And the ritual of the hearths had emerged as a central part of the process. On nights like this, when a group felt it was quorate, you would sit around a campfire, real or metaphorical, to drink, smoke, shoot up, make out—and, most important of all, you talked your heart out about what you had seen. Generally the sessions were transcribed by speech recognition systems and uploaded to what was left of the World Wide Web, to provide an expert oral history of the flood.

But Thandie said, "Nah. When we do the hearth later, we can embellish. In the meantime I'm comfortable here." She scissored her long legs in the crisp water. "You want to hear about South America or not?"

"Shoot," said Gary.

"To begin with, the glaciers are vanishing in the Andes . . ."

Even as the seas rose, global warming was increasing faster than ever. An immediate consequence was that cities along the Pacific coast of South America that relied on glacier runoff for their drinking water were running dry as the glaciers vanished. Others too, in similar locations in North America and the foothills of the Himalayas, were going thirsty.

Meanwhile on South America's east coast, Thandie said, there had been a major sea incursion at the broad mouth of Rio de la Plata. Coastal cities like Montevideo and Buenos Aires had long been drowned, but now the sea was pushing hundreds of kilometers northwards, flooding the lowlands of Argentina, Uruguay and Paraguay. An even more dramatic incursion had forced its way into the mouths of the Amazon and back along the river valley, creating a giant inland sea. "Even where it isn't drowned the rainforest is dying back," Thandie said. "Just rotting away."

"And so becoming another source of carbon dioxide, rather than our greatest land reservoir of carbon, as it should be," Elena said. Her specialism was global ecological cycles. "More greenhouse."

"Yep," said Thandie. "Every little helps."

And of course, Gary thought, ahead of each of these clinically mapped incursions a desperate crowd of refugees would be driven headlong, and behind it cities and towns would be left drowned and littered with corpses. Such things no longer needed saying.

Thandie said that after spending some time with Lily in Peru they had traveled together to the US, where they had tried to push on the search for Grace. But the federal government was in the middle of a major relocation from flooded-out DC to Denver, Colorado, the highest state capital. And there Thandie had formed an impression of what was becoming of North America.

Florida and Louisiana were all but gone now, nothing left but salvage crews working over the flooded ruins of the cities. The great plains of the eastern half of the continent were rapidly being inundated, and throughout the eastern states immense bands of refugees washed west. A major community was coalescing in the Appalachians, the highest point between the east coast and the Rockies and still above the floodwaters. America's single greatest problem was a savage drought, which was affecting much of the agricultural heartland. Meanwhile both coasts were battered by a plague of hurricanes, more of them and more intense every year, giant storms feeding off ocean heat that raged over the ruins of the abandoned coastal cities.

But there was also a gathering refugee crisis in Canada, as Hudson Bay spread inexorably wider, and the sea forced its way down the throat of the Saint Lawrence valley toward the Great Lakes, drowning Quebec and Montreal and Toronto. Elena said there was another extinction event going on there. The lakes were the largest bodies of fresh water on Earth; now their ecologies were poisoned by salt.

When it was Elena's turn, she began, "I myself have seen much of Europe in my travels . . ."

The plight of northern Europe was in fact the big story of the year. The inundation of Holland had been the beginning of a drastic flooding episode that now extended across the north European plain, through north Germany and into Poland. An immense population was in flight, head-

ing either north to Scandinavia or south toward the Latin
countries, a program of evacuation still more or less con-
trolled by the European Union, though national rivalries
were reemerging. But the south had problems of its own,
with an intense drought locked down from Spain to the
Levant. Meanwhile isostatic shifts were sparking off earthquakes and volcanism across the Mediterranean region. In
the Middle East a major war was brewing between Israel
and its Arab neighbors, the proximate cause being auda-
cious attempts by Syria and others to get their hands on the
Israelis' advanced desalination technology.

They spoke in broad-brush terms of other areas none
of them had witnessed in person recently, relaying sec-
ondhand accounts. Gary repeated Sanjay's description of
Australia.

In the Indian subcontinent, the misery of flooding and
war in India, Pakistan and Bangladesh had been augmented
by years of monsoons that failed or mistimed because of
shifts in the global ocean circulation system. In southeast
Asia there was great suffering. In Vietnam there had been
a tremendous evacuation from a drowning Ho Chi Minh
City to the highlands of the north. Cambodia and Thailand
were mostly gone. North and South Korea had abandoned
their fratricidal struggle and opened their common border, the better to manage the flows of refugees caused by
the rising of the Yellow Sea. In China, that same rise had
caused the abandonment of Beijing, and a huge wash of
refugees into Inner Mongolia and beyond.

Much of Africa was gripped by drought, while the Rift
Valley was flooding. The rainforests of the Congo were
dying back too, and Gary had heard of heroic efforts to
save the last colonies of African great apes.

"And in Russia," Elena said, "all across the roof of the
planet, the *taiga* is burning, the world forest."

"Great," said Thandie. "More cee-oh-two."

Elena said, "A number of us are as concerned about the
warming as about the flooding."

Thandie managed to laugh. "I love your Russian understatement. Yes, quite a number of us are concerned about
that. More sources of cee-oh-two, less available sinks as the
land drowns with its forests and marshes. Even in the sea
we're not getting any breaks. Higher temperatures reduce

the productivity of the phytoplankton, so they can't draw down as much of the cee-oh-two as they used to. Oh, and as the sea spreads at the expense of land and ice, the planet's albedo is reduced." The flooded world was getting darker. So it reflected less light, absorbed more of the sun's heat energy, and got even hotter.

"And so it goes," Gary said. "A whole interlocking set of feedback cycles, all of them set to 'positive.'"

"Yeah," Thandie said. "In fact I think we've reached a crucial point where the climate changes driven by the sea rise itself are starting to kick in major league."

"So what next? You think your sea-level rise is going to keep on coming?"

"In the longer term," Thandie murmured. "But short term we're going to see a pulse, an artifact of ice cap melting . . ."

The sea rise and the accompanied warming had together been enough to destabilize both the Greenland and Antarctic caps. The West Antarctic ice sheet, floating on the ocean, was beginning to shatter as the water steadily rose and warmed. But the seaborne sheet acted as a dam which blocked the glaciers, rivers of ice running off the frozen continent. Now those glaciers rushed to the sea, calving into icebergs. It would not be long before the huge East Antarctic sheet, anchored firmly to its base of rock for twenty million years, would also begin to crumble.

"So," said Elena. "Floods. Earthquakes. Vast refugee flows, which in turn bring resource shortages, the spread of disease and conflicts. Shifting climatic zones which, among other things, change the ranges of mosquitoes and other infection vectors. Our planet is failing us, and our civilization is under immense strain."

"Nicely summarized," Thandie said dryly. "You fucking Russians are a miserable bunch."

"We have a saying," Elena said. "The first five hundred years are the worst. I fear I am getting cold. We should go and unpack for the night. And then we can share this desolate news all over again." She clambered out of the water, her underwear sticking to her flesh.

Thandie watched Elena, and she saw Gary watching her. Thandie stood up, stretching, and walked over to Gary. She really was quite beautiful, he thought, in an athletic, hunter-gatherer kind of way. She murmured, "You keep your observations to yourself." But she grinned at him, not malicious. She walked on, showering him with droplets warmed by her body.

As they dressed, Elena said she had negotiated with the dacha staff for an evening meal. "There will be local delicacies, beetroot soup, and trout served in walnut sauce. Do not be concerned about the fish. Only the deeper parts of the Black Sea are poisoned by industrial hydrogen sulphide . . ."

43

The party crossed the Caucasus, heading north and east, skirting the foothills of the southern mountains. Then they descended toward the shore of the Caspian Sea, traveling over a steppe of sandy clay until they reached the lower valley of the Volga.

They lodged for a day at Astrakhan. Close to the border with Kazakhstan, this was a coastal town that sprawled across the delta of the Volga, spanning eleven islands. The Caspian Sea, cut off from the global ocean, had not yet risen, and the lands around its shore had not yet suffered the flooding experienced elsewhere. It was strange for Gary and the others to run around town and to see the cathedral, the city's kremlin, the bridges, all eerily intact, as if nothing in the world had changed. But the city was all but drained of its people, and they saw more soldiers than civilians. The Russian authorities knew the oceanic transgression was coming, and had taken what precautions they could.

The party split up here to provide distributed viewpoints to observe the incursion. Some of them, including Sanjay and Elena, stayed in Astrakhan. The rest broke into pairs or threes and spread out away from Astrakhan up the river valley or around the northern shore of the Caspian, where some thousand square kilometers of the coastal land was below the old sea level, a great band of lowland that stretched right around the ocean shore and spread maybe a hundred and fifty kilometers inland.

Gary was paired with Thandie. They set up camp at the shore, close to a sandy, deserted beach. There they waited for the expected breakthrough.

Days passed. The weather was good, and they swam in the landlocked ocean, but it was foul with industrial waste and oil. In fact they could see drilling rigs out on the water, gaunt shapes like floating factories. They worked. They had their laptops and satellite connections, and they spoke to their colleagues, spread around the shore of the sea and in the river valley. They held a number of virtual "hearths," where the scattered researchers sent each other webcam images of their campfires.

After a couple of days they were joined on the shore by more observers, in tents and mobile homes. Few spoke English; none seemed to be scientists. "Disaster tourists," Thandie said dismissively.

"Like us," Gary pointed out.

At night they discussed their lives, Gary's captivity, Thandie's ambitions, their shared memories, their mutual friends. And after a couple of days, in the dark of their tent as they tried to sleep, Gary dared raise the subject of Elena Artemova, and the swim at Krasnaya Polyana.

"I swing both ways, if you want to know," Thandie said. "But I don't swing for you. Sorry."

"That's OK," he said calmly. "There's something about Elena, though, isn't there?"

Thandie snorted. "What, her chest?"

"No. That sadness you see in her. She reminds me of Piers Michaelmas, on his dark days. I want to make her smile. Does that sound dumb?"

"No," Thandie said. "Since I feel the same way."

"Good," Gary said. "I mean it." He thought of her lost baby, and felt warm. "If you can find happiness with Elena—"

"Shut up, Boyle."

"Roger that."

So they drifted to sleep, both thinking of Elena, who for all Gary knew might be thinking of both of them, or neither.

On the fourth morning they woke to a distant roar. When they climbed out of their tent the rubberneckers were already standing by the shore, binoculars in their hands.

Sanjay made an excited webcam communication; he had to shout over a noise like a waterfall. "It's broken through! We let you sleep, we thought you'd like to discover the sound for yourselves. It was a storm in the Black Sea that did it . . ." The rising waters of the Black Sea, fed from the global ocean via the Mediterranean and the Sea of Marmara, had at last broken through the Caucasus barrier at its weakest point, forcing their way up the valley of the Don, flooding Volgograd, and then pouring down the Volga valley to Astrakhan. "The whole damn town's already inundated. It's extraordinary!"

The distant rumble continued, like a far-off war.

Thandie checked her data feeds. "The Black Sea had risen to around fifty meters above the old datum when it broke through the Caucasus. Whereas the Caspian was about twenty-seven meters *below* the datum. That's about seventy-seven meters of head. No wonder it's so damn loud."

"We've work to do."

"Yeah. But let's go see first." On impulse she grabbed his hand. They walked down to the edge of the sea.

All along the littoral the grubby water was advancing slowly, like a tide coming in, surging a little when a wave broke. They paced back before it, counting, timing their steps.

"At this rate it's going to amount to a half-kilometer advance per day," Thandie said. She pulled a handheld from her pocket and did some quick figuring. "A vertical rise of maybe ten centimeters a *day*."

"It's going to take a while to fill up to the global datum, then," Gary said. "A year?"

"More."

The tourists were baffled. They seemed to have expected a giant wave you could surf on. Well, if you wanted spectacle you should be in the Volga valley, Gary thought. But he had a scientist's imagination, the capacity to understand the numbers. "The Caspian is a thousand kilometers long. A sea that could swallow Japan. And it's filling like a bathtub. *Think* of the volumes that must be pouring down the Volga." And, Gary thought, it was just going to keep on pushing back and back, eating away at the land.

They stood there and let the rising water wash over their bare feet. Thandie said, "Nobody's seen a sight like this since the Ice Age. Do you think we're privileged or cursed?"

"Both, maybe."

"Listen, Gary. What's next for you?"

"What do you have in mind?"

"More of this." She waved a hand. "We're going to see a re-creation of giant bodies of water that haven't stood on the Earth since the last glaciation, when meltwater filled every hollow: the lost great lakes. From here the sea will eventually extend all the way north to the Arctic coast. In Africa, the ocean will force its way up the Niger and the Nile to re-form Lake Megachad, a sea the size of western Europe. And in North America Lake Agassiz will form again, a huge inland sea that stretched from Saskatchewan to Ontario, from the Dakotas to Minnesota. Sights not seen for five hundred human generations. Let's go see . . . Why, there's even good science to be done. Even if nobody will ever buy my book about it."

But he had already decided what he should do. He could keep working wherever he went: in the midst of a global transformation there was data to be gathered everywhere. He would still be part of the worldwide community of watchers. But he'd decided. He would go back to America. His mother had died and he had no immediate family there. But he thought he would see if he could help Lily find Helen's baby. At heart, he was discovering, he was drawn to people, not spectacle.

Twenty-seven years old, he wanted to go home. He tried to explain this. Thandie didn't press him.

The sea continued to advance, rising, until it soaked the cuffs of their trousers. A rubbernecker a dozen meters away glared in disappointment. "Is this all there is to it? What a bust."

44

From Kristie Caistor's scrapbook:

When he joined up in Omaha, Bennie Thornton didn't know much about the purpose of the crusade. As far as he was concerned it was a holy war, a chance to earn some grace by sticking one to the Muslims, a last chance before the world finally went to hell.

In fact, he learned during his orientation and training, the war in Jerusalem was all part of a grand scheme designed by a group of American Christian fundamentalists called the Third Templars—a project intended to bring about the apocalypse.

A little Googling showed Kristie that the religious response to the flood had been complex and multifaceted, even just within Christianity. How should a Christian act in these extraordinary times? Some commentators cited Bible passages that supported an argument that the devout should concentrate their efforts on ensuring that they and others were among those saved. And adherents of the modern "prosperity gospel," who believed that God rewarded faith with wealth and material success, argued that the time to use that God-given wealth was right now, to buy up the high lands and let the less worthy drown. But the US National Association of Evangelicals led calls for the government to take various actions regarding the flood and its effects, just as it had once led calls to act over climate change, actions it claimed were entirely consistent with Christianity.

Gradually an ecumenical campaign by Catholic and Protestant leaders won traction, arguing that selfish actions conflicted with basic Christian teachings of self-denial, humility and charity. They pointed to Christ's expression of the Golden Rule: "And as you would that men should do to you, do ye also to them likewise" (Luke 6:31). That was surely a mandate to help those afflicted by the flood, which was disproportionately affecting those of limited means, like the poor inhabitants of shantytowns and river deltas. Leaders of other great religions developed similar arguments.

It seemed to Kristie that the religions were in general doing a great deal to harness ethical and material backing for the vast relief efforts being mobilized around the world, and indeed to temper the thrust of some of those efforts, as some of the super-rich and the consultancies and multinationals continued to try to use flood emergencies as opportunities to extract profits and colonize fresh economic territory.

But the Third Templars had a more specific cause.

They claimed that, according to Revelation and other sources, the building of a Third Temple on the Mount in Jerusalem was a necessary prerequisite to clear the way for the coming of Christ, and put an end to this age of turmoil and disaster. So that was what they set out to do. They were joined in this purpose by a gang of Messianic Zionists.

Unfortunately the erection of the Third Temple required demolishing various Islamic monuments in place on the same site. So the mission had immediately sparked a war that involved all three of the monotheistic faiths, Judaism, Christianity and Islam. The war of Abraham, they called it.

It had quickly widened out to a regional conflict involving other issues, battles over high land and water and desalination technology. The Israeli state had been a pioneer in weapons and security technology since 9/11 and before, and fought back viciously against any threat. And the Palestinians in their walled-off enclaves were making one last attempt to win back the land they believed had been stolen from them. There had been many wars fought over Jerusalem, Bennie learned, all the way back to the ancient Romans and probably beyond. But this, one way or another, was likely to be the last.

All Bennie cared about was getting into the fight. Aged nineteen, his body a mass of muscle and testosterone, he whooped as he jumped out of the plane to make his first parachute descent into the burning city.

45

The AxysCorp chopper skimmed over the oily waters of Upper New York Bay, heading northeast toward Manhattan. The pilot banked the bird, and pointed out the Statue of Liberty. "Everybody wants to see the old lady," he called back.

Lily leaned against Plexiglas. The day was dull, the sky a solid mass of slate cloud from which rain fell steadily, rattling on the bird's hull. The gray of the sky was reflected in the gray of the sea, gray over gray.

And there was Liberty, tilted over by Hurricane Aaron two years ago but still standing on her submerged pedestal, surrounded by a turbulent sea. Lily didn't imagine the grand old statue could keep standing much longer; one good storm would probably do the trick. But, according to Thandie Jones, the statue herself would survive indefinitely, submerged and buried in sediment. Even when the green patina on the lady's copper sheeting thickened and turned to stone, her sculptor's design would still be visible to whatever strange undersea visitors she might receive.

As the flooded cityscape glided beneath the chopper's prow, Lily used Liberty as a reference point to get her bearings, trying to see how much had changed since she last flew in here over two years ago for Thandie's science presentation. There was no sign of the barriers and levees hastily thrown up in those early panicky months; they were covered by the water. There was Brooklyn to her right and Jersey City to her left, the ground now entirely submerged, and only a few tall buildings protruded above the water. Grand-looking vessels lay at anchor around the shallow coasts, some the metallic gray of navy ships, but also yachts, brilliant white, floating like toys in a bathtub. The last refuge of New York's super-rich, perhaps, lying at anchor above the wrecked city. And Manhattan was a reef, directly ahead of her, the tallest buildings thrusting out of the water like splinters of quartz.

The chopper ducked down into the Financial District, sweeping between the shoulders of battered, burned-out skyscrapers. It was like flying through a virtual-reality version of some great canyon system, simplified rectangular blocks and straight-line cliffs with the water lying in the rectilinear valleys below. The glassless windows of the buildings were dark, but there was activity on the water: powerboats raising wakes that lapped against the stained walls, and heavier, lumbering rafts. The water itself was littered with garbage, plastic scraps and bursting bin liners.

"Heading up Broadway," the pilot called. "I'll be setting you down at Union Square, or over it. Broadway and 14th Street. You know it?"

"I think so," Lily said, dredging up memories of tourist excursions. "Was there a farmers' market?"

"Yeah. Nice place, if kind of run down. That was how it was, anyhow."

His voice was crisp in her headset. He had a New York accent but of a cultured sort; evidently he was a native. Lily wondered what he had done for a living before the flood, before he had come to do what everybody seemed to do nowadays, which was work for Nathan Lammockson. She asked, "You're a New Yorker yourself?"

"I am, ma'am. Grew up in Gramercy, in fact. Nice place to live. My mother, she's still alive, she's been moved out to the Catskills. She's talking about going to stay with her brother in his hunting lodge in West Virginia, up in the Appalachians. That's pretty high, you know."

"That sounds like a good plan."

"Yeah, but AxysCorp says the hills are already full of woodsmen and survivalist types. You know, the kind of guys who loaded their pickups and set off as soon as the first raindrops started to fall. Mr. Lammockson says there have been more casualties in the US inflicted by gunshot wounds at illegal roadblocks than by the weather events themselves."

"I wouldn't be surprised."

And she wasn't surprised to hear him quote Lammockson. As the global crisis had intensified Nathan Lammockson had taken to broadcasting regular speeches to his worldwide network of employees and business partners, a mix of pep talk, hard news and his peculiarly British homespun-capitalist philosophy. In an increasingly fragmented world it was as if Nathan Lammockson was left standing like the Statue of Liberty herself, alone but still bearing the torch of hope.

"So," she said, "are you going to join your mother in the hills?"

The pilot snorted. He seemed surprised she'd asked. "No, ma'am. I'll be staying as close to Mr. Lammockson as I can. Isn't that what you're doing?"

46

In the diffuse shadow of the Con Ed building's clock tower a giant raft drifted over Union Square.

The raft must have been a hundred meters long. Its core was a slab, black as tarmac, bordered by barbed wire and with giant Stars and Stripes dangling limp and wet at its corners. There were shacks on its back, built of ply or plastic or corrugated iron and lashed down by ropes and cables. One of the shacks, a bit grander than the rest, rose to a couple of stories, glass-walled like a lookout tower. People seemed to be working all over the raft, hauling stuff back and forth from tarpaulined heaps of materials. Boats docked with the raft, everything from canoes and rowboats to sleek-looking launches in AxysCorp livery. The raft even had a helipad, marked by a big H splashed crudely in white paint.

The chopper ducked down to an easy landing on the H. Lily saw they were being watched all the way down from a kind of bunker of sandbags set up on the raft, with a slit window from which glass lenses glinted.

Lily stepped out into driving rain. It bounced off the surface of the raft, which was, she saw now, a quilt of ply and plastic tarps, roughened up to give firm footing. The raft bobbed massively, and the vertical lines of the buildings around her dipped and swayed. She pulled her poncho tight around her body, and shook her hood forward to keep the rain off her face; the rainwater tasted salty where it dribbled into her mouth. There was a stink of sewage, and something else, something more profound, corrupt.

She could hear the hissing of the rain on the floor, the calls of the people, even the cries of the gulls. They were sea-coast noises, she thought. Other than that the city was astonishingly quiet. But then Manhattan's traffic, the private cars and buses and flocks of yellow cabs, lay rusting meters beneath her feet.

Nathan Lammockson strode forward, here in person to meet her off the chopper, bulky and purposeful in a waterproof coverall. He was shadowed by an aide who made continual notes on a handheld. Lammockson shook the pilot's hand. "Bobby. Neat landing. Remember me to your mother."

The pilot grinned, pleased and flattered. "Thanks, Mr. Lammockson."

Lammockson embraced Lily. "Good to see you again. Let's get you out of this fucking rain." He led her toward the two-story building.

She glanced back at the pilot. "Look at that guy. You've made his day."

"The old tricks are always the best. I knew Tony Blair. Did I ever tell you that? I learned at the feet of the master."

The tower turned out to be a kind of two-level apartment, with a kitchen and storage area down below, and an open-plan lounge-diner-bedroom up top. It was small and basic, but furnished exquisitely. The white-leather armchairs had evidently been salvaged from Bloomingdale's, for a store tag sat like a trophy on a little coffee table. It must have taken one hell of an operation to retrieve these beasts from under the water without so much as a single mark; salvage was already hugely difficult in a city in which all but the tallest buildings were now entirely submerged.

Lammockson helped her out of her poncho, while he warmed up some coffee. "Welcome to my humble," he said. "Hey, you want something stronger than that? I have some Jack Daniel's that needs finishing." He showed her the bottle.

"No, thanks. Quite a place you have here."

"Costs me an arm and a leg in rent. The Collective claim to be a bunch of bohemians, but they're as sharp as any Lower East Side slum landlord ever was."

"What Collective? I just assumed you owned the whole raft."

He laughed and handed her a coffee. He poured a slug of Jack Daniel's into his own mug. "Hell, no. Cheaper to rent. Especially since, as you know, I've no intention of staying around longer than I need to. I still have some business here, supplying the remaining recovery and evacuation consultancies, but basically I moved out of New York after the hurricane."

For years Nathan had been steadily transferring his wealth into tangible forms, in power and land and other assets. As communications and transport links steadily broke down, the surviving financial institutions were under increasing pressure. Nathan always said he didn't want his wealth to disappear when the power failed in some bank's computer.

"The Greenwich Village Collective built this raft, mostly from automobile tires and oil drums. Planned and assembled it right here after the hurricane blew out, even while the waters rose steadily around them. Only don't call it a 'raft.' A raft is a kind of vessel, right? This raft isn't meant to go anywhere, too damn big to navigate down the city streets. Think of it as an island. People live here; they ain't just crew." He pointed to low buildings. "*That* is a water filtration plant. And *that's* a school. There are already kids in there who don't remember the world before the flood." He waved his mug at the flooded streets, the floating garbage, the cliffs of glassless windows around them. "To them, this is normal. Think of that! Time goes on."

"So how do people live?"

"Scavenging. We're floating above the carcass of the greatest city in the world. It will last for decades."

"I thought the federal government was in control of salvage rights."

Nathan raised his eyebrows. "Look around, Lily. The federal government's in Denver. It doesn't have a lot of control on the ground in a place like this."

"I see the Stars and Stripes flying everywhere."

"Oh, sure. The people here are still Americans. Who's going to be the first to haul down Old Glory? But they've been looking to their own defense and provision for years already. The federal government doesn't even collect taxes anymore, save from the likes of me who can't get under their radar. It's the same in Britain. The rump government in Leeds has no control over the ratty little salvagers who go scuba-diving in the Thames Estuary."

Lily shrugged. "I wouldn't know. I haven't had much news out of Britain since the tsunami, not since I got my sister and her kids out of there—thanks to you."

Lammockson nodded. "Where is Amanda?"

"The AxysCorp compound in Iowa. I thought I'd join her there, and take her down to Project City with me."

"Fair enough. You don't want to bring kids into a place like this, if you can help it. I mean there are hazards enough, the sewage. The other day, over on the east side, we found Freon bubbling up from an underwater mountain of rusting refrigerators, down on some dump. And every day you have the corpses bobbing up to the surface. The kids here earn a few Collective-scrip dollars by poking away the stiffs with boathooks. Five, ten years ago you would never have imagined you would live to see such scenes. And in another five years you won't either, when the fishes have eaten the bodies of the urban dead." He drank his coffee. "So what about your buddies? Piers Michaelmas is in the area, isn't he?"

"I heard a British chopper is bringing him in to Manhattan later today." Much to her surprise, Piers had finally abandoned his British army commission and had "taken the Lammockson shilling," as he put it, coming to work for AxysCorp, though he hadn't yet committed to come to Project City.

"And the scientist guy?"

"Gary's in the States too. He's in Colorado, at the NOAA headquarters there."

He nodded. "Look, I'll have Michaelmas brought here. You can use this apartment for the night. I have my yacht moored over at Coney Island, I'll be fine there. You can conference-call Gary and whoever else you want. My staff will show you how."

"Thanks, Nathan."

"It's not generosity, believe me, but calculated self-interest. I want you guys with me, you hostages, you who have already weathered a worse storm personally than any global-flooding shit is likely to unleash on us.

"The world is changing, Lily. This is no longer an emergency, because it has no finite duration. We are entering a new phase in human history. Earth itself has intervened in human affairs, trying to shake us off as a dog shakes off a flea." He was standing up straighter, apparently unconsciously, and his voice took on the sonorousness he adopted as he addressed his worldwide flock. Lily remembered Piers's observation that Nathan was a man who actively sought a crisis commensurate with the stature he perceived in himself. "Listen. The average sea-level rise is already up somewhere between seventy and eighty meters, depending who you believe, and still accelerating, still following Thandie Jones's exponential curves. And humanity is in flight. I've some satellite imagery I should show you, taken in the infrared. Whole refugee nations marching inland, dogged by thirst, famine, disease and brushfire wars. Before the flood, fully a third of the world's population lived at elevations below a hundred meters. Well, we're approaching that level of rise now, so there are two billion people who must be either dead already or on the move.

"The governments have at last shed their denial about what's happening, but it's too late for them. They are losing control over their own resources and populations, just as they're getting locked into a new kind of geopolitics. Suddenly altitude is a more valuable resource than oil. There are rumors that Russia and China are moving toward war over Tibet, for instance. Governments will soon become irrelevant. Governments will always be at a disadvantage because they have an obligation to deal with the whole population, to support it or suppress and control it, or whatever. Private organizations have much more limited goals—selfish goals if you will, but goals much more achievable by their very finitude. And so it's the corporations, the big consultancies and the multinationals, that will stand when governments crumble and crack."

"And you mean to stand with them, Nathan?"

"You can bet on it." He reached for the Jack Daniel's. "You sure you won't have a slug of this? You're not going anywhere else today. Relax. Take your boots off. The shower is hot. Come on, I'll get you a glass."

47

It was late in the day by the time Piers reached Union Square, and came to the raft. In Nathan's apartment, he stood before the window and gazed out at the view while cradling a glass of Lammockson's whiskey. He looked like he needed leave; his eyes were gray-rimmed, his stubble untidy.

The clouds had broken up. Behind the battered shoulders of Manhattan's surviving buildings the sunset towered into the sky in layers of pink and red, and the light shone in the oil pools on the surface of the waters.

"Quite a sight," Piers said. "Volcano sunsets, they say. All that dust in the air."

"Yes." Lily hadn't seen Piers for six months. She didn't much want to talk about volcanoes.

She tried to get a sense of him. He was the same Piers she had always known, the same mix of strength and fragility, of personal power and awkwardness. But he did seem a little more nervous than usual around her, however. As if there was something he wanted to say to her, but didn't know how.

"Piers, I'll swear you were wearing that same shirt when I last saw you in Newburgh." It was an AxysCorp-durable garment, in fact, already years old. As other suppliers fell away, Nathan Lammockson was clothing the world.

He shrugged. "It's a while since I've been shopping," he said with some of his old dryness. "Slowly but surely we're all turning into scarecrows."

"Which will make no difference to my dress style at all." That was Gary's voice, crisped by the connection.

They turned. Gary had appeared on the screen of the laptop Lily had set up on Nathan's coffee table. The image fritzed a bit.

Piers and Lily walked back from the window. Lily raised her Jack Daniel's. "Hey, Gary, you have a drink there?"

He reached out of the image and retrieved a cup of something steaming hot in a china mug. "Coffee. Only been passed through the perk about four times. And then there were three."

"Yes."

Piers raised his own glass. "To Helen, and John Foreshaw. Absent friends."

They drank together.

Lily said, "I suppose you're wondering why I asked you here today."

"Ha ha," Gary said.

"Well, we know why," Piers said. "You want to persuade Gary here to sign up with Lammockson, and for us both to come to the Andes with you."

"Yep. I happen to think it's the best option we have."

Gary said, "I have some unfinished business which has a bearing on that. We'll get to it." He looked past them. "Quite a sunset you have going on there."

They shifted so he could see out of the window. "New York City's not as pretty as it looks," Piers said. "People living like rats on a vast garbage dump."

"You always were a poet, Piers. So how's Newburgh?"

"An unhappy place too."

The new townships in the Catskills, vast sprawls erected at huge expense, had absorbed a good fraction of New York's fleeing millions. But they were now themselves under threat from the water that forced its way up the Hudson valley, lapping higher every day.

"We go through stages of abandonment," Piers said, and he made a dyke of his upright hands, and moved them back step by step. "We tried to save the city by building levees and river walls and drains and pumps. When that failed we moved the people to new towns up in the hills. And now that's failing in turn. Everybody's exhausted, I think. Worn out by the years of building and salvaging and rebuilding. Nobody wants to move *again* . . . I think there may be a danger of a kind of psychological collapse."

"That would be fatal," Gary said dryly. "Because the sea's continuing to rise whether we like it or not."

"So," Lily asked, "how's the science?"

Gary shrugged. "Thandie's models are being borne out by events. Data points sitting neatly on the curves. We need to nail a few parameters—the exponential rise rate seems to be settling down to a new value. And we've had some surprises. For instance because industry has collapsed globally in the last couple of years, the injection into the air of aerosols—ashes from fires, soot, smut, sulphates, all kinds of garbage—has stopped, suddenly. But a lot of that stuff was actually screening out the sun's heat from the ground. So the air's getting cleaner, but the downside is we've had an even stronger warming pulse.

"As to the future, we have nothing better than outline hypotheses on what's coming next. We just have to keep observing. NOAA managed to persuade the USAF to grant us a couple of ICBMs to launch clouds of smart motes. Microsensors that get blown on the wind, and embedded on the land or in the oceans. Fifty-year lifetimes, powered by motion, communicating and reporting through self-assembling sensor webs. With luck, before we lose the capability to do it, we'll saturate the planet with sensors, and never lose the capacity to monitor what's going on."

"Another grand gesture," Piers said.

Gary smiled, wistful. "It's an irony that just as we're starting to understand the planet properly, our civilization is being screwed. But if it's correct that the trigger for the whole event was anthropogenic activity, that's no coincidence. Thandie thinks it's our fault, for sure. But she also thinks we're losing the capacity ever to prove it."

"Where's Thandie now?" Lily asked.

"Watching the filling-up of one archaic inland sea or another. We do keep in touch."

They spoke of their plans.

Piers said, "Nathan has loaned me to the US government. After my work saving Sellafield I've been asked to go and consult on the nuclear plant at Palo Verde. Palo Verde is a big plant in the desert west of Phoenix—the biggest in the US, and the only American plant not on a river, bay or sea coast. They've stockpiled fuel there. Assuming the sea keeps away there will be power there for a long time to come without dependence on imports from anywhere else. A locus for civilization."

Lily asked, "And when you're done you'll come to Project City?"

"I'm thinking about it." He had a wary look. "I mean, yes, I'll come. But it's complicated."

"Complicated how?"

He hesitated. His expression was closed up, as if he longed to be hiding behind his towels again.

Lily held her breath, sensing how important this moment was to Piers. Gary looked away.

"Look, Lily—this is a whole new start, for all of us. We're going to be building a new life, one way or another, up in the mountains. I can barely conceive how it's going to be, save that it will be *different*. And you and I, well, you have your sister, but—"

"We're both alone."

It seemed to take an enormous amount of courage for him to cover her hand with his. "We may never love each other. We may never have kids. God, it's hard to think of a worse time *to* have kids. But—" He wouldn't meet her eyes.

She thought she understood what had brought this on. As Nathan understood in his own way, the pressure of the flood had become such that everybody was in flux, there was no certainty. Piers's own advice of only three years ago—that they should all move back to Britain—was now proven to be wrong-headed. That was why Nathan was relocating his core functions and staff to an enclave in the Andes. That was why the hostages were having this conversation now.

And that was why Piers had made this strange declaration. To him, refuge wasn't so much a place to be. To Piers, Lily herself was his haven, as perhaps she had been in Barcelona.

To mock Piers now would be fatal, terminal. She had to be honest, straightforward.

"Yes," she said.

Piers looked at her, surprised. "Yes?"

"Yes. I'll be with you."

"That's settled, then," Gary said, sounding pleased. "Good."

Piers blew out his cheeks, his face reddening.

*   *   *

"So what about you, Gary?" Lily asked. "You coming to make up the quorum?"

"I got something else to do first," Gary said. "I mentioned unfinished business. I had a message from Michael Thurley. You remember, the Foreign Office guy?"

Lily frowned. "I've heard nothing from him since Helen was killed."

"Well, he's still working on the case, still trying to track down Grace. To their credit, the British government kept up pressure on the Saudis, while they had a lot of other things on their minds."

Piers nodded. "Good old HMG. So what's happened now?"

"Said has been on the run for two years, since the coup. In the end he exchanged Grace in return for a safe haven, somewhere in the Rockies. And meanwhile Grace has been handed over to Thurley, who's in Denver, where the State Department is operating out of now."

"So Michael Thurley has Grace, at last." Lily shook her head. "I don't believe it. Poor Helen! She never saw her baby again."

"But Thurley doesn't know what to do with her. And she's not 'baby Grace' anymore; she's five years old. So Thurley contacted me. Here's my plan. I need to finish up my commitments here. Then I'll go to Denver to meet Thurley and Grace, and I'll bring Grace to Project City, and meet up with you guys."

Piers grunted. "Gary, don't leave it too late. It may not be possible to make that kind of journey much longer."

Gary nodded seriously. "I hear what you say." He glanced at his watch. "If we're done we ought to shut down, this link is costing Nathan a small fortune. You know, I can't remember the last time we were together in person—all of us survivors."

Lily said, "Once we couldn't get away from each other, now we can't meet."

"We will," Gary said. "Look after yourselves."

"And you look after Grace."

He reached over, his hand disappearing out of sight of the projection system, and his image dissipated.

Lily and Piers were left standing side by side.

"Well," she said. "Suddenly this is awkward."

"Oh, if you're going to be an idiot about it I'm taking a walk."

"Have a drink with me first—"

There was a boom, like an artillery piece firing. Both Lily and Piers ducked reflexively.

They turned to the window, where the sunset was fading. A billowing cloud rose up from some part of the abandoned city, far away. Maybe it was a building falling, Lily thought. Or maybe not. As the noise echoed from the flat concrete walls the pigeons took flight, rising from their nests in windowless rooms that had once been occupied by lawyers and Web designers and public relations representatives, lifting up in a great gathering flock that darkened the towering red sky.

Three

2025–2035
Mean sea-level rise above 2010 datum:
200–800m

48

Lily decided to talk to Amanda about Kristie. She was surprised when Piers insisted on accompanying her.

He was waiting for her at noon, when she emerged from her AxysCorp office just off the Plaza de Armas at the heart of Cusco. Piers kept his AxysCorp durable-wear coverall crisply laundered and ironed, so it had the look of the military uniforms he had discarded five years ago, when he had first come to work for Nathan and they had moved to Project City. He was forty-nine now, as she was, graying, his face gaunt, his posture so erect that his shadow under the blue Peruvian sky was like a sundial. He still had that air of brittleness about him, she thought. Like a dried-up cane ready to snap in the breeze, as Michael Thurley had observed all those years ago. Yet he survived.

"I'm not sure why you're coming," Lily said. "This is a family matter."

He stiffened a bit. "Ah. And there was me thinking we are family now."

In the five years they had lived together she had kept learning that he was extraordinarily easy to hurt. "I don't mean that. But this is sister stuff. A mother and a daughter, an aunt and a niece. Amanda hasn't spoken to Kristie for six months, not since Kristie headed off for the Titicaca commune."

"Or alternatively," Piers said, "not since Amanda moved in with Juan Villegas."

"Well, there you go," she said. "There are two sides to every story, aren't there? All I want is for my sister and my niece to start talking to each other again. And if you go implying that this is all somehow Amanda's fault then you won't be helping."

"But it is Amanda's fault, as you put it. Through her

own vanity she has taken up with this man and driven her daughter away."

"Piers, Kristie's twenty years old. She's entitled to make her own decisions. I mean, what were you doing when you were twenty? Not living with your mother, I'll bet."

He shook his head. "That's irrelevant. These are not normal times—things are not as they were. The old rules don't apply."

"Hm," she said. "Look—just leave Amanda to me. All right?"

But Piers stayed silent, making no such commitment. He smiled at her, and offered her his arm.

They set off to walk to Amanda's—or rather to the house of Juan Villegas, the *criollo* Lily's sister had moved in with. You walked everywhere in Project City, or you rode a bicycle or maybe a horse if you could get hold of one. Even Nathan Lammockson walked. There wasn't the fuel to spare for nonessentials.

They crossed the expanse of the Plaza. This was Cusco, once the capital of the Inca empire, later a Spanish colonial city, and in the twentieth century a tourist haven. Now Cusco was the center of Nathan Lammockson's Project City, his high-altitude enclave. But this sprawling square of paving and floral displays and streetlights remained the heart of the city, just as when it had been the center of a continent-sized empire the Incas had called Tahuantinsuyo, the Four Quarters of the Earth. They passed colonial churches full of vivid imagery in blood and gold, and climbed steep streets crowded with people in AxysCorp work suits, but also with locals, some of them Amerinds in bowler hats and ponchos. One woman pushed a huge barrow-load of yams. When she had first come to work for Nathan here, Lily had soon realized that despite his vast reengineering of the city and its environs—diverting the trans-Andean water pipeline that had once supplied Lima, for instance—Lammockson's vision, or madness, could never overwhelm the essential character of this place, any more than had the ideological drive of the conquering Spaniards, who, unable to demolish the Inca city, had built their own town on its monumental foundations.

She looked up into a sky as rich and blue as porcelain, and she drank in air like wine. She was three kilometers above the old sea level, three kilometers up in the sky, so high that even the flood, which it was said was now approaching two hundred meters above the old datum, made no difference to the character and the quality of this place.

At Villegas's home, Amanda greeted the two of them. "Lil, lovely to see you—and Piers, I wasn't expecting you." She gave them fluttery kisses on both cheeks.

"I hope I'm not intruding," Piers said politely.

"Not at all, you're always welcome, you know that. Do come in—it's turning into quite a party." They followed her in. Amanda looked good, Lily had to admit, her rich black hair tied back in what Lily thought of as an Eva Peron style, and wearing a black dress that was just a bit too low cut for noon. Her face was still beautiful but in a wistful, transient way, for she showed her age, mid-forties now.

She showed them into the living area. It was immense, having once been a hotel lobby. Juan Villegas welcomed his guests, raising a glass. "Join me in a drink."

Lily was surprised to find Nathan Lammockson himself sitting here, a glass of wine cradled in his right hand. He glanced up at Lily and Piers, then turned back to the flatscreen TV he was watching. It showed news from scattered locations across Peru, a broadcast provided by a division of his own AxysCorp.

A butler silently approached Lily and Piers with a tray of glasses and a wine bottle. Lily took a glass, but Piers waved it away. "It's a little early for me."

"Oh, I insist," Villegas said. "It's a very good vintage." Dressed in a crisp suit, his tie perfectly knotted, he stood poised as if for a society photoshoot beside the room's best feature, a two-meter-high stretch of original Inca wall, the stone blocks cut to a laser fineness. This small former hotel had been Villegas's reward for his part in the complex and shady dealings that had led to Nathan essentially buying up a Peruvian city.

"Juan's right about the wine," Nathan said, knocking back a slug of it himself. "Chilean. None of your Peruvian shit. And preflood. We send the subs down for it. If we go to all that trouble the least you can do is drink the bloody plonk."

"Come on," Villegas said, his smile broad, his teeth perfect. "If your boss says it is OK, how can you refuse?"

Piers accepted the glass reluctantly. He and Lily sat down on a small, leather-clad sofa.

Amanda fussed among her guests, bearing trays of nibbles, a paste of spiced meat on crackers. "Of course we should turn the TV off. Forgive me, Nathan." She clicked her fingers at the TV, and it died.

"Good riddance," Nathan said.

Piers took a sip of his wine, barely lowering its meniscus by a millimeter. "I thought you were encouraging everybody to sit at home and watch TV, Nathan."

"Well, so I am. I'm also encouraging them to exercise and eat vegetables. Doesn't mean I need to do it myself." He emptied his glass and held it out to the butler.

Lily knew the theory. Cusco was crowded, and, frankly, there wasn't much to do, nor spare power to do it with. Nathan had deliberately promoted a trend to stay at home, to consume movies and TV shows and games on big high-definition screens, to chat and mail and blog—to have a social life that was electronically mobile but physically static. "Battery humans," he had once called his cooped-up, interconnected citizens.

"And I," Lily said to him, "came to talk to my sister about Kristie. Didn't know you cared so much about our domestic life, Nathan."

He grunted. "You know I'll always care about you Barcelona folk. But you're right." He grinned, self-deprecating. "I'm not too good at girlie chat."

"Nor am I," Lily said ruefully. "So why are you here?"

"I needed to talk to Juan. We may have a problem."

"A diplomatic incident," Villegas said more smoothly.

"The *Prince of Wales* has come steaming into Amazonia," Nathan said. "Followed the old river course in from the Atlantic. Right now it's anchored somewhere over Iquitos. Word is the British are coming ashore and are talking to the Amerindians in the cloud forest."

The *Prince of Wales* was one of Britain's two CVF-class aircraft carriers, hastily fitted out even as the floodwaters rose, nine decks, forty aircraft, sixty-five thousand tonnes of projected military power. On the effective abandonment of Britain after the 2019 tsunami the British government had set up a seat in exile in Labrador, Canada. The Americans had kicked up a fuss about having the old imperial power back on the continent. But in an increasingly threatening world the transferral of much of Britain's military assets across the Atlantic had swung the argument for the Canadians. And with the Americans occupied with their own problems, there was nothing much they could do about it.

"It's a remarkable fact of the new geography," Villegas said smoothly, "that it is now possible for a ship the size of the *Prince* to sail by sea from the old Atlantic coast into the heart of the South American continent, all the way indeed into Peru."

Piers Michaelmas said smoothly, "I'm sure the incursion of the *Prince* is just a probing. As the world changes, the governments have to test new dispositions."

Lammockson grunted. "Well, the British can go test somebody else's disposition. As far as I'm concerned governments are now part of the problem, not the solution. Anyhow I'm going across the mountains later today to get rid of Admiral Nelson. Maybe you should come along, Piers."

"Then you can give me a lift to Titicaca," Lily said impulsively. "I can visit Kristie."

Amanda looked at Lily sharply.

"It's out of the way," Nathan said. "But—ah, the hell with it, why not? We leave at four."

Lily said, "I'll be ready."

The conversation turned back to the British. Villegas said smoothly, "I am sure we will find a reasonable solution . . ."

Lily expected he would. While he lacked Piers's experience and indeed Piers's sharp intelligence, he exuded a terrific air of competence. Amanda's latest man was quite a contrast to Wayne in Dartmoor. Juan Villegas was a widower, childless, aged forty-seven. He was known locally as a *criollo*, once one of the richest of the rich in Lima, with a family said to have descended from the conquistadors. If he had been fortunate in his birth he had made the right decisions in his later life, in supporting Nathan Lammockson as Peru's institutions disintegrated. As such he had been exactly the sort of man Amanda would be attracted to here. And she, still beautiful, with her bright and brittle social skills, and her connection with Lammockson dating back before the founding of Project City, had been a useful acquisition for him too. But Lily had detected some genuine affection between them. Amanda could have done a lot worse.

When the conversation stalled, Lily put down her wine. "I'd better say thank you and run. Sorry, Amanda, I know I said we'd have some time, but I want to try to talk to Benj before I go see Kristie."

Again Amanda's eyes flashed.

Nathan grinned maliciously. "Why? Isn't he talking to his mother either?"

"He's staying out of the feud," Lily said. "Which is why he may be able to help."

"Ah," Piers said with a surprising edge of bitterness. "That's Benjamin Caistor all right. Always trying to help. Always in the damn way."

Amanda flared at that. "He's a good boy, and always has been." She glanced at Villegas, evidently uneasy at this display of complicated family conflict.

He just smiled at her, indulgent.

Amanda followed Lily into the short hallway. Her face was a mask of anger, unrecognizable from the expression she had presented in public. She hissed, "What the hell are you doing? I invited you here to talk over this business with Kristie, at your insistence you'll remember. Now you're just taking over, are you? It's Dartmoor all over again."

Lily spread her hands. "I don't mean it like that. I just want—"

Amanda said furiously, "You want to meddle in my life because you don't have a life of your own. You want to screw around with my relationship with my kids, because you don't have kids of your own. That's all there is to it. This isn't about my needs, Lily. It's about yours. It always is."

Lily was stung. "Amanda, for God's sake—"

"Just go," Amanda said. She practically shoved her sister out of the heavy front door, into the Andean sunshine, and slammed it closed.

49

Benj walked Lily through the P-ville slums to the biofuel field. Shacks slumped around them, built of sheets of corrugated iron or plastic—there was never any wood to spare. A couple of AxysCorp cops accompanied them, wearing company blue like Benj and Lily. Unlike the cops Benj carried no weapon.

The biofuel field was an open rectangle in the middle of the shantytown's spread. Plants unfamiliar to Lily, green leaves on foot-high stalks, grew here in neat rows. Lily knew something about this project. She had a kind of floating role in Nathan's organization, with various assignments; she had done some work on the management and logistics of field experiments like this. But she didn't recognize these new plants.

She could clearly see the scar of the explosion, a blackened circle that spanned much of the field.

Benj walked her around the field boundary. In places the fence was broken down, overrun by the moundlike forms of shacks. AxysCorp cops patrolled, automatic weapons cradled; they looked tense, alert, waiting for trouble, maybe wanting it.

"You can see how they're pushing in, the shacks," Benj said. "Although Nathan has this area clearly marked out as Green Sector. Every few months we shove them out, rebuild the fences, but back they come; we don't have the manpower to keep them out."

"Like fighting the tide," Lily murmured.

"The encroachment into Orange is even worse, you can imagine . . ." Hands on hips, he looked around, at the field, the shacks, the children peering curiously at them from the shadowed interiors. He waved and smiled at the kids; some of them waved back. "Mostly up to now we've been growing stuff you could eat, if it wasn't used for fuel. Sugar cane, corn for ethanol, canola or soy for biodiesel. With those products the problem is mostly theft. We can deal with that, but Nathan got impatient with the losses. So he ordered a switch to this stuff."

"What is it?"

"Jatropha. Comes from Africa, places like Tanzania, Mali. Favors hot and dry conditions. A little gen-enging and it grows fine here."

"And Nathan prefers it because?"

"The oil it produces is poisonous," Benj said. "You can use it for fuel, but you can't eat it. So there's no point in stealing it."

"Right." Lily glanced at the fringing shacks, the round faces of the children. "But if you're a parent trying to feed her kids—"

"You see the problem."

"And now it's come to this," she said.

Benj was twenty-two now. He had grown taller even than Piers Michaelmas. He would never be good-looking, he lacked his mother's delicacy of features, but he looked competent, Lily thought, and kindly. He was quite unrecognizable from the withdrawn, gadget-hungry kid he had been in London, although that kid had always shown a lot of common sense when he needed it, such as at Greenwich, and a lot of compassion. And he had found a role that suited him, working here among the slums of Pizarroville, Project City's unrecognized and unwelcome doppelganger.

For all Nathan's boasting, Project City pretty much conformed to the usual standard of a rich Green Zone surrounded by a shantytown. The slum had grown haphazardly as all slums did, Lily supposed, congealing out of the vast flows of refugees coming up from Lima and the other coastal towns. However there was some order here. Once he had recognized that P-ville wasn't going away, that the flow of refugees up the valleys to Cusco and beyond wasn't going to stop for a long time yet, Nathan Lammockson had done what he always did and imposed his own vision. If this slum must exist on his doorstep, it was going to be a planned slum, designed for some kind of sustainability. It was either that or have it turn into a hinterland of starvation, disease and riot.

So there was now a crude communal water supply, rudimentary welfare and medical care, policing performed by AxysCorp guards and P-ville volunteers. There was even an economy of sorts, as the shantytown served as a pool of cheap labor for Project City. AxysCorp also rented space on shack roofs for solar-panel arrays, and paid for sewage to be used on the farms, a token fee for the slum's only pitiful export. A kind of internal economy was growing up as well, feeding off the drowned carcasses of the lowland towns. People trekked hundreds of kilometers for salvage, even all the way to the higher suburbs of Lima, a megacity become a submerged midden.

And in his boldest intellectual stroke Lammockson had sliced up the slum into sectors, the land area divided into rough thirds. The Silver sector was "residential," the core of the slum. The Orange third was to be left wild. And the Green third was agricultural. The idea was to make the place sustainable. But there was a constant tension between the need for basic living space and room for crops. Lily had observed that people always seemed to find it difficult to fulfill Nathan's visions for them.

It was thought that a *million* people might be living here, drained mostly from the eight million who had once crowded Lima—a number growing all the time, such was the continuing influx and the explosive birth rate, in contrast to the declining population in Project City itself, where Nathan was running a brisk campaign to discourage unnecessary propagation. P-ville was a fecund slum surrounding an aging Utopia. And a slum was still a slum, however the world changed. The children who stared out at Lily were sunken-faced and big-eyed with hunger. These were people who had been poor in the vanished cities and were poor here now, people for whom the flood had meant only that they had swapped a slum in a river valley for one in the mountains.

This city around a city had no name Nathan cared to give it. Those who lived here called it P-ville: Pizarroville.

"You know," Benj said, "there were people here who were glad when Lammockson walked in and bought Cusco. The government had been falling apart, because of the floods, and the droughts when the meltwater from the Andean glaciers was lost, and the border disputes with

Ecuador and Chile. Chaos, conflict, mass migration and no functioning democracy. The people were happy to swap a set of ineffective bosses for an effective one, especially when Nathan started making so many promises about how he'd look after P-ville. There's a widespread feeling of betrayal that it has come to this, Lily, soldiers keeping starving people out of fields of inedible crops."

"So what was it, a petrol bomb?"

He grinned. "An inventive use of our own fuel. Right now I'm trying to stop this incident blowing up into some kind of policing war."

"I'm flying to Titicaca later with Nathan. You want me to talk to him about it?"

"That might help. It's still the case that what Nathan says goes." He looked at her. "You're going up there to talk to Kris, I guess."

"That's the idea."

"Did Mum send you?"

"No." Lily pulled a face. "In fact she accused me of interfering."

"Well, you are."

"We can't afford to fall out, the family. Kris is finding her own life, and that's fine, that's what she must do. But in the end we're all we have, each other."

"But for you, 'we' means more than family," Benj said. "You have your friends—the hostages. You're always drawn to them."

"I see them as family too," she said. "You know that."

"Yes. But I wonder if Kristie feels—I don't know—that the others get in the way."

She frowned, wondering if he was trying to tell her something. "There's a problem with Piers? Is that what you're saying?"

He shook his head. "I'm just not sure what you're going to find inside Kris's head, when—" A screen embedded in his suit sleeve flashed pink; he tapped it and looked at a bit of scrolling text. "I need to go. Trouble in another bit of P-ville—another experimental field."

"You want me to come with you?"

"No. You go catch your flight with Nathan. Give Kris my love. Tell her I agree with you that she should call Mum, which will probably make her even more determined to do the exact opposite. And tell that Quechua chap she's with, Ollantay, that he owes me a glass of chicha."

"I will."

"Got to run." And with that he detailed one of the cops to escort her out of P-ville, and he was gone into the shantytown's winding streets.

50

I n Nathan's plane, Lily was lifted into the sky above Cusco.

She looked down at the old town, with its domes, cupolas and bell towers pushing out of a sea of red-tiled roofs. Beyond the fortified fence that circled the whole city she saw the brown smear of the shantytown, and the belt of agricultural land beyond, with its rough walls, banks of poplar trees, bright yellow fields, and dark scattered dots that were cows and llamas patiently feeding. Further out still, the dome of the spanking new nuclear reactor shone brightly in the sun.

But as she rose higher yet the town nestling in its basin was lost in the detail of a crumpled landscape of peaks and table mountains, draped with low cloudlike puffs of smoke. This was the Andes, a mountain range second only in scale and extent to the Himalayas, its grandeur unconquered by the flood. As they crossed the sierra they flew over a quilt of cultivation, neat fields of barley and maize with walls of tall eucalyptus and prickly-pear cacti. This high ground had first been terraced and farmed by the Incas six hundred years ago, and was still worked today, with crops of potatoes, and with herds of llamas and alpacas loping freely.

But peering east she thought she could see the sea of cloud that covered the new Amazonian ocean, a rainforest now submerged and rotting under a salt sea only a few years old.

Piers Michaelmas sat ahead of Lily. She could see the back of his head, the precisely shaven hair as he sat bolt upright in his seat. He had decided he was coming along with Lily to "sort this out," as he put it, and she hadn't been able to find a way to talk him out of it.

"Amazing what the Incas did up here," Nathan murmured. Sitting next to Lily, he looked over her shoulder. "I mean, their empire lasted only a few decades. But the Incas built fast and big, and left a mark. Just like the Romans."

"And just like you, Nathan?"

"Oh, don't push your luck, Brooke. Yes, like me. Some of us have a gaze that pierces centuries. I think that was a phrase of Churchill's." He gazed out at his domain, and the brilliant sunlight of the high air silhouetted his fleshy face.

The plane landed, businesslike, near the shore of Titicaca, on the outskirts of an ugly, functional town called Puno, once a base for silver mining and now the administrative capital of the altiplano. Lily and Piers clambered down under a sky of even deeper blue.

The lake water was calm today, turquoise and flat, stretching away. The light of the descending sun caught the yellow of the reed beds. On the horizon Lily saw a serration of glaciated peaks, and clouds bubbled up from the lower ground, cumulus clouds created *below* this body of water. It was a sight she always found astonishing, a whole lake seven hundred kilometers long complete with islands and fishing boats, suspended three kilometers up in the sky. But even here refugees had drifted. Even here there was a kind of fringe shantytown around the shore, people squatting in crude huts of reed or overturned boats, living on the fish they caught, or the potatoes that they grew on scrubby patches of cleared ground—and, perhaps, there was a little alpaca rustling going on.

Nathan stretched his legs for five minutes, and then got back aboard his plane with Villegas and his people, and took off for his confrontation with the intrusive British in their aircraft carrier. A few minutes later a company car arrived for Piers and Lily, a dawdling cell-powered buggy.

The last known location of Kristie Caistor was on the Islas de los Uros. The car took them to the place on the shore where they had to catch a boat to get to the islands themselves, another AxysCorp vessel with the planet-cradling corporate logo plastered to its hull.

The "islands" were artificial, just mats of reeds. On the largest was a kind of village of neat-looking huts of reed. Rowing boats were pulled up on the island's soggy littoral.

There was a faint smell of rot, and a stronger stink of the fish that hung on lines in rows, drying in the afternoon sun. AxysCorp's modern plastic-hulled boat looked entirely alien.

Kristie stood on her island home waiting for her aunt. Twenty years old, deeply tanned, she wore a tunic of brightly dyed wool and a black bowler hat. A young man stood beside her, shorter than she was, his skin a deep brown, his eyes black, wearing similarly colorful woolen clothes. Like Benj, Kristie was much changed from her Fulham days. But Fulham was vanished now, a name nobody need ever speak again; this was the reality, this eyrie lake, and this was what Kristie had become.

As the boat drew in Kristie ran forward. "Hi, Lily! Let me help you. It's a bit tricky to cross until you get used to it."

She was right. It was awkward to step from the bobbing boat onto the island, where the reeds gave way under Lily's feet, making the footing uncertain. Lily had a flashback to when she had clambered aboard the *Trieste* with Thandie Jones, all of eight years ago.

Piers followed, impatiently refusing help. Despite his insistence on coming along, he looked deeply unhappy to be here.

Kristie's young man held out a hand. "So you are Aunt Lily. Come, let me show you our home. We don't get many visitors!" His English was good, with the trace accent she remembered.

"Ollantay, isn't it?" Lily said. "We did meet once, in Cusco."

He looked at her, his eyes empty, his smile faint. "*Qosqo*," he said. "We call it Qosqo. Closer to the true Inca pronunciation."

"The town's name," Piers said stiffly, "isn't Qosqo or Cusco but Project City."

Ollantay turned to him, his bland smile unchanging. They shook hands, but Piers's expression was hostile.

They walked to a shack, bundles of reed heaped up for walls with more reeds spread in a rough thatch over a roof of corrugated iron. Birds had evidently been nesting in the thatch, and a small satellite dish sat on the roof.

Inside, the space was surprisingly roomy and clean, with

blankets hanging on the walls, and a kind of woolen carpet spread over the floor. There were boxes and trunks, and nods to modernity like nylon sleeping bags rolled up in one corner. Lily saw traces of Kristie's old identity: the handheld computer on which she'd once done her homework and compiled her scrapbook, her old pink backpack hanging from one wall, even her battered teddy bear stuck in a corner. And Lily smelled cooking, roast meat. She suspected it was guinea pig.

They all sat on the floor, cross-legged. Ollantay prepared a kettle to boil over a camping stove.

"So this is your home," Lily said.

Ollantay said, "Actually it's my parents'. In my culture it's the custom for partners to stay in the home of one set of parents or the other before marriage."

Kris cast an uncertain smile at Lily. "And it's not exactly practical to stay with my mother, is it?"

Piers said, "You should bloody well make it practical. That's why we're here."

"Piers," Lily said gently. She said to Ollantay, "Well, thank you for making us welcome."

Kris said mildly, "He is being a good host actually. The usual rule is that Quechua is the language spoken here." The tongue of the Incas.

Ollantay said, "The true language of Peru, before it was Peru." He poured boiling water into a pot, and set out cups, filling them with a green tea.

Piers snapped, "But you aren't a full Quechua yourself, are you?"

"Oh, everybody's mixed up here nowadays," Kris said with an effort at brightness. "Like everywhere, I suppose. You have the fisher folk who've been here generations. But now we have an influx of lowlanders, coming up from the coast. And there are *barbaros* too."

These were Amerinds from the Amazon forests, some of whom had managed to keep their distance from western culture through the long centuries of colonialism and industrial exploitation. They had tribal names like Mascho Piro and Awa and Korubo. But now the flood was lapping at the foothills of the Andes, and they were driven out at last, forced to ascend through the cloud forest to this unwelcoming plateau. Along with them came other inhabitants of the forest, birds and snakes and monkeys; few of these were permitted to survive by the human inhabitants, and the mountains witnessed the tip of an extinction event.

"Funny lot, they are," Kris said. "The *barbaros*. No idea of money or other languages. They don't even know what country they're in."

Lily nodded. "Nathan sends ethnographers and anthropologists. Even their languages are unknown, in some cases. And there's a danger of infection; colds can be lethal to them."

"It's all a great big flushing out, isn't it?" Kris said. "Forest Amerinds mixing with people from the cities who might have been lawyers or accountants or computer programmers a year or two ago . . ."

Such stabs of insight, Lily thought, made her sound like her brother—and made her seem wasted up here, by this beautiful, lonely lake.

But Piers was still angry. "None of which," he said, jabbing a finger, "makes *him* the genuine article. *Ollantay*. The name you were born with was Jose Jesus de la Mar."

Ollantay shrugged. "That's not the name I choose to die with."

"But what kind of name is Ollantay? Do you know, Kris?"

"Yes, I—"

"Ollantay was the great general who built the Inca empire for Pachacutec. Not exactly a subtle choice, is it, Jose? And is that what you dream of, taking back the land for the Incas?"

Ollantay smiled. Lily thought he was actually enjoying Piers's clumsy attacks. "Well, would we not be better off if the Europeans had never come? Or if the Incas had butchered Pizarro and his holy thugs? Would we now be huddled in shantytowns while you grow oil crops to drive your cars, and the world drowns because of centuries of your industrial excess?"

"Enough," Lily snapped. "For heaven's sake, Piers, what's got into you?"

Piers stood. "I am not the problem. *He* is. This addle-brained boy hero who's caught Kris like a fish on a line."

Now Kris blazed at him. "Don't you speak about us like

that, you dried-up old fool. Who do you think you are, my father?"

Piers looked astonishingly hurt. But before he could reply Lily stood, grabbed his shoulder and dragged him away. "Out."

"I'm not done—"

"Oh yes you are. Look—wait for me outside."

Still he glared at Ollantay. Then, abruptly, something seemed to break. He turned and pushed his way out of the hut.

Lily sat again and blew out her cheeks. "I'm sorry about that."

"You shouldn't have brought him," Kris said, subdued.

"I could hardly stop him."

"You shouldn't have come either." Kris was visibly angry, the blood flushed in her cheeks, under her black hat. "I've had all I can take from my mother about this. Can't you just accept that this is how I've chosen to live my life?"

Well, she had a point. But then Lily looked again at Ollantay, who was regarding her coldly.

She dug a cellphone out of her pocket and gave it to Kristie. "Take this. You've not been answering your old phone."

Kris smiled. "It's at the bottom of the lake."

"Please. You don't need to use it. Just have it. Let Amanda text you . . . It's a terribly hard punishment, Kris, to cut her off altogether. And besides, shit happens, love. There will be times when you need to speak to us, believe me."

Kris hesitated, for long seconds. Then she reached out, took the phone and tucked it inside her pink backpack.

Lily saw Ollantay watching this, and wondered if Kris would be allowed to keep the phone, if it had been he who had thrown the old one into the lake.

Kris said, "Actually I suppose I don't have a choice. If I don't take the phone Piers will probably arrest me and haul me back in plastic cuffs. That man is so controlling." She bunched her fists. "So meddling. I feel as if he's been there all my life. I wish he'd just leave me alone."

"Oh, he can't do that," Ollantay said. "Not ever. He can't help what he does."

Kris looked at him, surprised. "Why do you say that?"

Ollantay smiled. "Because he loves you. Can't you see that?"

Kris laughed. But the laugh died, and her face softened in astonishment.

And Benj saw it too, Lily realized. That was what he had been hinting at, in P-ville. But Lily had never realized it. She felt a deep, cold, savage surprise, and a sense of betrayal that thrust into her belly.

Piers pushed his way back into the hut, his phone in his hand.

Lily said, "My God, Piers, you pick your moments."

Piers looked at her blankly, and at Kris who wouldn't look back at him, and at his phone. "I'm sorry," he said.

"What for?"

"Nathan is sending the plane back. It will take you home. You too, Kris, if—"

"Leave me alone," Kris flared.

Lily was growing alarmed. "Piers. Tell me what's happened."

"It's Benj," Piers said reluctantly. "There was an incident. Another attack on a biofuel crop. The police opened fire—he tried to intervene—"

And Lily understood. She'd managed to save Benj from his conscience at least twice before, in Greenwich and then Dartmoor. But she hadn't been there for him this time.

"Is he dead?" Kris ran up to Piers. *"Is he dead?"*

51

March 2025

Ｆrom Kristie Caistor's scrapbook:
    The webcam focused on the round face of little John Ojola. He was six years old, but he looked much younger, three perhaps, his growth stunted by lack of food, his limbs like twigs, his belly swollen under a row of ribs. He lay cradled in the arms of a Christian Aid worker who had no food to give him, here in this refugee camp in Teso, Uganda. John's huge, luminous eyes, unblinking despite the flies that sipped at his tears, seemed to stare through the camera at the viewer.

John was a sight you could have witnessed any time since the 1960s. His brief life was a cliché of pain. Few visitors to this voluntary-agency Web site lingered for more than a few seconds.

But now John was distracted; his head tipped sideways against the arm of the aid worker. She too was looking away, at something much more remarkable than another hungry child.

This camp had been here for several years—but this year was different. This year there was flooding across a swathe of Africa, from the Sahel to the Horn, from Senegal, Mauritania, Mali and Burkina Faso in the west, to Kenya, Sudan and Ethiopia in the east, some of the continent's poorest countries. There was already little food to spare, and now the floods were making it impossible for the local subsistence farmers to plant for this year's harvest, the cassava, millet and groundnuts. The flooded roads hindered any attempts at relief. And as the rising water contaminated springs and wells, the numbers of cases of diarrhea and malaria were increasing fast.

John had no memory of the last great flooding episode in this part of Africa, back in 2007, caused by a La Nina

event in the Pacific. In 2007 the waters had eventually subsided. These new floodwaters were still rising.

And John stared at the family who had just walked into
the camp. They were dressed smartly, the two children in
robust AxysCorp dungarees, the woman in a loose dress,
though they were all dusty from their long trek. The man
actually wore a business suit, so rapid had the family's flight
been from the drowning city of Kitgum.

They found an empty space in the dirt and sat down.
The woman inspected her bleeding feet, and tended to her
children.

The man in the suit looked up at the aid workers. He
held out his cupped hands. "*S'il vous plaît?* Please?"

52

April 2025

Gary waited for Thandie Jones at the quarantine fence around Cadillac City. He spotted her behind the last gate, having her papers, prints and retinas checked over one more time by Lone Elk's Seminole guards.

He hadn't seen her for five years. She must have been forty now. Tall, lean, wiry, her dark hair scraped short close to her scalp, she wore a tough-looking, much-patched AxysCorp-durable blue coverall. Her only luggage was a small canvas backpack. For a week she had been stuck in Cadillac City's quarantine processing, and she looked as if she had run out of patience.

At last, grudgingly, the Seminole guard unlocked the gate. When she saw Gary waiting for her Thandie grinned and broke into a few running steps. "So this is where you've been rotting away."

"Good to see you too." When they embraced, she smelled of the antiseptic of the quarantine facility, but under that there was a deeper, earthy, coppery scent—a mélange, he thought fancifully, of all the places she had been, across Eurasia and Africa and Australia, North and South America, a witness to a flooding world.

He let her go, and they turned and walked into the tent city, heading for Gary's home.

"So," he said. "Welcome to Cadillac City."

"Yeah, some welcome."

Gary shrugged. "Sorry about that. Lone Elk's rules."

"Lone Elk? Oh, the local big guy. We live in a world owned by strong men now, don't we?"

"There are a lot worse than Lone Elk, from what I hear."

"This really is a city."

"Yep. Although the famous Cadillac Ranch is actually a couple of kilometers thataway"—he pointed east—"all those cars stuck in the ground ... Administratively we're a suburb of Amarillo."

Gary led her through the heart of the tent city, along a street of beaten earth between canvas walls. She glanced around, her gaze sharp, analytical.

It was the late afternoon of a spring day here on the Panhandle, and the landscape beyond the fence was flat and empty as it always had been, broken only by scattered pumpjacks and farmhouses, and the lights of more distant towns. But within the confines of the fence, with its barbed wire and watchtowers and patrolling Seminole guards, the weathered tents crowded in, with the big marquees of the communal facilities looming over the rest. At one gate a convoy of trucks had drawn up, laden with lumber mined from the drowned lowland plains. Wood was always in desperately short supply.

It was after the end of the school day, but it wasn't early enough for most adults to have made it back from work. Inside the tents electric lamps were glowing, and there were cooking smells, rice and beans and soya, the tinny voices of radios and TV sets. Voices murmured, in Spanish and English. There were plenty of Texans, but with a sampling from all across the drowned eastern US, from the southern twang of Alabama and Georgia and Florida, to even a few clipped Bostonians and earthy New Yorkers.

Today Gary saw all this through Thandie's eyes, and, as he often did in her presence, he felt oddly defensive. He knew her basic opinion of him, that he should be out in the world doing what she had been doing—science—rather than hide away in a place like this.

He found himself saying, "Lone Elk runs things by the book. He's kept this place functioning for years now, keeping us all alive."

"Paradise on Earth," Thandie said dryly.

"No," he replied sharply. "We've had our problems ..."

In the course of the great dislocation that had affected the eastern US, the aid money released by the federal government was generally siphoned away by consultancies and multinationals to advance grand Green Zone projects, designed to create industry and wealth that would someday, in theory, trickle down to the rest of society. But in the interim, unless you were super-wealthy, the choices were generally FEMA-villes, where at least you got a roof over your head and maybe basic amenities such as sewage, or a shantytown around some Green Zone where you didn't even get that. Such places didn't legally exist at all, being "temporary" in nature, even though some of them had persisted for years.

Lone Elk had had the ability, wealth and connections to reverse some of that policy, in this one place. He diverted money and resources into Cadillac City, and he was using the skills of the refugees themselves to build a place you could survive in—and indeed the act of rebuilding itself was a kind of therapy.

"Believe me, we appreciate Lone Elk for fighting in our corner."

"Well, he's right about the quarantine," Thandie said. "I've seen the plagues myself. You've got cholera and typhoid all over, and more exotic stuff: SARS, West Nile virus, Lyme disease, Ebola, even bubonic plague—and new diseases nobody has a name for, jumping across species boundaries. At least here in the US there is still an infrastructure capable of churning out the antibiotics and the trained staff to handle them. The great fear is of a major pandemic, an influenza outbreak, say. We'd fall like blades of grass."

"Some say it's bioterrorism."

She shrugged. "There might be some of that. I don't believe it's significant. It's surely a product of the huge mixing-up of the world because of the flood. On a fundamental level the biosphere is suffering, whole ecosystems collapsing. The equilibrium of the microbial world itself has been disrupted."

They stopped by Gary's tent. It was a boxy thing fixed to the ground by guy ropes and pitons that hadn't been moved for years. A lamp burned inside. "Home sweet home," he said. He felt he needed to prepare her. "Listen, Thandie. Lone Elk's coming here to meet you in an hour. He wants to hear your report in private before he decides how to respond to it in a more public forum."

"Fair enough." She patted her shoulder strap. "I had time to work on the material in the quarantine tank."

"I don't know him as well as Michael does, actually. It

was through Michael you were invited here. Oh, we get briefings on the flood's progress and the global situation from the government agencies in Denver, but the government has its own agenda, which is generally to persuade people to sit tight unless it's absolutely imperative. Everybody knows it's best to take what the government says with a pinch of salt."

"And Lone Elk thinks a storm might be coming."

"That's the judgment he needs to make."

"Look, I'm ready for him. Don't fret, it's going to be fine. Though there won't be too many laughs. So you going to let me in? I'm longing to meet Grace."

At the center of the tent, the roof was high enough for them to stand up straight. A single electric lamp augmented the daylight glow through the walls—Cadillac City had a mains supply—and there was a smell of coffee. The drink itself was foul, but Michael liked to keep a pot heating to drive out any worse scents.

Michael Thurley sat on his favored fold-up seat, watching a government news broadcast on a handheld screen. Grace was curled up on a couple of spread-out sleeping bags, drinking soda from a tin mug, and working through a homework assignment on a handheld of her own. They both got up when Thandie came into the tent. Gary saw how Thandie's eyes widened as Grace stood up. Ten years old, she was as tall as any of the adults, tall as her mother had been.

Clean-shaven, Michael wore dark trousers, leather shoes, and a white shirt open at the neck with a loosened tie. "Thandie Jones." He shook her hand. "It's good to meet you in person at last."

"You got that right."

Gary asked, "By the way, how's Elena?"

"Still a moody Russian. Last time I saw her was at Gujarat."

Michael asked, "Gujarat?"

"Where the waters of the Bay of Bengal, having invaded Bangladesh and northern India, broke through to the Arabian Sea. Leaving India an island, you see, yet another landmark hydrological event. I can't wait to get back to her."

"I'm sure. Would you like a drink? We have water, recycled and filtered, and what passes for coffee. Or maybe you'd like some of Grace's cola, manufactured right here in the city."

"Cadillac City Cola." Thandie grinned at Grace, trying to include her, but Grace looked away. "I tried some of that in the tank. Did you know they're still manufacturing Coke and Pepsi and stuff in Denver? God bless America. Thanks, I'll stick to water."

"Well, our recycled urine does have more fizz than that stuff. Look, let me take your pack, sit down . . ."

While he fussed, Thandie approached Grace, who submitted to a pat on the shoulder. "Wow, you're grown."

"So you knew my mom." Grace's accent was complicated, basically American, with a strong flavoring of the Texan she'd picked up in the camp, but laced with Michael's British correctness. And underlying it all was a more lilting intonation, a relic of her time with the Saudis.

"I only met her online. I'm very sorry about what happened."

"I don't remember her." Grace looked at Gary. "I've got my assignment to do. Can I go to Karen's?"

Michael frowned, bringing a mug of water for Thandie. "That shows poor manners. Do you have to run out straightaway?"

Thandie smiled and backed out of Grace's way. "You go, girl. We're going to be talking business here anyway. Get your homework done."

"Thanks," Grace said. She clutched her handheld to her chest and hurried out, pulling the flap door closed behind her.

The adults sat on lightweight fold-out seats. Thandie sipped her water, and Gary accepted a cup of coffee from Michael. Thandie glanced around the tent, at the Seminole rug that lay over the thick groundsheet, the plastic trunks and cupboards, the bedding rolls, the small kitchen area with their electric stove and grill, and the little crucifix that Michael always hung from the central pole, a symbol of his tentatively rediscovered Catholicism.

"So, welcome to our yurt," Michael said in his dry English way, watching her.

"I've seen a lot worse than this."

"I bet you have. Of course it helps that we haven't had to move for so many years. One puts down roots."

Thandie grinned. "And here you are in your shirt and tie, going off to work every day, it looks like."

"Lone Elk likes a bit of formality. He is running a city here. Though he doesn't insist on jackets, thankfully. I've worked my way up into quite a senior position, in what amounts to a mayor's office."

"Senior?"

He smiled. "Only Seminole above me. That counts for senior around here."

"And I'm a lowly technician," Gary said. "Mostly I work on the lumber collections, and the recycling programs. But I get to use my skills. I run a weather service for the city, of a sort."

Thandie watched him. Gary felt faintly embarrassed. Maybe he had come across as too earnest.

Thandie sipped her water. "Anyhow I'm glad I got to meet Grace."

Michael said, "Of course it's been difficult for her. Until the age of five she was brought up by her father's family, or a branch of it. An extremely wealthy family too. She had nannies, maids. They spoiled her to death. And then Gary and I took her in. I suppose we are something of an odd couple."

"I'll say," Thandie said. "But I'm impressed."

"Impressed?"

She looked at Gary. "You know, Boyle, before I came I never got why you stayed here. There's so much science to be done out there. But now I see it. You stayed for Grace."

Gary nodded, his feelings of defensiveness fading. "I was there at the moment she was born, in that cellar. There's nowhere else I want to be but with her. Nothing else I want to do but see her grow up."

"You made the right choice, pal."

A gruff throat was cleared outside. In this tent city it was a signal that had come to serve in place of a door knocker.

Gary stood up. "We got company."

53

Lone Elk arrived alone, though Gary suspected he would have a guard or two in the gathering shadows outside. Thandie stood to shake his hand.

The Seminole was shorter than you might expect, Gary supposed. He wore a straightforward shirt and trousers of tough artificial fabric. He was aged about sixty, his skin dark but not weathered, his black hair cut short and peppered with gray. He looked more like a Hispanic businessman than a tribal leader.

Michael served fresh coffee for them all. Lone Elk sipped his, probably out of politeness; the elders were used to better stuff than this. He and Thandie made small talk for a while. Thandie spoke of her background, sketched her career before the flooding began, and outlined what she had done since, her global eyewitness sampling. They were sizing each other up, Gary saw.

"Forgive me for prevaricating," Lone Elk said eventually. "Actually it's not my way. Generally I like to cut the bull and get to the point." His accent was like a lilting Bostonian.

"A habit of a busy man."

"But I know I'm going to have to listen carefully to what you have to tell me. I spent a small fortune in government scrip bringing you here because Gary tells me you're just about the best in your field. We live in a world of lies, of denial, of willful ignorance. My problem is that I have to judge what you tell me not only on the content of your words, but on *you*."

"Take me as you find me," Thandie said evenly, and Gary sensed she was close to taking offense.

"Oh, I will." Lone Elk sat back. "But what do you make of me, I wonder? You've seen the world. Did you expect to come home to America, and find your friend Gary in a camp run by an Indian?"

Gary had been surprised that Lone Elk and his people preferred to use that term.

Thandie shrugged. "Why shouldn't I expect it? Everything is so mixed up now."

"My people lived in the east, in Florida. We were among the first in North America to be confronted by the European settlers. It was not a happy experience, as you can imagine. We were hunted to near extinction in the Everglades. But we survived the dispossession, the plagues, the attempted genocides, the generations of discrimination.

"Then at the end of the twentieth century a miracle happened. Through gambling, we became wealthy—hugely wealthy. The money gave us power. We bought back, for instance, our sacred grounds which had been earmarked for ruinous exploitation by one concern or another, and we began a language reclamation project. It was the same for other tribes across the country. There was a new sort of tension between us and the whites, and between ourselves, our different nations. But we were heading, I believe, for a new equilibrium—a way of living in a new age."

"And then the flooding came," Thandie said.

"Then the flooding came. Again, we were among the first impacted, the first to have to move, the first to lose our lives. But money is still useful, isn't it? God gave me wisdom, I believe, and money gave me the power to buy what needed to be bought. Land. Tents. Portaloos." He grinned. "I used to mount music festivals. I know how to host thousands of people in a field. This is no different. A Woodstock of the flood.

"And so here we are, surviving where others have lost everything or drowned, because they were not decisive enough. And now I must be decisive again."

"Yes."

"Many of my family believe that this too, the flood, is the fault of the whites—if they had stayed at home, none of it would have happened. Do you believe this is true, that human agencies are to blame?"

Thandie shrugged. "There's still no concrete proof. Things are changing too quickly; there are too few of us, too many observations to make. I have the feeling we'll never know for sure. Anyhow, does it matter? What we have to deal with are the symptoms of this global sickness, whether we understand the causes or not."

"Quite so." Lone Elk steepled his fingers. "I am privy to certain confidential federal government briefings. I'm told the average sea-level rise is now around two hundred meters."

"That's the ball park."

"Then what is becoming of the world, Thandie Jones? Tell me what you've seen."

She nodded. She unfolded a screen.

All the world's maps had changed.

In South America, the flooding had taken big chunks out of the continent's familiar cone shape. The Amazon basin had been turned into an inland sea that lapped against the foothills of the Andes. In the north, lowland Venezuela and Colombia had vanished, and in the south another mighty sea was pushing in from the River Plate estuary, drowning Uruguay, Paraguay and western Argentina, and threatening to separate the Andean spine from the Brazilian plateau.

As west and north Africa flooded there was a flight to the high grounds of the south. Pretoria was emerging as a major regional player.

Australia was lost, all save high ground in the west of the continent and a fringe of mountains.

In Europe, vast populations continued to be driven from the northern plain, and were crowding into the high ground to the south and north, in Spain, the Mediterranean countries, the Alps, Scandinavia. The European Union was still functioning, just, out of a new base in Madrid, trying to cope with an unending crisis of refugee flow, shortages of food and land and water, disease.

"But Eurasia is the real cockpit," Thandie said. "We don't have good data on the ground; our best information comes from the remaining satellites. We know European Russia is gone, flooded from the Baltics deep into Siberia, save only for the Urals. And so there's been a vast flow of people east and south, into Kazakhstan and Mongolia. And meanwhile lowland China is flooded east of a line from Beijing through Kaifeng to Changsha, and refugees have been driven up from that direction. The Russians and

Chinese are facing each other in Mongolia. I don't think anybody knows what's going on there—even the respective governments, where they're functioning.

"Overall, the numbers speak for themselves. To date we've only lost something like twenty percent of the old dry land area, but that was home to around half the world's population."

Lone Elk nodded. "And North America?"

She brought up more maps. "In the west the coastal lands have been lost, and the sea has encroached through San Francisco Bay into the Sacramento Valley. But it's in the east the real damage has been done. Look at the map. You can see we've lost a swathe of land extending in from the Gulf and Atlantic coasts, covering Louisiana, Arkansas as far north as Little Rock, Mississippi, Alabama, Georgia as far north as Atlanta. Florida is gone, of course."

"I know about Florida."

"The Carolinas are gone as far west as a line through Charlotte. Of course the east coast is entirely underwater, Virginia, Washington, DC, Baltimore, Philadelphia, New York, all lost. The sea is now pushing up the Mississippi Basin beyond Saint Louis; pretty soon Chicago will be threatened from the south and from the north, by the rise of the Great Lakes, and a new seaway will cut the country in two."

Even so, America was surviving, comparatively. Much of the lost eastern lowland had been the nation's most populous, the most fertile terrain. But in the west there was plenty of room. On the Great Plains—the Dakotas, Montana, Wyoming—you had an area greater than France, Germany and the Low Countries combined, holding fewer than three million people before the refugees came. So the government was trying to look beyond the immediate imperatives and was devising a massive project of construction and relocation. The government had recalled advisers from the State Department's Office of Reconstruction and Stabilization, which over a couple of decades had acquired experience of rebuilding countries that had failed, through natural disaster or war. Now that expertise was being brought home, and resources recruited from what was left of the public and private sectors. The next few years would see whole new cities springing up on the Plains, with the agricultural and industrial hinterland to support them.

"It's a fantastic project," Thandie said. "Like a crash terraforming program."

"And," Michael said, "an awful lot of money will be filling an awful lot of corporate pockets."

"Well, yeah. But at least it's visionary."

Lone Elk nodded. "But in the short term, what of Texas? What of us?"

Thandie traced a contour on the map. "Right now the threat is becoming critical on a line running south down through Dallas-Fort Worth, Waco, Temple and Austin to San Antonio. Pretty soon all those people are going to have to move. Two million in San Antonio, for instance, best part of a million in Austin. There are six million in the Dallas-Fort Worth urban area, the fourth largest metropolitan area in the US—"

"All those people. And all of them coming this way."

"You've got to bet on it."

Lone Elk smiled. "I never gamble, actually. I just take the profits. I've heard the government is already talking of sequestering land in the Panhandle to cope with the anticipated refugees. Bringing in the army."

"So I've heard too."

"Well, the feds will dump half of Dallas onto us. They'll turn this place into a slum. And then we'll be overwhelmed by more fleeing hordes."

"That's what you need to plan for," Thandie said evenly.

Lone Elk nodded. "Then it's clear. We've done well here. But now we must move."

Gary looked at him. "Move? The whole city?"

"This place is too close to the rising human tide. We must retreat up the beach, a little further."

As Lone Elk discussed details with Thandie, Gary thought it over.

Moving the city sounded impossible. But it also sounded a better option than sitting here and waiting for the millions from Dallas to come climbing up out of the canyons. But that, of course, was the selfish thought of a man who had a full belly and water and a place to sleep looking down on those who had not.

Gary considered his own position. He had to get Grace and Michael out of here before the overspill arrived. That was the bottom line. Joining Lone Elk's unlikely migration sounded a better bet than going it alone, becoming just three more ragged refugees. But if that didn't come off, maybe they'd have to make their own way to higher ground, west to the Rockies. Or maybe they should even take up Lily Brooke's long-standing invitation to go down to the Andes . . .

Michael was watching him, grave, going through his own inner calculations.

Gary came back to the conversation.

"You've seen horrors," Lone Elk was saying to Thandie. "Populations in flight. Whole ecosystems destroyed. But you must have seen some wonders too."

"Oh, yeah. The whole world's being transformed, turned into something new. I've sailed ships over the North American transgression—I mean, over the flooded eastern states. The world's reverting into something like it was in the Cretaceous, before the dinosaur-killer asteroid fell, a world of shallow seas. But the new shallow-water ecosystems may not have time to bed in before they are drowned in turn. We don't know what comes next."

"*Why* don't you know? How high can this water rise? The government has no projections, or none it will release."

"The surviving governments have no credible models that I've seen. Even in Denver they don't want to face the worst possibilities—to look into a future that they won't be able to manage. It's become a matter of ideology, kind of like the old battles about climate change. Government advisers are flood deniers, because that's what the politicians want to hear, even while the waters lap around their feet. And denial makes for bad science."

"So what is the good science?"

"The data is patchy," Thandie said. "It always is. Masked by local surges, hot spots, other effects. Take what I say with qualification—"

"I'm no fool, Ms. Jones," said Lone Elk evenly. "Tell me what you believe."

"The sea-level rise is still accelerating," she said bluntly. "We seem to have settled into a long-term growth paradigm. For the last five years the rise has stuck pretty closely to an exponential increase at a rate of fourteen percent per annum. But of course the growth is compound."

He grimaced. "I ran casinos. Compound interest I understand. That means a doubling of the rise every five years. And if this goes on—"

"You can do the math."

He shook his heavy head and steepled his fingers. He didn't look as shocked as Gary might have expected. "Then that is what I must plan for."

"I'd say so. I have a more detailed report for you on my laptop."

He waved that away. "Later. Do you have children, Dr. Jones?"

"No."

"If you did, this would be harder for you, to witness the suffering of the world."

"I imagine it would. But I hope I'd do my job even so."

"Yes. But I do have children. And my job is different. My duty . . ."

They talked on.

The night deepened, and the lantern's glow filled the tent. Michael made more coffee. After an hour Gary started to wonder about food.

And after a couple of hours more Grace called Gary on his cell to say she was staying with her friend Karen for the night.

54

June 2029

From Kristie Caistor's scrapbook:

Sister Mary Assumpta's webcam, shakily held up in the air, gave a vivid impression of the crowds swarming around the monumental ruins of the palaces of the Roman emperors, here on the Palatine Hill. And occasionally, as the camera waved wildly, you could glimpse the rest of Rome, heavily flooded, the ancient city once more reduced to the seven hills from which it had originally sprung.

Italian police, stationed throughout the Palatino, watched nervously. Long experience had taught them that the devout were not necessarily well-behaved, and a surge, or worse a stampede, could be catastrophic. And on days like this there was always the possibility of terrorism.

The noise of the helicopter broke suddenly over the crowd.

Sister Mary's camera, searching, returned a blurred image of ruins and blue Italian sky. And then she found the chopper, done out in a combination of Italian police colors and papal yellow.

The helicopter lowered a cage to the Flavian palace. And when the cage rose up again, there was the Holy Father ascending into the air, surrounded by cardinals and security men in black suits, his robes dazzling white, his hand raised in blessing. A great murmur rose up from the crowd, more a groan than a cry, and the webcam's microphone picked up Sister Mary herself muttering prayers in rapid-fire Irish.

The rumor was that the Pope would now return to his homeland, America; he would continue to address his global flock through modern communications. But everybody there on the Palatino knew that this was the day the popes had finally abandoned Rome, with the Vatican already lost, an end to two millennia of turbulent history.

The chopper ascended into the sky and turned away, heading west toward the rising sea where an American aircraft carrier waited to collect the Holy Father. The police came to move through the crowd, trying to begin the process of dispersal.

Somebody cried, in a harsh Australian accent, "Next stop Mecca!"

55

A manda sent a car to bring Lily across Cusco to her home. Lily waited for it with some anxiety.

The car slid up to Lily's door. It was one of Nathan Lammockson's hydrogen-powered limousines, new, sleek, sweet-smelling inside. It pulled away silently.

Eleven years since they had come to Project City, six years after Benj's death, Lily rarely saw her sister in person. The tension between Amanda and Piers had become unbearable after Benj's shooting. And Piers's peculiar obsession with Kristie, obvious to Lily as soon as Ollantay had pointed it out all those years ago, hadn't gone away, and didn't help either.

But now Kristie had got in touch with her mother and her aunt, and asked them both to come down to Chosica, where Ollantay, Lily learned to her surprise, was working on Lammockson's Ark Three project. Lily didn't feel she could disregard such a request. She didn't imagine Amanda could ignore it either. So she put in a call to Amanda, suggesting they should talk it over. She was faintly surprised when Amanda agreed to meet her.

At least the car was comfortable. In a way it represented the core of Lammockson's vision for Project City, Lily thought, a vision that was at last being realized a decade after the city's establishment. The two nuclear stations and the wind and solar farms split water into oxygen and hydrogen that fueled the city's farm vehicles and a handful of private cars, their tanks themselves effectively serving as a mobile energy store. The car was an emblem of a new way of living, with systems that were distributed and adaptable, resilient, long-lasting, clean, no obsolescence or waste. That was the dream, anyhow.

And it was in this inward-looking, static, high-tech Utopia that Amanda lived all the time. She rarely ventured out of her house, and when she did have to attend some function or other she would rush straight into one of Villegas's limousines, barely breathing the musty, sewage-laden, carbon-dioxide rich air of the city. She certainly never saw the hinterland around Project City, the shantytowns like P-ville, or the suffering in the chaotic regions outside Nathan's remit altogether.

When she reached Villegas's miniature palace, Lily felt oddly reluctant to get out of the car.

The butler met her at the door and led her into the old hotel. The air-conditioning unit had been looted from the American embassy in Lima, and its chill was ferocious but welcome. Lily stripped off her hat and reflective poncho, and rubbed the sun cream off her face at a mirror by the door, trying to get the oily stuff out of the deepening lines on her fifty-five-year-old forehead.

The butler waited. Jorge had been in Amanda's service for years now. He was studying for a doctorate in biotechnology at Nathan's technical college, and was somewhat overqualified to be standing around taking coats. But if you were rich in Project City you could take your pick of the swarm of refugees who continued to struggle up from the valleys; there were bright, beautiful people who did far worse than this for a place on the higher ground.

Jorge showed her through to the big living room, the old hotel lobby with its wall of Inca stone, where Amanda sat on a leather sofa. She wore a loose trouser suit, her legs curled under her, a glass in her hand. The big plasma screen showed a soap opera, part of the unending streams of sport and computer-scripted dramas pumped out by Project City's broadcasting service, dubbed into English, Spanish or Quechua as you preferred. It was one of Nathan's many strategies to anesthetize his huddled population. Amanda didn't get up. She raised her glass; it was half full. "Sit. Have a drink. Jorge will get you what you want. This potato vodka isn't half bad, once you build up some immunity." That, at least, was a flash of the old Amanda.

"Give me what's she's having, please."

Jorge bowed and withdrew.

Lily sat gingerly on the edge of one of the room's sprawling sofas.

Amanda watched her soap opera. She was over fifty now, still beautiful, Lily thought, still slim, still possessing that unconscious flexibility of pose that men always found so attractive. But the bitterness that had been planted in her when Benj had been killed in P-ville was apparent in a tightness around her eyes, a smallness in the way she held her mouth.

This room of shining leather and polished floorboards was adorned with artifacts looted from the submerged cities. Juan Villegas, born a Catholic, had acquired a fine collection of church plate, stored in cabinets of bulletproof glass, a row of chalices lined up like sports trophies. Rumor had it that he had an entire door detached from Lima's cathedral.

Jorge returned with Lily's drink, and withdrew. Lily sipped it; it was very strong.

"So," Lily said, uncertain. "Where's Juan today?"

Amanda waved a hand, and the soap volume reduced. "Out with the Holy Guards. Should be back soon." She looked at Lily. "You don't change, do you? A bit more leathery."

"Thanks."

"You're pale, though."

"That's the sunscreen and the hats. It's *hot* out there, Amanda."

"Which is why I never go out. Still working on the gen-enged crops, are you?"

"That and Nathan's agricultural program in general . . ."

She spoke about Nathan's current schemes, as his scientists labored to resolve the pressure on the available agricultural land. Nathan's new cultivars of maize, corn and rice were resistant to drought, and more nutritious than the old forms. The most radical technique was to turn single-season crops into perennials: varieties of wheat and barley and maize that didn't need sowing. That would save hugely on labor, and permanent root systems would dig deeper and seek out nutrients and fresh water, ever more scarce on the surface. Argentina and Mexico had always been big on transgenic crops before the flooding, and recruiting genetic engineers for this sort of work hadn't been hard.

There was also a longer-term program of adaptation. As the sea level rose, it was as if the farmland was on a sinking elevator. For now the agriculturalists were cultivating crops suitable for montane conditions. But in the future, as ecological zones migrated upward, they might have to shift to a different suite of crops suitable for lower altitudes. All this was strange and scary to think about, but Nathan insisted they prepare even so.

Lily tried to tell Amanda how good it was to be out among green growing things—even if it was a strangely quiet countryside. There were few farm animals now; chickens and pigs were kept to consume vegetable waste, thus maximizing land use efficiency, but cattle, sheep and even the native llamas and alpacas were seen as too expensive. It was like this all over the world, it seemed. It was extraordinary that an extinction event was going on even among domesticated farm animals.

Amanda listened, but she clearly wasn't interested, and let her attention drift back to the flickering images of the soap actors.

Lily shut up, and sipped a bit of the vodka. Then she said, "So—Kristie."

Amanda raised her eyebrows. "She wants something. That's the only reason she ever gets in touch with me. Otherwise I have to rely on reports by the AxysCorp cops just to find out what she's up to. Juan has access to her crimint file. Surprising how much you can find out about people that way."

"Come on," Lily said. "Kristie's not a criminal."

"Maybe not, but last month that Quechua boy of hers was a millimeter away from a conviction for disrupting potato shipments from the Titicaca area. What an idiot he is. I had to pull strings with Juan to get him transferred to Chosica and the Ark project. Otherwise he'd have been exiled."

Exiled: banished from all the Andean communities under Nathan's direct or indirect control, and so cast into an outer darkness of chaos, hunger, flight and disease.

"And of course he took Kristie with him. Even if he'd been sent away she would have had to go with him. Oh, she'd have had no choice. Juan would have seen to it. He's very much a supporter of the New Covenant, you know.

It's all black and white with him now. If Ollantay hadn't shown a residual bit of common sense and backed off, I couldn't have persuaded Juan to spare him, or Kristie. Why should he?" She took another strong slug of her vodka, and put the glass on the arm of her chair. From nowhere Jorge appeared with a fresh, full glass, which he smoothly substituted; dew gathered on the chilled crystal.

"But this time it's different," Lily said. "I mean, she's contacted me as well as you. Maybe she's got some other kind of news. Or maybe she just wants to see us—"

"You're dreaming."

"Let's go together," Lily said impulsively. "I have to go down to the coast tomorrow. They're mounting another dive into Lima. Sanjay McDonald is supposed to be there, running the science for Nathan."

"Sanjay who?"

"Climate scientist. He was in London. An associate of Thandie Jones, who knew Gary. As far as I know Gary is still with Grace, somewhere in the US. With any luck Sanjay will have some news about them."

Once more Amanda's eyes drifted back to the murmuring soap. As the years had passed she had grown less and less interested in Lily's connections with the Barcelona hostages. But conversely, as her own family had disintegrated around her, Lily's bonds to those who had shared her captivity seemed to grow stronger.

"Never mind that," Lily said. "When I get back let's go see Kristie together, you and me."

"You and me and Michaelmas, you mean."

Lily said tightly, "Piers is my partner. He cares about us."

"He's a locked-in obsessive who 'cares' about Kristie."

"That's just foolishness. A weakness. Something Piers deals with." That was true enough; it was a trait in himself Piers despised.

Lily had long got over her own odd, surprising stab of resentment at his feelings for Kristie. She knew Piers had never loved her, and never would; in fact she had come to believe that despite a divorce and a couple of failed relationships he hadn't truly loved anybody before. Somehow, for some reason, presumably as a product of the last few impossible years, he had become fixated on Kristie, a girl he barely knew. But Piers was in his mid-fifties now, and Kristie only twenty-six. Such love of the old for the young was a kind of mourning.

Well, if I can live with it, Lily thought, so can you, Amanda.

But she knew that Amanda's problem with Piers was not only his peculiar, longing fixation with Kristie. No, Amanda's problem was that she had come to blame him for the shooting of Benj, caught in the cross fire that day in Pizarroville. Piers had been nominally responsible for the security operation. It was a responsibility he fully accepted, though in any moral sense it wasn't his fault. None of that helped with Amanda.

"Look, Piers isn't a bad man. He's shouldering as much responsibility as anybody else here. We all have weaknesses. We all make mistakes."

Amanda scrunched up her face and turned away. "Juan doesn't make mistakes. Or he doesn't think he does. Right now he's out with the Holy Guards, patrolling the eastern foothills for refugees."

As the sea-level rise had continued, now approaching an astounding four hundred meters, the flow of refugees was relentless. So Nathan had created the Holy Guard, tough, heavily armed units that went out into the chaos, doing whatever it took to deflect the refugee swarms. Many of the Guard were recruited from Pizarroville—the desperate poor fighting to keep what they had.

Lily said, "It's a tough job. I couldn't do it."

"That's the trouble," Amanda said. "Juan can't either—or he couldn't, until he fell in with the New Covenanters. He's a man of conscience, believe it or not. He needs to find a way to justify what he's doing."

Lily knew the theory. If God had broken the Covenant He made with Noah after the Biblical flood—Genesis 9:11: "Neither will there any more be a flood to destroy the Earth"—it could only be because humans had broken it first. But was God punishing *all* mankind? Surely those who had been wise enough to move to higher ground early were a kind of elect, raised out of the herd of sinners, and had a duty to preserve themselves for a new post-flood age to come. And conversely those who had not been smart enough to prepare showed their weakness as well as their sinfulness. So the high-altitude elect therefore had a holy duty to stay alive and hold onto their ground.

"They've had meetings about it here," Amanda said, fiddling with a lock of hair. "Business types like Juan, but also soldiers and doctors and priests. I have to organize drinks and nibbles while they talk about the best way to machine-gun refugees, and the moral justification for the culling."

" 'Culling'?"

"We had a doctor here who talked about 'apoptosis,' which is a phenomenon of the body, unhealthy cells committing suicide to make room for the healthy. It's got pretty elaborate, theoretically speaking. They've written up screeds of justification for what they're doing—it's all online, you can read it if you want."

"God, Amanda. I don't know how you deal with this stuff."

Amanda flared suddenly. "I hate it, if you want to know. Don't you? I hate everything about the way we live here. Living behind walls, behind wire and machine gun towers, while everybody else starves. Nathan with his mad schemes, his artificial crops and his ocean mines and his stupid Ark. People like Juan, decent enough once, now going slowly crazy because of what they're doing to stay alive. And me with a son dead and a daughter who won't speak to me except when she needs me to keep her out of prison. I *hate* it all. My life started going downhill when Jerry walked out on us, and it's got steadily worse since. When we were growing up in Fulham I never would have dreamed it would come to this."

"No." Lily had an impulse to go over to her, to comfort her. But Amanda looked away.

Lily stood up, setting down her drink. "I need to get ready for my trip to Lima. I'll call you when I get back. And we'll go see Kristie together, yes?"

"Whatever." Amanda sipped her drink and waved her hand, making the voices of the soap opera characters swell and boom so they filled the empty room.

56

With a bit of arm-twisting by Piers, Lily got a seat on a supply chopper flying out to Lima.

The coast was draped in the low, clinging fog the inhabitants of Lima had once called the *garua*, so the chopper descended into a white-out. And then the complicated, boxy superstructure of an oil rig came looming out of the fog. Lammockson had established this old rig *over* the heart of the drowned city as a base for his continuing salvage operations.

The chopper landed on the rig's upper deck, and Lily scrambled down.

She found she could walk to the edge of the platform, which was fenced off by a rail and sheets of Plexiglas. The sea, gray and rolling, stretched off to a horizon blanked out by the *garua*. She might have been in the middle of the ocean. In fact she was standing directly over the heart of a megacity, of which there was no sign at all.

An AxysCorp flunky came running to meet her, an earnest young man prompted with instructions from Piers. Sanjay was on the rig, but was supervising a deep-dive submersible descent into Lima, and she had some time to spare, maybe an hour. The flunky tried to persuade her to go down below where it was safe, to have some food, a beer even, watch some TV. She refused. She needed the air. She was given a thick coat to pull on over her coverall, and a cup of coffee, and she got away from Piers's nanny and went walking around the rig platform.

She passed among outcroppings of machinery, like open-air sculptures, attended by engineers in hard hats and coveralls. She recognized some of the operations going on here. Most of the salvaging operations were run remotely, with cranes lowering robot machinery with manipulator arms and cutting gear down among the drowned buildings. Even after years of systematic plunder, Lima, like all the world's lost cities, was still a tremendous lode.

But Lammockson always thought ahead, and more advanced technologies were being trialed on the rig. His surveyors told him there was gold, zinc, copper, silver and lead to be found under the ocean floor, raw materials for the long-term survival of civilization. The scientists even knew where to look, around big volcanic deposits called "sea floor massive sulphides" built up by hydrothermal vents, places where water circulated through deep cracks in the sea-floor rock, dissolving metals as it moved through the rock and precipitating them out in conical black chimneys. So Lammockson was creating an ocean-floor mining capability. He had other teams of experts working on locating undersea oil deposits. Sea mining had been frowned on in the past because of the damage the noise, sediment plumes and turbulence might do to fragile seafloor ecologies. Nobody cared about that anymore—or at least nobody was in a position to police it.

Lily was watching a fresh robot salvage machine being lowered over the side when Sanjay came up to her. "Lily! What's a landlubber like you doing on a rust bucket like this?"

As usual when she met a face from her past, Lily felt overwhelmed by a spasm of emotion, a peculiar kind of longing. She grabbed Sanjay and hugged him. "It's good to see you."

He submitted gracefully enough, and hugged her back. Sanjay, short, compact, dressed in a standard-issue Axys-Corp coverall, didn't show his forty-five years save for the gray in his beard. He said, "You want to go down into the rig? There are lounges, bars. Get you out of this breeze if you feel like it."

"Would you like that?"

"Well, I've been in that control room for hours, sniffing up cigarette smoke and stale beer and coca-plant halitosis. I'd rather stay out in the fresh air if you can stand it."

"Then let's walk."

They continued Lily's slow perambulation of the deck. Sanjay asked about Amanda, and he spoke of his children and their mothers in the Scottish archipelago, where an ex-

traordinary new amphibious society was emerging among
the clans.

Sanjay said the DSV dive just completed had gone well
enough. "Though these days I rarely have to make them
myself, thank Ganesh for that. Look, you can see the boat."
He pointed to an ungainly craft that dangled from a crane,
dripping; it looked oddly like a conventional submarine cut
in half, with manipulator arms, cameras and windows clut-
tering the cut-through cross section. "That's a COMRA.
Developed by the China Ocean Mineral Resources R&D
Association."

"A Chinese design?"

"Purchased by Lammockson for AxysCorp for a huge
price—along with luxury villas in Project City for its crew
and engineers. One of the most modern designs from the
preflood days. The dive into Lima went well. We went
down to the cultural center around the Plaza Mayor, and
the shops at Miraflores. San Isidro, the business district, is
pretty accessible. And we got some good science data. Actually the dive was paid for by a Quechua community, up
in the Andes somewhere. They had salvage targets of their
own."

That pricked her curiosity, and she wondered if it had
something to do with Ollantay, but she wasn't much interested in the mining of Lima.

He said now, "I heard from Gary Boyle."

"Via Thandie Jones, I guess? I haven't heard from him
for years."

"Well, he isn't in a place it's easy to send postcards
from."

"Where is he?"

"That's just it. Nowhere . . ." He told her how Gary was
now part of an itinerant community, thousands of people
wandering through the crowded western states. "They've
been on the road for years, Lily. After they were forced
out of their camp at Amarillo, they have failed to find anywhere permanent to stay." Sanjay shrugged. "It's happening
all over, from what I hear. Tremendous populations on the
move, washing back and forth in search of room to live."

"Gary still has Grace with him?"

"Oh, yes, according to Thandie. Michael Thurley too."

"Grace must be sixteen now."

"Yes. And a stroppy teenager, according to Thandie."

"That's healthy," Lily said firmly. "I wish there was something I could do for them."

"There's still a bond between you all, you survivors of Barcelona, isn't there? Gary's OK. He's probably wishing he could find a way to help *you*."

They agreed to talk this over more later. And Lily told him she was going to visit Lammockson's Ark Three to meet Kristie. She offered Sanjay a ride.

"I'd like that. Ark Three? I wonder what Nathan is up to now."

"You'll see what there is to see. Not that he tells us anything."

He glanced at her. "You seem uncomfortable about it."

She thought it over. "I keep away from Nathan's more baroque efforts. There's something *unbalanced* about his super-tech projects. Obsessive, you know? Here he is trying to master the world through technology. While all around us . . ." She gestured at the gray ocean that rolled over the drowned remains of Lima.

"I understand," Sanjay said, thoughtful. "But maybe at such times as these we need big thinkers like Nathan Lammockson. Because for sure we need big solutions." He grinned. "The insane as a last-resort evolutionary resource. But don't tell Nathan I said that. I'd better go sign out with the COMRA crew. I'll meet you at the helipad."

"Sure." But as he turned away she called, "Incidentally, you said a Quechua group put some funding into the dive. What were they after?"

"They guided a robot into the cathedral." He grinned. "They brought up a coffin. Pizarro's bones!"

57

Chosica, a thousand meters above the old sea-level datum, had once been an inland resort town for the residents of Lima. The Rimac River ran through it, but the landscape away from an irrigated valley floor was desert, the mountain slopes bare sun-bleached rock. To put up Nathan's workers, a rough community of shacks had grown up around the heart of the old town. Lily and Sanjay walked through the shantytown, guided by a satnav patch sewn into Lily's jumpsuit, seeking the hut Kristie shared with Ollantay. It was late afternoon now.

This was just another slum in a world of slums, where, in the roughly built shacks, pots boiled, children played, and dogs slept in the heat. There was a persistent stink of sewage. But above all this loomed the outline of a ship, the slim lines of a vessel big enough to be an oceangoing liner, covered in a bristle of scaffolding.

"I don't believe it," Sanjay said. "That thing must be three hundred meters long! I know you called this project 'Ark Three' but that could have meant anything—something metaphorical—a seed bank, maybe, a vault of frozen zygotes. I didn't think it would be an actual damn ship. We're a kilometer above the old sea-level datum! How's Nathan planning to launch the thing?"

Lily had no idea. "Whether the ship goes to the sea or the sea comes to the ship, it's going to be a spectacular sight, isn't it?"

"There's something about the lines of that tub that remind me of something. I'm no marine engineer. Maybe I'll think of it." He took out his old phone and paged through its memory.

"Actually Nathan is building it in conjunction with a consortium."

"A consortium of who? People like him?"

"Nathan isn't saying," she admitted. "But I think that's the idea. Even the super-rich have run out of places to build Green Zones. So they're looking for other solutions."

"I guess if this is number three, there must be other arks."

"I wouldn't know."

He couldn't take his eyes off the boat. "I can't believe what I'm seeing. A ship, halfway up the Andes! The man has to be crazy after all."

Lily's GPS patch bleeped. They came upon the shack Kristie shared with Ollantay. Amanda must have been here already, for, remarkably, Jorge, Amanda's butler, was standing outside in a suit and tie; he looked entirely unaffected by the dirt around him.

Lily glanced at Sanjay. "This might be bloody."

"Families."

"Yes. Come on, let's get it over with."

The shack was a box, with plastic sheets for walls and roof, cluttered with junk, heaps of clothes, a bed, a table, cupboards. There were vents and windows, and a fan was running from some power source, but it was ferociously hot. The teddy bear stuck on top of a cupboard was a small reminder of a lost past.

In this tiny one-room hut, four people were pressed into the corners, sitting as far from each other as they could get: Piers, Amanda, Ollantay and Kristie. Amanda was wearing her black trouser suit, and Kristie a grubby but colorful dress of woven wool. Piers and Ollantay wore AxysCorp coveralls, and looked oddly alike as they faced each other, separated by the diagonal of the room. Nobody spoke as Lily and Sanjay walked in.

"So," Lily said. "You remember Sanjay McDonald, from London?"

Nobody responded.

Sanjay seemed unperturbed. He nodded at them all, and sat on an upturned plastic crate in a corner, flicking through images of classic ships on his phone.

Lily said, "I have the feeling we walked into the middle of a row."

"You could say that," Amanda snapped. "Or a joke."

"Oh, Mum—" Kristie said.

"Of course you missed the punchline," Amanda said. "Why don't you tell Lily what you just told me?"

Uncertain, distressed, stubborn, Kristie glanced at Lily. "We're getting married," she said. "According to the traditions of Ollantay's people—"

"She's pregnant," Piers said. "That's what she's told us. *Pregnant.* By this man." He couldn't bear to look at Ollantay, evidently, or even to speak his name. Stiff, immobile, Piers looked more brittle than ever, Lily thought, desiccated and fragile. And now she saw how heavy Kristie looked, gravid beneath her loose woolen clothes.

Ollantay was thirty now; his neck was thicker, his skin heavier, his boyish looks gone, but he was as cocky as he had ever been. He smiled.

Lily blew her cheeks out, and sat down herself. "So that's why you called us here, Kris."

"You're family," Kristie said. "You're my aunt." She took a breath. "*She's* my mother. I wanted to tell you in person. I hoped you might be happy for me."

"Happy!" Amanda snapped. "Oh, you bloody little fool."

"Ollantay's family are happy. His mother—"

"For God's sake, Kristie, I couldn't care less about a pack of flea-ridden alpaca herders."

Ollantay glared at Amanda. "In my culture," he said, "lovers live together before the wedding. It is a period we call *sirvinakuy*, which means 'to serve each other.' We marry only when we conceive, and have demonstrated we will bear strong children. Everything about our relationship has been honorable, in my tradition."

Piers stood up. "Oh, this is all— it's not to be tolerated." He stalked out, ducking to get through the low doorway.

Amanda glared at Kristie. "What's it going to take to make you give this up? Shall I speak to Juan, or Nathan? Shall I have this clown who's knocked you up arrested?"

"Oh, Mum—"

Amanda stood and closed on her daughter. "How about a forcible abortion? I could do it, you know."

"Mum, I'm seven months gone!"

"You think that matters? I'm not talking about an NHS hospital. It would only take a word to Nathan. Is that what you want?"

Kristie turned her face away. Ollantay stood up to protect her. Lily got up quickly, trying to get between them before it turned to violence.

And Sanjay, in his corner, peering into his phone's screen, was laughing. "I knew I'd seen that profile before. It's the *Queen Mary*. Nathan Lammockson is rebuilding the *Queen Mary* halfway up the bloody Andes! Oh, thank you, Ganesh, for keeping me alive long enough to see this!"

58

September 2031

Gary set one foot after another on the cracked, dusty blacktop. Grace walked at his side, sixteen years old, slim, erect, almost feral. Between them they pushed the shopping cart that contained the inert form of Michael Thurley. Michael slept uneasily under a plastic tarp, curled up in the big wire mesh basket.

And before them and behind the walkers shuffled, a line that stretched for kilometers. The mayor's guards walked parallel to the main column with their shotguns and pistols visible. Around them the flat desolation of the Great Plains stretched to the horizon.

This was Walker City, a city on the move. To walk was the world. To walk was life.

Much of Gary's time passed in a kind of daze. So long as the walk itself wasn't too strenuous he would lose himself in its slow rhythm, the gentle rock of his body, the working of the muscles, one foot after another, walking his youth away over this tremendous, continent-spanning, mind-numbing plain. Gary thought sometimes that this excursion was a karmic response to his experience in the cellars of Barcelona, that age of enclosure now balanced by these years of semi-infinity, the plain beneath his feet, the huge sky above.

And every morning, after a couple of kilometers or so and the muscles were warmed up, his mind wandered away like a balloon cut loose of its tether. At thirty-nine years old he seemed to have shed so much, his obsessive questing for meaning in the past, his fears over what was to come for himself and Grace and Thurley. None of it meant anything when all you could actually *do* was walk, put one foot after another, a slow propulsion into the real future.

But every so often he came back to himself.

He had long since shed every gram of excess fat. His feet

were like pads of leather, the muscles of his legs and but-
tocks hard as rock. His boots were so worn and supple and
polished they were like part of his skin. He wore his old
AxysCorp-durable jumpsuit, so faded it was the color of
the dust itself. On his back was his pack containing another
jumpsuit, his single change of clothes, underwear washed
so often you could see through it, and other lightweight
gear, plastic sandals, a silvered poncho that could keep out
the rain or the sun's heat, a thin but warm sleeping bag
and inflatable bed roll, elements of a blow-up tent, cooking
gear. He had a few things that wouldn't fit into the pack, a
light spade and pick, and another bag was slung at his waist,
heavier, holding food and water canteens.

All his stuff had self-selected in the long years of walking, surviving a Darwinian filtering based on utility, robustness and lightness, where other junk had broken down or
proven too awkward or heavy. All of it products of a civilization that had pretty much vanished, all of it unbearably
precious.

Which was why, of course, Thurley had got himself into
so much trouble a few days back. You couldn't afford to let
your boots be stolen, even at risk of your life.

This country wasn't like Iowa, where at harvest time
they had walked through country that glowed with life, the
red barns bright in the yellow and green fields, the gleaming water towers, the mighty white grain elevators. There
had always been a good chance they could find work, for
nobody had any gasoline now. The big harvesters stood
idle, and the gathering had to be done by human and animal muscle.

But in Nebraska there was nothing but emptiness, a
plain that went on and on. The towns were little one-street
places with not much more than grain silos and defunct gas
stations and dead cars, with ad billboards painted over with
uncompromising messages: NO FOOD. NO GAS. WE
SHOOT. KEEP WALKING. DOGS. Between the towns
the roads were empty save for an occasional motor home
or SUV abandoned where some earlier emigrant had run
out of gas. The population was gone, save for those who
found it easier to prey on those who passed by than to produce anything for themselves. And in the end Thurley had
been preyed upon.

That was why, today, Gary couldn't switch off his aware-
ness of the walk, because of the burden of Thurley. The
shopping cart, that had traveled far from the supermarket
where it belonged, was on loan to them from the mayor.
It was just big enough to carry Michael with his thin legs
tucked up to his chest, though he was jolted when the small
wheels jammed. Michael's boots were lodged underneath
his body at his own insistence. Michael had nearly given his
life for the damn things, and he wasn't about to lose them
now.

Gary was sharing the burden of pushing the cart with
Grace. But walking like this was unbalancing him, and as
the kilometers clicked away he could feel that asymmetry
niggling in his hips and back. He resented it, he admitted it
to himself, as the long day bore down on him, and his aches
grew worse.

By mid-afternoon he felt so bad he was actually relieved
when the F-15 came screaming down the road over their
heads.

Everybody ducked, stumbling. Gary let go of the handle,
and the cart tipped off the blacktop. Thurley was rattled
around, and groaned in his pain-filled sleep. The column
stopped, raggedly, and a murmur of conversation replaced
the steady shuffle of feet.

"Wow," said Grace. She took off her worn baseball cap
and wiped sweat off her brow. The plane was a glittering
jewel, receding along the dark stripe of the road. "What do
you think? Denver or Salt Lake City?"

Gary grunted. "Far as I know the Mormons haven't got
an air force yet." But, he reminded himself, he actually
knew very little, and that plane had been an antique.

Grace checked on Thurley. He had fallen back into his
deeper sleep. He was drooling, the spit clinging to the pa-
pery flesh of his thin cheek. "Yeck," Grace said, pulling her
face; sometimes she looked much younger than her sixteen
years. But she bent and wiped his mouth with the collar of
his own jumpsuit. Then she dug a canteen out of her pack
to give him water.

Gary stepped away from the road, treading over the
scrub grass of the prairie. A city guard eyed him, but made
no move to intervene. Looking down the line Gary tried to

see what was going on at its head. Vehicles in military olive were lined up on the road, blocking it, and a quite enormous Stars and Stripes hung, unruffled by any breeze.

"Roadblock," he murmured.

"You got it," said the guard.

From the head of the line, whistles started sounding, blown by the mayor's officials. "That's it for the day," the guards called along the line of the column. "Break the line, form up, everybody off the road." An electric car came driving down the line with a tannoy broadcasting the night's instructions. "Surnames E to F on latrine duty, I to K on water sourcing, please report to the guards for local details. E to F on latrines . . ." The line split around the axis of the road, people clearing the tarmac, plodding into the dust. Packs were dumped on the ground, and the components of tents were drawn out, groundsheets and inflatable struts and guy ropes. Reluctant-looking men and women came out of the column bearing shovels and picks, preparing for the chore of digging the night's latrine trenches.

Gary helped Grace shove their cart away from the road. They moved back fifty meters or so until they found a clear space. Grace threw their plastic tarp on the ground and lifted Thurley out of the cart. Wasted, worn out by walking, he was light enough for her to lift by herself.

Gary got out his cellphone. He pressed the power button gingerly, wincing at the single pip that showed how low the battery had run. But he left it on, and set it on the blanket beside Thurley, letting it make its connections and figure out where it was, and pick up any messages.

The sun was still high; that was one advantage of the unscheduled halt, earlier than the mayor generally planned. So Gary dug his mirror stove out of his pack and began to set it up. They had no fuel for a fire. Gary sometimes imagined the whole of the North American continent had been scoured clean of lumber by the clouds of human locusts that had passed back and forth across its face for years. But the mirror stove was a valuable piece of gear. It was a parabolic mirror with hollow struts, blown up with a few brisk breaths, that sat on a little wire stand. If you positioned it right, face up to the sun like a silvered sunflower, you could set a small pan of water to boil on a wire frame at its focus.

Grace said, "I think he's OK. He's not lost any more blood. And the wound hasn't reopened."

Gary grimaced. "Well, that's good." In fact it was a miracle, given the only doctoring Michael had had, for a wound that would have seen him in intensive care back in better days, had been first aid from Gary and Grace.

"Let's let him rest a bit," Grace said. "Then we'll try to feed him."

"Sure. Later I'll walk up the line and see if I can get some time from a doctor."

Gary dug in his pack for their tea leaves and tin cups, and he checked over their food. It was travelers' fare, tough, difficult to chew, long-lasting: a jerky of rabbit meat, slabs of hard unleavened bread provided by the mobile city's bakeries, and sun-dried fruit, raisins and apricots.

Grace saw he had his phone turned on. "So where are we?"

He picked it up and paged for the GPS functions. "A few kilometers north of Lincoln. I don't think we would have made it tonight. Tomorrow, for sure. All depends on the holdup by the roadblock."

Such a blockage was a genuine problem. The mayor had negotiated a stay on open ground north of Lincoln for a few weeks at least, with lodging and food and water in return for labor on flood defenses and harbor work around the Nebraska town, as well as work in the fields. The walkers could carry little in the way of supplies, and they were running low on food. A holdup of more than a day or two could see real hunger setting in. But there was nothing Gary could do about that now.

He took his boots and socks off, always a key moment of the day. He dug out the plastic sandals he wore around camp, open and soft, so his feet had room to breathe and relax. He hid his boots under a blanket, and took out his penknife and rasp, meaning to get to work on the hard skin of his heels. Like a soldier, he thought absently, maybe like the guys in the roadblock up ahead, and every infantryman right back to Alexander. You always took care of your feet.

"You're daydreaming," Grace said. "Switch your phone off."

"Yeah." He held it up regretfully. Its small screen shone

like a window to a better place. Here was his only connection to the rest of the world beyond the walking city, the family he hadn't heard from since his mother had died, his science colleagues, Lily from Barcelona. He had a charger but no power source. It had broken his heart when he had had to trade away his portable solar-cell array for food when the city had been going through its worst time, trapped by a dust storm somewhere near Dodge City. Occasionally, very occasionally, you came across a community where there was power, from the sun or biofuels or the wind or geothermal heat, and he was able to top up the phone's battery in return for labor. But the last charge-up had been a long time ago, and the few seconds or minutes each day he allowed himself to turn it on were steadily draining the energy.

He held his thumb over the power button. But then the screen sparked to life, with a text message. "Don't switch off. Am coming. Will find U." It was from Thandie Jones.

59

A jeep came barreling along the road, open-topped, driven by some guy in uniform, with Thandie and another woman in back. The jeep was at least fifteen or twenty years old, and looked a lot older. But evidently the Army at least still had access to gasoline. People stared. Aside from the city's own little electric carts, you rarely saw a moving vehicle nowadays.

This was a thrill for Gary. He hadn't seen Thandie for five, six years, not since the time she had briefed Lone Elk in Cadillac City. He knew she'd been roaming the shore of America's gathering inland sea, studying its formation and advising the Denver government on its navigability, ecology and other issues. He'd actually been expecting to meet up with her in Lincoln, if the mobile city got that far. Now here she was coming out to find him.

The car pulled up alongside Gary's little encampment. Gary could *smell* it, smell the rubber of its tires and its oil and the sickly sooty exhaust, the scent of an American childhood.

Thandie swung her legs out of the jeep and came striding over. She had to be forty-five now, or more. But though the hair she wore scraped to her scalp was now shot through with gray, and her face was grooved and tough-looking, almost mannish, she moved with strength and grace. And when she gave him a hug, wrapping her arms tight around his chest, he felt his ribs crush.

"Jeez, Thandie, you're keeping fit."

She stood back and held him. "Well, so are you. The life we live nowadays, huh? The global extinction event has claimed the couch potato."

Her companions followed her. The slim ash-blond woman who came to stand by Thandie, about forty, her expression serious, was Elena Artemova. The Russian ecologist was just as Gary remembered from all those years ago when he had met her en route to the Caspian Sea, if anything her beauty enhanced by the lines around her mouth, the hint of silver in her hair. When she stood by Thandie their arms brushed, but Thandie didn't move away; they both seemed unconscious of the touch.

"You know," Gary said, "what I remember of you two is how you fought the whole time. When we were in that dacha by the Black Sea—"

"That's dykes for you. Women without men, eh, buddy?" This was the soldier who had driven them. He was a strong-looking man, stocky. He wore a sergeant's stripes, and his face was hidden under a helmet and behind big dusty sunglasses. "Gary Boyle, right? You don't remember me." He took off his helmet, rubbed a grizzle of gray stubble on the scalp of his head, and plucked the glasses off the bridge of his nose. He was older than the others—sixty, maybe, Gary thought. He had striking bright blue eyes in a suntanned face, but the eyes were bloodshot, and his fleshy nose was marked by crimson blood vessels. "The *Trieste*, remember?"

"Gordo," Gary said, remembering. "Gordon James Alonzo."

"That's me." He tapped the stripes on his arm. "Sergeant Alonzo now. I joined up again when the Mormons started kicking up shit. I'm too old, but hell, they aren't going to turn away an astronaut." He glanced around at the linear encampment, the people scratching in the dirt. "And I guess there are no spaceships to fly around here, right?"

"No," Thandie said. "But soon there's going to be a harbor for oceangoing ships at Lincoln. A harbor in Nebraska! Makes you boggle. Gary, it's thanks to Gordo that we made it out here to find you. I'm not sure you're going to reach Lincoln anytime soon."

"Why not?"

"Because there's a war a-brewing," Gordo said. "So you going to invite us in? Some hospitality you're showing here, fella. You got anything to drink?"

Gordo walked into Gary's little camp, glancing around at Thurley and Grace and their bits of gear. Grace sat by Thurley, uncertain; she was always wary of strangers, and Gary saw she had the hilt of her knife showing at her belt. To Gary's relief Gordo didn't show much interest in Grace. Perhaps older women like Elena were more to his taste.

Gary fussed about, spreading more of their blankets on the dusty ground, setting rolled-up sleeping mats for the guests to sit on. He showed them his solar stove. "Hot drinks we can do. Tea, if you like it stewed. Otherwise it's water. We filter it well enough." He looked at Gordo. "Alcohol, no."

Gordo grunted. He dug out a hip flask, unscrewed its cap, took a slug. He held it out to Gary. "You want?"

Gary stared at it longingly; he could smell the whiskey. But he shook his head. "I guess not. When we started walking it took me a while to kick a habit I didn't know I had. Probably isn't a good idea to go back to it now, right?"

Thandie and Elena came into the camp area and sat down, side by side, cross-legged. "We're not going to impose," Thandie said. "We can see how you're fixed. But we'll stay the night, if that suits you. Look, we brought gear of our own in Gordo's jeep. A tent, other stuff. I'll take a tea, Gary, but you can be our guests later."

"Courtesy of me," Gordo said, lifting the flask again. "Me and Uncle Sam."

Thandie turned to Grace. "I don't know if you remember me, honey. You would have been about ten when we last met."

Grace looked away, studiously unconcerned. Gary knew the look. She was always uncomfortable whenever relics of the past showed up. She preferred to dwell in the present, this dusty world of camps and walking and latrine ditches and bandits—the only world she had known, save for those strange early years when she had been a hostage of a Saudi royal family.

Elena got up and looked more closely at Thurley, where he slept under his blanket. "This man—"

"He's Michael Thurley," Gary said. "Once a UK government guy who tried to help Helen and Grace."

"He is injured," Elena said. She lifted the blanket cautiously to inspect Michael's wound.

"We ran into bandits," Gary said. "A couple of days and

a few dozen kilometers back. We've been walking down from the prairie, the Nebraska Sandhills."

"They must have wanted something pretty bad," Gordo said.

Gary forced a smile. "His boots. That's all. But he fought back."

"And he won," Grace said.

"That he did. But he took an injury."

The bandit's knife hadn't gone deep into Michael's belly; it had been a swiping slice rather than a stabbing, which might have been fatal. The wound was clean, but it was long and had spilled more blood than Michael could afford in his weakened state.

Gary hadn't been able to get hold of a doctor, so he and Grace had had to handle it themselves. Gary had pushed the flaps of sliced flesh together, while Grace had sewn it up with a length of their fishing line, precious stuff liberated from a broken-open sports store hundreds of kilometers back. With her finer fingers and clearer eyesight, she made a much better fist of jobs like that than Gary ever did; it was always Grace who patched their clothes. They had had no anesthetic, no disinfectant save the heat of water boiled by their mirror stove. But they had got it done.

Elena nodded gravely. "Well, it was necessary. Good work. But now we live in a world in which it is commonplace for a sixteen-year-old girl to perform lifesaving surgery on a wounded man."

"We do the best we can," Gary said sternly, feeling as if he was being criticized.

Grace stood up sharply. "Gary, I'll go find my friends."

"Sure, honey, if you like," Gary said. "But you don't have to go—"

"Yes, I do. Then you can all talk about me to your heart's content. I can see that's what you want." And she stalked off, heading down the line of the column away from the roadblock.

Gary said, "Sorry about that. I have a feeling she did the same thing last time you visited us."

"Don't apologize," Thandie said. "She's got spirit. Why the hell shouldn't she ditch us old stiffs? Hey, Gordo, couldn't you get one of the Army medics to come out and see Michael?"

"Nah-ah." Gordo shook his head. "Strictly against regulation to treat refugee injured or sick."

Elena sighed. "The Army gets the best medical treatment. It is just as it was in Roman times. And the best food."

"Yeah, yeah."

"Oh, come on, big man," Thandie pressed. "What's the use of being an astronaut if you can't pull a few strings? Get it done."

Gordo looked irritated. But he got up, walked back to his jeep and spoke into its radio.

Thandie winked at Gary. "Still thinks he's a hotshot."

"Yes," said Elena, "and he seems to think every woman on Earth finds him irresistible. Once he even made a pass at me. A 'bull dyke,' he called me. It took a fist in the testicles to get him off me."

"You just have to know how to manage him," Thandie said. "You've got to admit he's useful."

The pot boiled. Gary threw in some leaves, swilled the potion around, and poured the drink into tin cups. He took rabbit jerky from his pack, and set it on their thin plastic plates.

Gordo came back. He stood for a moment, sipping at his flask, and he surveyed the long roadside camp, his free hand curled into a fist on his hip. "Jesus," he said. "I can't believe you people live like this. Just hobos tramping in the dirt. Is it true there are women who've had kids on the move? Got knocked up, gone to term and pupped, all on the road?"

"Nicely put, bozo," Thandie said.

Gary said, "Look, we might be on the road, but we still have to live. And for most people life means having kids. Anyhow we aren't just wandering around. We're organized. You can see that. We're a city on the move. We have a mayor, who we elect, although it has to be a show of hands. We have cops and medical facilities, and we barter with other communities. When we stop we get organized, we dig latrines, we post guards. We have chaplains in every denomination, and imams and rabbis. We help each other; we bury our dead; we care for our children. And we stay out of trouble. The first mayor was a man called Lone Elk, a Seminole Indian—"

"I remember him," Thandie said. "Evidently a smart guy."

"He got taken out by a sniper, but the system he established endures. We're not beggars. We're Okies. We work in return for lodging or food. It's not ideal, but it's not meant to last forever. We're looking for a place to put down some kind of roots. Until we find that, we're on the move. An Okie city, but a city nevertheless."

But Thandie glanced at Elena as he said that, and Gary knew what she was thinking.

The inland sea that had swept across North America from the east now lapped as far west as a line running north to south from the Dakotas through Omaha, Wichita and Oklahoma City, and on down to the Gulf. East of that ragged shoreline, save for scraps of the Appalachians, there was nothing left of the continental United States until you reached the old Atlantic shore, nothing but sea. Even America was running out of room.

"You always get turned away," Elena said.

"That's true. One place we came to, the mayor mobilized his National Guard against us. Said we deserved to die."

That made Elena angry. "Was the mayor a man? Only a man would say a child deserved to die."

There were other places they had chosen not to stay.

The federal government's brand new cities on the Great Plains, which had come to be known as "Friedmanburgs," had turned out to be corporate playgrounds and enclaves for the rich, like experiments in raw capitalism. The usual shantytowns gathered around the gated Green Zones, living off the garbage of ages past, or providing cheap labor for the burgs. But a year ago, Gary had heard, things had started to change, at last. By now it wasn't only the dispossessed poor who wound up in the slums, but many of the old middle classes of America, finally washed up, dwelling in cardboard shacks like the rest. There had always been opposition to the nature of the Friedmanburgs and their corporate dominance, from religious and civil rights groups among others. Now the former lawyers and accountants and teachers in the shanties grew vocal and articulate, and put pressure on their elected government. At the same time the power of the corporations began to flake as the complex international networks of information, money and resources on which they relied finally began to break down.

The federal government was exhausted by the years of crisis and hollowed out by the money it had had to spend to save its citizenry from the flooding, at the very time its tax base was dwindling to nothing. But now, under intense pressure, it finally assembled the resources to act. The Friedmanburgs were forcibly nationalized, with National Guard units, tanks and fighter aircraft. The super-rich fled—but there were a diminishing number of enclaves they could flee to. Nathan Lammockson took in some of them, in Project City, repaying old debts; he always said he had got out of the States in anticipation of just such an outcome.

But it didn't help Gary and the others. By then Walker City was far away from the burgs, tramping down another dusty road.

Gary asked Gordo, "So why the roadblock? Refugees?"

Gordo shook his head. He took a bit of rabbit jerky and spoke while chewing. "Not that. It's the fucking Mormons. It's coming to a head over the I-80 . . ."

Gary had heard little of this. "What have the Mormons got to do with it?"

"Utah is high enough to have survived pretty much intact," Thandie said. "They're self-sufficient up there. And now the Mormon community has thrown up some hotheaded leadership. They couldn't see what the Denver government was doing for them. First they blocked any incoming refugees at the state line, unless they were Mormon or would convert. Then they stopped paying their dues altogether. When Denver sent in the police and FBI and eventually the Army, the Mormons fought back."

"A war of independence sparked by a tax dispute," Elena said. "American history is a wheel."

"Raised their own fucking army," Gordo said. "'The Soldiers of the Angel Moroni.' I joined up when it looked like we were going to get an honest-to-God war out of it."

Gary asked, "And it's a war over an interstate?"

"Not just any interstate." Thandie started sketching maps in the dirt. "At Lincoln you're at the terminus of what is still a major cross-continental route. Look, the I-80 used to run across the continent, all the way from San Francisco to New Jersey. Right? And it still survives for most of its length to the west of here, from Lincoln, Nebraska, over the Continental Divide, all the way to the hills over San Francisco Bay."

"But," Elena said, "not much further *east* of here it runs underwater. Lincoln is the new terminus."

Gordo said, "Denver is thinking ahead, about how to use that sea, the new coastline. I'm talking trade, projecting military force. And a harbor at the terminus of the interstate would be ideal for trade and troop movements and the rest. But the trouble is—"

Gary finished for him, "The trouble is Salt Lake City has the same idea."

"Exactly," Thandie said. "The Mormons have set up a camp outside Lincoln itself. And now Buzz Lightyear here and his army buddies have sealed the area off. They're still talking, is what I hear. There's still hope of avoiding conflict."

"A hope not shared by all of us," Gordo growled. "Some of us want to just stick it to the Mormons and get it done." He screwed the top on his flask and shoved it back in his pocket. "I'll get our tent set up. Hey, Madame Brezhnev, you want to give me a hand?"

Elena scowled at him. But she got to her feet, dusted herself off and followed him to the jeep.

Gary was left sitting with Thandie. "All this strategic thinking. Planning for war and the projection of power. But if the sea keeps rising . . ." It was the same question climatologists had been asking each other around their hearths for fifteen years.

As the flood approached four hundred meters, some forty percent of the preflood land area had now been lost, removing the living space of at least seventy percent of the human population—four billion people. And amid the vast displacement of the flooding itself there was an ongoing carnival of tectonic events—volcanoes, quakes, tsunamis—as huge masses of water settled their weight over the drowned lands.

Thandie said, "Then there are the climate shifts. Multiples of feedback processes are working to drive carbon dioxide and other greenhouse gases into the air, and there is a continuing failure of the mechanisms that might remove them. Even if the sea-level rise ceased tomorrow, those changes would continue to work through. We don't actually know what the end state will be like. Certainly like nothing we've seen before."

"But the sea-level rise isn't about to cease."

"No. For sure there are going to be more wars like this one. More squabbling over scraps of high ground. We're all going to have to choose where we make our stand." She glanced around at the encamped city. "A group this size isn't going to be viable much longer."

"I know that."

"You decided where you'll go, you and Grace?"

He eyed her. "Have you?"

"West," she said promptly. "West to Denver. The highest state capital, the capital of the federal government, the strongest enclave of high-technology civilization left anywhere in the world, probably. That's the place to be, I figure."

"The place where any solution to all this is going to come from."

She pulled a face. "I don't believe in 'solutions' anymore. I just want to be in a place where I can keep having hot showers for as long as possible. How about you?"

He hesitated. "I've had bits of contact with Lily Brooke. We've an open invitation to join her in Nathan Lammockson's fortress in the Andes."

"Project City." She grinned.

"Yeah. Look, I know there's something screwy about Lammockson, but he's a tough, resourceful guy who's committed to protecting us, I mean our group of hostages. He's stuck to that line for fifteen years now, and Lily and Piers are pretty close to him. I'm going to try to make it there, I think."

She frowned. "That means going south. Through Mexico, Panama . . ."

"I don't imagine it will be easy. But there are no easy choices, are there?"

"That there aren't. Come on, let's help those two idiots fix the tent."

So they got the tent up. Gordo let Gary charge up his phone from a battery in the jeep. And an Army doctor came out to check Michael's wound; he cleaned it up and replaced the stitches with a plastic adhesive, but told Grace she'd done a good job. Michael stayed unconscious through the whole thing.

As the night drew in Gordo set up a camping stove, and they cooked chicken and pork and stir-fried vegetables, military supplies; it was better food than Gary had tasted for years.

Grace came back with a girlfriend. They listened to music, by headphones plugged into a little power-free crystal radio set. The girls sang along with the song they were hearing: " 'I love you more than my phone / You're my Angel, you're my TV / I love you more than my phone . . .' "

The Denver government broadcast music through the surviving network of satellites, but nobody was recording music anymore, and you heard nothing newer than fifteen or twenty years old. Gary missed it badly. Always a big music fan, when he'd come out of the Barcelona cellars he'd spent a lot of time catching up with the output of his favorite bands, and devouring the best of the new stuff. Now that was no longer possible. Gary wondered how much the girls understood of the lyrics they were repeating, the phrases that casually referred to a vanished world. But he envied them their discovery of stuff that was at least new to them.

The girls started improvising dance moves, and the adults clapped along. Gordo produced more alcohol, wine this time, and Thandie and Elena accepted some. Even Gary relented. Grace took a sip, her first-ever alcohol so far as Gary knew, but pronounced it bitter.

They talked on, drinking quietly, as the stars came out over the Plains. There was one mild eruption around midnight when Elena got to her feet, noisily accusing Gordo of putting his hand on her thigh. It turned out to be Thandie playing a malicious joke.

Then they settled into their tents, Michael, Grace and Gary squeezing into the small orange dome they had carried in pieces on their backs for years, and Gordo and the women in the big, sturdy, bottle-green military tent he'd borrowed for the night.

It was around three in the morning when Gary was woken by the crashing noise of low-flying aircraft.

He scrambled out of the tent. Gordo and Thandie were

already out, Gordo pulling up his pants, his head tilted up. The planes roared over, their lights like constellations in flight. Their noise was more than loud; it was oppressive, crushing.

Gary yelled at Gordo, "Ours?"

"Hell, no. That's a Russian design, MiGs. Fucking Mormons." He grabbed his jacket and started hauling down his tent.

Gary faced Thandie, for one last moment. He said, "Denver, then."

She replied, "Project City. I'll remember."

"Good luck—"

He heard a boom, like a crash of thunder. He looked southeast, toward Lincoln. Fireballs blossomed in the night.

"Shit," said Gordo. He threw stuff in the back of the jeep and jumped behind the steering wheel. "So it's come to this," he said as he started the engine. "A civil war over a drowned interstate. You know, we should have been flying to Mars, right now, tonight. NASA had this schedule. I could have been on the flight, not too old yet . . ." He looked up at the stars and gunned the engine. "You two dykes getting in or what?"

60

May 2034

From Kristie Caistor's scrapbook:

The footage on the Toodlepip.com Web Site was ambiguous. It was hard to be sure of the details or of the precise sequence of events, in a murky panorama of broken, slushy polar ice under a leaden sky, the blurred figures of the humans, the small, scrambling bear.

The flood was causing an extinction spasm, an event that was gathering pace rapidly. All over the world animals were driven from vanishing habitats, or slaughtered when they came into competition with humans for the remaining high ground. Birds were more mobile, but their nesting and feeding habits were always fragile; birds had been suffering since the beginning of the event, when a teenage Kristie had noted plunges in the populations of blue tits and other garden birds. As climate zones shifted or were drowned, vegetation was forced to relocate or succumb; the changes came much more rapidly than the life cycle of most trees, and the forests which burned or drowned were not replaced. Even the microbial world was stirred up, a cause of the new plagues which afflicted mankind.

Much of the dying was out of sight, however; coastal and shallow-water life was being erased all but invisibly, for example. Toodlepip.com's unique selling point was that it gathered images at the very point of these extinctions: pictures of the last of a kind succumbing to the dark, transmitted painlessly to the site's remaining subscribers in Green Zone enclaves around the world. Some of these images were unspectacular. It was hard for most people who weren't actually ecologists themselves to grieve over the destruction of a coral reef. But cute mammals were always a different story.

The polar bears had been the poster stars of the global

warming crisis that had afflicted the planet long before the flood itself. Now, all around the Arctic Ocean, every spring Toodlepip and other agencies watched anxiously, or eagerly, for the bears to emerge from hibernation, the crux point of the animals' survival. If the sea ice melted the mother bears wouldn't be able to get to the seal cubs whose meat they relied on after a winter's hibernating. And if the mothers couldn't feed, their babies starved, and that was that.

The last wild bear of all, it was commonly agreed, was a wretched starveling cub, stained yellow by the urine of its dead mother. And since the zoos had long been abandoned as expensive luxuries, the last in the wild was likely the last in the whole world, and the bears would join the elephants and the tigers and many, many more species in their final refuge in gene banks and zygote arks.

What wasn't clear from the Toodlepip footage was whether the cub died of natural causes, or whether it had been shot by the Inuit hunter who had guided the camera team to this remote spot in the Canadian Arctic in the first place. Even that was a story, the last Inuit bringing down the last bear. There was so much chatter about the event that it broke into international news summaries.

61

June 2035

The AxysCorp chopper descended from a turbulent sky. There was a pad ready for it on the Nazca raft, marked out by bright yellow paint on a cluttered surface that heaved and swelled gently. The bird set down gingerly. Lily, watching from the raft, knew that the company pilots disliked having to bring their birds down on the town rafts, and you could see that reluctance in their flying.

As soon as the engine died and the rotor blades slowed, Juan Villegas clambered down and ducked under the slowing blades, hauling a crate out after him. The pilot, insectile behind his sunglasses, stayed in the safety of the gleaming bubble of his cockpit; he didn't even release his harness. Lily ran in, head down, and took hold of the crate with Juan. Villegas stumbled on the heaving surface. The crate wasn't heavy, but it was bulky and awkward. Together they made their way to the edge of the helipad, two elderly people hauling luggage, Lily thought, over this rough, swelling surface of plastic tarps.

"Thanks," Villegas said with feeling. "I wasn't expecting it to be so unsteady underfoot."

"You're doing OK," Lily said, and she meant it. He was fifty-seven now, only a couple of years younger than Lily herself. There was very little left of the sleek blackness that had once made his hair shine, and he wore an AxysCorp coverall as battered and patched as Lily's own, rather than a sharp suit. But he was still a handsome devil, she thought with a rare pang of jealousy. "I mean, you're here. A lot of Project City folk won't set foot on the town rafts."

He nodded. "I know. Tell it to my pilot." The raft heaved again, making the two of them stagger, and Lily almost dropped the crate. "The storm is coming," Villegas said. He glanced to the west, toward the Pacific, uneasily. "We could see it from the chopper, a sheet of black cloud. The weather forecasts have predicted it for days. And when the surge comes, that will be the end of Nazca. You're confident the raft will hold together?"

"As confident as I can be. Maria's hut is just over there—that's Maria Ramos, the mayor. That's the best place to leave this gear."

"I'm in your hands."

They pushed on.

Lily had been involved in the construction of the raft, leading a team of AxysCorp engineers. The raft's skeleton had been laid down in a great sprawl in the heart of the old town, the basic pontoons of tires and oil cans overlaid by girders scavenged from ruined properties, and then topped by plastic tarps and treated corrugated iron, anything nondegradable. Shacks and huts constructed of bits of garbage and tied down by guy ropes clustered over the raft's broad back like frogs clinging to a log. A Red Cross flag fluttered over one larger building, the medical center, and a few more advanced structures towered, a transmitting mast, aerials, a wind turbine.

When the project had begun, two years before, the sea had still been remote, its waves breaking far below Nazca's altitude. It seemed absurd to be building a raft so high above the water. But after twenty years of the flood the sea-level rise was approaching some eight hundred meters above the old datum, and it was now rising at an astounding *hundred meters per year*, a rate that itself continued to increase. And suddenly here was the water, worming its way even into this mountainous region, and with its huge, implacable strength already starting to lift the raft up from the town that had given birth to it. The place was crowded and frantic as the final evacuation approached. People hurried everywhere, laden with mattresses, sheets and blankets, bundles of clothes, baskets full of food, pots and pans, bits of furniture, bales of string, coils of wire, spades, hoes, anything that might be useful in the long years to come, when the raft would be adrift on the face of the ocean.

They found Maria Ramos's home and set down their crate. Lily stepped up to the rough doorway. "Maria? It's Lily. We have the AxysCorp gear for you."

As they waited Villegas peered curiously at the detail of this raft-borne dwelling. The mayor's residence was just another shack built of corrugated iron and doors taken from some abandoned building. Chickens and pigs were restless in cages made from plastic mesh. Bowls had been strapped to the roof with bits of rope, to catch rainwater. People came and went in a hurry, adults and children, loading up here as everywhere else. Lily vaguely recognized Maria's grown-up children and grandchildren. She had been working with this woman for years.

A child ran across their path, making Villegas start. She was no more than five, but she carried a wicker basket full of clothes on her head. There were many, many children here, toddlers, infants in papooses on their parents' backs.

Villegas said, "Nathan will be disappointed his birth-control programs and his 'voluntary limits' lectures are not working."

Lily grunted. "Deeper drives kick in when you're threatened, it seems."

"I suppose so. It is said that after every war there is a population surge. And what is this but a world at war? Nathan should tell more of his inner circle to come out of their high-tech fortress and take a hard look at what's actually happening out here."

Which, to his credit, Juan did. As the years had worn by Lily had come to see strengths in him she hadn't discerned in the dandyish socialite she had first encountered. Juan had always thought of himself as a weighty figure in his community, regardless of Nathan's patronage, and that was how he behaved. And his Christianity, having been through its harsh New Covenant phase, was now expressing itself more generously. He had become a useful ally for Lily in Nathan's court. And despite her own occasional pangs of jealousy she was pleased that he had brought a kind of stability for the last few years to the ever-troubled life of her sister.

Maria came out of her house. She wore a faded woolen shift, her face was grimy, and she looked tired, tense. "So you came," she said to Lily.

"As promised. This is Juan Villegas. Juan, Maria is—"

"I know you," Maria said, peering at him. "You used to be in the society pages, back in the day. A playboy, weren't you? Dating pop stars and tennis girls." Her English was good, and lightly accented with a mix of Spanish and Quechua intonations.

Juan shrugged, looking embarrassed. "That was a long time ago. In a different world."

"Well, that's true. But you're surviving, evidently, aren't you?"

"As are you," he said gently.

A breeze whistled among the guy ropes, and a few drops of rain spattered on the plastic sheeting under their feet. They looked to the west, where, just for a moment, the light strengthened, the sun trying to break through the storm clouds. Maria pushed a stray lock of gray-black hair back from her forehead, and when the light caught the planes of her face this fifty-year-old woman was beautiful, Lily thought, with something of the look of a *mestiza* despite her Christian name. But her eyes were black with tension, her full lips pursed.

Lily had seen this all through the Andes. Maria was of a generation that had already seen one huge dislocation. Driven out of Lima as a young woman, she had come here to build a new home, and had endured half a lifetime of withering work breaking new land. But now the sea was rolling over farms established scant years before, and Maria had to move again. It was hard for people to take. Older folk felt exhausted, unable to face another uprooting. The young, conversely, resented being driven from the only homes they had known, and blamed the old for the wastefulness that may have caused this global convulsion. Even as the huge work of evacuation continued, there were family arguments, divorces, suicides, murders.

"The storm is coming," Maria said. "You'd better leave before it hits."

Lily felt obscurely hurt by this curt farewell. "We brought you the standard AxysCorp package. Radio equipment with backups, all solar powered. A GPS navigation suite. Fifty cellphones . . ." All products of Project City's high-tech factories, equipment designed for robustness and longevity, though many of them were assembled from the components of scavenged older gear. This was Nathan Lammockson's standard gift to each new raft community, a way to keep in contact with them, and maybe retain some control.

Maria glanced at the crate. "Thanks," she said flatly.

"I hope we'll keep in touch, Maria. There is a chopper rota. If there are emergencies, medical needs Project City can help you with—"

"This raft could not have been built without the advice of your engineers, Lily," Maria conceded. "But let us not lie to each other. AxysCorp encourages drowning communities to build rafts because otherwise we would all become refugees and wash like a tide up the valleys, and then what would happen?"

"Come on, Maria. You know how it is. We're already beyond the theoretical carrying capacity of the higher ground. We have to find other solutions."

"I know, I know. But is there not room for one more town, one more family—one more child?"

"We must all make judgments," Villegas said.

Maria shrugged. "Indeed we must." Another gust of wind, more raindrops. That golden light faded, clouds raced overhead, and again the raft heaved under their feet, restless.

Juan glanced at Lily. "Perhaps it is wise to get moving before that pilot loses his nerve and lifts without us."

"Go, go," Maria said, and turned her back on them.

The raft was surging constantly now, and Juan fell flat on his face when he was tripped by a bit of plastic rope. The Nazcans were rushing, gathering children indoors, strapping down the last bits of loose gear. By the time they reached the chopper the wind was gusting, the rain coming down solidly. The chopper's blades were already turning, and inside his rain-streaked cockpit the pilot waved at them to hurry.

As soon as Juan had the door closed the pilot gunned his engine and the chopper lifted. The raft's muscular surging was replaced by a sharper buffeting as the chopper's blades bit into the turbulent, stormy air.

The bird dipped, turning north, and Lily looked down at the Nazca raft. It was a ramshackle island that rose up amid the rooftops and drowned streets of this sun-bleached old colonial town, its back studded with shacks and wind turbines, every flat roof gleaming with rainwater pails and buckets. At the raft's center topsoil had been spread out over a bed of stones, a splash of pale brown that would become a seaborne farm. Almost everything of which the raft was constructed predated the flood, Lily reflected, over-manufactured imperishable junk now lashed together to make this new home, rising like a dream above drowning Nazca.

And then the sea surge began, tall waves washing in from the west, and the raft heaved. She saw ropes break, bits of the structure splitting and separating, and people scrambled to make hasty repairs. But the chopper swept north and the raft and the drowning town receded behind her.

The pilot found some smoother air, and his confidence seemed to lift. After a few minutes' flying he pointed down. "Last chance to see," he called back.

Lily glanced down. Some twenty-five kilometers from Nazca, flying north away from the storm system, they were passing over a plain that once must have been arid, desolate, but was now awash with gray sea water.

Juan leaned past her to see. "The Nazca lines. They were discovered from the air, you know. Have you seen them?"

"I let Nathan fly me around up here a couple of times."

This was the pampa, once one of the world's driest deserts. It had been an immense sketchbook for the ancient folk who had lived here, and their scribbles, made by lifting stones to reveal the lighter earth beneath, had been preserved by the intense aridity. But now, of the strange millennium-old geometric markings trampled in the high dirt, of the monkey and spider and flower and the elaborate birds, there was no sign, all of it erased by salty ocean water.

"Another of mankind's treasures lost," Juan said without emotion.

The chopper rose higher still. Looking back to the south and west, Lily could see the storm-lashed Pacific surging against the foothills of the Andes. But to the north and east too she saw ocean, calmer, steel-gray, an extension of the Atlantic that had pushed across the continent and was now lapping against the mountains. Pacific and Atlantic visible in a single glance. And all along the new shorelines, to east and west of the mountains, the rafts clustered, like ghosts of the towns beneath the water.

Juan Villegas leaned back in his seat and closed his eyes.

62

" I am confident," Domingo Prado said. Moving ahead of Gary, with Grace bringing up the rear, he pushed through the green shade of the Panamanian forest. He had his machete in his hand, and his revolver tucked into the band of his pants under the pack on his back.

Domingo was around forty-five, a bit older than Gary. He was a big man but lithe, and he took the downward slope of the ground in long easy strides. Well, Gary thought, after so many years on the road they were all lithe at best, skinny to the point of skeletal at worst. But though it was still morning, only ten a.m., Domingo had already sweated through the back of his shirt and the brim of his battered straw hat, and even through his canvas pack. He sweated as he had when Gary had first met him, hundreds of kilometers to the north and years back in time.

"Tell me why you're confident," Grace called ahead.

"Because I know this country. Panama, the canal zone. I used to be a ranger in the Chagres national park, which is on the Colombian side of the canal, east of Alajuela Lake. You will see. Once we get over there I will guide you well. I know it like the back of my hand."

"Sure," Gary said. "Like you knew Guatemala and El Salvador and Honduras and Nicaragua—"

"Hey," Domingo said, and he turned to grin at Gary. His face was so dark in the green-shadowed light his expression was barely visible. "Have I ever let you down?"

"Every fucking day, pal," Gary said ruefully.

There was some truth in that, and some untruth too. As they had trekked south through the Americas the Okies had quickly learned that they needed guides. You couldn't rely on the precious old maps the mayor carried in her locked trunk; even the GPS data that came down from an

increasingly patchy satellite network wasn't sufficient, for
the world was changing constantly as the sea bit away at
the lower land.

And then there was the politics, such as it was. As they
had headed south they had soon passed far beyond the
remit of the two more-or-less functioning governments in
what was left of the US, the rump of the federal government
still holed up in Denver and its deadly rival, the Mormon
administration in Utah. Law was enforced locally or not at
all. In some places you could work in return for land to set
up camp in, food and clean water. In other places bandit
communities did nothing but prey on passing refugees—
although the walking city, still a thousand strong, was generally numerous enough to deter any but the most determined
raiders. The world was a constantly changing quilt of opportunities and threats. So you needed local knowledge, somebody who knew the ground.

Domingo Prado had attached himself to Walker City
at the Mexican border. There were worse than Domingo.
He really did have some travelers' knowledge of Central
America. He made plenty of mistakes, mostly through his
habit of bluffing rather than admitting his lack of knowledge. But at least they were honest mistakes, Gary always
thought. He never spoke much of his own background, how
he had lost whatever home he may once have had, if he had
had a family, a wife, kids. There were plenty of people like
him in the world, dislocated, survivors of a drowned past.
All he wanted in return for his guiding was food, and the
chance to travel, a bit of adventure.

Anyhow, stuck in this forest, he had no choice but to
trust Domingo, and they pressed on.

Something scurried through the undergrowth, startling
Gary—a possum maybe. And a bird flapped overhead,
a flash of color, crying. He had no idea what these creatures were. This was the Panama isthmus, a place where
two continents had collided only three million years before, and where biotas separated since the breakup of su-
percontinents had mashed together. The Great American
Interchange, they called it. The result, here at the bridge
between worlds, was exotic and unfamiliar to Gary. The
rainforest was like a cathedral, he thought, the green canopy like stained glass, the filtered light shining on trees slim

as Gothic columns. Most of the time he just had to concentrate on where he put his feet. But it was beautiful, all beautiful.

And he heard a subtler rustling, somewhere behind him. Parties of the mayor's guards, out to shadow them. You never traveled alone.

Then, quite suddenly, they broke out of the jungle. And Gary realized that Domingo might, today, have made the mother of all his mistakes. For they faced open water.

The slope fell away until it reached the water, only ten or twenty meters below their position. You could see how the jungle had been flooded; the green carpet, broken and patchy, cloaked the slope even as it descended into the water, and some surviving trees pushed above the surface. And beyond that the water stretched away before them, gray and calm, until more green-clad hills rose, far to the northeast, kilometers away.

In the open air the sun was intense. They retreated to a scrap of shade, and wiped their brows, loosened their shirts, pulled sweat-soaked cloth away from their flesh.

"Shit," Domingo said. He squatted down on his haunches, swatting at flies with his hat.

Grace asked, "So what is this?"

"The canal zone," Domingo said. He gestured. "We are looking northeast, roughly. Yes? Just here the isthmus"—a word he could barely pronounce—"takes a detour. It connects North and South America, but here it curls to the northeast for a couple of hundred kilometers. So you have the Atlantic to our west, over *there*, and the Pacific to the east. This whole area was transformed by the engineering of the canal—which was more than a mere canal. It was a kind of liquid bridge, with locks to lift up the ships on either side. The Gatun Lake was right here, formed by damming on the Atlantic side."

Gary glanced down the slope. "This isn't Gatun Lake. Best case it's some kind of inland flood. Worst case the sea has broken through."

"Either way we are in trouble," Domingo said.

"Only one way to find out which," Grace said. She stood, fixed her ancient baseball cap back on her head, and walked cautiously down the slope toward the water.

The sun was high, and cast dazzling highlights from the water. From Gary's point of view Grace was silhouetted, the brilliant light around her body making her seem slimmer, even taller than she was. She wore her arms bare, and he could see her muscles, the wiry biceps. She was twenty years old now; a difficult teenager had grown into a strong woman. She could not be called beautiful, Gary always thought, not conventionally anyhow. She looked like an athlete, a worker. But he recognized beauty in her health and strength and poise, a kind of Cro-Magnon beauty fitting to the world she had grown up in—a world where she had been a refugee since she was five years old.

Watching her, Gary felt proud. He could never have saved her from the flood—he and Michael Thurley, poor Michael who had died far from home of the knife wounds that had been inflicted on him in Nebraska. But they had got her through to adulthood confident, competent, healthy, equipped for a dangerous world, *sane*. There were probably a lot worse fates for a young woman growing up in this dislocated age.

She reached the edge of the water. She crouched down, dipped her hand into the lapping water, and lifted a palmful of it to her mouth. She spat it out. "Salt," she called.

"So that's it," Domingo said bitterly. "The most magnificent of all mankind's engineering creations—gone! Drowned like a sandcastle on the beach."

"And the isthmus is severed," Gary said. "North and South America separated for the first time in three million years. Astonishing when you think about it."

Domingo raised an eyebrow at that. "Our problem is," he said more practically, "if we are ever to reach your friends in the Andes we must cross the water. But how?"

"How about we sail?" Grace stood and pointed, east along the shore of the strait.

A boat, a battered-looking cruiser with a gleaming mast, lay on the water, tied up loosely to a dying tree.

63

They were hailed from the boat. "How many are you?"

Gary glanced at Domingo. "American accent. Florida maybe?"

"Could be."

Gary cupped his hands and shouted back, "Three of us here. Others in the forest."

There was a pause. Then, "I got you covered from here. And some of my boys are above you, they have you from the back. Got that?"

"Got it."

It was always this way, at best, when you encountered strangers. A show of strength, a posturing of weapons and warriors that might or might not exist. On a bad day you'd get shot at before you realized there was anybody there.

"So what do you want?"

Domingo answered now. "Passage." He pointed. "Across the canal zone to Darien."

Gary called, "We just want to pass through. We're heading for Peru."

"Peru, huh."

"Yes. We've no intention of staying here."

There was a longer pause. Then Gary saw a rowboat being let down into the water, lowered on ropes from capstans. "I'll come talk it over. Remember, I got you covered. This is my country, and I know it a damn sight better than you do."

Gary spread his hands. "We're no threat."

Two men clambered down a rope ladder into the boat, one moving a bit more stiffly than the other. They rowed briskly across the few hundred meters to the shore. Gary, Grace and Domingo walked down the slope and along the littoral to meet the boat as it came in. It ran aground in a place that, Gary could see, had been cleared of tree stumps and rotting lumber to be made suitable for landings.

The two men in the boat looked alike, both black, heavy-set, square-faced; they wore tough-looking denim jeans and jackets and battered, salt-faded caps. The older man had a face twisted into a wrinkled glare. The other, younger, more nervous, had an open expression, wide eyes. Father and son, Gary guessed. The father seemed to be unarmed, but the son bore some kind of automatic weapon, and he stood back, out of reach of the newcomers. He kept the muzzle pointed at the ground.

Gary stepped forward, hand outstretched. "The name's Gary Boyle."

The older man took his hand and shook. "Sam Moore. My boy Tom."

The boy nodded.

Domingo cautiously fingered the straps of his backpack. "May I? I have gifts."

Moore glared harder, and the boy waved the automatic around. But they let Domingo take off his pack. He drew out two cans of Diet Coke, the walkers' standard gift for Americans. "A token of friendship," he said.

Moore was still wary, but he took a can, and passed the other to his son. "Shit, haven't seen this stuff in years. How old is it?"

Gary said, "They're still manufacturing it in Denver."

"No kidding." Moore popped the can, listened to the hiss of the carbonation. "Needs to be cold, really." He took a deep slug of the soda.

The boy fumbled with the tab, spilled some of the soda on his face when he tried to drink out of the can, and then pulled a sour expression.

Moore had drained his can. "Shit, that's good." He crushed the can in one hand and tossed it in the water. "So much for saving the planet! You guys remember that stuff? Gifts, huh. So, Gary Boyle, who are you and what do you want?"

Gary said they were a scouting party for a band of travelers. "The rest are back in the forest."

"You're on foot."

"Yes, aside from barrows and carts and the like."

"You folks come far?"

Gary glanced at Grace. "Depends where you start from. I'd call it from Lincoln, Nebraska. We've been walking south since then."

Moore whistled. "All the way to Peru, right? Down the spine of the Americas."

"That's the idea."

"When I was a young man I once drove down the Pan-American Highway, from Laredo, Texas, down through Central and South America, all the way to Paraguay. Hell of a trip. And the only stretch we had to hike was back there." He pointed his thumb back across the strait. "The Darien Gap, eighty kilometers of jungle. Was then, is now. But I knew the country, grew up here. On the other side we hired a car and drove on into Colombia."

"The Highway is mostly flooded now," Domingo said. "We have had to trail through higher ground. It wasn't easy."

Gary asked, "What about you? You say you grew up here?"

"Yeah. My grandfather was a canal zone shipping agent. I was born and raised here, and worked on the canal myself. But we moved to Florida in twenty aught aught when sovereignty over the canal passed back to Panama. But I came back on contract, and things weren't so bad as everybody thought they were going to get with the locals in charge, and eventually I settled again." He turned. "Tom, go get these folks some water."

Tom looked doubtfully at the newcomers. But he went back to the boat, his automatic held loosely in one hand, and returned with a clutch of canteens suspended by neck straps which he passed to Gary. Gary shared them out, and gratefully sipped clean-tasting water.

"And you stayed here when the flood came," Grace said.

"Nowhere else to go. This is home, for me and my family. When the sea started rising over the lower locks, and the canal got screwed up, the Panamanians just abandoned the place. Could have been kept working long after that, but once it was given up, without maintenance, it didn't take long to fall apart."

He pointed over his shoulder, to the Darien area. "Big

dam up there called Madden, bottled up the river Chagres and created the old Alajuela Lake. When the Madden dam failed it was a real torrent that came down the valley and poured into Gatun." He gestured at a landscape now drowned. "Gatun flooded its locks, undermining them, and eventually broke its own dam on the Atlantic side. Then river Chagres came curling down through the wreckage, and found its old path back to the sea, on the Pacific side.

"But then the sea rose up further, and covered everything over. Now you'd never know it was ever there. Damn shame. But we always had to work hard to stop the jungle from taking it back. The canal was a wound in the Earth that was always trying to heal, my daddy used to say."

"And now you make a living off your boat?"

"We fish. Me and my family, my boys." His eyes narrowed, still suspicious. "There are a whole lot of us, all around this shoreline. Boats and rafts and houses on the coast. We look out for each other."

"I'm sure you do."

"So what is it you want? Passage to the other side of the strait?"

"That's about the size of it, if you can do it. There are a lot of us, however."

Again that suspicious frown. "How many?"

"A thousand."

Moore's mouth gaped. "A *thousand*. Are you kidding me?"

"There used to be a lot more."

Walker City had still been tens of thousands strong when they started their long walk south from Lincoln, though many had followed Thandie Jones's footsteps to Denver, and others had gone to try to find refuge in Utah. As they had walked south, more had split off when they had found somewhere permanent to stay, often following spur roads off the route of the Pan-American Highway. On the other hand others had joined the marching community, people displaced or simply unhappy, seeking a kind of order among this exodus of Okies.

Many had been born, many had died. Slowly, over the years, the numbers had dwindled. But there were still a thousand of them, a mobile township still run out of the mayor's office with its guards and doctors and daily rotas, all following Gary's vision of Project City, an enclave at the roof of the world where there would be room for them all.

Moore said, "Can't be easy lodging all those people in the damn rainforest. Well, a thousand's more than can fit in my little boat."

"You can manage," Domingo said. "Fifty, even a hundred at a time. It isn't so far. You can run a ferry service."

Moore's suspicion was replaced by calculation. "Well, hell, I suppose I could. But why would I want to?"

Gary kept his voice pleasant, his expression relaxed. "We don't expect charity. We'll pay."

"What with? Diet Coke?" Moore laughed.

"Yes," said Gary frankly. "We have other goods. Otherwise we'll work. There are a thousand of us; we have skills, tools." He looked around. "We could transform this place for you. Make it future-proof. You need to think about what's to come. I used to be a climatologist, I know what I'm talking about. We can give you a better chance of surviving the sea-level rise." He glanced uphill. "Such as by building wharves further up, a hundred meters, two. Ready for when the sea reaches that altitude."

Moore seemed uncertain, and that was a look Gary was familiar with; even now people didn't wish to believe in the flooding. "You think that's going to happen, it's going to get that far?"

"Oh, yes. And you need to plan for it, right? Let us help you."

Moore eyed him, calculating again. He stepped closer, so his son couldn't hear. "Tell you what I got a need for. Women. Wives for my boys. You understand?" He cast a sideways glance at Grace. "A couple of my boys are too young yet, but maybe you got some little girls you can leave here to ripen, so to speak. Take 'em off your hands. Or failing that"—he tilted his hand back and forth—"a little action. We are kind of isolated up here. You see what I'm saying?"

Gary said evenly, "We don't run brothels. And we don't sell people."

"Seems to me I got the boat you need."

"And it seems to me," Domingo said, smiling broadly, "that we are a thousand strong, and you are a handful. You could kill the three of us, you could kill ten times our number, and you would still lose your lives. *And* your boat."

Moore stepped back. "So is that the game? You said you were no threat."

"So we lied," Domingo said.

Gary said firmly, "We're not bandits. We want to trade or work, Sam. We think of ourselves as Okies."

"Had a great-great-uncle was an Okie in the Depression."

"Yes. It's not dishonorable. But the bottom line is—"

"We have no choice but to go on," Grace said unexpectedly. "We have to cross this strait."

Moore looked at her. "And that means I have to do business with you."

"You'll get a good deal," Gary said. "But, yes, you have to do business with us."

"Sorry, man," said Domingo. "Hey, it could be worse."

Moore seemed to accept the reality. "All right. Come back here tomorrow, talk terms and work out some kind of schedule. There's more you need to know, as well."

"Like what?"

Moore gestured at Darien. "Tough country there. Always was. Now you got indigenous types, and paramilitaries, and a bunch of Marxists from that Commie group that mounted the coup in Colombia. You don't want to be caught in the cross fire."

"I hear what you say. Any help you can give us we'll pay for."

"Fine. Tomorrow." Moore and his boy turned and went back to their rowboat.

Gary blew out his cheeks. "I hate this horse-trading, Domingo."

"You're good at it, man. Hey, nobody got shot today. That's a result!"

Gary looked down at the strait, the single boat moored to its drowned tree. "No more Panama. You know, some geologists used to say that the formation of the isthmus was the single most important geological event since the end of the dinosaurs. It changed the pattern of ocean currents, globally. Instead of the old equatorial flows, water exchanging between Atlantic and Pacific, now you had great interpolar streams. Ice caps formed, and the Ice Ages began. Without the cooler climate forcing us out of the trees and onto the savannah, no humanity, probably. All because of a sliver of land. But now it's drowned again, and everything's going to change."

But Grace looked at him blankly.

And Domingo couldn't care less about global ocean currents. He grumbled, "I hope they take the girls and leave the Diet Cokes. I myself like Diet Coke, and don't want it all given away! Is it a sin to wish for that?"

They climbed back toward the line of trees, and the relative cool of the forest.

64

ater on the day of Lily's last visit to the Nazca raft,
Nathan Lammockson held what he called an "equator-
crossing party" at Chosica, in a lounge of his still-
unfinished ship. Lily was drained after the jaunt to Nazca.
But it wasn't the sort of event you could get out of, if you
were as close to Nathan as she was.

Nathan played host beneath a huge animated wall-map
of the world, which showed the rising sea and the continents drowning, over and over. Lily, as smart in a trouser
suit as she was capable of getting, stood uncomfortably
with a glass of fruit punch in her hand. Juan Villegas
looked the part in a dapper lounge suit, as did Amanda at
his side. Slim and elegant in her brittle way, Amanda was
still beautiful in her mid-fifties. Age suited her, in fact, Lily
sometimes thought; she looked *good* with the wrinkles in
her brow, the lines that framed her eyes, the stretched flesh
at her neck, even if she did color her hair.

Nathan had a string quartet playing soothing classical
pieces. The players had been filtered out of the refugee
streams, their skills detected and tested for by Nathan's efficient personnel department. You could find any skill you
wanted in the crowds washing up from the lowlands, if you
were patient.

And through the unglazed portholes that lined this
unfinished lounge you could glimpse Chosica and its
sprawling shantytown of workers, a grim contrast to the
glittering atmosphere aboard the ship. Lily was all too
aware about the muttering over Nathan's grandiose folly.
In the 1930s the original *Queen Mary* had absorbed the
industrial output of sixty British towns, and was built in
a shipyard with decades' experience. Nathan had had
to build not just his ship but the shipbuilding industry

around it too, and he had sucked Peru's technological resources dry to do it.

Given the atmosphere, it really wasn't much of a party.

Lily plucked up the courage to say something about this to Nathan. "We're so tired, Nathan. Dog-tired. The endless pressure of events, you know?"

"It is kind of relentless, isn't it?" He took a healthy slug of his drink, a mash whiskey with water. "But, hell, that doesn't mean you shouldn't have a good time. That's why I call these landmark parties. Every time we have something to celebrate, let's roll out the barrel."

She had to smile; just for a moment he sounded like the archetypal Londoner. *Rowl aht the barrull.* "Yes, but Nathan, I don't even understand what landmark we're celebrating here. 'Crossing the equator'? What equator?"

He grinned. "I'll announce it later, but since it's you ... According to the boffins, today's the very day the sea rises past eight hundred meters above the old datum. Now, you know as well as I do that that kind of data is always iffy. I mean, the measurement of the rise itself is getting patchier as those radar satellites fall out of the sky, and altitude measurement was always shit besides. You've been to Nazca today, which is just going under and isn't that supposed to have been six hundred meters up? ... However. The brainiacs say it's eight hundred meters today, and so it's eight hundred. Now you see why it's an equator to cross?"

She nodded. "Because eight hundred meters is the fifty percent mark."

"Right. Today is the day we lost fifty percent of the world's old land surface. Of course the percentage of *useful* surface lost is a lot higher; we still got Greenland and old Antarctica, ice deserts poking uselessly above the waves, and all the mountain ranges ... Still, fifty percent. And about five-sixths of the human population displaced or dead. What a mess. Cheers." He drank more whiskey.

"You can be a cold-hearted bastard, Nathan."

"You think? Maybe I'm just getting tired too. I mean, look at that fucking map." He snapped his fingers.

The big wall display froze at a projected eight hundred meters. The map was mostly blue, with the shapes of the old continents showing in a paler tint—new continental shelf, carpeted with drowned river valleys and deserts, forests and cities. The Andes were an eerie tracery down the western shore of South America.

Nathan said, "Look what's left. In North America the Rockies states are surviving, from New Mexico up through Colorado, Utah, Oregon. In Africa you have that big slicing from southwest to northeast, sparing South Africa and the eastern nations, through Tanzania and Kenya up to Ethiopia. In Asia you have the Himalayas, Mongolia, the Stans, just a pit of warfare, chewing up lives like a meat grinder. Aside from that nothing save for scattered mountaintops and bits of high ground in Britain, Australia, India, Indonesia. Europe's gone outside the Alps, pretty much. Russia gone, even the Urals."

"Mountaintops and bits of high ground," Lily repeated.

"We still get messages. Beacons from the high places. Hell, I never heard of most of these places before they started transmitting to each other over the world ocean." He glanced at her. "Something I have to tell you. The highest city in Spain is called Avila. And guess what?"

"Tell me."

"We got a message from there. When Madrid was evacuated the Spanish government collapsed, and there was a final power struggle. And the faction that came out on top was—the Fathers of the Elect."

"You're kidding."

He shook his head. "They've been asking for help. They heard I've been sheltering you and the others. Maybe they thought that was enough of a connection." He laughed. "They've asked for your forgiveness, you and Piers and the rest."

She was astonished. "What do they want?"

He shrugged. "The usual. A place on the high ground. I doubt if we could help anyhow. But it's your baby. What would you say?"

She considered. "They kept me in a hole in the ground for years. They killed one of my friends, they raped another, and they left us for dead. Fuck 'em."

"Fuck 'em." He raised a glass and drank to that. He looked at the map once more. "There's still a ways to go before we run out of land. Lhasa in Tibet is four kilometers up. La Paz is just as high . . . I think we're seeing an end game to the wars, though. In each of the main surviving highland zones, the Americas, Africa, the Himalayas, you'll soon see control established in the hands of a few strong governments, or individuals. There'll be order, of a sort. And maybe a bottoming-out in the deaths. We're nearing the final end of the corporate feeding frenzy too. Things have broken down too far for that to be sustained any longer. The survivors among the rich will be those who were smart enough to have converted their wealth to power and security by now.

"There are some who say, you know, that this global collapse is a good thing. Or at least it will look that way in the long run. Maybe our civilization was overcomplicated, like a mature forest, with every scrap of land occupied, every convertible bit of matter turned into biomass, the trees, worms, beetles all locked into a complex web of dependencies, everything living off everything else. Maximum efficiency but minimum resilience. So then when the shock comes, the fire or the earthquake or the drought, the dieback is huge. But what survives is stronger, more adaptable, robust."

"Hm. I'm not sure it's a good analogy, Nathan. Anyhow I can't imagine you embracing any dieback. I bet you're thinking ahead. You're always thinking ahead."

He glanced at her. "Well, I always have a plan B. I guess you know that much about me by now. And where I don't have plans, I have options. Such as, I managed to buy up the Svalbard vault from the Norwegians, before the government there collapsed."

"The what vault?"

"A post 9/11 if-the-apocalypse-comes thing. A worldwide project to establish a seed vault, three million samples, a hundred meters deep inside a mountain on some Norwegian island. It was a smart design. Even if the power failed it would have been kept cooled by the permafrost. But they didn't see the flood coming."

"So where are the seeds now?"

He grinned and pointed down. "In the hold."

"On the *ship*?"

"Nice touch, don't you think?"

"All right, I'll buy it. When the flood goes down, Nathan Lammockson plays Johnny Appleseed and restocks the world. What else? Give me one headline."

"Race-specific weapons."

That shocked her. "Jesus, Nathan."

He glanced out of the window at the laborers in their shacks. "I've had a team of experts working on the problem for years. An application of pharmacogenomics, they call it. If the shit really hits the fan, I want to be sure me and mine survive."

"You really are crazy."

"Everybody says that," he replied, unperturbed. "But you've all followed me from Southend-on-Sea to this damn place, and nobody close to me has suffered so much as a day's hunger. Who's crazy, then? I pray I don't have to use such weapons. But I know I wouldn't forgive myself if I didn't prepare for what I can foresee. Naturally this is confidential."

At that moment Piers approached Nathan. He was dressed in his grubby field coverall, and looked as out of place in this glittering lounge as a tramp in a palace. "Trouble at La Oroya," he said.

"Shit," said Nathan. "We need that smelter."

"A chopper's waiting." Piers glanced at Lily. "You'd better come."

"Why? Oh. Ollantay's involved?"

Piers said nothing.

"I'll find Amanda," she said, and pushed her way through the crowd.

65

The smelter facility dominated the high valley of La Oroya. The mountains surrounding the valley made a natural bowl which stopped the breezes blowing the pollution away, so that smog hung thick over the town, visible from kilometers away. And as the chopper swept in you could see the columns of white smoke rising from the stacks, rising into the clear air. The land itself had been turned into a grubby industrial site, scarred by waste dumps and vehicle tracks.

On the ground, Ollantay greeted Piers confidently. Ollantay had his own private army with him, Inca-costumed thugs armed with rifles. He simply ignored Piers's squad of AxysCorp troops with their formidable-looking weapons. And behind Ollantay, sitting on the ground in rank after sullen rank, were the workers who had blockaded the smelting plant. Ollantay looked magnificent, Lily thought. He was in his mid-thirties now, a man in the prime of his life. He wore the clothing of an Inca noble: feathers in his tied-back hair, a huge, elaborate gold plug in each pierced ear, and a tunic of dyed vicuna wool embroidered with some kind of heraldic symbol.

And Kristie was at his side, in vicuna-wool clothing of her own, her child in her arms. Manco, her half-Quechua boy now nearly four years old, was almost too big for her to hold. For all the longing glances Amanda gave her, Kristie looked as if she belonged here, at her man's side.

Ignoring Ollantay, and very obviously keeping his distance from Kristie, Piers walked up to the workers and their families on the ground. He put his hands on his hips and spoke in clear, clipped English. A couple of the AxysCorp squaddies stepped forward to interpret for him in Spanish and Quechua. "Now look here—this is all unnecessary, and very unhelpful. I know things are difficult for you up here, but then things are difficult for all of us.

"And what you do is very important." He waved a hand at the smelter, which would be idle soon, when the Axys-Corp management team running the blockaded plant ran out of feedstock. "Refining your arsenic, lead, cadmium, copper, you are an essential link in the industrial infrastructure of Project City and its environs. Without you, the high-technology civilization we've been able to maintain here will fail. As simple as that. And if that happens it will affect all of us. Why, right now on the other side of the world, the final battle for Jerusalem is being fought out between Christian, Jew and Muslim with wooden clubs and chunks of rubble from the smashed holy monuments. Is that what you want to see here?"

A woman stood. She held up a child, an infant maybe two years old. It hung limply, its head lolling. "Lead in baby," she said in heavily accented English. "In bone, liver, kidneys, brain. Doctors say." She pinched the child's leg. "No feeling in legs, arms. No speak. Lead in baby."

"I'm sure there are treatments—solutions, filters, face-masks—"

Ollantay said, "There were pollution problems even before the flood, when this place was owned by a US corporation, before Nathan Lammockson bought it up. It's one reason Lammockson came to Peru, isn't it, Piers, for the high-altitude mining facilities that were already here? Back before the flood, at least they used to save the worst of their emissions for overcast days, or nights. Now they don't care; there is no law, no environmental legislation, no government to stop AxysCorp polluting as it likes." Piers tried to interrupt him, but Ollantay shouted him down. "And the population affected is so much larger now, with the refugees crowding from the lowlands into the valley, begging for work . . ."

While they argued, Lily approached Kristie. "You shouldn't be here," Lily said. "Ollantay's just making trouble."

"He's a leader," Kristie said confidently. "The Oroyinos respect him. Everybody in the high valleys respects him, all the way to Puno, even the *mestizos* and Spanish." Thirty now, there was nothing left of the English girl who had first come here, Lily thought, save her trace of accent.

Amanda could barely look at her daughter, or her grandson. "You're an idiot, and so is he." She still wore the black dress she'd donned for Nathan's party, under a waxed coat and incongruous rubber boots.

Kristie hissed, "And you think speaking to us like that is going to help, Mum? Listen to me. You, and Piers and Lily and Nathan, you're all going to have to take the feelings of the people up here more seriously. What do you think is going to happen—that you'll be able to force people to work at the smelting plant, and in the shitty mines at Puno, at gunpoint? How long do you think that will last?"

Lily felt utterly dismayed at the scene, the filthy air, the people sitting in the dirt, the limp, damaged child. It was the sort of place that, unconsciously or not, she kept away from in the course of her work for AxysCorp. "No wonder people are drawn to Ollantay, if they have to live like this."

"Yes," Kristie said in triumph. "And Ollantay represents history, Lily—it's personal for these people. Despite all the Spaniards and other colonials could do, it's a history that never went away. Ollantay calls me his *aclla*."

"His what?"

"His chosen woman. His holy companion, like the Vestal Virgins of Rome." She hefted her child. "Though less of the virgin in my case . . . And maybe I will become his *coya*, wife of an emperor."

"A holy companion," Amanda said. "An emperor's wife. Oh, for God's sake, Kristie, you bloody little fool!"

There was trouble. Somebody got up and swung a punch at Piers. The AxysCorp guards dived in to protect him, and Ollantay and his men rushed in after that. Lily hurried over, hoping to separate the men before any shots got fired.

66

From Kristie Caistor's scrapbook:

Nathan's Ark Three project was supported by a global organization of like-minded individuals that had evolved out of the old LaRei rich man's club into a survivors' network of resource flows and shared information. And, just as Nathan was supported by his colleagues, so he supported other initiatives. Kristie, curious about this and the other LaRei projects underway around the world, tried to hack into Nathan's systems, and scoured his in-house news channels for snippets of information.

She was intrigued by a feed from an astronomy camp on a peak in the Chilean Andes called Cerro Pachon. In the clear air up here, no fewer than three great telescopes had been operating since the beginning of the century, known as Gemini South, SOAR, and the immense Large Synoptic Survey Telescope, which was capable of taking a survey of the entire sky several times a week. As the site was a relatively near neighbor of Nathan's, he undertook to maintain support chains to the astronomers, adapting and improvising as the flood washed out lowland roads, airports and rail links.

Kristie, more interested in other arks, didn't linger long over her images of bundled-up astronomers, laboring under spectacular skies framed by glacier-topped peaks. She did wonder briefly why a community of the rich in a time of global flood should devote resources to searching the sky.

67

"My name is Gary Boyle."

"Sorry, buddy. You're not on any list I got."

"I know Nathan Lammockson. He helped me—I was a hostage in Barcelona—he sprung us out, vowed to support us . . ."

But this coca-chewing guard, his face hidden by his immense sunglasses, looked too young to have heard of Gary, or even Barcelona.

And the fence he and his companions defended was a good three meters tall, concrete panels topped by barbed wire and studded by machine gun towers. It stretched from horizon to glass-clear Andean horizon. This was the boundary of Project City, of Lammockson's empire. And it was sealed shut against Gary Boyle.

They were alone in a vast empty landscape, Walker City's advance party led by Gary and Grace and Domingo, the AxysCorp guards who had come out from behind their fence to deal with them, and a handful of locals, young Andean men, standing idly by in colorful wool ponchos, watching. Gary, dizzy with the altitude, felt desperate. His phone had been dead for months. If the guards wouldn't let him pass, he had no way to contact Lily.

"I'm Gary Boyle! I know Lily Brooke! And this is Grace, Grace Gray! We walked down two continents to get here. The walk consumed my life. I'm forty-three years old. My whole damn life. But now we're here, now we need help." He felt absurdly like crying.

"Look, guy, you can see how we're fixed." Gary wondered how he had managed to pick up a Brooklyn accent, since he couldn't have been more than five years old when New York drowned. "We ain't got room for no more. We ain't got room for *you*. Just because you can throw a few

names around makes no difference to that. Mr. Lammockson is famous all over the world, anybody can say they
know him, right?" He leaned closer to Gary. "And let me
tell you something else. Even supposing you and your lady
friend here are buddies of Mr. Lammockson, even supposing you could prove it, there's still no way you would be
allowed in with your army of bums."

"If you'd just take a message to Lily Brooke—"

"No." The guard started shouting now, exerting his
authority. "I'm not some runner for you. *You* take a message. You take a message back to your 'mayor.' You tell
her that if you don't shift your thousand asses, they'll be
shifted for you." He looked Gary up and down, contemp-
tuously staring through his sunglasses. "You been warned.
You got forty-eight hours. You got that straight?" And
he turned and walked back to the gate in the wall, held
open for him by more AxysCorp goons.

Suddenly Gary was exhausted. The world yellowed. He
bent, felt the blood pound in his ears, retched.

Grace rubbed his back. Domingo squatted down beside
him.

"Well, you tried," Grace said.

"This damn altitude," Gary said. "I can't *think* straight."
He sat on the grassy ground, and gazed up at the wall that
excluded him.

"Nobody's going to blame you, my friend," Domingo
said.

"Nathan's breaking his promise to me," Gary said. "And
that means I'm breaking my promise to you all, the mayor,
the thousand people who walked all this way with me."

Grace looked at the blank wall, her expression empty.
"It makes no difference," she said. "If we keep walking. Not
to me. I spent my life walking. I don't believe I ever thought
it would end."

"But listen," Domingo said more urgently, leaning close
to Gary. "Never mind broken promises. You heard what
the fool with the gun said. Suppose there were a way to
get in, to make contact with this Lily, or Lammockson. If
we persist we might find a way. Suppose they allowed you
in—you, and Grace, a handful of others. Suppose it was as
the guard said. If they let you in, but you had to leave the
others behind—"

It was just the kind of deal Nathan Lammockson might ask him to make, Gary thought. But he had made his choice long ago, when, even as times became so hard, he found he was unable to abandon Walker City. "No. It's all of us, or none."

Grace shrugged. "Then I guess it's none of us. We're a thousand strong, but we're no army."

"But armies do exist in this world."

Gary turned, still sitting. He saw woolen trousers, boots, a figure standing over him. One of the locals, a Quechua, had spoken to him. Gary tried to stand, but staggered, and Grace had to help him.

The Quechua must have been in his thirties. Not tall, but a strong face—no, arrogant more than strong. He wore a woolen tunic, brightly dyed. Huge golden studs stretched his earlobes. Behind him were more young men, similarly dressed, watching cautiously. They wore ponchos though the day was warm, and Gary wondered if they carried concealed weapons.

"So who are you?"

"My name is Ollantay." He smiled. "The name means nothing to you. That's fine. But your name means something to me, Gary Boyle." He turned to Grace. "And you are Helen Gray's girl, yes?"

Reflexively, Domingo stood between Ollantay and Grace. "You know about us? How? Are you from Project City, from Lammockson's people?"

"Quite the opposite. I've never met Nathan Lammockson. But I have met your fellow hostages, Piers Michaelmas, Lily Brooke."

"Oh? How so?"

"Kristie Caistor is my wife."

Gary gaped at him. "Kristie—" Lily's niece, whom he had last seen as a kid in London—who must now, he reminded himself, be in her thirties herself.

Domingo said, "And what was it you said about armies?"

Ollantay's eyes narrowed. "You have been excluded by Lammockson. So have we, we Quechua. And we have been exploited by him for a generation now, as he huddles in his palaces, and builds his absurd mountain-stranded boat. Here, on a land that used to be ours, we suffer the last spasm of western colonialism. But times are changing. A final battle approaches, a final reckoning, before the sea closes over us all."

Gary was bewildered by this exotic young man, and his head spun with his mentions of Lily and Kristie. "What the hell are you talking about? What boat?"

Ollantay gestured at the fence. "There is no room for barriers like this, not any more. Now is the time to right wrongs. It will not be vengeance. Simply justice."

Domingo looked him up and down. "And how are you going to fight this battle, mountain boy? Will you ride llamas and throw spears?"

Ollantay faced him, and Gary sensed the silent conflict between them, a contest for dominance. "Not spears," Ollantay said at last. "I will tell you one thing, one fact to take back to your footsore mayor. We have Kalashnikov rifles. AK47s. They were extracted from a saved cache in Lima, our drowned capital. We used Lammockson's own salvage submarines to achieve this, right under his nose. We have the guns, and the ammunition. That is how we will fight our battle. Perhaps we could win without you, though we are not numerically strong. But you, who have come walking out of nowhere, are an opportunity for us. With you we will overwhelm Lammockson and his AxysCorp guards and his Project City, his technological Utopia."

"We didn't come here for this," Gary said.

Domingo, determined now, said, "No, but this is what we've found, Gary. Before, we always walked away when we came to a crisis. But this is the end of the journey. You always knew it would come to this, some day, when the land ran out, and people crowded together tighter and tighter, like goats on a mountain summit. You heard what that guard said. If we're driven away from here there's nowhere else to go. It is the crunch for us. Fight or die."

"I won't take this back to the mayor."

"But I will," Domingo said. "In fact it's not your choice." He glanced at Ollantay. "Are you ready to come with us now?"

Ollantay smiled. "I have been waiting for this all my life."

Gary looked at Grace. Her expression was closed up, unreadable.

And suddenly he was retching, his head pounding, the altitude beating him again. He leaned over, resting his hands on his knees, while Grace rubbed his back.

68

From Kristie Caistor's scrapbook:

All along the flooded fringes of the Andes the rafts drifted. Nobody knew how many there were, how many people were struggling to survive out there on the breast of the sea.

Nathan Lammockson posted troops along the shifting coastline to stop them landing. There was never any shortage of volunteers for that duty.

And he sent out boats among the rafts. The boats carried doctors, but not to administer to the sick.

Nathan had long been digging up old population-reduction philosophies and techniques. Even before the flood began there had been voluntary human extinction movements, developed by those who believed mankind was essentially a scourge and that its sole remaining duty was to restore Earth to its pre-human condition as best as possible, before submitting gracefully to the dark. Lammockson argued that here you had a rationalization for not fleeing from the encroaching flood, for submitting to it. So the doctors in the boats were "suicide missionaries," trained to counsel refugees to accept their fate. They were equipped with appropriate medications.

Other missionaries, not sanctioned by Lammockson, sailed among the desolate raft communities. One motorboat carried a preacher, gunning up and down the shore, haranguing with a loudhailer. This is how it feels to live in a world with an intervening god, he said. How mankind was back in the days of the Old Testament. Nathan considered shutting him up, but decided he was doing as effective a job as his suicide doctors.

The population of the rafts wasn't fixed. Rafts broke up, or were cannibalized by others. Or they drifted away, over the horizon, to a fate nobody on the land cared to imagine. But there were always more, rising up from the flooded towns.

Kristie watched this. Isolated from Cusco for years, she wondered if there was anybody in there who fretted as she did about how long this could go on.

69

August 2035

Ollantay's ragtag army broke through Project City's outer perimeters near the airport.

The invasion force had no armor or heavy weapons. But it did have a lot of people, the Quechua and the other dispossessed from the highlands, and a good number of the resentful poor from P-ville, as well as hundreds of able-bodied adults from Walker City. And it did have an awful lot of AK47s and ammunition to spare.

Few died in the desultory exchanges of fire around the airport. Nathan's forces were too well dug in to be vulnerable to Ollantay's crude tactics, but on the other hand they seemed reluctant to deploy the heavy weapons they must have possessed. When the skirmish was over, the rebels left a significant detachment of Lammockson's forces pinned down, holed up in the terminal building. Ollantay presented the stalemate as a victory, because it left this quadrant of Cusco largely undefended.

Then he led his army into the city from the southeast.

The invaders worked their way up a broad, deserted street called the Avenida El Sol, which, according to the elderly maps downloaded into Gary's sleeve patch, ran straight into the old center of Cusco.

The rebels broke into two files which proceeded down either side of the road, in the cover of the buildings, keeping away from the center line where they would be vulnerable to sniper fire. Such rudimentary military tactics had been grafted into Ollantay's thinking by a handful of military veterans among the Okies of Walker City. But inexperience showed in the cowering, nervous way the invaders huddled in doorways, clinging to scraps of cover, peering fearfully at shadows and at the sky. Most of them had Kalashnikovs, weapons they waved around with a casualness that scared Gary.

Walker City's current mayor, Janet Thorson, was a tough fifty-something who originally hailed from Minnesota, graying blond, short, strong-looking, wary. Now she walked with Gary in the van of Ollantay's army. They both wore their antique AxysCorp-durable coveralls, still their most flexible and enduring garments and, dirtied down as rough camouflage, the nearest they had to battle dress—garments whose purchase had once made Nathan Lammockson that little bit richer, now worn by an army come to bring him down. Neither of them carried weapons save the handguns tucked inside their coveralls. They had no armor, no flak jackets or helmets, and Gary, who was no soldier, felt very vulnerable.

"Shit, these kids got a right to be wary," Janet Thorson said. "Let's face it, we're none of us used to cities anymore. Some of the Walker kids have *never* been in an environment like this, never in their young lives. And I guess most of these Andean hill-folk types are first-timers too."

Gary imagined that was true. And it was true that Cusco was a better functioning town than any he personally had seen for years. The buildings were reasonably intact, the road surface maintained. There were even *shops* lining this long avenue, shut up and boarded now but obviously still working. But there was nobody around, no adults or children, not even a dog; even the birds were quiet. "I guess the town itself is a reflection of Nathan Lammockson's will," he said. "Willpower and discipline and leadership, applied across decades."

Thorson grunted. "Yeah, that and the money he managed to vacuum up while the world was going to hell. But discipline, foresight, yes. Which is why this lull makes me uneasy." She pointed to a CCTV camera on a stand; it panned silently, viewing the advancing army. "They know we're here. I think Nathan Lammockson knows exactly what he's doing. He must have seen that a day like this would come, when the workers in the shantytowns and the mountains who've been spending their lives for his precious city would rise up—even if we walkers are a joker in the pack. No, he'll have foreseen this; he'll have prepared. We're walking into some kind of trap, is what I think," she said grimly. "It just hasn't snapped shut yet."

As they pressed on the advance units came up against more defensive perimeters, at intersections of the El Sol with transverse roads called the Avenida Pachacutec, just north of the rail station, and the Avenida Garcilaso a few blocks further on. At each halt Gary, maybe a hundred meters back from the advance guard, was able to hear the popping of gunfire, screams, yells before the column was waved on. Evidently Nathan's resistance was proving no tougher in the town than at the airport.

When he came through the intersections himself Gary saw the remains of barbed-wire fences, smashed-open roadblocks, pillboxes of sandbags and concrete slabs. And at the Garcilaso intersection he saw a dead man, some guy in a bright blue AxysCorp uniform that looked as if it had rolled out of the factory today. He wore a white helmet, and had a sergeant's stripes on his arm. He was flung over the road surface, face down, limbs sprawled like a doll's, a deep crimson stain spreading over his back. This was the first corpse Gary had seen today. He had seen plenty of death in his time with Walker City, and enough violent death, but he never got used to it.

Now the column halted again. The order came to hole up. People looked for shelter, from the sun as much as from sniper fire, in doorways and alleys. Doors splintered and windows shattered as the invaders began to help themselves to whatever they could loot from the shops and residences, offices and churches. But Gary started to hear complaints that there was no food or water to be found.

The mayor told Gary she was going forward to see what was happening, and left him.

Gary went back twenty meters to find Grace, who had been walking with Domingo. Grace looked more uncomfortable than nervous. Domingo looked like some kind of pirate, grinning hugely as he cradled his own AK47, which he had polished until it gleamed in the clear Andean light. He had a looted necklace, a string of chunky aquamarine blocks, wrapped around his head like a bandanna.

"You really are an asshole, Domingo," Gary said with faint disgust.

Domingo laughed. "But this is a day for assholes. What next, O great non-asshole gringo?"

"The mayor's going forward. I guess Ollantay's plan-

ning the next step. Come on, we'll go up with her." He took
Grace's hand.

"We are mere foot soldiers," Domingo said.

Gary shook his head. "We got friends in this city. Anything we can do to reduce the body count today, we're
going to do."

Domingo bowed. "Then I follow your lead."

Holding Grace's hand and followed by Domingo, Gary
worked up the line until he caught up with the mayor's
party. They had stopped at another major intersection, beside a green space beneath the shoulders of a monumental-
looking church.

Standing before this blocky pile, Ollantay held court.
He was in his Inca finery, gaudy woolen tunic and trousers,
those gold ear-studs bright in the sun, and he had a gold
helmet on his head, looted from some private collection
during the bee-sting raids he had mounted on Cusco before
this main assault. He stood erect, his face dark and proud,
here on this day of his apotheosis.

Mayor Thorson stood before Ollantay dubiously, listening to the conversation that passed between Ollantay
and his senior generals, such as they were. They were a
pack of thugs and troublemakers who had been attracted
to Ollantay's cause from the highland communities, farms
and mines, here to settle old scores. There were even a
few of the dispossessed from the raft communities offshore. This core group stood around a wooden box that
looked like a coffin, hauled here on a cart.

Among them was a man Gary didn't recognize, in a
fresh-looking AxysCorp uniform. Aged maybe thirty, he
was overweight, an unusual sight nowadays; he had a puffy,
resentful face, and he stood by Ollantay nervously.

And Kristie was here. Her little boy wore feathers in
his hair and had his own Inca-prince costume. He held his
mother's hand, one free finger probing a small nostril. It
had been a shock this morning, the first shock of the day,
for Gary to see Kristie Caistor at the side of a man like
Ollantay. In fact, he saw, she wore a pink plastic backpack,
incongruous amid the Inca stuff, and Gary had a faint
memory of how she had carried the thing as that bright,
pretty London kid, long ago.

Gary murmured to Thorson, "So what's the plan?"

"Ollantay has spies in Project City," she said. "Moles. Like that fat guy, evidently. Lammockson and his senior people have holed up in a sports stadium a few blocks that-away." She pointed northeast along the transverse avenue.

And that was where Lily and Piers must be, Gary thought. What a strange reunion this was going to be. "So we're going to lay siege?"

"Yeah. Although Ollantay seems to think he has a way in. Meanwhile Ollantay has some kind of ceremony to carry out here."

"A ceremony. Some Inca thing?" Gary glanced around, at the blank faces of the buildings that surrounded them, the empty roads. He heard the distant buzz of a chopper. "The longer we wait here the more vulnerable we are."

"Tell me about it. But you know Ollantay. Look at these guys. A lot of them aren't thinking at all. They're dispossessed, they've slaved for Lammockson, they're refugees— as we are. The guys from the rafts in particular have got nothing to lose. This is their moment in the sun, their chance to strike back at *something*, somebody. The events of today have as much to do with testosterone as lebens-raum, I'd say."

"That's a grim thought."

Her face was hard. "Well, we're here to maximize our own gain. We owe nothing to Nathan Lammockson."

The fat thirty-year-old broke away from Ollantay's cir-cle and approached Gary. "I know you," he said. "You're Gary Boyle. One of the hostages from Barcelona."

Gary stared at him, startled. "Have I met you?"

"I was just a kid when you got out. Maybe you don't remember. I'm Hammond Lammockson."

Gary immediately saw the likeness to Nathan, which had been pricking his memory. He even spoke with a trace of his father's London accent. "Wow. Yes, I do remember you. What are you doing here?"

"With AxysCorp's enemies, you mean? I guess you don't know my father well. The game's up for him. He will be put on trial by the newly constituted government of Qosqo."

"Trial, huh. And what are you, a witness for the prosecu-tion?"

Hammond's face was resentful, angry. "I don't know what you think of Nathan Lammockson. I don't care. As a father he's a disaster. He spent his life putting me down, belittling me, marginalizing me."

Gary could imagine that. "Maybe he thought he was toughening you up."

"Well, he succeeded."

Gary said, "Lily Brooke, Piers Michaelmas—they're here, they're still alive? I've not been able to contact them since we came to the area."

"Oh, yeah. Still alive. Still my father's favorites. Whereas I'm just a passenger. He was always closer to you people than to me, you hostages." He sneered. "Like pets."

Gary recoiled from this man's bitterness. "You're his son. I remember Nathan saying that everything he did he was doing for you, you and his grandchildren."

"Grandchildren. Yeah. You should have seen the frigid bitch he chose for me to have those grandchildren for him. Well, I failed to oblige."

"I can't believe you're planning to betray him."

"Watch me." And he walked away, back to the Quechua group, as Ollantay began his ceremony.

Ollantay climbed up onto the coffinlike box. The murmur of conversation around him ceased.

"So we begin the end-game," Ollantay said. "The show-down with Nathan Lammockson, and the eradication of the stain of colonialism. And it's fitting that we make ready for the final battle here at this historic site." He waved a hand. "This is Qoricancha, the temple of the sun—the most important place of worship in the Inca empire. Once, seven hundred sheets of gold covered the walls. The mummified bodies of emperors sat on thrones of gold and silver. Even in this patio where we stand there were golden statues of beautiful women, and llamas, trees, flowers—even golden butterflies. The Spaniards desecrated the temple, seeking only gold, caring nothing for the Incas and their gods, and they turned this stone husk into a Christian church.

"But now the Inca sun rises once more." He raised a military boot, and slammed it down on the coffin lid. The lid splintered and broke open. Ollantay reached down and hauled up a tangle of bones, broken and dusty, fragments threaded together with bits of wire into a loose representation of a skeleton. Ollantay grasped the skull, its jaw gaping open, and rattled the bones in the air. "Behold Pizarro! Behold Pizarro!"

There was a huge roar from his followers. Two men pushed upright a gibbet improvised from tent poles, and a noose was passed around the neck of the conquistador, five hundred years dead, his bones yellowed and splintered.

As the skeleton was hoisted aloft before the mighty walls of the temple, Mayor Thorson murmured, "God help us all."

70

It had been an awfully long time since Cusco's Estadio Universitario had been used for the purposes it was designed for, Lily reflected. Now the stadium's pitch was crowded by tents and Portaloos. The grass was trampled and cut up by vehicle tracks, where it wasn't covered by duck boards. Stocks of food and water had been laid in, the gates sealed shut, and gantries that had once hosted television cameras were home to machine gun nests. Lammockson's private army was short on heavy weaponry, but the pitch was ringed by small artillery pieces.

This was where Nathan Lammockson would make his stand. Since the reports had come in of Ollantay's approach with his ragged army, Lammockson had put in place a kind of scorched earth policy. He had retreated to this preprepared fortress with a couple of thousand people, his most trusted guards, his closest advisers and supporters, everybody that was precious and loyal to him, in fact. The rest of Project City had been evacuated, the citizens either holed up in churches and cellars or sent to Chosica where they were sheltering on the unfinished Ark. After that the town had been emptied of supplies. Nathan was convinced the rebels would disperse as soon as they got hungry and thirsty.

Inside the stadium the atmosphere was strange. The sky above was bright blue, and the sun, low this winter day, cast a golden light into the stadium, making the polished weaponry gleam, and the murmur of the thousands gathered in this echoing bowl gave it the feel of a sports crowd. It all made Lily feel peculiarly cheerful, as if it were a Saturday afternoon in London and she was taking Amanda's kids to a football match, at Fulham or Queen's Park Rangers. But a different sort of fixture was being planned today.

Lammockson himself was at the very center of the pitch, where once soccer teams had kicked off their matches. He was sitting in the sun on a fold-out canvas chair, sunglasses masking his face. But he was ringed by troops, and he sat only a few meters from two AxysCorp-livery helicopters that rested on the grass. Piers was with him, and Juan Villegas with Amanda sitting in the background, and Sanjay McDonald. Though he rarely spoke Piers had the distracted look of a man listening to a dozen conversations at once, probably through a mil-spec version of an Angel. Other advisers came and went, especially Nathan's top military people, informing him of the disposition of the rebels. Nathan seemed cool amid the tension, like a director on some unlikely film set.

As Lily approached, Sanjay got up and hurried to her, small, intense, nervous, his beard ragged. "Lily, thank God. There's news. I've been speaking to Thandie, in Denver."

That cut through her preoccupation. "Thandie?"

"A Comsat drifted into the right position and we got a contact . . . It's surging again. The sea-level rise."

For years the rise had roughly followed Thandie's rule-of-thumb exponential curve, doubling every five years. But the reality was always more ragged, more uncertain than that.

"Another subterranean sea broke open, I guess," Lily said.

"Something like that. Actually it backs up reports we had from Chosica. There have been flooding episodes below the town. Seems Nathan's Ark Three might be floating off sooner than he expected. But that's not all Thandie had to say. Listen, Lily. She's made a place for herself in Denver, got in with government circles."

Lily smiled. "That sounds like Thandie."

"And she's discovered—"

"So you showed up, Brooke." Nathan had spotted Lily and cut across Sanjay.

Sanjay, anguished, had to break off.

Lily mouthed, "Later." She turned to Nathan. Once she would have bridled at his goading, but over the years she'd hardened to his insults. "You know where I've been, Nathan. Touring the perimeter."

"And?"

She shrugged. "You know the situation. The perimeter's secure, all units in place, armed and provisioned. But the rebels are in place too." She had looked down from the old TV gantries at the grubby army Ollantay had assembled, a band that stretched right around the walls of the stadium. They were like fans waiting to be admitted to a sports event, a cup final. But most sports fans didn't go noisily looting surrounding properties, or letting off potshots at the stadium.

"So we're under siege," Nathan said, unperturbed. "Fuck 'em."

"Ollantay himself is there," Lily said, glancing at Amanda. "You can't miss him, strutting around in his Inca feathers, that golden helmet gleaming. Kristie is with him. And the kid." She admitted, "A sniper could take Ollantay out. You don't even need the spotter scopes."

Amanda looked away, her face white, her eyes shadows. Juan put his hand over hers.

Nathan shook his head. "No. I want him alive so he can surrender. That's the most orderly way out of this." He grinned at Lily in that cruel way of his. "And besides, to you he's family."

"Oh, shut up, Nathan," Lily snapped. "And speaking of family, your own son's been spotted out there too." There had been rumors that Hammond had gone over to the rebels.

Now it was Nathan's turn to look away. "Ah, the hell with him too. My boys are under instruction to keep him safe. When all this fizzles out he'll come around. I'll make him eat a little shit, and that will be that."

" 'Fizzles out,' " Lily repeated. "You're confident about that, are you?"

"Why not?"

Piers put in, "We planned for this, Lily. You know that."

Project City had been preparing for Ollantay's assault for weeks, putting into place operations that had been worked out over months and years, plans drawn up for the event of a rebellion. The rebels' reinforcement by the Walker City Okies was just a complication. Nathan wanted minimal resistance, no fighting at all if possible, and he had forbidden the use of heavy weapons or mines unless absolutely necessary. He wanted to preserve his city intact, he said. Lily was among the few who knew Nathan had a plan B.

She glared at him. "No need for any last resorts, then, Nathan."

"Not unless circumstances change," he replied smoothly.

A single scream pierced the air like a bugle call.

Nathan stood. Amanda clung to Juan's arm. Lily heard the rattle of weapons being cocked. There was a crump, a sound like distant thunder, and people flinched. Lily turned, scanning, looking for the source of the scream, the bang.

Suddenly AxysCorp soldiers fled from the tunnels where once the players had come out onto the sports field. Smoke gushed after them. They were pursued by people spilling out of the tunnels, ragged, mostly men but some women, even a few children. The men wore bright woollen tunics and cloaks. They all seemed to be armed, even some of the kids, and Lily recognized the deadly, simple form of Kalashnikovs.

Lammockson's fortress was breached, just like that.

AxysCorp troops took shelter behind sandbag heaps and Portaloos. Gunfire began, the popping of small-arms fire, the rattle of automatic weapons. The first shots landed home, and people twitched like puppets and fell to the dirt. The troops around Lammockson drew in, their weapons at their shoulders. Lily heard the slicing noise of helicopter rotor blades cutting into the air.

But pandemonium filled the stadium. The rebels were still pouring in through the tunnels, and the AxysCorp troops were struggling to figure out what was going on, to get into position.

And now there was a charge by a handful of men in bright Inca costumes. They cut through the AxysCorp lines, heading straight for Lammockson's party. Piers screamed orders, and the AxysCorp troops responded, lined up and fired. Inca types fell, but they fired back.

Lily heard a round hiss past her ears. She threw herself to the ground. "Down! Get down!"

The engine roar intensified. Lily squirmed and looked around. From a circle of people lying flattened like corn stalks in a gale, one of Nathan's helicopters was lifting into the sky. She saw a bullet ping off its hull, leaving a dent in its armor, but it rose smoothly, and Nathan Lammockson was already gone. The other bird still stood on the ground, the blades turning vigorously. Everybody was down on the ground—*everybody but Amanda*, Lily saw with horror.

Amanda was standing up, looking bewildered. She called her daughter's name, over and over: "Kristie! Kris!"

Juan Villegas, on the ground himself, plucked at her arm. "Amanda, for God's sake—"

Her forehead exploded, red-black blood and tissue fanning out in front of her face. For a second she stood, trembling. Then she fell, limbs loose, tumbling to the ground.

Lily got to her knees and crawled toward her sister, through the noise of the chopper, the screaming, the shots. "Amanda!"

Piers Michaelmas lunged across the ground and hit her with a rugby tackle around the waist, forcing her flat on her belly.

Lily struggled. "Let me go!"

Piers held her down. "It's too late for her."

She balled her fist and punched him in the mouth, but still he wouldn't let go. "You prick, Piers. So much for your siege defense. It didn't last five minutes."

"Listen to me. Just listen," he shouted over the noise. "You can see what's happened. We've been betrayed."

"Who by?"

"Hammond Lammockson. It was always a risk not to hunt him down after he absconded. He betrayed his own father—gave Ollantay plans of the stadium, the military preparation, got him through the gates."

"Then it's finished."

"No." He shook his head, as if to clear it. "The city is lost. Nathan's out of here already. You can say what you like about him but he's decisive. And that second chopper is going in a few minutes."

"Going where?"

"The Ark at Chosica, I think. That's still well defended. We've a chance to be on it, you and I. But he's given me a mission."

"To do what?"

"Bring in Hammond."

"You're kidding."

"No. You know Nathan: blood's thicker than water.

Hammond's already in the stadium, with the rebels. Ollantay has the advantage of surprise, but these aren't trained military units. A handful of us ought to be able to get through, retrieve Hammond, and make sure Ollantay is down.

"Listen to me, Lily. This is our chance. Kristie is there, and her kid. We think they're close to Ollantay—well, they must be. There's nothing you can do for Amanda now. But if you want to save her daughter—"

She didn't hesitate. "Let's go."

He grabbed her arm. "Wait. Take these." He took a handful of lightweight gas masks from his pocket, shook them so they folded out into shape. "Put one on. We should be safe, it's the Quechuas who are targeted by Nathan's ethnic weapons, but—"

"Nathan wouldn't do it."

He pointed upward. "He already is."

Looking up, she saw that the chopper in the air was venting a yellowish gas. Heavier than the air, it descended quickly. The chopper banked and circled, spreading its gas throughout the stadium.

"Shit," Lily said. She pulled a mask over her face.

"Quite. And take another. Kristie should be immune. But her kid—"

As Ollantay's son, Manco might be half Quechua. "All right."

A party of AxysCorp soldiers got to their feet and ran past Piers and Lily toward the rebel concentrations, yelling through their own gas masks, guns blazing.

"That's our cue," Piers yelled. "Come on!"

He hauled her to her feet. Reaching for the handgun at her back, she staggered after the troops, Piers dragging at her arm.

71

The rebels were numerous, but they were a mob, ill-trained, most of them lacking any sense of formation and discipline. And now that the Quechua leaders were falling, choking as the yellow gas filled their lungs, panic was setting in even amongst those who must be immune to the ethnic-specific toxin.

The AxysCorp squad cut through this rabble like an arrowhead burrowing into flesh, leaving a trail of dead and wounded. Lily, hurrying behind the squad, could see how many of the fallen wore remnants of western clothing, even battered AxysCorp-mark garments. They must have been the citizens of Walker City, Americans like her own father's family, stranded as far from home as she was, and dying here today.

It wasn't hard to find Ollantay in his golden helmet, his proud Inca plumage. As those around him fell, choking, their swollen tongues sticking out of their mouths, he stood unaffected with his AK47 raised and spitting fire, until the AxysCorp squad overwhelmed him and got his weapon out of his hands. A couple of the AxysCorp guards dragged Hammond Lammockson to his feet. He had been trying to hide among the Quechua corpses.

And here was Kristie, kneeling on the ground, her boy clasped to her chest. Lily hurried to her with the mask. "Put this on him, Kristie—do it!"

Kristie stared at her, eyes wide with shock. But she took the mask and, with trembling hands, looped it over the boy's head and pulled its elastic tight. "Lily, what is this? People just started *dying*."

"Nathan's genomic weapons," Lily said grimly. "An ethnic-specific toxin, targeted at the Quechua. Supposed to be lethal even to a quarter ancestry. You and I should be OK, but your boy—"

"That's monstrous," Kristie flared.

"More so than an AK47? Look, you need to come back with me. Your mother—"

"To hell with her." She looked up at Ollantay, who stood between two guards, his hands behind his back in plastic cuffs. "Why isn't Ollantay hurt by the gas?"

Piers, his gun pointing square at Ollantay's face, sneered at him. "Maybe because this Inca hero isn't the pureblood he'd have liked you to believe, Kristie. As I tried to tell you long ago." The muscles of Ollantay's arms bunched against the tension of the cuffs. "Maybe because you've thrown away your life on a lie—"

"Enough," Lily said, putting a hand on Piers's arm.

"I won't go," Kristie said.

"Oh yes you will," Lily snapped, and she hauled her niece to her feet by main force.

"Lily . . ."

She turned. It was Gary Boyle, standing there in plastic cuffs like Ollantay. Beside him was an older woman, short, tough-looking, likewise cuffed.

Despite the bedlam around her, Lily ran to Gary and embraced him. He smelled of dirt, cordite, blood. "Jesus, it's good to see you. Even in circumstances like this. When the spotters warned us Walker Okies were coming—I didn't know if you were still with them. They wouldn't let me try to contact you."

"Lily, this is Mayor Thorson. Of Walker City."

Lily eyed the woman, who met her gaze proudly. "I'm ashamed we didn't welcome you here."

"It wasn't your fault," Thorson said dismissively. "You don't call the shots, do you? Besides, the game's up for you."

"That it is," Piers said. He ordered the AxysCorp troopers to remove the cuffs from Thorson and Gary. "Look, Lammockson is abandoning Project City. I think he always intended to if, when, the sea reached his Ark. The city served its purpose in building the Ark for him. I don't know what kind of order will emerge here now. Lammockson doesn't care anymore, I suspect. But we know about you people, Walker City. I believe you would make a responsible contribution to—"

"You don't know anything about us," Thorson sneered at him. "Go on. Run away with your feudal master. We'll sort this mess out."

Piers's face worked, but he backed off. "Whatever you say. Lily, we must go. We have Hammond. That chopper's going to lift in a few minutes whether we're there or not. Gary—"

Gary shook his head. "These are my people now. The walkers. I'll stay. But take Grace." He glanced around.

Lily said, "Who? *Grace*?"

A young woman emerged from a crowd of rebel prisoners, cuffed as the others had been. She was the image of Helen Gray. She stared at Lily, wide-eyed. Lily's heart melted. She had had no idea Grace was here.

Gary said, "She'll be safe with you—safer, anyhow, if she's close to Lammockson. He's a bastard, but a smart, surviving sort of bastard."

"Gary—"

"Just go."

"Come on," Piers said. He raised his weapon and led the way to Nathan and the helicopter.

Lily took Grace's arm. She was reluctant, but, numbed, she followed. Kristie was more resistant, but Lily didn't give her the choice; she simply dragged her away.

The AxysCorp troops followed, making a fighting withdrawal, pushing Ollantay and Hammond along with them. As they ran Kristie sheltered her son's head with her arm. Lily reminded herself that Kristie still didn't know about her mother.

Lily looked back. Gary was already lost in the confusion. She'd spent only minutes in his presence, the first time she'd seen him in years and years.

They were almost back at the chopper, its clattering rotors adding to the roar of noise in the stadium, when Sanjay came blundering up to Lily.

"Lily! I have to tell you—Nathan didn't give me a chance—"

"What is it, Sanj?"

"When Thandie called—she spoke about the sea levels—and about the Ark."

"What Ark? Ark Three, Nathan's ship?"

"No—listen to me—*Ark One*. The Ark they're building in Colorado. In the end, Thandie says, that's the only chance. In the end . . . She said you needed to know. She tried to tell Gary—"

There was shouting. Lily turned.

Ollantay shook himself free of his guards and whirled around. Lily saw that he had a weapon held behind his back, in his cuffed hands, a revolver that must have been hidden under his tunic. He shot blindly, aiming for Piers.

And Sanjay screamed and fell; he lay twitching, his breast laid open to the bone, bloody masses bubbling within.

Piers raised a revolver and shot Ollantay point blank in the head. The Quechua fell. Kristie hid her son's eyes. Piers lowered his gun. "Should have done that a long time ago."

Lily yelled, "Sanjay!" She tried to get to him; he was still alive, it seemed, still struggling to breathe.

But Piers grabbed her. "No more time!" He pushed her into the chopper's open hatch, where AxysCorp goons grabbed her and hauled her in. Kristie and the kid were bundled in after her, and Grace, Hammond, Piers, a few others.

The chopper lifted with a surge that sent Lily tumbling to the floor. She wasn't strapped in, wasn't even in a seat. She found herself looking out of the open hatch at the receding ground. There was Sanjay, sprawled in blood like a fallen fledgling. She swore to herself that she would get word of this to his family in Scotland, his children. And further out the ring of AxysCorp troops were still fighting to defend the scrap of land from which their employer had already ascended.

As she rose the bowl of the stadium opened up. Everywhere people fought and died in a cloud of toxic dust and gunsmoke, fighting for the right to exist on this dwindling scrap of ground. And still the chopper rose until the stadium shrank into the detail of Cusco, a carpet of red-tiled roofs where more battles continued in the squares and in the streets, a whole city abandoned by Lammockson now that it had served its purpose. Higher still Lily ascended, until Cusco was lost in its bowl in a spine of water-lapped mountains.

Grace sat, still cuffed, bewildered. Ark One, Lily thought,

looking at Grace. That's it. Whatever it is, Grace has to be aboard. Sanjay gave his life to tell me about it. And I have to get her there.

Kristie was coming out of her shock. She looked around wildly. "Where's my mother? Is she on this chopper? *Where's my mother?*"

Four

2035–2041
Mean sea-level rise above 2010 datum:
800–1800m

72

August 2035

In the chaos of the boarding of Ark Three, Piers put Lily in charge of Grace Gray, Kristie and Manco. They had been assigned numbered cabins on what was called the main deck, three levels down from the bridge. After they were hurried through Chosica's riots and flooding and rushed over a gangway onto the ship, they were dumped into a kind of foyer on A Deck, which was, Piers said, one level lower than the main deck. Then, having delivered them, Piers handed Lily pass keys and ran off to help with the embarkation.

Lily was left in an absurd situation. After all the bloodshed and loss of Project City, the abrupt termination of years of her life and her work, suddenly she found herself blundering around a crowded, half-finished cruise liner in search of a staircase. But she held Grace and Kristie firmly by the hand, and Kristie in turn hung onto Manco, and hauled them through the ship's tangle of corridors.

The Ark was clamorous, crowded, confusing. The crew in their snug AxysCorp uniforms, mostly young, mostly Quechua, were loading stores, sacks of grain, haunches of butchered animals, anonymous pieces of equipment wrapped in plastic foam. Some of these items were so heavy they formed human chains, passing the loads from one to the next, chains which snaked deep into the ship's interior. And then there were the passengers, the final evacuees from Project City and the rest of Nathan's collapsing Andean communities, pushing through the corridors with children and bundles of belongings. Everybody was grimy, sweating, some bloodied from the battles in Cusco and the scramble in Chosica. To add to the confusion dogs and cats were being brought aboard; the dogs' barking was a clamor. And the ship bucked and rolled, groaning, responding to

the sea that was already drowning Chosica and floating the
Ark loose from her mooring.

Grace and Kristie gave Lily no trouble; they just followed where she led. They had both spent the last few
years in tents and shacks; they were disoriented too in the
guts of this restless steel whale, and that suited Lily fine.

At last Lily found a staircase, and they clambered up
to the main deck. It was quieter here, an area Nathan had
reserved for those closest to him; it had the feel of a hotel.
When Lily read the designations on the doors it wasn't
hard to figure out the layout. She hurried her charges
along the corridors. The doors were a long way apart;
these rooms, or suites, must be big. The finishing was better here, the carpets more complete, hidden electric lamps
casting a soft uplight on the ceiling. But still the ship surged
and creaked; you couldn't forget your situation, not for a
second.

She came to their rooms, and took out the pass keys
Piers had given her. She showed them to Kristie and Grace.
"These are just temporary. Later the locks will be config-
ured to your DNA markers and other personal indicators. Look, I'll be in the room just down the corridor." She
pointed to the door, a room she hadn't even seen herself
yet. She swiped the doors open, and pushed Grace inside
her room. "I'll come see you in a minute." She pulled the
door closed, and swiped the card again to lock it from the
outside.

Then, trying to be gentle, she put her arms around Kristie and her son, and shepherded them into their room. She
kicked the door closed behind them, and subtly swiped it
locked. The noise was shut out. Suddenly they were in silence, calm. Perhaps the walls were soundproofed.

They were in a kind of sitting room, wood panels on the
walls, soft uplights casting a glow over a plastered ceiling,
a carpet thick under her feet. The furniture was modern-
looking, a sofa and armchairs before a big wall-mounted
TV screen. Connecting doors revealed a bedroom with a
big double bed and a smaller child's cot, and a bathroom
where halogen light gleamed from polished tiles. There
was a real feeling of luxury, Lily thought, like the homes
of the very rich in Cusco. In the bedroom there was a net
sack of plastic toys, soldiers and animals, footballs and puz-

zles, brightly colored stuff probably salvaged from Lima or Arequipa.

In the middle of all this Manco stood holding his mother's hand. They still wore their Inca costumes, the colorful wool with the heraldic designs, now splashed with blood and stinking faintly of cordite. They left dusty footprints on the new carpet. They looked utterly alien here, a surreal displacement.

Lily said, "Piers said there are clothes for you in the cupboards. They thought of everything, I guess. Look, toys." She tried to smile for the boy's sake. Manco just looked at her, eyes wide. Lily reminded herself that this poor little boy had just seen his own father gunned down, right before him.

Kristie still had her small pink backpack. She slipped this off now, rummaged, and drew out her battered old teddy bear. She handed it to Manco, who grabbed it, and stuck his thumb in his mouth.

Lily asked, "Do you think you're going to be OK?"

"OK?" Kristie looked at her blankly. "It's all gone. My whole life. Everything I built up with Ollantay at Titicaca. Everything we planned and dreamed about. All just cut off. My husband gunned down in front of his child's eyes." Absently she placed a hand on Manco's forehead. "My mother, shot dead too. OK? No, Lily, I don't think I'm going to be OK."

"Look, Kris, it's just us now. All that's left of the family. You and me and Manco. We've had our differences—"

Kristie laughed in her face. "Differences! We were on opposite sides in a war!"

"Not a war of my making."

"No. Well, it wouldn't be, would it? You've always been the same, haven't you, Aunt Lily? Always off to one side. Never taking a stand, never taking responsibility. But always meddling in other people's lives. You abducted me—"

"I saved you."

"That isn't how I see it. If you didn't notice, my side *won*. Even without Ollantay I could have gone back to his family. They're Manco's relatives too. Gone back to my own life."

Gone back to drown, Lily thought bleakly. "Kris, we'll have to talk."

"Just go away," Kristie said dismissively. She was the image of her mother, Amanda in one of her stubborn moments, the set of her lips, the angle of her head, the unyielding eyes.

Lily's heart broke. She turned to the door.

"Lily. One thing."

"Yes?"

"Keep him away from me."

"Who?"

"Piers. I don't care how big or small Nathan's damn boat is. Just keep him away."

Lily withdrew without saying any more.

Outside, she paused in the corridor, leaning against a wall. She hadn't stopped moving since spilling out of the chopper in Chosica. She felt breathless, exhausted, the muscles in her legs trembling, her head stuffy and full, the blood in her ears singing. She was coming crashing down from the exertions of the day, the combat, the shock of the deaths. I'm too old for this, she thought.

She hadn't even had time to think of Amanda, of her random, unlucky gunning-down. Her sister was dead, a vivid, complex, different, *unfinished* life terminated in a second by a scrap of lead. Lily felt as if something had been removed from herself, an amputation. She was going to pay for this later, when she stopped moving at last. But she had one more duty first.

She knocked on Grace's door, then let herself in with the swipe card.

Grace's suite was similar to Kristie's. Grace was sitting on an upright chair, perched right on the edge, as if she was afraid of dirtying it. She hadn't changed; she was as dusty as Kristie. But she had kicked off her boots and put them by the door.

Cautiously Lily sat down opposite her. "This must be very strange for you, after Walker City."

"I haven't been in a room like this since I was five years old. And I don't remember much about that." She was shut in on herself, her hands bunched into fists and pressed into her lap. Her accent was strange, a mixture.

"There's no need to be frightened."

Grace just looked at her, and Lily wondered how often

in her life she had heard such assurances. "I took off my boots," Grace said.

"I noticed."

"They always made me do that. My father's family, in the palaces. If I came in from playing, from the gardens . . . I do remember that."

"Well, you can wear your boots as much as you like in here." Lily gestured. "This place is yours. There are clothes to change into in the cupboards. And if you don't like them—"

"Gary passed me to you like he was handing over a parcel."

"I'm sure he didn't mean it like that."

"I was with him fifteen years. He just passed me over to you, to this." She looked at Lily, not angry, wondering. "I know about Barcelona. How you and Gary and my mother were hostages."

"Yes. Well, so were you. You were born into it."

"I know. *You* were passed around from one group to another, a token, a trophy. That's what you've done to me today."

"We only wanted the best for you," Lily said desolately. "We're trying to save you. That's all we've ever wanted. No harm will be done to you here. You're safe now, Grace. I swear it."

But Grace's gaze became unfocused, as if she was looking inward.

Lily got up. At the door she looked back. Grace had not moved from her chair, sitting alone in the silent, pointlessly opulent room.

ily took a walk around the ship, alone, avoiding people. There was a pervasive stink of sawdust, lacquer, paint and fresh carpets. The floors were covered with synthetic rubber or linoleum or rush matting. Some of the walls were painted or paneled with wood, decorated with geometric designs and murals, clumsily executed. But, years after the keel had been laid down halfway up an Andean hillside, the ship was not finished, and as she walked past bare steel walls Lily estimated maybe fifty percent of the internal fitting-out was yet to be done.

Lily had never been aboard this ship of Nathan's, the most stupendous of his many projects. Was this great beached vessel really the best use of all the resources he had commandeered? Lily had just avoided the controversy and stayed away. Well, she had been wrong, as she had been wrong about Nathan before. Now she wished she had taken up his offers of tours and training; today it would have been useful.

With difficulty she found her way back to her room.

She stripped off her filthy coveralls and took a shower. The faucet had an option she'd never seen before, for salt water. Figuring that must put less stress on the ship's systems, she chose it. The water was hot but oddly sharp, and the briny smell made her think of seaside days as a child. She stayed under the shower for a long time. Then she rinsed off the salt with a quick flush of cold fresh water.

As she dried off, she found she couldn't bear the thought of facing anybody else, not Piers, not Grace or Kristie, certainly not Nathan. Today had been long enough already. Though it was early, she locked her door.

She explored the room. It had a little alcove with a kettle and coffee and a miniature microwave oven, almost a tiny kitchen. Unbelievably, there was a mini-bar. She really was in a floating hotel at the end of the world. She wondered how long this kind of thing could possibly last.

She tried the TV system. It showed a patchy US government news channel, broadcast from Denver. Behind the live feed was an on-demand movie service, including some titles that went back to the 1930s, when this boat's original was launched. She glanced at *King Kong* and *Things to Come*; their monochrome images were digitally enhanced. But she had lost interest in movies when they stopped being made, when every movie ever made became an old movie, set in an unreal world that didn't matter anymore. She snapped the system off.

She made a dinner of a chocolate bar and then worked her way through the little bottles of gin from the mini-bar. By the time she fell asleep, she wasn't sure if she was crying or not.

The next morning Piers came for her. He said they had an hour to spare before some kind of maiden-voyage ceremony to be hosted by Nathan. "Attendance compulsory, of course." In the meantime he offered to take her on a tour of the ship. "Welcome to your new home."

"Welcome to the madhouse, more like," she snapped, hungover, grieving.

"We must each make our judgment about that." He put a hand on her shoulder. "Are you all right?"

"I'm functioning."

"Most of the time, that is all one can hope for," Piers said dryly. "Come on. The VIP experience . . ."

They found their way to a grand staircase that punched through the upper decks like an elevator shaft in a mine. They climbed up to the very top deck. This was the smallest in area; the boat's upper levels were tiered in a stepped effect.

The bridge was up here, a roomy pillbox with tinted picture windows. Around the feet of three towering red funnels utilitarian buildings clustered, like a small industrial facility. Radar dishes turned silently. Over their heads were big solar panels that could be tipped and tilted independently, like the slats of a Venetian blind; their upper surfaces sparkled in the sun.

Lily walked to the edge of the deck and looked toward

the shore. They were only half a kilometer, less, from where the water lapped around the rooftops of Chosica. She could hear gunfire, but the battle that had accompanied the Ark's impromptu departure was already over. Some of the offshore rafts drifted close to the Ark, and a few small powerboats buzzed back and forth on the water, probing, but, deterred no doubt by the Ark's armory, none came near the ship.

Piers saw her looking. "Nathan has an impressive arsenal on board. We shouldn't be bothered by that shower."

"Those people built the ship for Nathan, and now they're to be abandoned."

Piers shrugged. "They were paid. Fed and housed, for years. You know there's little point debating the ethics of such things. These are ruthless times, Lily." They walked on.

Piers looked as if he belonged here, oddly, on this reincarnated 1930s cruise liner. He had always had a David Niven look about him, like a relic from a more elegant age. He showed no sign of the traumas of yesterday, the battle that might so easily have ended in his own death, the fact that he had killed a man. She wondered how much of it showed in her own face.

Piers said this level was called the sports deck. "Once you actually would have found chaps playing sports here, deck tennis and so forth. Not now, though. The space is too useful for other things.

"However Nathan has made every effort to build a ship that emulates the Cunard *Queen Mary* as closely as possible—that is, the ship as she was launched in 1936. She served as a troop carrier during the Second World War and was gutted; the restoration after the war differed in some details. But this is obviously a modern vessel—really a facsimile of the old *Queen Mary*, built with modern methods and materials, features like a self-healing coating on the hull and propellers to minimize the need for dry dock."

"And a nuclear power plant in the engine room," she said. "Or so I've heard."

"Well, quite. Scavenged by Nathan from a nuclear submarine." He gazed up at the three red funnels, his hands shielding his eyes. "Even those beauties are just for show."

"And the solar panels?"

"Designed to fold away neatly in the event of a storm. Nathan is planning to stick mostly to tropical waters, so there will be plenty of sun. Should enable us to eke out our uranium supplies that much longer, always assuming resupply will be difficult."

"Resupply? What kind of world does Nathan think he's living in, that he's going to be sailing around in a cruise liner buying up uranium stocks? And why build a mock-up of the damn *Queen Mary* in the first place? This is all unreal, Piers."

He eyed her. "Is it?"

They went down a staircase to the sun deck. Here they followed a broad walkway around the edge of the deck. Lifeboats were suspended over their heads. The boats' keels were white, but they were a thoroughly modern design, with bright orange Kevlar superstructures, first-aid boxes and robust-looking electric motors. They passed a gymnasium, and a squash court.

"A squash court! Jesus Christ, Piers."

"Well, we're going to need exercise. Nathan has been careful to restrict the numbers on board. Three thousand in total, two thousand passengers, a thousand crew. You'll get a chance to use the court. We'll figure out a booking system."

"You're laughable, you know that, Piers? After all that's happened to us you're talking about squash. Laughable."

"Maybe we could run a squash ladder," he said mildly.

At the stern of the ship, on this deck, was a restaurant. It was elegantly styled, its exterior wall a white-painted sweep, and glancing inside she saw an array of tables and a dance floor, all curves and wood panels and chrome. But it was only half-finished, the tables covered in dust sheets, the floor unpolished, a mural of dancing figures on the wall incomplete.

"This is the verandah grill," Piers said. "A feature of the old ship, a place to see and be seen. Nathan put a lot of effort into re-creating it."

"I don't think I packed my fucking ball gown."

"Gowns will be provided. You know Nathan. He likes to realize his dreams in every detail."

"Nathan was born in the Thames Estuary. What does he know about 1930s cruise liners?"

"He's allowed to dream, I suppose," Piers said. "Cats looking at kings and so forth."

They descended a flight of stairs to the promenade deck. Another wooden walkway ran around the circumference of this deck, Piers said, a half-kilometer in length. Lily eyed it up as a running track. They went indoors and wandered through huge chambers. The "cabin-class lounge" was a vast, ornate room with the feel of a hotel lobby. It was dominated by a giant frieze showing two unicorns locked in elegant combat. Doors led off to a ballroom, all gilt and silver and a parquet floor, a bar, and a "smoking room," as Piers called it, a kind of fantasia of a London club, with wood paneling, a domed ceiling—and a *fireplace*.

"Unbelievable," Lily said. "I mean, where are we going to get the wood to burn in that fireplace?"

"Ah, but that's hardly the point. Even the fire will be a facsimile."

They passed on through an observation lounge and a drawing room, half-finished shells but nonetheless crammed with detail. The observation lounge seemed attractive to Lily, a room whose curving design fitted its function. The drawing room was overwhelmed by a portrait of a Madonna and Child, a simulacrum of a work commissioned for the original ship; the Virgin was haloed by compass points, and stood amid navigational instruments.

The ship was big enough, but you couldn't walk far before coming to a wall or a rail, and it was already starting to feel stuffy to Lily, enclosing, static. And its unfinished opulence seemed unreal after her bloody experiences of yesterday. And yet for all the surreality here they were, aboard Nathan's extraordinary ship, once more living inside his dreams, just as in the Andes.

They went back to the staircase well and descended further, hurrying down through the main deck, and decks A and B—the lower decks went down to G before you got to the machinery rooms, holds and stores in the belly of the ship. They paused on C deck, and Piers brought her to the restaurant, a tremendous room with a dome set in a towering ceiling. It was divided by columns into a nave and side aisles, like a church. One wall was dominated by a huge decorative map of the Atlantic. But a side door opened to reveal a glimpse of a shabby, stuffy-looking kitchen, and a Quechua girl hurried through laden with a sack of rice.

"This was once the largest public enclosed space afloat," Piers said. "Large enough on its own to have held all three of Columbus's pioneering transatlantic ships. Imagine that! There's a swimming pool on D deck below. And a Turkish bath, next to the hospital—"

"Enough, Piers. Jesus!"

"The use of the ship is certain to evolve. We have time to work it out. The ship herself will be rebuilt as we sail. We have facilities to handle that too."

"Rebuilt? What about raw materials?"

He smiled. "You'll see. One of Nathan's surprises. Our position is clear, however you feel about it." He raised his hands. "This is our world—this ship, the sea she sails on and the air, and whatever we can extract from those resources, this is all we have. And in such a closed world there are rules to be obeyed, if we are to survive."

"Control our population growth, for instance."

"Well, quite. And now we can begin the job of defining those rules."

"You're going to enjoy that, aren't you? Working out how people should live."

"Somebody has to take the lead," he murmured.

Studying him, she saw again the paradox in him. He was the one who had arguably coped worst with Barcelona. Now here he was nineteen years later, aged fifty-nine, actually relishing a new confinement. It was like a neurotic wish-fulfillment, Lily thought, the captive returning to his cage, this time as captor.

"You know, this ship is everything I thought it would be. Insane. A grandiose folly. This is why I stayed away from Nathan's mad project all these years."

"Wait until you hear what Nathan has to say about it himself," he replied mildly. "And wait until the fitting-out is finished. I think you'll be impressed." He glanced at his watch. "Come on. We don't want to be late for the boss's party."

74

Nathan's maiden-voyage party was held on an open area at one end of the sun deck, where a big helipad H had been painted.

Waiters circulated, doling out glasses of champagne. Lily took one and sipped. She was no fan of champagne, but it was a novelty nowadays to say the least. Something in the fizz, the alcohol, seemed to ease her lingering hangover from the mini-bar gin. From here Lily was able to look back at the ship, at its rising stepped decks and that row of ornate funnels. It was like a mixture of an aging hotel and a half-finished shopping mall. It was hard to believe she was really here, floating away on this thing, and that she was perhaps doomed to spend the months and years of the rest of her life on this ship.

The party was small, restricted to Nathan's closest companions. So here were Lily and Piers, and his closest aides like Juan Villegas. Villegas wore black today; his partner Amanda had died only yesterday, and he cast a regretful glance at Lily. Her sister could have done a lot worse, Lily thought, not for the first time; Villegas really had cared for Amanda.

Grace Gray stood by Villegas. She wore a trim white dress. She showed no interest in her surroundings. Even when her gaze passed over Lily there was no recognition. Lily felt a stab of anxiety, a premonition of guilt. She had sworn to keep Grace from harm. Was that promise already being violated, just by her having been brought here?

And there was Hammond Lammockson, looking even more uncomfortable. He kept his eyes downcast, his hands bunched in fists. He actually wore a suit, as did his father, and you could see a superficial resemblance between them, but Hammond was stockier, darker. At least he wasn't cuffed, but two burly-looking AxysCorp guards stood behind him. Lily wondered uneasily what Nathan planned for him today.

Nathan chimed a glass and cleared his throat. "Thanks for coming. Not that you had a choice." It was one of his characteristically disconcerting sallies aimed at those dependent on him, and there was a nervous murmur in response. "I got to tell you first we've had some news, relayed from Denver. We're not the only ones who have been at war. Jerusalem has gone, drowned. Of course most of it was ruins by now anyway, but yesterday the sea closed over it. So that's the end of the war of Abraham, and all the wars over Jerusalem I guess, wars going back to the Romans, a war extinguished by the sea as a rising tide puts out a campfire on a beach.

"That's the way it's going to happen now, all over the world. The water level is rising at somewhere over a hundred meters a year. A hundred meters! That's going to put enormous pressure on human societies. Governments and corporations and cultures will crack and crumble under the strain.

"And that's why I built this ship," he said, pacing. "First of all as a refuge. This was always meant to be a place we could live if we ever got kicked out of the Andes. Well, we've achieved that so far, haven't we?

"But I have other objectives. I want to bring hope." He waved a hand at the deck, the funnels rising above them. "I saw the old *Queen Mary* as a boy, concreted to her wharf at Long Beach. For all I know she's still there now, trapped and drowned under the sea. I fell in love with the old girl immediately."

So that's it, Lily thought. Nostalgia for a boyhood adventure.

"And that's why I brought her back now, in this new form. The *Queen Mary* was the culmination of a shipbuilding tradition in Britain that went back to Brunel and beyond. People were fascinated by her, by her construction, her launch, her feats, the records she set. She was a technological triumph, a moon rocket of her day. And she was beautiful, a marriage of art and engineering, a synthesis we lost somewhere along the way.

"And *that's* why I wanted to build a fine ship to sail out

of here on, not just some tub, another shabby raft. Every other damn ocean liner has long run out of gas and been turned into a floating refugee center. The *Queen Mary* represents the pinnacle of her age, the technological civilization that spawned us. Now she's back, and she's underway, although I was hoping to wait another year so she could be launched on her centenary, but there you go. And as we sail around the globe I want her to represent hope in the minds of those who see her, an aspiration of civilization presented to all those ratty raft communities on the water and the drowning refugees on the land, hope that beauty like this can be brought back into being someday in the future when this damn flood lets us all go."

"I'm trying not to laugh," Lily whispered to Piers.

"You've always been skeptical of Nathan's ambition," Piers murmured. "Just remember—"

"I'm on his boat. I know, I know."

And now Nathan came to his final motive for building the boat.

"She's for my son," he said, without looking around at Hammond. "For all I know my only surviving relative. The repository of my genes, and my dreams." Now he turned to Hammond, who glowered back. "I did it all for you, Hammond. It was always for you, you know that. Even when I denied you, or turned from you, or punished you, or spoke to you harshly, it was all for your own good. I spent my life telling you so. You understand that in your heart, don't you?"

Hammond glowered back.

"But you betrayed me." Nathan spoke softly. Everybody on deck was so silent now that every word rang out clearly. "You allied with my enemies, that fool Ollantay. You let them into Project City. Your actions resulted in the smashing up of what it took me twenty years to build. But you know what I have to do? I have to forgive you. Kneel before me, son."

Hammond didn't move. Lily saw his hands flexing, his big muscles working.

Nathan nodded to his guards. One of them produced a nightstick and whipped the back of Hammond's legs. He grunted with the pain, and his legs folded up, spilling him into a clumsy kneeling posture. The guards stepped behind him and grabbed his shoulders, holding him down in the kneel.

"Before you all," Nathan said, "before my closest friends here, you must purge yourself, son. I have to hear you apologize, in public, in full." He smiled. "If you come back to me, you will have everything. All I own when I die. A princess to carry on my genes—our genes—through her children." And here he glanced oddly at Grace. A faint alarm bell rang in Lily's head.

"But I do have my authority to maintain. If you persist in your betrayal you're no use to me, and it's the fishes for you, son." He glanced out to sea. "So what's it to be? Love or hate? Life or death?"

Hammond tried to look away, but a guard grabbed his chin and tipped his head up. Father and son locked gazes. It was an extraordinary moment, Lily thought, pure primate drama.

Hammond cracked first. "Very well," he hissed, his jaw clamped by the guard's grip.

"What was that?" Nathan gestured for the guard to release his mouth.

"Very well. I apologize. I apologize for my betrayal. You win."

"Yes, I do, don't I?" Nathan grinned and stood back.

The guards released Hammond. He slumped forward, rubbing the back of his legs.

Nathan turned. "Now that's done and we're a family again, we can get on with our cruise. The cruise of a lifetime, ha! . . ."

Lily felt rather than heard the engines start up, a deep thrumming that came vibrating through the decks. Glancing at the shore, she saw it begin to slide away, as the Ark pushed itself through the water under its own power. The ship's whistle sounded, a deep bass note like a whale's bellow. Birds flew up in a cloud from drowning Chosica.

Nathan raised his glass, and a ripple of applause broke out among his friends.

Hammond got slowly to his feet.

75

December 2035

From Kristie Caistor's scrapbook:
The first scrapbook entry Kristie made during the voyage of Ark Three was on Christmas Day 2035, the first Christmas at sea. Until then she hadn't been able to bear to touch her handheld, not since the death of Ollantay and her mother on that calamitous day in August.

But Nathan made an effort for Christmas, with a big party for the ship's children in the restaurant, hundreds of them. And then Kristie gave Manco his own little party in their cabin, with seashell-paper streamers and a toy Inca warrior she had made herself, a doll knitted from the vicuna wool of their old clothes. She let Lily see her great-nephew too. Lily brought sweets. Kristie recorded some of this, for Manco's sake in the future. It seemed churlish not to.

But she caught Lily looking at the handheld, and her old pink backpack that she had brought from London and had later risked her neck to retrieve from under the nose of Wayne in Dartmoor.

The backpack and its contents meant a lot to Kristie in a way she wasn't comfortable thinking about. Her little bag of souvenirs was a last link to her own deepest past. And she had brought it with her into Cusco, on that fateful August day. Why would she have done that if she hadn't already sensed, on some deep level, that that day would mean another break with the past? She suspected Lily was mulling over the same ideas.

Kristie wept again that Christmas night, as she hadn't since August. Wept for Manco and for the loss of Ollantay, wept for the arrogance and foolishness that had killed him, as she had always known it would. And she wept for London, for how far she had come, and how she could never go back.

76

Lily came out to the promenade deck's walkway. It was seven thirty a.m. The day was overcast, gray, drizzly, but not cold, and the Ark heaved slightly on a steel-gray sea. They were underway; she could feel the screws' turning in a faint vibration of the deck.

Piers emerged to meet her. He wore a lightweight coverall, the sleeves rolled down. He handed Lily a John Deere baseball cap, once deep blue, now faded to a kind of gray.

She took it reluctantly. "Must I? I never liked hats, my head's the wrong shape."

"Precipitation over a millimeter per hour."

"Piers, we're under cover, for God's sake. I can see the rain, but there's not a breath of wind. We're dry as bones under here."

"Ship's rules. Acid rain. You know the score. Better a hat on your head than a burned scalp. You're a sourpuss today," he said with good humor.

She grunted. "It's just such a lousy day. The whole world is gray. Well, come on, let's get it over with." She put the hat on her head.

They took their places side by side. Piers set his watch and off they went, heading anticlockwise on their usual circuit around the hull, their pace not too fast, their running shoes padding over the polished wood of the deck. Naturally it was always Piers who ran the watch, who paced them, who kept control; Lily had long since given up arguing about that.

They passed a couple of walkers, people Lily knew vaguely—after seven months at sea she "vaguely" knew all of the few thousand people in this floating village. Lily and Piers broke their run as they passed the walkers, who nodded and smiled. This was friction-reducing behavior Nathan always encouraged, an excess of politeness that reminded Lily of Japan, another intensely crowded environment.

When they reached the stern Lily saw the ship's long wake streaming behind, a highway cut across the ocean.

They turned around the stern and headed back up the ship's starboard side, past the gangways that led to the OTEC energy plant. This was a raft in the water towed alongside the sleek flank of the ship. The OTEC was Lily's area of work; she had senior responsibility there. Nothing was on fire or sinking, and she was content it could survive another hour without her.

She asked Piers, "Any idea where we are?" She had long lost interest in the details of the Ark's wanderings.

"The North Sea. We're steaming south toward the Dutch coast. Then we're going into Europe. Heading down the Rhine valley, toward Switzerland. There might be some scenery for a change." He glanced at her. "You're not the only one who's a little stir crazy."

As if to prove the point they passed their starting line. The circuit around the deck was less than half a kilometer, and even at their modest pace they finished it in just a few minutes. Off they went again, completing their minuscule laps.

Piers was panting hard. "Finding this tough today."

"Maybe it's the carbon dioxide."

The unending rise in cee-oh-two levels in the atmosphere was one undeniable consequence of the flood, though there was no climatologist aboard to explain the link. Aside from the warming pulse it caused, acid rain burned the leaves of the plants in the ship's gardens and little farm, etched away at the solar cell panels, and, sometimes, stung unprotected human flesh.

"The young don't seem to be bothered by it," Piers said. "But then the young never are."

"No. You ever wonder why we do this, you and I, Piers? Running around this stupid track, day after day? We're such creatures of habit. Christ, we even run the same way, anticlockwise every time."

Piers sighed. "You're not going to get deep, are you?"

"Well, you have to face it, Piers. We spent five years in cellars. Now we're in confinement again, and here we are, running around the walls. As if we're testing the boundaries of our cage."

"Or maybe we're just trying to keep fit."

"Kristie says we should have had more therapy when we came back from Barcelona."

Piers snorted. "I seem to remember London was flooding at the time. It was hardly an opportune moment for long sessions on the couch, was it?"

"Maybe not, but—"

"It's not us who have the flaws, Lily. It's not us who are psychotic, however long we spent chained to radiators. It's the world. The world is psychotic. I mean, is this how you imagined spending your old age? And besides, frankly, Lily, you're one of the sanest people I know on this ship. If you're going crazy, we're all doomed."

"Maybe so." But it didn't always feel as if she was so sane, not when she lay awake in her bunk in the small hours, alone in her head, listening to the deep groans of the ship's hull as she forged endlessly over the deepening world ocean.

Looking back after seven months of the voyage, the first few days and weeks had been extraordinary.

The intense social life of upper-crust Project City had transplanted itself to the Ark, brittle, gossipy, somehow desperate, as if this was simply some exotic cruise. Four-course dinners had been served in the great restaurant every night, and Nathan's pet refugee string quartet played in the verandah bar. Amanda would have been in her element in those early days, Lily thought sadly.

But that veneer of cruise-liner luxury hadn't lasted. Lily had been able to keep her suite, but it was an awfully long time since anybody had come to fill up her mini-bar. In fact she now used it to keep her socks in. The always artificial barrier between "passengers" and "crew" had broken down in a farcical scene when Nathan had tried to discipline one of the kitchen staff for getting a passenger pregnant. They were all crew now, all of them had a job to do.

And as the relationship of the crew with each other had sorted itself out, so the internal functions of the ship had been reorganized. Nathan had ordered that a few areas be kept aside for recreation and exercise, like the promenade deck track, but others had been given over to vital functions like desalination.

One of the swimming pools was now being used as a mineral extraction area. Electrical currents were passed through sea water to make the minerals dissolved in it accrete out on metal mesh. The water was full of calcium carbonate, the relics of the shells of tiny sea creatures, which could be used to make a kind of concrete. And there was magnesium too, present at a concentration of a kilogram or so per ton of sea water. Nathan's plan was to use these materials to maintain the fabric of the ship itself. Lily thought it was miraculous to see these substances appear out of nothing; she had had no idea that sea water itself was so rich.

Her own OTEC plant was an experiment in extracting another resource from the water: energy. "OTEC" stood for Ocean Thermal Energy Converter. There was a temperature difference of a few tens of degrees between the warm surface of the sea and the deeps where the temperature was only ever a few degrees above freezing; just as it was always dark down there, so it was cold. The idea of OTEC was to extract usable energy from this temperature difference. The floating raft topped a stalk that plunged more than a kilometer deep into the ocean. The warm surface water was cooled a little, the cold deep water warmed a little, and the flow of heat between them could be tapped. The temperature difference was greatest in the warmth of the tropics, which was where Nathan hoped to sail his Ark for most of the year.

There was a side effect, however, in mixing up the nutrient-rich deeper waters with the surface. Around the OTEC algae bloomed in a frenzy of feeding and breeding. These algae were harvested, especially a variety called spirulina, optimal crop plants with almost their whole substance being edible, nothing wasted on such fripperies as leaves or trunks or stalks. But the algal protein needed some heavy preparation before it became palatable for humans.

There was something even more exotic going on in the old verandah bar on the promenade deck. With the dance floor covered over, the bar had been converted into a lab where more of Nathan's pet scientists were trying to develop a radically new form of solar cell. The panels on the

Ark's sports deck, conventional titanium-coated polymer cells, had an efficiency of ten percent, but photosynthesizing algae could trap up to ninety-seven percent of the incoming solar energy. Nathan's bioengineers hoped to be able to grow bright green solar panels like leaves, coated with the light-harvesting pigment molecules to be found in the algal cells. Nathan intended that in the long term these new solar arrays, with the support of the OTEC, could make the ship independent of resupply of uranium for its primary power plant. And in a world where sunlight was about the most easily accessible energy source of all, the new technology could be hugely commercially valuable.

But Nathan had deeper purposes in mind than trade. All these projects were facets of his greater vision.

Nobody expected the voyage to last forever; sooner or later this new Ark would come to rest on its own Ararat. But in the meantime Nathan wanted to make his floating city entirely independent of the land. He could feed himself from the sea, and collect fresh water from the rain. With the OTEC and his solar cells he hoped to harvest useful energy from the sea and the sun, and with his sea concrete and magnesium he hoped to be able to maintain the fabric of the ship herself from the resources of the sea, without resupply of any kind from the land. Lily imagined a day off in the future where every bit of the ship had worn out and been replaced by materials extracted from the sea. It would be the ultimate defiance of the flood and the damage it had wrought to human ambitions.

For all his faults, Nathan was a kind of genius of foresight, Lily acknowledged. Maybe the world needed such dreamers, as she remembered Sanjay McDonald once saying to her. She often wondered how long she could have survived without the shelter Nathan had given her since Barcelona.

Of course that wasn't to say that his dream of his ship-city sailing endlessly on the sea was actually going to come true, any more than his Andean enclave had ultimately survived its greatest challenge.

They completed their usual twenty laps, a distance of around eight kilometers. On the last lap Kristie came out to wait for Lily, leaning on the rail.

Lily pulled up beside her. Kristie let her aunt get her breath. Piers ducked indoors, heading for his cabin and a shower—salt water, that was the only choice now. Kristie didn't acknowledge him, didn't even look at him. She had brought a couple of mugs of coffee substitute. Lily drank gratefully, though she would have preferred fresh water, even the vaguely chemical-smelling stuff that came out of the ship's reverse-osmosis desalination plants.

This morning Kristie was ready for work. Over a regular AxysCorp coverall she wore a light protective suit with a hood and goggles, and had thick gloves tucked in her waistband. She worked in a plant that had been built into the ballroom, where the shells of crab, shrimp and lobster were processed for their chitin, a substance that was used as a cellulose substitute in the manufacture of paper and cardboard. It was one of Nathan's more ingenious schemes, a product of his endless quest to find ways for the Ark and its passengers to make a living: they could sell crustacean-shell paper to other seaborne societies. Lily thought this wasn't as good an idea, however, as the little optical workshops Nathan had set up elsewhere aboard the ship, where spectacles lenses were ground; people would need to be able to see long after they had given up writing things down.

"Wasn't expecting you," Lily said, recovering. "So what's up? Manco all right?"

Kristie pulled a face. "Little bugger's a pest this hour of the morning." Occasionally, mostly when she swore, Kristie's London roots showed through the vaguely transatlantic veneer she had picked up. "He's in the jungle gym. It's better when we're not underway, and he can go swimming. But I have to wear him out before I can deliver him to school with a clear conscience . . . Lily, I came to find you. I thought you'd like to know."

"What?"

"It was on the ship's news. The Scafell Pike beacon was lost overnight."

"Oh." Scafell Pike in Cumbria was, had been, the highest point in England. "The Welsh mountains, the Scottish Highlands must still survive."

"Yes, and full of bandits, according to the news. Britain's still there. But England's gone, every scrap of it. It's astonishing, isn't it?"

"Yes, it is. And we were there at the beginning for England."

Kristie smiled. "When you had to come and save us from Greenwich."

"Well, you'd done pretty well yourselves. And now here we are at the end."

"We went to Cumbria a few times, the Lakes, Mum took us."

"I remember the postcards."

"But we never climbed Scafell Pike."

"Climbing wasn't your mum's thing, was it?"

" 'What, in these heels?' "

Lily laughed. Suddenly she longed to hug her niece, this damaged thirty-one-year-old, an abrupt, powerful impulse. But she knew she mustn't, this contact must be enough for now.

The problem between them was Piers. Just as her mother had never been able to forgive him for the death of Benj, so Kristie had never forgiven him for killing Ollantay. Lily had tried to talk her down out of that, but Kristie *knew* how much satisfaction Piers had got from gunning down his rival. She had seen it in his face, in his eyes, as he pulled the trigger. She had even come to blame Piers, it seemed, for the death of her mother.

In any other age Kristie could have got away from Piers, simply moved out. But they were stuck on a boat that felt very small if you shared it with somebody you hated. In that way, Lily thought, the Ark was like a scale model of the whole reduced world.

"Well, so much for England," Kristie said. "Time for work." She allowed Lily to kiss her cheek. Then they broke to begin their day. Lily headed to her cabin to change, and Kristie made for the ballroom, where the day's batch of dead crustaceans was already being prepared for processing.

77

April 2036

With great caution, the Ark approached the coast-line of Europe.

Nathan's purpose was to reach Switzerland, where he hoped to establish trading relations with the nearest thing to a functioning national government left in western Europe. Then he wanted to pass on east to the high ground of central Asia. His destination there was Nepal: the gateway to the Tibetan plateau, a place he believed he could do good business. "It's the most extensive upland in the world," he declared. "And the pivot of the future for mankind. That's why we've got to be there." But the news out of the region had been fragmentary since reports of a disastrous three-way war between China, Russia and India over the precious high land—a war that was rumored to have gone nuclear before it was done. A number of the crew were concerned about what they would find, if they ever got there. But that was far in the future.

The ship passed from the ocean into the Westerschelde estuary. Sonar and radar tracked the drowned landscape passing beneath the prow, and the inboard TV system relayed heavily processed images to Lily's cabin, a ghostly carpet of houses and roads and rail tracks. This was Holland, its dykes and canals finally overwhelmed after centuries of defiance, all slowly sinking beneath a layer of ooze. The flood was now so deep, in fact, that the submerged landscape was starved of sunlight by the column of water above it. If you had stood in the submerged streets of Antwerp or Arnhem you could not have seen the Ark's hull pass overhead, like a lenticular cloud.

But on the ship, you always knew when you were over what had been dry land. Birds fell on the ship in flocks,

finches and starlings and crows, land birds deprived of their
roosting territories. The children earned extra food rations
by going up to the sports deck and knocking the birds away
with brooms. And a thin scum of oil and rubbish coated
the waters, still seeping up from the wrecked cities below.
Much of it was plastic, brightly colored and as indestructible as the day it was manufactured, or masses of rotting
cardboard or gray food scraps. Seagulls came out of nowhere to descend on this stuff. And occasionally you saw
darker, lumpier shapes, bloated remains released from the
unintended tombs below, swimming up to float among the
purposeless garbage.

Manco and the other children were forever badgering
to be allowed to go swim among these intriguing floating treasures. To them, born a decade or more after the
flood had begun, such things as aluminum soda cans and
plastic microwave-meal formers were exotic marvels. Of
course it wouldn't have been safe, even if the ship were not
underway.

The Ark passed southeast, crossing the German border.
Wherever possible the Ark would follow the courses of the
river valleys, still incised into the drowned landscape, and
every so often the ship stopped to allow a manual sounding,
made by the ancient expedient of lowering a cable. Nathan
always ordered extreme caution in navigation, and didn't
trust electronic systems alone.

On the animated maps the passengers were able to
count off the cities over which they were cruising: Duis-
burg, Dusseldorf, Cologne. By the time they reached the
vicinity of Bonn they were floating over the higher ground
through which the Rhine valley was incised. The naviga-
tor stuck rigidly to the center line of the valley. Now, to
east and west, scraps of high ground protruded above the
waves, hilltops reduced to low islands. Lily saw remnants
of the urban landscape of once-crowded western Europe,
houses coating the islands like coral, factories and power
stations, pylons and phone masts, occasionally the glitter
of a modern development like a shopping mall. Nathan's
bridge crew looked out with telescopes and binoculars,
and sometimes sent a boat party to explore. And the ship
sounded her mournful whistle, the deep bass note rolling

across the sea without echo. There was never any reply, but birds would fly up from the islands in great clouds.

At last Ark Three sailed into the heart of Switzerland.

The Ark came to anchor somewhere over the flooded remains of Geneva. The northwest of the country was now dominated by a salt-water merger of the old Lake Neuchâtel and Lake Geneva, itself just another bay of the hugely extended North Sea.

A shore party was to be taken to meet federal and canton government agencies in a mountainside community called New Geneva. Set well above the waterline, this was a temporary site, tents and houses of clapboard and corrugated iron, but nevertheless was a functioning city. The Swiss were in a position to deal with Nathan and his offers of trade. Some of the cantons in the mountainous regions had not been directly touched by the flooding at all, and the Swiss had quickly organized themselves to keep at bay the waves of hungry refugees who had come flooding from the lowlands of Germany, France and Italy. Nathan intended that the Swiss should be treated as valuable long-term trading partners. He even intended to put forward a proposal for the Ark to do some deep-sea mining on the Swiss's behalf.

Lily wasn't in the official party, but she did get the chance to go ashore briefly. After eight months at sea it felt very odd to stand on land, not to feel the world swaying under your feet. The lake was a mirror, deep blue, surrounded by mountains that stretched into the distance, still sharp and vivid, even if they had lost much of the snow that had once coated their lower slopes. If you hadn't known Switzerland before, Lily reflected, you'd never know that anything was *wrong* in this scene, that anything had changed, that beneath the waters of this brilliant lake whole cities lay rotting.

And before this backdrop the Ark floated on the water like a toy, gleaming in the brilliant clear sunlight. The ship looked at her best today, with those stacked decks and the bright paintwork of the funnels reflected in the water. With typical showmanship Nathan had had the superstructure draped with fluttering flags. It was at moments like this that Lily glimpsed the insane genius of Nathan's vision. In this drowned-out world from which so many of mankind's achievements had been erased, the Ark looked like a visitor from another age, not an oceangoing ship but a time machine.

Piers was the de facto leader of the shore party. But Nathan put his son Hammond into a suit and tie and sent him along too. This was part of Nathan's slow wooing-back of his estranged son, after the betrayal and humiliation of a year ago. Lily thought that Hammond was coming to an accommodation with his father. But a grain of bitterness was lodged in Hammond for good, like a bit of seed between his teeth.

She was more disturbed by Nathan's order, on this trip, that Grace should accompany Hammond.

Nathan clearly wanted Hammond to take a woman, to start a family. It was entirely self-interest. Nathan thought a suitable relationship would domesticate Hammond, as well as providing a conduit for Nathan's genes to pass to the future. Hammond had rejected the candidates Nathan had produced so far. But since the beginning of the voyage, Nathan had had his eye on Grace Gray. She did have Saudi royal blood. And maybe it was a way, for him, of uniting two of his pet projects, his son and the loose family of former hostages he had been sheltering for two decades. And Hammond, Lily could see, didn't mind the idea of having Grace at all.

But Grace wanted nothing to do with Hammond. She had emerged from her peculiar life in Walker City reclusive, withdrawn, and, Lily thought, almost certainly a virgin. When she was forced to be with Hammond, earthy and grasping, she retreated even further into herself.

Lily didn't like to oppose Nathan, or even Hammond. But she felt a duty of care to Grace. She tried to talk about this to Piers. He was much more of a politician than Lily would ever be, and would say only that things were "complicated."

She couldn't see what harm Grace could come to on this trip, however, as she and Hammond were going to be out in public the whole time they were together. She returned to the ship and got on with her own job, her concern about Grace niggling quietly at the back of her mind.

Then, twenty-four hours after he had gone ashore, Piers

called her. Grace had done a runner, and disappeared into
New Geneva. "Lily, it sounds as if she's been waiting for the
chance to get away from Hammond. The trouble is, if the
Swiss find her before we do they'll throw her in the lake.
They have *very* tough laws about refugees."

"I'll be there," Lily said, and she folded up the phone.
"Shit, shit."

Grace was found quickly by the Swiss, and handed over to
the Ark crew.

They spent months on the extended Lake Geneva, trading, training, refurbishing the ship. Throughout that time
Grace was restricted to the Ark, and watched by AxysCorp
guards, and Lily remembered Barcelona.

78

June 2037

From Geneva, the Ark cautiously crossed to the head of the Danube at Donaueschingen. From here the navigators guided the ship east along the track of the drowned river valley through southern Germany and Austria, crossing the sites of Ulm, Regensburg, Linz and Vienna. Each city was marked by the usual scum of garbage and bloated corpses, and by a cluster of starveling raft communities who competed with the seagulls for scraps. It was a sorry end for Europe, Lily thought. Nathan gradually tightened security on the ship. He ordered that the city sites be given a wide berth, and he set up a twenty-four-hour armed patrol of the promenade deck. Any boat parties sent to the high ground went heavily armed. The mood aboard became tense, fearful, fretful.

It was a relief when the Ark crossed the site of Budapest, and ran south over the lower ground of the Hungarian plain. The cities here, deeply drowned, left no sign of their existence on the surface of the placid sea. Beyond Belgrade the Ark had to pass through a relatively narrow valley where the Danube traced the Romanian border. Communities of some kind survived in the Carpathians to the north, as you could see from rising threads of smoke, but there was no response to Nathan's radio hails.

By now, nearly two years after leaving Chosica, the ship was accumulating problems. The OTEC, the aquaculture experiments, even the sea-concrete plants proved cumbersome and problematic, and the ship's limited factories could never keep up with the demand for spare parts. Without the spares they had picked up in Switzerland many systems would already have failed, Lily judged. Even so the ship's systems had had to be cannibalized, internal partitions ripped out for repairs to the hull and the major bulkheads. The ship started to have a shabby, decaying look.

The Ark came through a broad valley in what had been Walachia, and sailed beyond the scummy patch of debris that marked the site of Bucharest. Once they had passed the old coast of the Black Sea, Nathan had the ship anchor, and launched a review of every aspect of the ship's operations.

During the refit the onboard debate about the ship's future intensified. The big main restaurant was used for weekly "parliaments," as Nathan called them, where anybody could raise any issue they were concerned about. At these sessions Juan Villegas was the most senior of those who challenged Nathan's unmodified fundamentalist vision of the future.

"Let us be realistic, Nathan," Villegas said. "Our needs are elemental. Fresh, land-grown vegetables. Seeds if we can obtain them. Topsoil, even. Basic supplies of all kinds. And whatever we can get to refurbish the ship."

"No. You know my philosophy, Juan," Nathan said. "If we go back to sucking on the teat of the land the first chance we get, we'll never wean ourselves off it. What we need is people. Engineers, biologists, doctors. Visionaries to drive forward the great project of independence."

"We can't eat vision! Dreams don't float! And we do not need more people. We need the precise opposite. We need *less*. We must find ways to offload crew. You have seen the figures, the way our basic supply is not keeping up with our internal demand . . ." He produced a twenty-year-old handheld and began scrolling through tables. But Nathan wouldn't focus on the results. Villegas grew steadily angrier.

In their time at sea, once he had got over his own shock at the events surrounding the abandonment of Project City, Villegas had grown in seniority among the barons around Nathan. Lily wondered if in some way his relationship with Amanda had actually been holding him back in Project City. Now Lily saw the insight and decisiveness that must have made Villegas his preflood fortune in the first place.

But at the same time his view of the ship and its crew, their mission and their needs, was diverging from Nathan's. Villegas wanted the voyage to end as soon as possible, before some terminal accident befell them, as surely it eventually would. Nathan wanted it never to end at all. As time went on their differences were becoming overwhelming. Villegas and Nathan were like two dinosaurs, Lily thought, the last of their kind confronting each other. After one of these parliamentary sessions turned into a near-riot, Nathan had his loyal AxysCorp cops man the stage with him, their sidearms visible.

It was typical of Nathan that in his heart of hearts he was developing a compromise. Lily, still in his inner circle if only because of Grace, detected this shift in small hints, the tone of his conversation, subtexts of briefings he asked to be prepared. He was not about to give up on his dream of a floating city, but he was starting to accept that in the short term at least he was going to need support from the shore. But it was also typical of Nathan that he shared none of this evolution in his thinking with his most senior officer and most significant challenger, Juan Villegas.

Lily had her own subplots to deal with, meanwhile.

A day came when Grace refused to eat. Lily was twisted with guilt. She'd told Grace how she'd used hunger strikes against the Fathers of the Elect, in her Barcelona dungeons. She herself had put the idea into Grace's head. Now here was Grace, held hostage in another floating cell, under pressure from Nathan, doing exactly that.

But Nathan wasn't about to be beaten by a mere suicide threat. He threatened to have his doctors force-feed Grace, if that was what it would take to keep her alive. Lily spent a lot of time with Grace, trying to find a way through this mess, a way to have her come down of her own accord.

The sea-level rise topped a kilometer, another ghastly and unwelcome landmark. There were surges and lulls, but it still showed no signs of slowing from Thandie's doubling-every-five-years exponential increase. Nobody talked about this hard fact, however.

The Ark sailed south over Istanbul and the Sea of Marmara, and through the Dardanelles to the Aegean. From there she passed over Suez and along the course of the Red Sea to the Indian Ocean.

Then she turned northeast to cross India, following the river valleys, heading for the frontier with Nepal. Much of

India was deeply submerged, but nowhere was free of detritus, the slicks of oil, the islands of indestructible plastic
garbage slowly spinning in the torpid currents, and the bodies, bloated and naked, that floated up like balloons from
the rotting ruins below. Billions had once lived here; billions must have died.

Lily found it a great relief when land was sighted on the
northern horizon, the foothills of the Himalayas, their summits brown and jagged. They had reached Nepal.

79

Landing craft from the Ark took ashore one of the ship's hydrogen-fueled armored trucks, and Lily was driven in toward Kathmandu with Nathan, Piers and a few AxysCorp goons. Villegas was left in executive command of the ship.

They drove along tight, winding roads that climbed into green-clad hills. In small, crowded villages, people watched apathetically as they passed. Every so often the view would open up, and Lily glimpsed the higher peaks to the north. But these summits did not gleam white as they used to in picture postcards; now the brown streak of bare rock scarred the mountains' faces all the way to their peaks.

Before they got to Kathmandu they were stopped at a military perimeter. Serious-looking hardware peered down at them from watchtowers. A polite young man in an orange tunic introduced himself. He was a representative of Prasad Deuba, Nathan's contact here. He apologized for the inconvenience of the security. Tense negotiations ensued, led by Piers.

Lily stayed in the truck and kept out of it. The Nepalese guards stared in at her, their faces hard, blank. Their drill looked competent, the way they held their weapons assured. Lily recalled that the Gurkhas, a mainstay of the British army for decades, had come from Nepal. Evidently the training and tradition had rubbed off. But some of these young men bore facial scars that looked like radiation burns.

In the end a deal was done. The AxysCorp troopers were not made to give up their weapons, but they had to proceed under armed guard. So they drove on, with silent Gurkha-type troops sitting composed in the rear of the truck, their own weapons cradled in their uniformed arms, and they were tailed by a couple of Nepalese army jeeps.

Kathmandu, when they reached it, astonished Lily. It was a sprawling city that had once hosted a million souls, and might still do so now—a major conurbation that had been more than fourteen hundred meters above sea level. And on the skyline the profile of the higher mountains loomed, still the highest in the world. Deuba's polite young man acted like a tourist guide now, and pointed out memorable sights. Streets that ran between delicate pagodas were crowded with pedestrians, cyclists and peculiar three-wheeled motor cars. Holy men still lived in their ashram near the great temple complex by the river, and on the opposite bank families still gathered around the greasy smoke of the funeral pyres.

But the place had evidently become astonishingly rich. In among the temples, Hindu and Buddhist, were modern buildings, glass-fronted office blocks and villas, sprawling private residences behind tall automatic gates. The people in the streets, their features delicately Indian, wore expensive-looking clothes. Even the beggars squatting in the road, their hands held out for food as the truck passed, wore fine clothes, if dusty. Some of them even wore jewelry that glinted at their necks.

"But you can't eat diamonds," said the young guide.

They passed a residence of the King, guarded by carved stone elephants. A band played in the street.

"Fuck me," said Nathan. "Bagpipes!"

Prasad Deuba, Nathan's business contact, welcomed them to his home. It was actually a complex of new buildings, a grand villa at the heart of the old city. Lily thought its fortifications looked more formidable than had the country's border's. Deuba fed them tea and cake, British style, and offered them a yak's-milk liqueur. "Very rare and valuable, now that the Russians have eaten all the yaks!"

"I bet you managed to turn a profit even out of that, Prasad, you old dog," Nathan said with an admiring growl. He said to his companions, "You'd be lucky to get out of a deal with Prasad with a shirt on your back."

Deuba smiled, but Lily saw his eyes remained cold. He wasn't going to be fooled by a little flattery.

Prasad Deuba had clearly been a businessman, in the old days. Aged around sixty, he had the expansive gestures, quick smile and penetrating stare of a salesman. He wore a western-style suit, very well kept, and his hair was gelled flat against his scalp. His accent was smooth, almost British. He had been sent to England for his education.

Nathan made his pitch. By now he was not looking for trading partners, as in the deals he had struck in Switzerland. What he wanted, he said, was sanctuary.

"Look, Prasad, you can see how we're fixed. Ark Three—you must come and see her, you'd be my honored guest, we put on a hell of a dinner in the restaurant—"

Deuba inclined his head. "It would be my pleasure."

"She's a fine ship, and she might last years, decades. But maybe not forever. We need shore support. I accept that." He waved a hand at Deuba's villa, the reception room they sat in, expensively furnished, servants standing silently in the corners. "And I can't think of a better place than this, a better partner than you. What I need from you is a liaison with your government, those Maoists who run your country now. We have a lot to offer." He began running through the Ark's assets: the nuke plant, the pioneering OTEC and manufacturing gear. The ship was a floating city full of the latest technological sophistication. "And then there are the people, my engineers and doctors and craftsmen and sailors—"

Deuba held up his hand. "My question is simple. It is the only datum the government would ask of you. How many are you?"

Piers said evenly, "Three thousand. That includes a nonproductive percentage, the elderly, the very young, the disabled, the ill. I can give you precise figures."

Deuba nodded. "*Three thousand*," he said mournfully. "You have seen our ever-changing shoreline, where the rafts of the dispossessed cluster like seaweed."

"The Ark is no raft," Nathan said, irritation growing.

But Deuba spoke to them of what had become of his country. "Nathan, you must understand our situation.

"It started even before most of us knew of the existence of the flood: a slow trickle of refugees coming across the border from India. Not that we would have called them refugees then. They were rich people, coming from India's coastal cities, and they had access to the best science data and predictions. They knew what was coming. They sought to escape the regional wars and the disruption of the flooding in the short term, and to preserve their own comfortable lives in the longer term. They came here with money, intent on buying property and land in our higher provinces. Those who sold them land quickly grew rich too. I admit I saw the straws in the wind earlier than most. I bought up a good deal of land for a pittance, before selling it on to rich Indians for a healthy profit. The result was a last explosion of twenty-first-century affluence, a building spree in this city. A country that had been one of the poorest in the world actually became, for a brief interval, one of the richest, per capita. All because of its altitude. I myself used my wealth to buy and reinforce this place, my fortress."

"You were wise."

"Yes. Because then the trickle became a stream, as those of lesser means came pouring in. The middle classes, I suppose you would say, of India, Pakistan and Bangladesh. They too handed over their wealth for a place in this scrap of a country of ours. Many more grew rich, at least in paper and credit and gold, but gave up their most precious possession, in return, their own land.

"And still they kept coming, refugees from the Indian plains, millions on the move now, the poor, the dispossessed, the desperate, swarming through the drowning provinces of Utar and Pranesh and Bihar. We accepted some, we set up refugee camps. We were rich, we were humanitarian. But every effort was overwhelmed by the sheer masses on the move. The government tried to seal the border, but it is long and difficult to police. So in the end corridors were established."

"Corridors?" Piers asked.

"We granted the refugees safe passage through Nepal to the higher ground, the crossing points to Tibet. We Nepali have always been a trade junction between India and Tibet."

Piers frowned. "What then? What became of the refugees?"

"Ah—" Deuba spread his hands and smiled. "That is the responsibility of the properly constituted government in Tibet."

It was hard for Lily to dispel his manner, his patter, and think through the implications of what he was saying.

"It must have gone on for years. Whole Indian provinces draining through your country. It must have taken its toll."

"Oh, yes," Deuba said easily. "It began with food riots—all those people had to be fed while on our soil—we actually had a revolution. Perhaps you heard of it. Our Maoist insurgents, who for decades had been a troublesome presence in the hill country, managed to leverage the popular unrest to overthrow the government. Now we are treated to lengthy lectures on the philosophy of the great leader," he said urbanely. "But little else has changed. The Maoists retained the old civil servants and junior ministers, and ride around in their government limousines. They even kept the monarchy, the symbol of the nation. But the Maoists have been able to maintain a productive dialogue with their counterparts over the Tibetan border, with whom they share an ideology, of sorts.

"And of course, in the end, the flow of refugees from India dried up, though we still get a few stragglers by one route or another."

"Like us," Piers said grimly.

"Indeed. My friend Nathan, we have done good business in the past. But I have to tell you I cannot help you now. I know exactly what the government's response will be. They will not turn you away out of hand, but will set a quota. Three hundred, say, ten percent. The most skilled of your doctors and engineers and so forth. They can stay, they will be welcomed on shore. No children, however; we have enough of them. The rest must sail away."

Nathan was angry now. "You'd cherry-pick my crew and tell me to fuck off? What kind of deal is that?"

Deuba shook his head sadly. "Not my terms, my friend. My government's. Our country is full!"

Nathan reined in his temper. "Come on, Prasad. I know you better than that. Is this just some hardball game you're playing here? Because if there's anything you need—"

Deuba adopted a look almost of pity. "Look around you, Nathan. What do you have that I could possibly want?"

Nathan stood up. "All right. Then what about passage through the country to the Tibetan border?"

"I can certainly arrange that for you."

"For a price?"

"A toll. Not a ruinous one. The journey will mostly be by

foot, I am afraid. I can of course hire porters and so forth.
We are not short of casual laborers! But you will need to
go on ahead and arrange your own passage through the
border itself."

Lily touched his arm. "Nathan, is that really a good
idea?"

"It's an option," Nathan said, visibly trying to calm himself. "Maybe we can do business with the Chinese if not
with this lot."

Deuba made placatory gestures. "Actually the Tibetan
government is no longer Chinese, strictly speaking . . . It
will take twenty-four hours to organize the journey. Please,
accept my hospitality in the meantime. For friendship's
sake."

Nathan glared. Then he softened, subtly. "The hell with
it. All right. I need a shit, shower and shave anyhow. But
look, Prasad, I still haven't taken no for an answer. We are
decent, resourceful, law-abiding people who would be an
asset to your country."

"I'm sure that's true," Deuba said smoothly, "and if only
it were in my power to make it so. In the meantime—come.
I'll show you to your rooms."

Piers and Lily stood, uncertain. Lily felt humiliated by
this out-of-hand rejection. Humiliated and scared.

They followed Deuba out of the reception room, shadowed by flunkies.

80

B efore they set off the next morning Nathan came around his group, checking they had been taking the anti-radiation pills doled out by the Ark's pharmacy. It wasn't a cheery way to be woken up, Lily thought.

Another of Prasad Deuba's bright young men, looking Chinese by extraction, was assigned to lead them to the Tibetan border. For the first few hours they drove. Then, all too soon for Lily, they ran out of road, and the party set off on foot, the three of them from the Ark, a few AxysCorp guards, Deuba's guide, and a handful of sherpas carrying their luggage, wiry young men who carried huge bamboo baskets using straps across their foreheads.

The hike was a steady climb, hour after hour, broken only by dips into green valleys, descents which always ended, frustratingly, in yet more climbing. Lily had tried to keep herself in shape on the boat, with her daily kilometers with Piers on the promenade deck and hours on the weight machines and treadmills in the gyms. But it only took half a day of this trudging climb to expose the limits of that fitness, to make her legs and back and lungs ache—to remind her that she was, after all, sixty-one years old. Nathan, now sixty-seven, was the slowest of the group and couldn't even carry his own backpack. But sheer stubbornness wasn't about to allow him to give up.

Always ahead of them, floating beyond the horizon like a dream, were the gleaming Himalayan peaks.

Lily's sherpa was called Jang Bahadur. Aged about thirty, he was handsome, strong-looking, apparently content. He wore a white scarf around his neck, and effortlessly carried a tremendous basket full of goods, clothing, tent equipment, food. "I used to be a lawyer," he said. "I specialized in patent law. Now I can carry forty kilograms for twelve hours at a stretch. My professors would never believe it!" His accent was some strong Indian dialect Lily didn't recognize.

"I keep expecting to get altitude sickness," Lily said.

Jang shook his head. "Unlikely nowadays, unless you climb the mountains themselves. Effectively we have lost a kilometer of altitude, thanks to the flood, and the atmosphere has been pushed upward. So, you see, while Kathmandu was once fourteen hundred meters above the sea, now it is only four hundred meters—nothing.

"It isn't altitude sickness that causes us difficulty, in fact, but *lowland* sickness. The older generation, my own parents for instance. When they came down to the sea they always found the air too thick, too rich for their blood, like altitude sickness in reverse. My mother always said she could never sleep while air like a suffocating blanket pressed down on her face. You could acclimatize, but it took time. Now it is like this even in my parents' home, the air thick everywhere."

"Not everybody can adapt."

He shrugged. "The old ones die. My parents died. And it is true in the natural world." He pointed at the mountains on the skyline. "As the sea ascends, so it drives zones of life ahead of it, up into the higher altitudes, until at last they are forced off the very summits of the mountains and, with nowhere else to go, must vanish. It is a peculiar mass extinction we are witnessing, a montane catastrophe."

She glanced at him. "You understand a great deal."

"For a sherpa?"

"I was going to say, for a lawyer."

He smiled. "Well, most of my customers don't particularly want to talk to me. When I walk, I get plenty of time to think."

That night they slept under stars, in air as crisp and clear as any Lily had ever known.

The next day they reached a picturesque bridge across a deep valley, called the Friendship Bridge, the only remaining crossing point, they were told, between Nepal and Tibet. There was a formal entry barrier here, with a red hammer-and-sickle flag fluttering over a spectacular red and gold frontage. The barrier was manned by a handful of soldiers in brown uniforms. Their faces, in contrast to the essentially Indian features of the Nepali, were flat Mongolian. Nathan's party and their guides were passed without much fuss, and only a small bribe in Nepali currency. They were made to understand, however, that a tougher scrutiny would follow later.

They spent one more night on the road.

And then, in the middle of another hard day's walking, they broke out of the green valleys at last, and climbed up onto a flat, ruddy brown, rock-strewn terrain. There were no trees, only clumps of tough grass. Lily remembered spacecraft pictures of the surface of Mars; this place had exactly the same rusted, dust-strewn, wind-eroded look. But when she looked up she saw a range of foothills, lumpy and brown, leading away to a sawtooth row of higher mountains, a celestial beauty on the horizon. It was an astonishing sight. This was the Tibetan plateau. Lily found it hard to believe that she was here, that her own strange journey had propelled her all the way from those basements and cellars in Barcelona to this, the roof of the world.

But the plateau was cut across by a barrier, a Berlin Wall of concrete slabs, barbed wire and machine gun towers. Beyond, Lily saw a splash of communities stranded on this bare high ground, clusters of tents and shacks, a few threads of smoke rising up into the still, clean air.

Jang pulled up his white scarf so it covered his mouth. He glanced at Lily. "Fallout from the bombs," he said. "My mother always made me wear this."

"You had a smart mother."

Nathan, wheezing from the exertion, led his party toward the big, imposing gate set in the fence. The Nepali sherpas were quiet now, even Jang, keeping their eyes averted from the guards who glared down from the gun towers.

Before they got to the gate the party converged with a line of porters coming across the plain, heading for the gate from a different direction. They were laden as heavily as Nathan's sherpas, with bulging bamboo baskets on their backs. The porters were flanked by armed men, Chinese, like sheepdogs controlling a flock. As they walked, mournful bells clanged.

Jang murmured to Lily, "Once those bells hung around the necks of yaks. When the Russians and Chinese and Indians came here to fight over this place, they ate all the yaks, or killed them with their bombs. Now men and women wear the bells."

"Are these people slaves?"

Jang shrugged. "What does that word mean? Too many people, too little room, too little food. Those who hold the high ground can do as they will."

At the gate the column of bearers was passed through, but Nathan's party was halted. Deuba's young man spoke to a commander in rapid-fire Chinese, but the guards showed no inclination to raise the barrier.

After maybe half an hour another man came out through the barrier, an older man, a European but dressed in a kind of Mao suit, as Lily thought of it, though cut of good cloth. Aides shadowed him.

"At fucking last," Nathan muttered. He strode forward confidently. "Harry! Harry Sixsmith, you old dog." He greeted Sixsmith exactly the same way as he had Prasad Deuba. Lily imagined him having a series of near-identical business relationships with men like these, studded around the planet. "You old dog!"

Harry Sixsmith submitted to a handshake. "Good to see you, Nathan. How long has it been?" His accent was cultured, upper-class British. He was tall, fit-looking, maybe Nathan's age, but Lily couldn't read his expression. Certainly he didn't look too happy to see Nathan.

They began to confer in English, with a Chinese translation for Sixsmith's aides.

Piers whispered to Lily, "Harry Sixsmith is another business contact of Nathan's. Once based in Hong Kong, but moved to the mainland after the British handover. An Englishman who made it in China. He and Nathan made a small fortune out of property speculation during the Chinese economic boom. But he's also said to have worked on government advisory panels concerning crackdowns on dissent."

"Nice guy. I can't make out what they're saying."

"Perhaps my ears are sharper," Jang said. "Mr. Lammockson's friend is insisting that Tibet is *not* a place you would want to bring your people. He is trying to persuade him of this, even though he personally, Harry Sixsmith, would make a profit from it."

Piers murmured, "And why would he do that?"

Jang gazed at him blankly. But Piers's radio phone sounded before he could reply, and Piers walked away, speaking quietly into the mouthpiece.

"Tell me," Lily said to Jang.

"This was a battle zone," Jang said. "You know that. A strategic war was fought over this place by Russians and Chinese and Indians, when it became clear how drastic the flood was likely to become. Nuclear weapons were used. Local people, the Nepali and the Tibetans, caught in the middle of a three-way invasion, had to find ways to survive, or be erased. There was huge loss of life.

"In the end a new administration emerged, a hardline Maoist faction, basically Chinese but not attached to the Beijing government. The Maoists are supported by some Russians, Indians, westerners as you can see—even Nepali, their former enemies. Since it won power this administration has conducted campaigns against the people under its control. Cleansings. Campaigns of indoctrination. All on a landscape made barren by altitude and poisoned by radiation.

"Nevertheless the Maoists are able to impose whatever conditions they like on those who would come here. Harry Sixsmith is telling Mr. Lammockson that if he brings the crew of his Ark here, he will be expected to pay a tithe."

Lily stepped closer to hear for herself. Lammockson was trying to bargain with technology, his advanced manufacturing techniques, his Norwegian seed bank. But Sixsmith said the Maoists cared nothing for seed banks. The tithe would be in drugs, weapons, women. And "underclass."

Lily asked, "Underclass?"

"There are rumors of still more drastic tithes imposed on the refugees," Jang said. "This is a poor place, crowded with people. How are they all to be fed?" He looked at her steadily.

"Cannibalism? We've heard of this. Desperate communities stranded on high-ground islands—"

"There is no desperation here, not among the rulers. The Maoists have borrowed notions of castes from the Hindus for a theoretical justification. Here the farming of people is systematic."

Lily stared at Sixsmith. "Jang, why didn't you tell us any of this before we came here?"

"You did not ask. I am a mere sherpa. In any case you might not have believed it if you did not see it for yourself."

"But you knew."

He smiled. "We Nepali imagine the future. The sea-level rise is over a hundred meters a year. Kathmandu is only four hundred meters above the sea now. In four years, or five or six, where am I to go? Perhaps I will be standing here, with my mother's scarf over my mouth, begging for entry into this ideological Utopia."

Nathan came away from Harry Sixsmith. "Jesus Christ on a bike," he said, glowering.

"We heard enough," Piers said grimly.

"Harry risked his own neck to come and warn us off. And he risked his neck again to persuade those guards to let us go. I never imagined anything like this." He was pale, trembling, the muscles in his cheeks working. He glared around, at the arid ground, the mountains. "Maybe this is where the last act of humankind will be played out. The last survivors fighting over human bones, while the sea laps around their feet. Christ. Well, we can't stay here."

Piers said, "Nathan, I had a message. There's trouble at the Ark. Some kind of mutiny. An attempt to scuttle the ship, so we would have to disembark."

"They're forcing my hand. What's that prick Villegas doing about it?"

Piers's face darkened. "According to the captain, he's leading the revolt."

"Christ, Christ." Nathan shook his head. For a moment he looked utterly weary, his shoulders hunched, his head dropping, as if he couldn't take another step. But then he straightened up, glanced around as if figuring out where he was, which way to go. "No time to waste. Piers, get these fucking sherpas lined up again." He strode off.

As they moved away, Piers walked beside Lily. "It's like a concentration camp," he said. "The whole plateau. Worse than anything the Nazis dreamed up."

"There has been so much horror in the world, Piers. We've been spared it, mostly, haven't we? The drowning, the starvation, the plagues, the utter desperation—"

"That's true."

"Why? Why us?"

Piers looked at her. "Lammockson's strong arm, and blind luck that we found ourselves in his shelter. And if we hadn't been spared, we wouldn't be here to ask the question, would we?"

Lily glanced back at the Maoist border. The big gates opened to allow Harry Sixsmith back inside. A road led away from the entrance, through whitewashed, flat-roofed buildings. The road was lined by posts, on each of which had been placed a human skull, jawless.

81

From Kristie Caistor's scrapbook:
The rise of the sea past a kilometer seemed to change the attitude of the Ark crew to the flooding.

In the year after the Ark sailed away from Nepal, the seas rose another hundred and fifty meters. The crew watched Nathan's animated maps as one by one more lights were extinguished. Tehran. Cabramurra, Australia's last surviving town. The great cities of southern Africa at last coming under threat, cities like Harare and Pretoria. Even South American cities like Caracas. Nathan's onboard news services still picked up broadcasts from wherever he could find them, notably Denver, and other surviving high-altitude enclaves. But the logs showed that the crew were tuning in less to the images of human suffering, the endless migrations, the raft colonies, the petty wars, and more to altitude records and graphical summaries of the tremendous event unfolding around the world. As it approached its terminal phase the flood was becoming an abstraction in people's minds, a thing to be tracked through numbers and grisly milestones.

Lily Brooke and Piers Michaelmas held a kind of private wake when the beacon from Avila was lost and Spain fell silent, and the Fathers of the Elect were defeated at last.

82

The prow of the Ark plowed into the crust that covered the sea.

Lily stood with Piers on the foredeck, watching. It was as if they stood on an icebreaker pushing its way through the pack ice of the Arctic. But the crust on this ocean was not ice but garbage. Lily had small binoculars, and through them the surface scum resolved into a mess of plastic netting, soda bottles, six-pack rings, bin liners, supermarket bags, bits of polystyrene packaging. In the watery sunlight the colors were bright, red and orange and electric blue, artificial colors characteristic of a vanished world. Lily thought she could smell it, a stink of rot and mold and decay, but that was probably her imagination; this far from land not much would have survived the hungry jaws of the sea but indestructible, biologically useless plastic.

Lifted gently on the ocean's swells, the rubbish stretched all the way to the horizon, where a small, ragged fleet of boats prowled. And beyond that was a band of dark cloud, ominous.

The sun was high, the sea warm. The Ark was in the Pacific, between Hawaii and California. This was the middle of the North Pacific Subtropical Gyre, a huge swirl of ocean currents that ran so deep that even the drowning of the land hadn't made much difference to them. And this was the place where all the trash that got swept down all the drains into all the rivers into all the seas finally ended up.

"The world's rubbish bin, two thousand kilometers across," Lily said.

"Yep," Piers said. He looked out, his prominent nose peeling from sunburn, his much-patched AxysCorp coverall shabby and faded. "What we see isn't the sum total of the waste, actually, not even a fraction of it. Plastic itself is indestructible, but a plastic bag can be reduced, shredded, chewed and eroded, ripped to bits. It ends up as a cloud of particles in the water, all but invisible, passing through the stomachs of fishes and out again but never reduced or absorbed. Almost all the world's plastic produced since the 1950s, a billion tons of it, is still in existence somewhere in the world."

"Amazing. Well, it's outlasted the civilization that produced it."

"Oh, easily. It will outlast mankind, no doubt. A million years, maybe, until some bug evolves the capacity to eat it. What a contribution to the biosphere!"

"And here we are sailing into the middle of it."

"Needs must, my dear," Piers said. "Needs must."

She glanced around. The Ark was accompanied by other craft, a small flotilla of sailing ships, solar-cell power boats, and rafts cobbled together from detritus, old tires and bits of corrugated iron, sailing under tattered blankets and sheets. Some of these vessels were so ramshackle they were barely distinguishable from the garbage through which they sailed, as if they had accreted out of it. "We could do without our escort. Following us like sea gulls after a whale. Kind of embarrassing."

"Well, it's not us they're following but the typhoon." Piers pointed to that black smudge on the horizon.

He was right. As the water warmed the ocean became less productive, the yield of fish and plankton diminishing, the surface waters becoming lifeless. But a typhoon stirred up the water across which it prowled, dragging up nutrient-rich colder layers from below, and in its wake there could be a brief bloom of life. So boats and rafts and ships, even the mighty Ark, were forced to dog the steps of the storms for the shoals they stimulated.

But it was a risky business. The warmer sea fed more powerful storms, and the loss of so much land surface gave the typhoons more room to play. A typhoon was an angry and unreliable provider.

Piers took the binoculars from Lily, and scanned the horizon.

"So what are you looking for?" she asked. "A Barbie doll to complete your collection?"

"I'm looking for the *New Jersey*, if you must know." One of the nuclear subs operated by the rump US government in Denver, still patrolling the global ocean. "We got a ping earlier; we tried a sonar hail but there was no reply. There's so much activity here in the Gyre you'd expect the government to take some notice."

"They'll probably start taxing us for the garbage we collect," Lily said.

"Nathan might have something to say about that," Piers murmured, the glasses pressed against his eyes.

The Ark neared the little group of craft at the heart of the garbage continent. The deck's deep vibration dwindled as the turbines were throttled back. Lily heard a rattling of chains as the sea anchors were dropped, and felt a faint tug of deceleration as the ship slowed, shedding her huge inertia.

When the ship was still, Lily heard some kind of loudhailer, an amplified voice bellowing out: ". . . orderly process. I repeat, you, the newcomers, the big fancy cruise ship and the rafts, pay attention please. Do not attempt to trawl the plastic, to scoop it up or upload it or extract it in any way. The plastic is the property of the commons. You may negotiate to purchase processed material from the trawling consortiums. Any attempt to primarily extract plastic without authorization will be met by lethal force. Please respect our laws and customs, and follow our orderly process. I repeat—"

A huge blast of feedback heralded the Ark's reply. "This is Nathan Lammockson of AxysCorp aboard Ark Three. May I politely ask, who the hell are you, who appointed you, and who do you speak for? And by the way you split an infinitive."

The answer came drifting back, uncowed. "You can call me the boss, Mr. Lammockson. My name doesn't matter. I work for the licensed trawlers in this Gyre. They appointed me, in order that I and my police forces can keep order for the common good."

" 'Keep order.' We're all on a garbage tip, and you're the boss of the rats, right? Listen, pal, there's a million tons of plastic washing around out there. Why the hell should I pay you?"

"You're paying for the service of extraction, sorting, baling and loading, Mr. Lammockson. If you don't like our service you're welcome to go elsewhere."

Nathan fell silent. Lily could almost hear his anger in the empty air. The boss resumed his peroration about his orderly process. After a time his voice was joined by parallel calls in other languages, Spanish, Chinese, Russian, Malay, Japanese.

The Ark's engines didn't start up again. For all Nathan's blustering he wasn't going anywhere.

The only effective legitimate power left on the global ocean was the US Navy, always overwhelmingly more powerful than the rest of the world's forces. But those surface ships that were still operational hung around the shoreline of the reduced continental United States, acting as offshore bases, assisting with evacuations, guarding the shore from unwelcome emigrants. Only the nuclear subs still roamed the global ocean, and even they rarely intervened in disputes that didn't directly affect the interests of the US. In the resulting vacuum, the only authority was local, bosses like the self-appointed controllers of this Sargasso of plastic waste. Nathan wasn't in a position to challenge them.

And, like any bum, he needed the garbage. Already small craft were pushing out of the deeper mass of the encrusted sea, rafts and trawlers and factory ships, sailing to the Ark to hawk their wares. Some of the rafts were quite extensive, Lily saw, with slabs of bright green on their backs, floating farms around which birds fluttered. The Ark crew let down rope ladders, and the lifeboat hawsers lowered launches into the litter-strewn sea. Soon the trading would begin.

A small hand tugged at Lily's leg. "Aunt Lily! Mum says I can go swim in the sea."

Lily looked down. It was Manco, now seven years old and cute as a button. He had turned out blond, astonishingly, further proof that his father Ollantay had been rather less than a true-blood Quechua. But like most of the children growing up on the ship he had been burned nutmeg-brown by the sun. And, barefoot, dressed in ragged shorts and an ancient replica football shirt, he was full of restless energy.

Every time the ship dropped anchor, so long as the seas were reasonably safe, the kids were allowed to go swimming. Now that the last of the onboard pools had been turned into an electrolysis tank there was no opportunity to swim otherwise. But this was a crowded, messy sea.

"I'm not sure, Manco. Did Mum really say it was OK?"

He thrust out his lip; he had his father's stubbornness, and his grandmother's. "Well, I wouldn't *lie*. Mum says if you take me I'll be all right."

Lily sighed. "She did, did she?" This was typical of Kristie, who wasn't above using Manco in this way to win another cheap victory over her aunt. Now Lily had a choice of either disappointing her great-nephew, or spending hours in a rubber suit bobbing around on a shit-covered sea.

Piers raised an eyebrow, looking amused. "Oh, you'll be fine, Lily. Look, the divers are clearing the water."

Lily glanced down. A squad of the Ark's divers had dropped into the water, and were pushing back a rope perimeter, supported by orange floats, scraping a cylindrical volume of the sea free of garbage. More divers plunged into the depths, armed with harpoons to keep off any predators, human or non-human.

"I'll wear my rubber suit," Manco promised. "And my nose filters! Oh, please, Lily. Mum says I can't go unless you take me."

"Here." Piers tossed her a radio phone. "I'll keep in touch."

"Thanks." Lily sighed. "Oh, what the heck. Come on."

Manco scampered across the deck, heading for the stairs down to the robing room. Lily followed, trying not to give Piers any satisfaction by looking too reluctant about it.

ily got herself and Manco into off-the-shelf rubber suits, and despite Manco's protests spent long minutes checking the suits over. The wetsuits were one item that were wearing out fast, and it paid to be careful. And she made Manco put on an orange flotation belt, even though he insisted they were for "babies."

Then they went back out and clambered down a rope ladder that dangled into the water from the deck beside the foremast. Manco let himself drop the last half-dozen rungs into the water, where he splashed around with the other children already there, squealing.

Lily descended more cautiously, and stepped into the small dinghy a diver held steady for her, drifting in the garbage just outside the float cordon. Once in the dinghy Lily blipped its electric motor to move a few meters away from the cordon. The little boat's prow pushed aside soda bottles and plastic bags and cling film. None of this debris could have been much younger than twenty years old; most of it looked as fresh as if it had come out of the factory yesterday. Now she was down and dirty in the vast scum, she found it didn't smell of anything but the briny seaweed tangled up in it.

She let the boat drift. She found the rhythmic rise and fall of the swell, the lapping of the water, almost comforting. She watched the kids playing beneath the vast gray wall of the ship. Some of them had a ball, and were belting it back and forth, yelling, arguing over the rules of some game or other. But others, including Manco, just swam, ducking under the water for long intervals—dives that would have been longer if not for the buoyancy of the flotation belts. It was a common observation that the new generation of kids, the very youngest of whom had never set foot on dry land, were drawn to the sea, the endless mysteries of the depths that always surrounded them. Nathan fretted about the work ethic among these dreamy oceanic kids, who might have to become the Ark's next crew once the present complement grew too old to serve.

Lily glanced further down the length of the Ark's hull. It was like drifting beside a sheer cliff. All along the ship's length, hatches had been opened, rope ladders let down and small cranes deployed, as the scavengers nosed cautiously in to trade. It was like a movie scene, Lily thought fancifully, like South Sea islanders come to offer shells to a Navy ship.

But there was nothing cute about the trade going on here. It was a question of survival, on both sides. The Ark needed the produce of this Texas-sized rubbish island. She hadn't been allowed into any port since Nepal; she had had to rely solely on her internal resources, and the produce of the sea. Nathan's sea concrete and magnesium plants still worked, just. Slabs of the concrete patched faults in the hull, and were being used for partitions within the ship itself. But there was no replacement for plastic or various metals, for aluminum or steel or iron. So here was the magnificent Ark reduced to trading fresh water or sea concrete or spectacle lenses or a visit to the ship's dentists for reclaimed plastic fishing net and sacks of polystyrene fragments.

The mood on the ship had been dreadful, too, since Nepal. Nathan had tried to keep quiet about what had happened in Tibet, but of course news of it had got out to the Ark's crew. It was a confrontation with the nightmare that had plagued most thinking adults since the beginning of the flood itself: the extreme end that might yet come to all of them. The encounter in Tibet had shattered Nathan's plans. The Ark had got away from Nepal intact. But without a destination the voyage became purposeless.

On the gathering world ocean there were new hazards to be survived. Vast burps of methane, released from melting permafrost, could send chunks of fizzing clathrates to the surface, and fill the air with a noxious stink—lethal if it got too strong—or even create down currents that could sink a ship. As the weight of the water settled over the submerged lands, there were quakes and vast landslides, huge events that created tsunamis and whirlpools, events magnified if you happened to be drifting anywhere near the old drowned continents.

And at the very top of the Ark's command structure relationships were near breakdown, with Nathan, Hammond and Juan Villegas locked together in a triangle of mutual loathing. It had been typical of Nathan not to do the obvious thing and throw Villegas overboard after his attempted mutiny at Nepal. Nathan seemed to see betrayal as a challenge, not a terminus. Villegas kept his life, and his job, no doubt after suffering some unspoken private humiliation. But Lily had not seen Villegas and Nathan share a single conversation since then, outside of formal exchanges on the bridge or in the crew parliaments.

Lily had come to think that the Ark was a classic example of the flaws in Nathan's thinking. He always followed his vision and his grand impulses, but failed to think a project through to the end. The ship had never been designed in the kind of modular, multiply-redundant way that might have made her truly self-sustainable, over years or decades. Obsessed by his civilizing dream, Nathan had gone for style and looks, and had left function to sort itself out. Now here was the result, this ridiculous clone of the *Queen Mary* towering over the rafts that lived off this sea of garbage, steadily consuming herself to stay alive, like a starving body metabolizing its own internal organs.

And as the world became more dangerous, as the ship's fabric and matériel corroded, so did the morale of those crowded aboard, surrounded by shabbiness and peril and the endless sea . . .

A salty wind stirred her hair. She looked to the north, to the storm system that was a brooding band across the horizon. Was that cloud band growing thicker? In which case—

Her phone pinged. She dug it out of her wetsuit, opened it up. "Piers?"

"Lily. Get back here."

She heard a deep thrumming, a growl of turbulent water. The wall of the ship's hull edged past her, and her dinghy bobbed. Unbelievably, although she and the kids and the divers were still in the water, the Ark's screws were turning.

*   *   *

"Piers? What the hell is going on? Is it the storm?"

"Not that. Fetch Manco and get back aboard, *now*. There's trouble. I think—"

A boat roared past her, painted gray as the sea. Its wash nearly turned the dinghy over. Lily had to grab the sides to keep from being thrown overboard, and she dropped the phone. She scrabbled for it in the water that puddled in the bilge.

The motorboat turned in a tight circle, sending a spray of foam over the Ark's hull. Lily thought she heard children scream. Then divers lunged out of the boat and into the water, two, three, four of them. They carried weapons, big tubes like bazookas. One of them started firing before he hit the water, and she heard bullets sing, splashing into the sea. The AxysCorp divers were struggling to form up, to respond. But she saw trails of turbulence, like the wake of miniature torpedoes, stitching through the crowd of AxysCorp divers, and they writhed and died while crimson blood seeped out. Conventional shots rang out, Nathan's crew firing down from the decks, but the sea blocked their bullets and unless they happened to catch a bandit out of the water there was little chance of hurting them.

All along the length of the hull more of the bandit craft were racing in, more divers with their unwieldy weapons hitting the water.

Lily just watched, shocked into immobility by the attack's suddenness, and by the effectiveness of the bandits' weapons. She knew that Nathan's technicians had been working on the problems of underwater combat. You could, for instance, insert a pulse of high-pressure gas into the water, and your bullet would drag the air with it, slipstreaming its way through. Or you could use the water itself, shoot out high-pressure pulses that moved so fast they cavitated, creating low-pressure volumes of vapor that would go zinging through the ocean, the world's deadliest water pistol . . .

On the Ark, all this was still experimental. The AxysCorp divers had no answer to this attack, no operational weapon save harpoons, like bows and arrows against flintlocks, like Incas against the Spaniards. We were complacent, Lily thought. We aren't tough enough to compete out here in a world of ocean scavengers, and now we're going to pay the price.

And then she heard a cry, a boy's voice. She came out of her shock in an instant. That had been Manco.

Inside the swimming rope, while the divers fought at its perimeter, the children were scrambling out of the water, dragging themselves up a rope ladder which was itself being hauled up into the ship. But one boy still thrashed in the water, leaping for a rope ladder that was passing out of his reach. It was Manco. He didn't have his flotation belt on. He'd probably taken it off so he could dive.

Lily didn't think about it. "I'm coming, hold on!" She fired up the boat's engine and surged over the sea scattering bits of vividly colored garbage. If she could get to the rope cordon she might be able to reach Manco, and haul him in. Then if she could get away, around the far side of the Ark—

The bullet spray stitched the length of the dinghy. Without thinking she dropped over the side, through the shallow crust of garbage and into the water with a shock of cold, and her head filled with the noises of the sea.

And then she was hit. She actually felt the shot enter her leg, above the ankle, and pass through her flesh and out through her wetsuit. She didn't know if it was the pirates or her own side. The wound wasn't painful. It just felt cold.

More bullets ripped through the dinghy, a drifting shadow above her, and sang through the water like diving birds. And she was sinking. She felt the water push into her ears, its salt stinging her eyes, washing in her mouth, salty, bloody. She wasn't far below the surface, and the light was strong; she watched as a plastic cap emblazoned with a soft drink logo turned in the water before her face, more indestructible than the pyramids, pointless and beautiful. This was the nightmare she had dreaded since splashing through drowning London, which she had climbed mountains and boarded a damn cruise liner to escape. At last the water had got her, she was immersed, and sinking into a boundless ocean.

Manco. She had to find him. She thrashed and inhaled water, spluttered, coughed, and inhaled more. She felt a tearing in her chest, a burning. Water in the airway. She worked arms and legs, trying to complete breaststrokes, but her wounded leg pulsed with pain when she tried to move it.

Something rose past her, bright orange—a flotation belt. She couldn't tell how far away it was. She reached out, grabbed it. It pulled her up, like a balloon. Trying not to inhale again, she looked up to the surface, seeking the ship. She saw it, a black wall that divided her universe in half. She was dimly aware of the churning screws; she had to keep away from them for fear of being dragged in and cut to pieces.

She broke the surface at last. She emerged gasping, spewing out water, into a riot of noise, of gunshots and cries, Nathan ranting over his loudhailer, the deep churning of the screws. The waves closed over her face, and she was submerged once more. But she came up again, coughing, the water spilling from her mouth, her chest aching. This time she stayed up, clinging to the belt.

She saw the rope cordon with its orange floats. It had been cut adrift of the ship. She ducked over it, kicking despite the pain in her leg. And she saw a body under her, a small figure descending, unresisting, into the darkness of the deeper water. It had to be Manco. She dived, kicking, dragging at the water with her arms, chasing him. She managed to get her hands under his armpits, and pulled his small face against her chest. He was limp, unbreathing. She kicked again, and screamed into the water at the pain in her leg, her breath bubbling out of her mouth.

And she saw a deep flash, far beneath her, under the hull of the liner. She knew what that signified, what Nathan had done. She tried to kick again, to get away.

Then the shock was on her, a silver wall that slammed through the water and over her, and a huge noise that penetrated deep into her aching chest, and turned her thinking to mush. That was Nathan's acoustic mine, his latest weapon of last resort, a high-pressure bubble of plasma driving an intense shock wave. Good old Nathan. Always thinking ahead. It seemed to go on and on, a dinosaur's bellow. Kick, and hang on to Manco. Kick, kick, kick . . .

She broke the surface again. She gasped for air, the salt water splashing in her eyes, a deadening cold ache spreading through her leg. She was surrounded by debris, drifting boats, what looked like corpses, and potato chip packets and condoms and nappies.

The Ark was receding from her, a gray cloud. Further

out, more motorboats roared, fast and lethal. And behind it all the storm system gathered. She saw boats darting away, like flecks of scum on stirred-up pond water. She felt a laugh bubble deep inside her. If the bad guys didn't get her, the storm would.

A new wave washed over her from her right-hand side. She came up coughing, clutching Manco helplessly to her chest.

And there was a new shape in the sea with her: a great black fin like a shark's, water streaming from its flanks. Not a fin. A conning tower. People climbed up through a hatch, and stood behind a Plexiglas screen. One of them waved, and an amplified voice washed over her. "Hi, Lily. What an entrance. Talk about a *deus ex machina*, huh?"

The drawl was unmistakable. It was Thandie Jones.

The world folded up and fell away, and she drifted into a dark deeper even than the sea.

84

June 2038

Lily woke up in a hospital room.

Some of it was familiar, the bed, bits of furniture, medical monitoring gear, regular hospital stuff. But the walls were steel. The battered paperback books on the shelf beside her bed were held in place with a wooden bar. And there was a constant regular thrumming, as of vast engines.

She wasn't sure where she was, but she felt vaguely reassured. She drifted back into unconsciousness.

When she came round again she found herself looking up at a medical officer in a blue coverall.

"Welcome to the SSGN *New Jersey*," he said. Aged about fifty, he was a round, smiling, reassuring man with a broad Texan accent. He told her he'd set her up in a kind of private ward. "Look, it's just a storeroom. But we sleep in nine-man berthing spaces on this boat. Believe me, you don't want to be recuperating surrounded by a bunch of enlisted guys snoring their ugly heads off."

"Manco . . ." Her voice was a scratch.

"The little boy? He's fine. A lot better off than you, in fact. Get some rest."

The next time she woke, Thandie Jones was there.

In her fifties, Thandie was still slim, tall, a handsome woman, her graying hair worn long and brushed back into a bun. She wore blue coveralls and sneakers, as the MO had; this seemed to be the standard-issue uniform here.

She leaned over Lily's bunk and gave her a hug. "Hi."

"We're in a submarine, aren't we?"

"Yeah. Bit of a change from the *Trieste*, right?"

"The coffee's no better," Lily whispered.

Thandie laughed.

Lily longed to ask her about Ark One, whatever it was, and Sanjay's cryptic message about Thandie's connection with it, over which she'd been fretting for years. She'd never wanted to discuss it over the radio. But now wasn't the time.

Thandie insisted Lily had to rest. "The MO says your problem isn't only the shooting, though that was a clean wound, or your near-drowning. You're over sixty—"

"You're no spring chicken yourself."

"Doc Morton says you're having a kind of crash. A system breakdown. You're exhausted, Lily. I guess living with Nathan Lammockson is hard work, huh?"

In the humming, fluorescent-lit calm of this undersea boat, Lily thought back to Ark Three, the perpetually fraught atmosphere among the commanders, the slow deterioration of the fabric of the ship, the deepening sense that they were all stuck on a cruise to nowhere. "Hard work. Yes, I guess it is."

"Look, you don't need to worry. We contacted Nathan. We told him you're OK—and so's the Ark, if you want to know. Nathan says they fought off those pirates without significant losses."

"Nathan would say that."

"Well, there's nothing you can do about it anyhow. We couldn't get you back to the Ark, things were kind of chaotic after the pirate attack and the storm. We're off on our own course, and it's going to be a while before we cross the Ark's path again."

"A while? How long have I been out of it? . . . *Kristie*. My niece. Manco's mother. I need to speak to her."

"I'll arrange it. But she knows Manco's OK; Nathan told her. For now just take it easy." Thandie stood and made for the door. "Sleep, read, kick back, watch TV. It's not as if you're missing anything. A nuclear sub isn't the most exciting place to be."

"Take care of Manco for me."

Thandie grinned. "I will—not that he's going to need it."

Lily lost count of the days she dozed away.

She tried to watch TV on the big plasma screen on the

wall of her cabin. She still couldn't bear old movies. The crew put out a kind of inboard broadcast service, where you watch them indulging in sports like wrestling and poker, or read their blogs, and look at their comics and artwork. All this was mostly incomprehensible in-jokes by a crew who seemed to be mostly middle-aged men who knew each other very well, with little news of the outside world. It meant nothing to Lily.

She tried the books on the shelf by her bed. They were mostly novels, yellowing paperback editions. The contemporary fiction made no sense, contemporary meaning any time from the last few decades before the flood, every single assumption made about the world having been proved wrong. But she found a few historical novels, accounts of worlds that had vanished even before her own, and older fiction, "classics." There was a Dickens omnibus, and for a while Lily lost herself in complex tales of a vanished England.

There was also an astronomical almanac, tables of star declinations and eclipses through to the end of the century. A sailor's book. Sometimes she found a study of the meaningless celestial precision of the almanac tables more comforting even than Dickens.

The engines hummed, the lights never flickered. She felt cradled. Sometimes as she dozed she felt her bunk tilt, the whole boat tipping as it undertook its maneuvers. So that was why the bookshelf had a bar across it.

Manco visited her. As it turned out, for the first couple of days after their rescue he had stayed close to the sleeping Lily. After so long on the Ark new faces freaked him out, and he clung to familiarity. The medical crew accepted this and set up a cot in Lily's room for him, and even installed a little chemical toilet so he wouldn't have to go out in the night.

But he came around. Being on a submarine didn't bother him fundamentally. After the Ark he was used to living in a machined environment, to living at sea. And the crew befriended him. Supplies ran him up a kid-sized version of the standard-issue blue coverall and gave him a red SSGN *New Jersey* baseball cap to wear. Lily learned that only the captain was ordinarily entitled to the grandeur of a red cap, so it was quite an honor.

After maybe a week, the medics let Lily out of her cage. She was issued sneakers and a blue coverall of her own, and Thandie took her on gentle walks.

The boat's interior was all corridors, brightly lit by fluorescent strips. The curve of the pressure-hull walls was obvious. The roof was a tangle of ducts and pipes and cables, and the walls were paneled with instrument boxes. It was a noisy place, the crew's voices echoing from the steel walls, overlaid by the rasp of a tannoy system relaying orders mostly incomprehensible to Lily. She was surprised that most of the doors were rectangular, ordinary-looking, unlike the curved wheel-handled hatches of the submarine dramas of her childhood. Thandie said there were only a handful of watertight doors on the boat, separating the big compartments, and those doors were circular, not oval.

The *New Jersey* was a hundred and seventy feet long, beam forty-two feet—the US Navy still worked in feet and inches—which made her a big boat, but you could walk her length in minutes. Despite some artful paintwork there was a continual sense of claustrophobia, and you could never forget you were in the guts of a machine.

"I hope Manco's not making any trouble down here."

"The men think he's terrific."

"I guess they would. But he's used to the space of the Ark. And he gets to go swimming whenever we heave to. He must be rattling around in this tin can like a wasp in a jam jar."

Thandie shrugged. "Don't worry about it. There are sports facilities. Exercise machines like treadmills and bikes, virtual reality systems where you can play tennis and so on. The guys wear him out. Mind you, since he was shown the control room, he's been nagging to have a crack at piloting the boat. The helm is a joystick, like a games console."

"He'll have us leaping out of the water like a salmon if he gets the chance."

Thandie laughed. "There are simulators, a big educational suite in the galley. We're allowing him time on that. Don't worry about him. The Chief of the Boat told me he would take personal care that Manco doesn't get into any trouble."

"Well, thank him for me."

This was an Ohio-class boat, Thandie told her, her keel

laid down long before the flood. Once she had carried Trident nuclear missiles, but she had been refitted as an SSGN, her mission to launch guided missiles and other conventional weapons: Tomahawk cruise missiles, unmanned air vehicles, various reconnaissance systems.

The nuclear submarines, designed for cruises lasting months with minimal resupply and refurbishment, continued to patrol the world. They were used to maintain physical contact with the scattered communities that were the refuge of mankind—and to protect the interests of the US. The subs were armed, some of them still bearing nukes, and this crew had seen action, Thandie said, mostly escorting convoys or driving off attempted forced landings on the US coastline. But most potential aggressors were far away from the remnant continental US, and the Denver government rarely intervened in third-party conflicts. The days when the US had acted as a global policeman were over.

And the boats served as floating platforms for scientists like Thandie, oceanographers and climatologists and biologists studying the fast-changing world—even historians and anthropologists recording what was becoming of the remnants of mankind.

Lily grunted. "Recording for who?"

"Well, we never ask such questions."

The crew was a hundred and forty enlisted men and fifteen officers, all men also, and a handful of passengers, mostly scientists like Thandie, men and women. They all wore the ubiquitous blue coveralls and soft sneakers, though the officers wore khaki belts rather than black, and had rank insignias on their lapels. Many wore baseball caps, faded souvenirs of long-disbanded sports teams.

Traditionally the enlisted men on a boat like this would have been young, but aboard the *New Jersey* there were few under thirty, and the mean age seemed to be late forties. Recruitment into the Navy had been wound down in recent years, Thandie said. As the subs and ships approached the end of their operational lives, the Navy just kept on the men until they retired with their boats. And besides, the men themselves didn't want to be anywhere else; where on Earth was there a better environment than this?

The boat seemed cramped to Lily, but was roomy enough for courtesy; as she and Thandie passed the men got out of

their way, smiling. Everything was spotlessly clean, brightly
lit. And with everybody wearing those same blue coveralls,
everybody being about the same age, it was a faintly eerie
environment. It was like being in a hospital, Lily thought,
an institution.

As they walked the corridors, and Lily slowly rebuilt her
strength and walked off the ache in her healing leg, they
spoke of their lives since they had last met.

Thandie had always tried to keep in touch with those she
had known in the old days, the slowly diminishing network
of scientist types—including Gary Boyle, who was still holding out in the Andes—and Nathan and his community on
the Ark. When Thandie had noticed that the *New Jersey*'s
course was going to cross the Ark's, she had persuaded the
captain to make a minor detour; the Ark was a significant
enough vessel for the Denver government to take an interest in. It had been no coincidence that Thandie and the sub
had shown up when she did, though fortunate for Lily.

Thandie listened to Lily's accounts of the Ark's voyage,
the seaborne communities of aging boats and disintegrat-
ing rafts, what she had seen of the brutal regime emerging
in Tibet. She encouraged her to relate all this to the anthropologists on board.

"Things are better than that in the US, for now. Much
of Utah has flooded now, and that's put paid to the Mormons. But you still have this relentless pressure of refugees
from the lower lands, crowding into the last scraps of high
ground—or trying to."

"You can't take them all."

"No, we can't. We've not yet fallen into the barbarism of
Tibet. But we have pretty rigid border control, Lily. We do
take doctors and engineers and the like, if you have a proven
qualification of some kind—but that's rare since most col-
leges shut down long ago. Otherwise you're turned away."

"How long can it last? Even Denver will go in the end."

"Something else we don't talk about. It may not come to
that, however. Not for all of us."

Lily looked at her. "Sanjay said something about Ark
One."

Thandie nodded. "I told him to get a message to you, if
he could. I wasn't sure if I should send such news through
Nathan ... Whenever I'm in Denver I keep hearing ru-

mors of some kind of last-ditch program. The Arks, they
call them. Supposedly top secret but it's leaky as hell, because that's the way of the engineers and scientists who are
working on it; we talk. Nathan himself was involved at one
time."

"Hence Ark Three."

"Yes. I think it began as an initiative of the rich, a global
network of them trying to find ambitious, high-tech ways to
save themselves. I briefed some of them, years back. They
shared ideas, technicians, resources. The operations on US
soil were taken over by the Denver government long ago,
but the program has continued. So I hear."

"So what is Ark One?"

"I don't know. But *whatever* they're doing at Denver has
got to be a better long-term bet than Nathan Lammockson's schemes. I remembered your pledge to your fellow
hostages, to Helen Gray's daughter. Gary made the same
promises."

"Grace, yes. She's on Ark Three."

"I don't have any idea how you'd get Grace into Ark
One, whatever it is. Maybe I could find out, though. I have
contacts back in Denver. Gordo Alonzo, for one. He's
involved."

Lily held her breath, choosing her words carefully, not
wishing to extinguish this flickering flame of hope. "It
would be a hell of a challenge."

"Oh, I like challenges."

More days passed. Lily wasn't always sure if she was awake
or dreaming. She found she read passages of Dickens until
some sentence or memorable image stuck in her memory,
and she realized she was reading the same page as yesterday. Gradually, however, day by day, she felt fitter in mind
and body.

It was just as she began to feel restless that Thandie invited her to come view her work area.

This was an extensive science bay that had been cannibalized from part of the missile compartment. There was a
well-equipped biology lab, with glass flasks and tubing and
pipettes and white-box equipment Lily didn't recognize.
An area for geology and hydrology stored shallow sea-bed
cores and minute samples of sea water from the changing

oceans, held in neat racks, and Lily remembered going to New York with Thandie to present a bank of evidence like this to the IPCC, a visit all of twenty years ago.

The pride and joy was the in-cruise observation area, a curtained-off room lit only by a dim red glow. Those sitting here in near silence were mostly scientists, supplemented by a specialist crew like sonar operators. All middle-aged men, they glanced around as Lily and Thandie entered, irritated at the light they let in. Then they went back to their work, mostly simply monitoring the screens, making occasional notes verbally into microphones or scribbled on paper blocks—seashell paper from the Ark, Lily was pleased to see, if surprised.

"At last," she said in a whisper. "Red lights, bleeping sonar, guys huddled over screens. This is what I've been waiting for. *Red October* chic."

"Oh, shut up. Listen, the boat has its standard complement of sensors." Thandie pointed to displays labeled BQQ-6, BQR-19, BQS-13. "Bow-mounted and active sonar, navigation arrays. But for these cruises that's supplemented by science gear. We have a towed array, robot vehicles, and we're shadowed above the water by various surface drones and UAVs."

Lily guessed at the latest acronym. "Unmanned air vehicles."

"Yes. With pressure, temperature, density, chemistry sensor suites, imaging in various wavelengths, sonar, radar, and a link to the surviving GPS network. We can put together quite a picture. Look at this." She pointed to a screen that displayed a kind of false-color map, an archipelago of scattered islands isolated in an immense ocean. A flashing green splinter was, Lily guessed, the position of the *New Jersey*. "This is what I brought you in to see, Lily. This submerged landscape. Thought you'd be interested."

"So where are we?"

"Britain."

Thandie showed Lily to a seat, and handed her a china mug of coffee.

All that was left of Britain was a scattering of islands over what had been Scotland, the peaks of the submerged highland mountains.

"Ben Nevis still shows above the sea. But England has long gone, and all of Wales—even Snowdon is a couple of hundred meters down by now."

"Britain? But you picked me up in the Pacific. What's the speed of this boat?"

"Around twenty knots cruising."

"So how long have I been shambling around like a zombie?"

"Longer than you think, I guess. Ask the MO . . ."

They looked over the operators' shoulders at screens that showed external views, from cameras mounted on the hull. The water was murky, full of floating fragments which sometimes glimmered with bright, unnatural colors, indestructible plastic detritus speckling the sea. But it was midmorning, the sun was high, and the particles in the water caught the light, creating long beams like the buttresses of some immense church. It was quite beautiful, and rendered in the boat's screens in true colors, a deepening oceanic blue. And in the further distance, dimly visible, Lily made out a hillside, with a tracery of rectangles that might have been field boundaries, and blocky roofless buildings.

"This is what we call the photic zone," Thandie said. "Top of the water column. Water is pretty opaque; ninety-nine percent of the sunlight is blanked out in only a hundred and fifty meters. Below that you're in permanent darkness."

"But the flood's around a kilometer deep, isn't it?"

"A bit more than that."

"So most of Britain isn't just submerged, it's in darkness."

Thandie said gently, "Does that make a difference?"

A darting shape shot across the field of view of one of the screens, making the operator jump back.

Lily asked, "What was that, a seal?"

"No . . . Bill, you want to play that back in slo-mo?"

It turned out to be a child, a boy naked save for a pair of shorts, his lithe body sliding past the boat's hull. Aged no more than eight or nine, he actually turned and waved into the camera.

"Cheeky little bastard. Visitor from a raft up above us. Fisher folk, probably."

"Wow. How deep are we?"

"Oh, a hundred and fifty feet," an operator said.

Thandie grinned. "This is nothing. You get the kids following you down as far as three hundred feet, and I've heard reports of deeper dives yet. It's happening all over the world. The kids are figuring out breathing techniques for themselves, and passing them on through radio networks, and they're going deeper and deeper. This is innocent enough. We do get less welcome visitors, people trying to damage the sensor arrays, even plant limpet mines on the hull."

The freeze-framed kid reminded Lily faintly of Manco, another avid ocean swimmer. "The world was flooded before these kids were born. The ocean is all they have to explore."

"So long as they stay away from my sensors, they can play Aquaman as much as they like," Thandie said sternly.

Lily watched the maps as the boat turned south, and began to track the length of Britain.

Thandie said, "We'll skirt the highlands to the east, cross the Firth of Forth over Edinburgh, and then track down the east side of the country over the Lammermuir hills. Even the Lammermuirs will be hundreds of meters below the prow. Nothing's going to foul us. Then we'll cross the border to England over the Cheviot Hills. There's a point to the voyage, Lily. We're surveying the topography of the country, studying how it's adjusting as the water mass settles over it, mapping the quakes and the landslides as the isostatic load changes. It's part of a global portrait that we hope will help us predict future quakes, and hence tsunamis."

The boat sank deeper, and the glimmering light from above dwindled to darkness, those cathedral columns dimming. At last, somewhere below two hundred meters, external lights mounted on the boat's hull flared to life, and picked out a sparse array of living things, Lily saw, things like fish and jellyfish and eels. It was impossible for Lily to believe that she was effectively poised in the sky above southern Scotland, flying in a submarine, surrounded by these wriggling creatures.

"This is the midwater," Thandie murmured. "There's no sunlight down here. Photosynthesis is impossible. So there are no plants, only animals and bacteria. And with no primary production these creatures have got nothing to eat but each other. They have evolved all sorts of strategies to evade predation—invisibility for instance. The water is full of gelatinous creatures, there's even an invisible octopus. Hey, look at that." She pointed to an unprepossessing-looking fish. "That's a bristlemouth. Thought to be the world's most common vertebrate, the most abundant animal with a backbone."

"Really?"

"And you'd never heard of it, had you? Lily, the ocean is where the action has always been. There are whole categories of life out there, probably, entirely undiscovered. It was only in the 1970s that we found black smokers, biospheres entirely independent of sunlight, only in the eighties that we found methane seeps, and more chemosynthesizer communities. What else is there? Who knows? *We* never will, that's for sure. Mine's the last generation to be privileged to be able to conduct science in this way, probably. Our children and grandchildren will be back to counting types of jellyfish." She laughed, an empty sound. "Hey, Bill, can you douse the lights? Let's see the bioluminescence."

"Sure."

To taps of the operators' fingers on their keypads the screen images faded to darkness, which were then stopped up to gray. The ruddy light of the observation room dimmed further too.

"It's tricky to see until you get cued in," Thandie said. "And life down here is sparse ... There. See that?"

There was a scattering of lights like a drifting toy submarine, too dim for Lily to make out their colors. And then a more spectacular sight, a blue spiral sparkling yellow.

"That's a siphonophore," Thandie said. "Kind of a colony, hundreds of jellies strung out along a central cord. Uses those glowing tentacles to lure in its prey. It's thought that eighty percent of the species down here in the midwater are bioluminescent. You use it to attract food—"

"And predators, surely?"

"Well, some species use their lights to attract *bigger* predators to fight off their own hunters. Lots of intricate strategies."

Lily saw a thing like a jellyfish, illuminated by its own spectral light, swelling and diminishing like a puff of smoke. It was extraordinarily beautiful.

Thandie said, "Actually there is an ongoing extinction event out there. As the world gets warmer there's a reduction in the volume of the big cold currents from the poles that plunge under the lighter, hotter water from the lower latitudes. That displacement used to carry oxygen into the depths, and fuel life. Now that vast transport is shutting off. Everything down here is suffocating and starving. But it's happened before. The fossil record shows there were similar pulses of excess warmth ninety million years ago, sixty million. But an extinction is also an opportunity . . ."

Traveling steadily south, they passed over a mountain called the Cheviot in Northumberland, an old volcanic mound, its summit once twenty-seven hundred feet above sea level. Now the cairns built by climbers on its crown were twelve hundred feet down. But life gathered over the mountain's ice-carved slopes, a loose column of fish and gelatinous predators swimming over the summit. Lily thought she saw a shark.

"An oceanographer would call the Cheviot a seamount," Thandie said. "Ocean currents are forced up and over the hill. That causes a cycling of the water above, called a Taylor cell, an exchange of nutrients and life forms. Stimulates the biota. Makes for good fishing too." One of the operators confirmed there was a human raft community drifting on the surface above them. Thandie said, "From the air you can still make out the topography of the drowned countries, from the fishing fleets clustered over the peaks of the hills."

"A shark, swimming over Northumberland," Lily said, wondering.

"That would once have seemed unusual," Thandie conceded.

The *New Jersey* slid deeper into the water. Forty or fifty kilometers further south from the Cheviot, around the latitude of Newcastle, a remote camera swimming alongside the boat picked out a ridge on the landscape, its crest marked by a cluster of colorful sponges.

Thandie punched the air. "Ha! I knew it. You know what that is?"

"Surprise me."

"Hadrian's Wall. We're near the fort called Housesteads here. Most of the countryside is coated by calcareous ooze, cruddy sea-bottom stuff. But there are some species that prefer bare rock, they seek out ridges and slopes where the ooze won't settle. Corals, sea lilies, specialized starfish, sea squirts, crinoids. So there's a whole carnival colonizing the ridge the Wall stands on, as well as the stones of the Roman Wall itself." Her grin widened. "Even in the circumstances that's a remarkable sight, isn't it?"

"Show-off."

Lily and Thandie took breaks to eat and sleep. But Lily was always drawn back to the observation room, this red-lit hive of mystery and quiet monitoring, of screens like windows into a changed world. She marked their progress as they sailed inland toward the Pennines, a chain of mountains that ran down the spine of the drowned country. They detoured to pass over the carcasses of Leeds, Bradford, Manchester, cities that had once glowed with the furnaces of the Industrial Revolution, now lost in the abyssal dark. And still the *New Jersey* sailed on, heading for the lowlands of southern England.

Over Nottingham Thandie showed Lily a recording of a creature they had just observed, picked out by the boat's lights. It looked like a vase, maybe, or a flowerpot, with the seams bristling with spines. "Sorry you missed it ... That's a vampire squid."

"A what?"

"A real relic—like the coelacanth, the fossil fish that turned out not to be a fossil at all. You see these things in deep strata two hundred million years old. We're somewhere near an oxygen minimum, Lily, around fifteen hundred feet down. Right here, not much can survive."

"Save this vampire squid."

"Yeah. A peculiar niche. It's a strategy to avoid predators, just hide out where nobody else can breathe. And when the mass extinctions come your descendants can radiate out into all those empty niches." Thandie shook her head, marveling. "It's like finding a living dinosaur, to see this thing. I wish you'd seen it live. You think Manco would be interested?"

"You could try."

But he wasn't.

Over the Midlands, over Leicester and Northampton, the submerged land was two thousand or twenty-five hundred feet down. Thandie got unreasonably excited when she spotted various exotic life forms wriggling in the "calcareous ooze" that now blanketed the streets and fields of central England. One of them was a sea spider, with yellowish legs that Thandie said had a twenty-centimeter span. "Antarctic fauna in Leicestershire! It's astonishing that they found their way this far north in just a few years . . ."

Remarkably, Lily learned, the southern English lowlands were now deeper than the offshore continental shelf had been before the flood, and the life forms that had inhabited those undersea plains around Britain couldn't survive here. But the shelf around Antarctica had always been deeper. The whole continent had been thrust down into the body of the Earth by the sheer weight of the kilometers-thick ice sheet it carried, and the life forms on the shelf had adapted to the greater depth. Now those polar creatures were colonizing new environments, like Leicestershire and Northamptonshire.

The final target of the journey was London. But at more than three thousand feet down the city was too deep for the *New Jersey*, which had a hull crush depth of eighteen hundred feet. So the scientists planned to send down ROVs, remotely operated vehicles, self-propelling platforms laden with cameras, lamps and sensors for temperature, pressure, salinity and other indicators, while the *New Jersey* hovered over the city's streets like a wartime barrage balloon.

On the day the ROV flotilla was scheduled to launch, the Chief of the Watch made an announcement about it over the tannoy. There was a lot of excitement among the crew, who usually behaved as if the world outside the curving walls of their boat didn't exist at all. But the fate of a great city like London stirred imaginations. The captain arranged for the images returned from the ROVs to be piped through the ship, to the flat screens in the galley and elsewhere. Even Manco was interested, though he barely understood what was happening, and he came with Lily to the observation room.

Thandie waylaid Lily before they went in. "Listen, Lily. I've had some luck."

"With what?"

"With finding out about Ark One."

"Tell me."

"It's something to do with Pikes Peak—the USAF base there. And there's some kind of operational center in the town of Alma, Colorado, which happens to be the highest city in the continental US. I got a few hints because some of my buddies at NOAA are involved. It's evidently a major operation."

"So what is it, another ship, a submarine, a refuge?"

"I don't know. Nobody's speaking. But the leaks are coming because they're recruiting a crew. Tough selection for skills; sounds like you have to have two doctorates just to make the short list. And single people only, no families, no kids. But they are taking pregnant women, early term anyhow."

"Why?"

"Genetic diversity, I guess. As large a variation as possible given the size of the crew. If I'm pregnant I'm carrying the father's genes along for the ride."

"So how do I get Grace onto this program?"

"I've no idea. Tell you who I'd ask, however."

"Who?"

"Nathan Lammockson. If anybody can pull the strings to swing something like this it's going to be Nathan, right?"

Maybe, Lily thought. But there was also Hammond in the equation, Nathan's own son. Wouldn't Nathan put him ahead of Grace in the queue for this miraculous sanctuary? Thinking quickly, she said, "Can you get me through to Ark Three? I'll try to speak to Grace direct. And I need to get back to the Ark myself."

Thandie pursed her lips. "That depends on the captain and ship's orders. Might be months away."

"I know. Whenever you can."

Bill called from the observation room. "Show's starting, you guys."

86

The observation room was crowded. The captain, his XO and other senior officers had come to witness this robotic jaunt live. When the door was closed, and the dim red glow was the only light, Lily felt vaguely oppressed by the unseen bodies around her. Manco's small hand crept into hers.

"Oh, shit," Bill said. "Here it is." He sang the Big Ben melody. "Ding dong ding *dong* . . ."

Everyone peered into the screens.

It was as if the ROV were flying along the bed of the Thames, heading downstream. Many of the bridges still stood, but the river bed itself was empty, the river vanished—or rather it was as if the river had risen up to drown the whole world. Boats littered the bed, sunken and abandoned. On the banks, Lily thought she saw rows of hummocks that must be cars, immobile and silt-covered. Everything was draped in a murky ooze that blanked out color and softened every profile, obscuring detail.

To the left the ROV's powerful lights picked out spiky ruins, a splintered tower like a tremendous stalagmite. This was the Palace of Westminster, home to the British parliament for centuries. The ROV swept away from the river and roamed over the north bank. It followed Whitehall, the government buildings outcroppings of encrusted sandstone amid the ubiquitous slime, and came to the open space of Trafalgar Square. Nelson still stood proud on his column, which was draped with sponges and weed. The ROV descended to the pavement of the square. The ooze was thick here, and there was a surprising density of life.

Thandie spoke enthusiastically. "Remember there's no plant life down here, only animals and bugs. So the 'forest' you see is actually animals, sea anemones, corals, tubeworms. And the 'browsers' are sea cucumbers and sea urchins."

Lily remembered standing in the square with Piers and the others just after the storm that flooded London. Now the living things of the deep sea, entirely alien to Lily, struggled and squirmed in the slime.

The ROV rose like a helicopter, returned to the river and nosed forward, heading downstream. At Tower Bridge Thandie had the crew pause the ROV and douse the floodlights. After a few minutes the familiar profile of the bridge became visible, illuminated by bioluminescent creatures that clung to its stonework or swam through its broken windows. You could even see how the bridge's carriageway had been left raised when it was abandoned, like a salute. It was a strange, magical scene, Lily thought, as if the bridge had been draped with Christmas tree lights.

The ROV passed on downstream, over Wapping and Bermondsey, heading for Greenwich. To the left its lights glinted from the smashed glass of towering City buildings. Then the ROV rose up and panned, returning a panoramic view. As far as the lights penetrated the great reef of London spread away, its low hills covered by hummocks that were houses and churches and shops and schools, the work of centuries dissolving in the ooze. Every few minutes one of the other ROVs would drift through the field of view, probing, inquisitive, like an alien explorer.

"Hey, there's the Dome," Thandie said.

Lily peered to see. The Dome itself was long imploded, its fragile fabric structure crushed and decayed away. But the circular profile of its site was still clear, like a lunar crater, and you could see the remnants of the structures within, the concert halls and the outer band of shops and restaurants. Lily considered telling Manco that this strange place was where Lily had gone to retrieve his mother, uncle and grandmother, sweeping in on a chopper that had flown far below the present height of the *New Jersey*. But she couldn't find the words.

In the plaza just outside the Dome, near the entrance to the North Greenwich tube station, there was activity, a blur of motion raising a cloud of colorless murk. Bill tapped the screen. "Look at those guys feed!"

Thandie said, "You get this sort of thing around a whale

carcass. The deeps are basically starved of nutrition; a good fat corpse can feed whole biotas for centuries."

Lily asked uneasily, "But that's no whale, is it?"

"Not likely," Bill said. "I've seen this in the cities before. Probably something like a subway station cracked open. All those packed-in bodies, you know? Preserved for years. The sharks and hagfish come first, for the decomposing flesh and the bone. Then you get the snails and worms and crustaceans, and then the clams and mussels that like the sulphides you get from decay. A big tomb can last for months. Feeding frenzy!"

Lily held Manco close, covering his ears with her hands.

87

From Kristie Caistor's scrapbook:

The *New Jersey* rendezvoused with the Ark in July 2039, a bit more than a year after rescuing Lily and Manco from the pirate raid. Kristie had a heart-wrenching reunion with her son.

After that, Kristie's relationship with Lily became even more tangled. She had to be grateful to Lily for saving Manco from drowning in the first place, and looking after him on the sub. But Kristie was jealous. Lily had had Manco to herself for a whole year of his young life. He came back older, a bit calmer, taller, more experienced, *changed*. And Kristie hadn't shared those changes with him. She showed him recordings she'd made on her handheld in the months he'd been away, but he showed no interest.

Nathan persuaded the *New Jersey* captain to stick around for a few weeks. He allowed the sub crew on board the Ark for rest and recreation, and threw some celebratory events in gratitude for the sub's assistance, and to mark the fourth anniversary of the Ark's launch. On the last night of the *Jersey*'s visit, Nathan threw a party in the restaurant, for senior officers and special guests only. The submarine crew looked spick-and-span in their whites, and Nathan's crew did him proud in their best surviving uniforms, tuxedos or ball gowns.

And in the middle of it Nathan stunned everybody by getting up on the stage and announcing that his son Hammond had become engaged to Grace Gray.

Kristie, amazed at this herself, recorded people's reactions: smug satisfaction for Hammond, a kind of resigned bewilderment clouding Grace's pale, freckled face—and a look of ice-cold satisfaction in Lily's eyes.

88

Ark Three pushed cautiously toward the turbid, debris-strewn waters that covered the western coastal strip of the continental US.

Captain Suarez guided her ship over the submerged coastline somewhere above the position of long-drowned San Diego, and made eastward, tracing the valley of the Gila River and roughly paralleling the US-Mexico border. She was making for narrows that ran between the Colorado plateau in the north and the Sierra Madre to the south, a new seaway between the US and Mexico. It was a gap the mariners were calling the El Paso Strait. Once through, somewhere over Texas, the Ark would turn north, sailing up the east coast of the Rockies archipelago, heading for Colorado and a rendezvous with the *New Jersey.*

The flood now approached eighteen hundred meters. That was more than a mile above the old sea level. There wasn't much of North America left save islands and plateaus that were remnants of the Rocky Mountain states, from Idaho to Arizona, from Nevada to Colorado. The progress was slow, watchful. Lily knew that Nathan was well aware of how dangerous the shallow waters of the North American archipelago had become, especially since the city of Denver had at last gone under, and the rump of the federal government, relocated once again, had started to lose control of the masses who thronged the surviving higher ground.

As for Captain Suarez, she had cut her teeth out in the open sea. She had actually captained the pirate convoy that had attacked the Ark in the Gyre before being recruited by Nathan in a typical Lammockson stunt of absorbing his enemy. Suarez didn't like coming too close in to shore, which was always fringed by boats and rafts or whole floating cities. She didn't like sailing through the muck that still came bubbling up from the drowned cities hundreds of meters below her keel. And, as a former pirate, she definitely didn't like the idea of making another rendezvous with the *New Jersey*. But that was the plan and like all Nathan's followers, in the end she did pretty much as she was told.

The ship no longer much resembled the brilliantly painted liner that had been launched from its montane dockyard in the Andes six years ago, scarred, much patched, its interior gutted and its hull and decks bristling with weapons. But Lily had managed to keep her cabin on the promenade deck. Long before noon each day she was usually exhausted by the heat. So she would sit in her cabin's shade—no air-conditioning now—and follow the ship's progress on the flatscreen on her wall, courtesy of Nathan's onboard narrowcast system.

And, as the ship made its slow traverse, Grace got in the habit of joining her.

Grace was three months pregnant with Hammond's baby, and worn out by morning sickness. It was obvious that all she wanted was somewhere to sit, somewhere comparatively cool where she wouldn't be hassled. Lily made Grace welcome, and kept her supplied with water, fruit and dried fish. She didn't expect friendship from Grace, still less forgiveness for engineering her marriage to Hammond Lammockson, an act that must have felt like an immense betrayal by a woman who had, after all, promised to keep Grace from any harm. Lily took anything she could get. Silent company was enough.

There were the same kind of relationships all over this decaying boat. You got along with the next guy, or you got rid of him; there wasn't enough room to escape your enemies.

Grace was looking at her. "What did you say?"

"Nothing." Lily wasn't aware she had spoken out loud. "Sorry." She was sixty-five years old, no great age before the flood had come, but after a quarter of a century as a refugee she looked and felt a lot older. Everything was softening for her, she sometimes thought, the border between thought and speech blurring. "Just maundering."

"The map is fritzing again."

Lily looked at the screen. The main display showed a

composite view of the archipelago of the western US, assembled from satellite images, with an outline map of the old continental coastline projected onto it and the position of the Ark shown as a bright green dot. The system was still pretty smart, and if you pointed at the screen little labels would pop up to tell you what you were looking at. Lily learned to recognize the complex inland sea that had formed over the Great Salt Lake Desert, covering Salt Lake City and much of Utah, and the convoluted tangle of inlets and bays that had resulted from the flooding of the Colorado River valley, Grand Canyon and all. The surviving dry land as seen from space was a gray-green hue, the color of crowded humanity and its shanty cities and scratch farms. It was strange to think that aside from this mass of islands there was nothing left of the western hemisphere save the Sierra Madre, stretching south, and some of the Andean plateau down the spine of South America, the mountain ranges north and south like shadows of the vanished continents.

The map projection flickered again as the processors went offline and limped back on, balky after years of heat and salty sea air.

Grace sighed. "I don't know why we're watching this. Maps are really for people like you who remember how it used to be. But they don't matter to the children." She stroked her bump idly.

"They may have maps of their own someday," Lily said. "Of ocean currents, maybe. Gyres."

"You don't need a map of the sea . . ."

Their tentative conversation broke down.

It was like this a lot these days, Lily had observed. As if it was too hot to think, to speak, as if everybody was exhausted the whole time. You spoke a bit, and then you just gave up. Her thoughts dissolved again, wandering.

The map recovered. The two of them sat and watched in silence as the Ark's brave green pinpoint edged its way eastwards through the treacherous waters of the El Paso Strait.

89

The Ark anchored a few kilometers to the east of the drowned cities of Colorado Springs and Pueblo. It was standard operating procedure to stand so far off-shore. This far out, few of the dismal throng of boats, junks and rafts that haunted every shoreline were able to reach the Ark.

A day after the Ark arrived, the conning tower of the *New Jersey* rose smoothly above the water. A flagpole was thrust into the air, and a brave Stars and Stripes unfurled. An inflatable launch was set in the water and came pushing toward the Ark. The launch was manned by officers and ratings in crisp white uniforms and peaked caps. Lily wasn't surprised to see Thandie in there, in an orange life jacket.

As the launch neared Nathan stood on the promenade deck with Captain Suarez, and Piers and Lily, Grace and Hammond, all dressed in coveralls as smart as the Ark's one remaining laundry could turn out. Lily glanced over at Grace. She felt like warning her to take one last look at the Ark, to say goodbye. She knew she must not say anything about what was to come today.

It was three years since Thandie had fished Lily and Manco out of the water in the Gyre, and nearly two years since the *New Jersey* had made its rendezvous to disembark Lily and Manco back aboard the Ark. Lily had kept in touch with Thandie about the tentative scheme that the two of them had been developing ever since. It was a scheme that none of the others, not Nathan, not even Grace herself, yet knew anything about. But by the end of today, Lily thought with a faint tremor of excitement, if all went well, it might be all over. And she could rest at last.

The launch drew nearer. The Navy crew stared up at

Suarez and her men. The sense of challenge in the air was palpable.

"Look at those shirts," Nathan grumbled. "Christ, they're ironed." He sniffed his own armpit, his fleshy nostrils twitching. "This better be worth it, Lily, whatever deal it is you're cooking up with these arseholes."

"Oh, it will be," Lily promised.

"I can't believe they're still flying that damn flag. I mean, how many American states have even a scrap of land above the waterline? They ought to cut out all but half a dozen of those stars. And what kind of navy is reduced to one boat?"

"We all cling to the past," Piers said. Where Nathan, over seventy, was melting with age into a wrinkled, grouchy slob, a kind of Walter Matthau stereotype, Piers, in his mid-sixties, was going the other way, Lily thought, ever more upright, his voice ever more clipped. "If we don't have the past, what else is there?"

Grace wrinkled her freckled nose. "The future?"

The launch pulled up alongside the Ark, and Nathan led the way down rope ladders to meet it. Captain Suarez and Piers stayed aboard, watching as the others descended. A couple of kids came paddling around the boat, having somehow found their way off the Ark and into the water. The navy crew watched them cautiously. The children looked like otters gliding through the water, aquatic creatures naked and brown, a species entirely distinct from the stiff uniformed humans in the launch.

Nathan and Hammond shook hands with the senior officer aboard. And Lily embraced Thandie. Unlike Lily, who felt her years weighed heavily, Thandie didn't seem to have aged a day, as if she had reached some kind of plateau.

The crew handed out life jackets, and the launch put about and headed for the shore, off to the west. Lily saw they were to be escorted by a couple more launches from the submarine. She could see why; the inshore waters were black with shipping.

Thandie glanced back at the Ark, at Captain Suarez. "I can't believe Nathan hired that damn woman. That he made her captain! She tried to sink him out at the Gyre, and she might have managed it if the *New Jersey* hadn't shown up."

"That's Nathan for you," Lily said. "When he beats you he assimilates you. I've seen him do it again and again." She glanced at Hammond, thirty-five years old and sullen, sitting stiffly beside Grace. "Even to his own son."

"Hell of a management strategy, to surround yourself with people who've got a grudge against you."

"It's kind of Darwinian, I think. You have to be strong to survive being close to him."

Thandie nodded. "Well, you've all survived this far."

"Yeah. But Nathan's not going to last forever, and neither is his Ark. Which is why—"

Thandie covered Lily's hand with her own. "I know. Look, I've done my best to set this up. There's at least a chance it will work, with luck and a bit of goodwill, and imagination on all sides. We'll just have to see how it plays out . . ."

They fell silent, for they were approaching the shore.

They came in somewhere over the flooded remains of the town of Pueblo. Lily could already see mountains shouldering above the horizon to the west. The mountains had a bare, brown look, stripped of the ice cover they had had only a few years ago; the snowline was somewhere above their summits now, a wholly theoretical plane in the air.

And as they approached the dry land they passed among the drifting offshore communities. The launches drew closer together for protection, and crewmen stood up, their weapons showing, pistols and nightsticks. There were boats and smacks of all sizes, and many rafts, improvised from the detritus of the drowned towns. One family even sat on what looked like a roadside billboard, its gaudy laminated colors still advertising a hot dog brand. There were very few old people on these vessels, few as old as Lily was, and there was a stink of sewage. As the launch passed, kids came rushing to the edge of the rafts, their hands out. Lily saw the dismal potbelly signature of malnutrition.

"My God," Hammond said. "This is a zoo. Can't we help these people?"

"We don't have the resources," Thandie said. " 'We' meaning the Navy, the government. It isn't possible to help everybody anymore."

"What a pack of losers," Nathan snarled. "You got a raft,

you sail out to sea and you can catch all the fish you want. Stay this close in to shore and you'll get nothing but scraps off the land. Pathetic."

"Not everybody's as tough as you are, Nathan," Lily murmured.

"Then the hell with them."

Lily saw how Hammond gazed at Nathan, his face black with loathing.

The shore, a rocky slope that pushed steeply out of the water, was fringed by barbed wire and concrete blocks, like tank traps. Troops in faded olive-green uniforms patrolled the barrier, carrying clubs that they evidently used to beat back anybody who tried to land. They wore helmets with a Homeland Security logo. Their actions were the ultimate expression of that particular department's historic function, Lily thought.

Looking along the shore, however, she saw how more troops and civilian workers were moving the barricade back, rebuilding it, retreating from a sea that now rose around a meter every single day.

The launches came in on a roadway that climbed up out of the sea. The troops moved wire and concrete blocks out of the way to let them land, and then hauled the launch out of the water and up onto the tarmac. The party aboard stepped out gingerly. Hammond made a show of helping his wife, but Grace refused him. Lily stood straight on the tilting road surface, and flexed her toes, testing her balance.

Thandie led the way to a small fleet of electric cars, emblazoned with Homeland Security and US Army and Navy logos. The Ark crew got into these vehicles, bemused; Lily couldn't remember the last time she had been in a car, even a beat-up electric jeep like this. Thandie said they would drive a few kilometers further inland to an old mining town called Cripple Creek, a center of population hereabouts where they would make their rendezvous.

As they drove away from the shore Thandie pointed out the sights to Lily. "That's Pikes Peak. Cripple Creek is on its southwest face."

"I haven't been ashore in a while," Lily said. "Those rafts, the starving people—I didn't know things were so bad."

Thandie grunted. "It could be worse. Sounds like it *is* worse, in central Asia. In America it's been a slower tragedy.

For all the abuse, the inequality and the corporate ripoff, Americans gave it their best shot. They built a homeland up there on the Great Plains in a decade, a whole new nation, and then in the next decade they had to abandon it again."

"Like the troopers at the beach. You build your barrier, then a little later your have to build it again further back."

"Just like that."

They drove on, climbing higher. Faded signs announced that this was State Highway 67. The road narrowed, becoming a pass through the mountains; some of the views were vertiginous.

Thandie said, "Things are fraying. The government has shifted its resources to a few special projects it's trying to sustain. Otherwise, before the government liquefies altogether, it is simply trying to help people prepare for the next phase."

"Rafts."

"Yes. There's nothing else to be done."

They were approaching the town.

Nathan leaned forward from the back. " 'Special projects,' " he growled. "What kind of projects?"

Lily said, "That's what we're here to discuss, Nathan." She glanced at Thandie.

Thandie shrugged. "It won't be a secret much longer anyhow. Tell him."

Lily said to Nathan, "A project like Ark One."

90

Cripple Creek had been a poor settlement that had become briefly rich when gold was discovered on Pikes Peak in the 1890s. Then when the gold was gone it became a tourist trap. The heart of the town was a row of storefronts that looked like a set from some western movie, with what had been gift shops and ice cream parlors. A faded sign promised tours to the Mollie Kathleen Gold Mine.

Now, in the age of the flood, a shantytown of tents and shacks spread far beyond the core of the old town, a vast community of refugees clinging to the face of the mountain. Homeless were camped right in the heart of town, in the streets and parking lots and the forecourts of disused gas stations.

Thandie's party was taken to a requisitioned restaurant that had once been a Denny's. A young soldier was posted at the door, and the window was plastered with signs saying the place was for the sole use of US military personnel and federal government officials. The nestlike shelters of the homeless washed right up to its door. Walking through mounds of canvas and plastic, Lily took care not to step on anybody.

Inside, the restaurant was clean, serviceable, but lacked any character. And sitting alone at a table here, cradling a china mug of coffee, was Gordon James Alonzo. He stood as they entered.

Nathan took command, as always. He walked straight to Gordo and grabbed his hand. "Gordo, you old dog. I haven't seen you in years."

Gordo embraced Nathan back. "Yeah, and you owe me my last paycheck, you rascal."

The former astronaut had to be in his seventies, Lily cal-

culated, but he was as upright and fit-looking and intimi-
dating as he had ever been, his blue eyes still bright. All his
hair was gone now, leaving a scalp that was nutmeg brown
and polished smooth, an egg carved of wood. He wore a
crisp USAF officer's uniform.

They sat at Gordo's table, Nathan and Lily, Hammond
and Grace, Thandie. The *New Jersey* crew who had accompanied Thandie set themselves over in the corner, and
took off their peaked caps. A young enlisted man came out
and offered them all coffee and bagels. As Nathan worked
through a round of introductions, Lily tried the coffee. It
turned out to be aromatic and fresh, the best she had tasted
in years.

"You can thank the Cold War for the coffee," Thandie
murmured.

"I don't get it."

"A joke at my expense, Miss Brooke," said Gordo. "I
work at the Cheyenne Mountain Air Force Station, specifically at the Cheyenne Mountain Directorate. Air and missile warning centers, space control center, and a shitload of
other functions, all buried behind concrete bulkheads and
steel walls two thousand feet under the mountain. When
the Cold War calmed down the base was put on warm
standby under NORAD. Which is the North American
Aerospace Defense Command."

"I know what NORAD is," Lily said testily. "Was once
USAF myself, you know, Gordo."

"My apologies. Anyhow when the flooding began the
base was reactivated, to handle security concerns arising
out of the new situation. And eventually I myself was reactivated, so to speak, taken out of the Army, brought back
into the Air Force, posted here. And now we're working
through seventy-year-old stocks of coffee and beans and
candy bars in the nuclear bunkers."

"And," Thandie said, "Gordo here is integral to Ark
One."

Gordo glanced around. "We never refer to it that way.
Code word is Nimrod."

"Nimrod, then."

Nathan was studying Gordo. "I was involved when
we conceived the Ark program in the first place. So was
Thandie, who was hired to give a briefing. It was an idea

somebody cooked up in the LaRei. Which was a rich guys' club. History now. Anyhow we all came up with projects, ways to beat the flood, and supported each other to get them done. It was always so damned secretive. I *built* Ark Three, and even I never found out what the other Arks were going to be or where they were built. And then the whole program got taken over by the federal government and I had even less chance of figuring it out. It's the same now, isn't it? You're not going to tell us what this Project Nimrod is, are you, Gordo?"

"Classified, sir."

Nathan glanced at Thandie. "So why are we here?"

Thandie's look was guarded. "I know more about Project Nimrod than I should. Oh, don't look at me like that, Gordo. I've been working around the military for years. You only have to keep your ears and eyes open to pick up a hell of a lot. What's left of the US military is up to something, deep in the heart of Cheyenne Mountain. I won't say what I think it is. You might want to ask why they would enlist *this* man as a consultant, however. But one thing is clear. It is designed to save a number of people. A small number, selected for their genetic diversity and their skill sets."

Nathan snapped, "Save them from what?"

"The worst case."

He frowned. "Which is?"

"Extinction," she said.

That stopped the conversation.

Extinction. It had always been a possibility, and then a growing probability, as the flood had kept relentlessly on, and mankind's ability to cope with its effects had crumbled. Civilization falling was one thing, but if the land itself were covered, if there were no rocks to bang together, no savannah for a roaming primate to inhabit, what then? It was a word nobody used, as if to say it might bring that very event about. But it was there, Lily knew, in the minds of everybody on the planet with any sense of perspective.

Lily watched Nathan. She saw what he was thinking. After all these years, she knew Nathan inside out. If extinction were to threaten, this Project Nimrod might be the only channel by which one's genes—specifically Nathan's genes—could pass to the future. *That* was what Nathan was thinking.

And that was what would drive events now, Lily hoped, Nathan's usual ruthless calculation impelling him to form fresh plans. Lily could achieve her own purposes by riding on those plans.

But Gordo Alonzo was frowning. "Just what's going on here? I was told by Miss Jones that we were here to discuss a donation to the project. By you, Mr. Lammockson."

"That's news to me," Nathan said, looking at Lily and Thandie. "You think we've been set up by these ladies, Gordo? Anyhow, what kind of donation? I can't believe you're asking for money."

"Not money, Nathan," Lily said gently. "Something much more precious. Seeds. Zygotes. Your Norwegian archive in the hold on Ark Three." A treasure Nathan had been protecting all these years, even as the world disintegrated around him and his cruise liner turned into a battleship.

"So why would I give that away?" Nathan asked. But Lily saw him work it out. "Oh, I get it. It's not a donation. It's a purchase."

Gordo was slower on the uptake. "A purchase of what?"

Thandie said, "Gordo, Lily and I cooked this up together. Look—here's what I know. Ark One needs what Nathan has: the root stock to rebuild a world. It's one thing the US government programs were slow in securing. And I know you have influence in the project, a lot of influence. There's a list of candidates for the crew, isn't there? You can get people off of there, if you put a word in the right ear. That probably isn't hard. But more important, you personally have at least a chance of getting somebody new on the list."

Gordo's eyes narrowed. "So that's it. In return for this freezer full of grass seed and pig embryos, Nathan wants to buy a place in Nimrod."

Nathan held his hands up. "Hey, don't look at me. I didn't come in here wanting anything." But, hooked by the prospect of a deal, he was watching Gordo's reaction. "Just as a theoretical possibility, however. If Nimrod exists at all, if you have this kind of sway. You think it's possible you could do this?"

Gordo shrugged. "I could maybe get a certain *class* of

people on there. And it doesn't include you, Nathan. There are various categories you have to fit—such as, young enough to have a kid. That rules out you." He stiffened, subtly. "And me."

Grace spoke for the first time. "You're working on this project knowing you won't be included yourself?"

"It's what we call duty, ma'am," he said.

Thandie caught Lily's eye and shook her head. Was there anything more corny than an astronaut being a hero? But Lily found herself moved even so.

But Nathan's thoughts were surging ahead. "Not me, then. But Hammond here." He clapped his son on the shoulder. "He's only thirty-five. You could take Hammond, right?"

Hammond's blocky face showed an extraordinarily mixed expression, relief he might be saved from a danger he evidently hadn't been imaginative enough to consider before, and resentment as his father reshaped his life once again.

Gordo's face worked. "It's possible—"

"No," Lily snapped. They all turned to look at her. She leaned forward, her heart beating. This was the crux of the situation—of her whole life, in a sense, since Barcelona. "Not you, Hammond. *Grace*. Send Grace, Nathan. That's who you must save."

Nathan immediately saw what she was doing. "Right. And so you'll fulfill your promise to Helen, all those years ago. With you people it always comes back to those days in the fucking cellars, doesn't it? It always comes back to that."

Lily shrugged. "You know us better than anyone."

"All right. But why should I do this? Why should I bump my own son out of this safe haven, whatever the hell it is, and put her in instead?"

"Because she's carrying Hammond's child." She pointed at Grace's belly. "Your genes are in there, Nathan."

Thandie glanced at Gordo. "She's actually a better candidate than Hammond, in terms of Nimrod's criteria. She's not academic, but she has shown independent survival skills that Hammond never has, frankly. And with a pregnant woman you're getting two for the price of one, two sets of genes—twice the genetic diversity. She will be an easier sell."

Grace looked utterly shocked. "*You planned this*," she said to Lily, and she touched her own belly. "You set up my relationship with Hammond—even the timing of my pregnancy, to get me onto this Ark. You've been planning it for years!"

Hammond snapped, "And what about me? Why should I allow this to happen? If I push you, Dad, you'll give me that place. I know you will. Why should I help *her*, knowing I might not survive myself?"

Gordo Alonzo said, "So that you will be remembered."

After that, nobody spoke for long seconds.

Lily felt the decision congeal around them. She felt a vast relief. I did it, Helen. I kept my promise to you after all this time. I did it.

Gordo stood up. "We ought to break this up. I got a lot to talk about with my superiors, if, *if*, I can swing this."

Thandie said, "I know you won't say anything about the nature of the project, Gordo. But why Nimrod? Why that name?"

Ramrod straight, he looked down at her. "I guess you skipped Bible studies at school. Genesis 10, verses 8 to 10: 'And Cush begat Nimrod: he began to be a mighty one in the earth ... And the beginning of his kingdom was Babel, and Erech, and Accad, and—' "

"Babel?"

"It was only generations after the Flood of Noah. Chapter 11, verse 4. 'And they said, Go to, let us build us a city and a tower, whose top may reach unto heaven.' "

"But God struck them down when they built the tower."

"Yes. But why? 11:6. 'Now nothing will be restrained from them, which they have imagined to do.' That's what God said about mankind. He feared us, and so He struck us down. We have that verse up on the wall on big banners, to motivate the workforce. 'Nothing will be restrained from them, which they have imagined to do.' "

"Wow," Thandie said. "You're challenging God?"

"Why the hell not?"

Nathan's radio phone went off. And then Lily's, then Hammond's.

It was Piers, calling from Ark Three. The ship was under attack.

91

Gordo and Thandie rustled up a helicopter to take them all back to the shore. As the bird came down in Cripple Creek it scattered some of the flimsier shanties that crowded the narrow streets. But the population didn't seem too scared. Lily supposed that the neighborhood of NORAD was one of the few places on the planet where helicopters would still be commonplace.

They hurried aboard. But Grace was staying behind, with Gordo Alonzo, to be taken away into Project Nimrod, into Ark One, whatever that meant. And Lily knew that this was it, that she would never see Grace again. There wasn't even time to say goodbye, and anyhow the noise of the bird drowned out everything they said. Lily mouthed, "Forgive me." Then Thandie pulled Lily into the chopper, and Gordo Alonzo held onto Grace, and the ground fell away, diminishing Grace's upturned face to a point.

Then the ride itself overwhelmed Lily. She couldn't remember when she'd last flown. It brought back a rush of memories, the smell of leather and canvas and oil, the shuddering vibration of the turning blades.

From the air, Lily could see Ark Three was listing. Smoke was pouring out of the engine room, oil spilling onto the ocean surface. The bridge was in ruins, and there was a fire in progress on the sports deck. Lily could see the lifeboats being launched, the orange craft swinging from their davits.

And rafts and boats were gathering like sharks around a wounded whale. More were on their way, a fleet of rough vessels making for the stricken ship. Such was the scale of the disaster that it could be seen for kilometers around.

"It looks like she's been torpedoed." Nathan turned on

Thandie. "Why didn't your damn sub do something about it?"

"She's doing something now," Thandie said. She pointed to a slim hull. "The *New Jersey* will be going in for your seed store if nothing else, Nathan."

A sub officer said to Nathan, "We'll save as many of your people as we can, sir, you can be sure of that."

As the chopper descended Lily saw the first boarders taking on the crew on the rope ladders and the promenade deck. She thought of Piers, and Kristie and Manco, and everybody else she cared for down there, the only world she had known for years. And me, she wondered. Where am I going to live now? A shack on some mountainside, a raft?

"Get us down, damn it." Nathan was hanging in the open doorway, a pistol in his hand.

Five

2041–2052
Mean sea-level rise above 2010 datum:
1800–8800m

92

August 2041

Nathan and Hammond personally carried Piers out of the wreck of the Ark. He was limp in their arms, tall, frail, his long legs folded up like a cricket's, a length of bony forearm protruding from each sleeve cuff. The Lammocksons had to clamber across a gathering archipelago of lifeboats and rafts, some of them Ark inflatables, others improvised from wreck debris. The crowded boats bobbed and dipped under their steps, and it was a miracle they didn't end up in the water, the two of them and the man they were carrying. But they kept going.

Lily, Kristie and Manco had a liferaft to themselves, much patched but serviceable. Manco and Kristie cowered in the shade of the raft's tentlike cover. Kristie's battered pink backpack was at her feet, following her into yet another new phase in her life. Manco, ten years old, was wide-eyed, naked save for swimming trunks and his bulky life jacket and his precious red *New Jersey* baseball cap. Kristie held him close, and when the popping of the guns or the screams got too loud she put her hands over his ears and pressed his face against her chest.

The Lammocksons reached Lily's raft. Gently they laid Piers down in the bilge. "Found him on the prom deck," Nathan said, panting, sweating hard. "Out cold. Got him in his jacket, hauled him here."

Hammond just stood there, massaging one arm, his face crunched into a scowl. He looked as if he might be carrying some wound himself. Every so often he looked to the shore, back to where they had left Grace with Hammond's unborn child.

"Well, you did the right thing," Lily said. She threw Nathan a bottle of water from the raft's small emergency supply. He swigged down a big mouthful, and poured more over his head before handing it to Hammond. Lily winced a bit at the waste, but it wasn't the time to make a fuss about that.

She looked down at Piers. It was wet on the floor of the raft, but there was nowhere else to put him. She scrunched forward and took his head on her lap.

Kristie sat staring at Piers's pale, motionless face. "Maybe it's best not to move him."

Hammond grunted. "Take a look under his life jacket."

Lily leaned forward, unzipped the jacket, and exposed a mess, Piers's overalls and ripped flesh mingling in a pool of sticky blood. "Oh, God."

"Actually I think he got shot in the back," Hammond said in a matter-of-fact way. "That looks like an exit wound to me."

"He went down fighting," Nathan said. "Always knew he would."

"Is there a medic? Dr. Porter, or Doc Schmidt—anybody nearby?"

"No idea," Nathan said. "And I don't see any way of finding out right now. Sorry, kid—you're on your own." Suddenly the steam seemed to go out of him. "Ah, Christ." He folded up and sat down on the boat's inflated hull, and wiped his brow with the back of his hand. "We've got to go back in there, there are still people trying to get off the wreck. But I'm beat. Just give me a minute, son."

Hammond shrugged. As ever in the shadow of Nathan, he wasn't about to go anywhere without his father.

Lily glanced over at her niece. "Kris, the raft has a medical kit. Look, the zipper behind you. Can you pass it over?"

Kristie sat for a long second, cradling her boy. Then she squirmed around to fetch the kit. "You don't want to waste it. We don't know how long it has to last, the stuff in there."

She was right, of course. With the Ark dying, with the crew unlikely to be allowed into Colorado, with even the *New Jersey* standing off, there was nowhere they could go, nowhere they could land—no place where they could ever get off this raft. But Lily put the thought aside. What else could you do?

Kristie handed the kit over. Lily opened it.

"No." There was a touch on her wrist, cold and wet. It was Piers. His eyes open, he was looking up at her, his face upside down from her point of view, his mouth twisted with pain. It was as if a dead man had come to life.

"Piers?"

"Kristie is right." His voice was a gurgle, indistinct, and the very act of breathing seemed to cause him pain. "You know it, and so do I. I'm sixty-five years old, for heaven's sake."

"So am I." Lily began to unroll a bandage.

"Be sensible, Lily. That's an order, by the way."

Lily forced a laugh. "I haven't taken orders from you since Barcelona."

"Please. For me."

She hesitated. Then she pushed the box toward Nathan, with a nod. Surreptitiously, out of Piers's eye line, Nathan prepared a syringe of morphine.

Piers asked, "How is the ship, the crew?"

"Well, we lost her." Lily looked up. The ocean was littered with orange boats from the Ark. The shabbier-looking craft of the attackers moved through this crowd like shark fins, and small battles were going on everywhere. But Lily could see that one by one the attackers were withdrawing, and the Ark survivors were pulling on plastic ropes to bring their boats closer together. The Ark herself was sinking into a bubbling oil slick.

She said, "I guess we got most of the people off. No way of counting right now."

Nathan jabbed the syringe into Piers's leg, right through his pants. Piers didn't seem to feel it. Covering, Nathan said, "We'll count it up later, when the arseholes who did this have got what they wanted and pissed off. I hope they're proud of themselves. They sent a fucking ship to the bottom of the sea, nuclear reactor and all. What a damn waste. A vessel that could have lasted decades yet, and all for a few scraps of wood and steel and plastic so they could make more of their shitty little rafts."

"The Americans," Piers said softly. "The submarine. Couldn't they help?"

"They wouldn't," Lily said. "Thandie Jones did speak to the captain."

"They stay out of fights," Nathan said. "That's how you

keep alive, for year after pointless year at sea. So much for the US Navy. Well. What's done is done. I always knew this day could come, when we lost the Ark. Now it's time for the next phase, is all."

Kristie asked, "What next phase?"

Nathan gestured at the scum of debris. "Rafts, that's what. Survival on the open sea. And the raw materials we need to do that are waiting for us, right over there." He pointed back at the Ark. "We always arranged it so the stuff would just float off if we lost the ship suddenly. I'm talking about seaweed. Algae, gen-enged, by the boys in the Ark's labs. From seaweed you can get algin, that is alginic acid, from which you can make emulsions, fibers . . . Construction material for rafts that will grow out of the sea, you just have to let it float there. You'll see." He stood up, and the raft rocked gently. "In the meantime we need to get back. Come on, boy."

He stood and strode away, back toward the center of the scatter of ships, the graveyard of his Ark, working his way across the cluster of rafts. Hammond followed reluctantly, wincing at the pain of his shoulder.

"They wasted our water," Kristie said. "Now we haven't got a drop in this damn raft."

"There'll be more water," Lily said, but she was uncertain. "Maybe it will rain."

"No rain today," Piers murmured. His eyes were wide, the pupils dilated, and he stared up at the sky. "Do you remember how it rained when we came out of the vault under that cathedral, how it rained in London . . ."

"I remember."

Kristie grabbed the medical kit, closed it and stuck it back in the zippered compartment. Piers watched Kristie, tilting his head. He actually raised his arm, reaching out to her.

"Come on, Kris," Lily whispered. "Just hold his hand, just for a moment."

But Kristie turned her boy's face away from the dying man.

Piers lasted through the rest of the day, and into the night.

As the light faded, Manco complained of thirst and hunger, but at last fell asleep. Kristie kept him in the shade of the cover, and soon it was too dark for Lily to make out either of them.

Nathan didn't come back to the raft. Lily just sat cradling Piers's head. There was no moon, no cloud. The stars were extraordinary, set in a sky from which humankind's pollution had all but washed out. Lily had spent years on a ship at sea, but even she had never seen the stars like this, for on the Ark there was always some nearby light or other to dazzle you.

Around the raft there was quiet, broken only by the soft lapping of waves, a murmur of voices, somebody crying, far away. It was a night to rest, a night many no doubt wished would never end, for tomorrow a new struggle would begin. But for now there was stillness.

Piers woke once more, in the dark. "Have you got it?"

"Got what, Piers?"

"For my face. You know. In case they come back." He tried to shift, his hands lifting feebly. "It must have fallen on the floor."

"Your towel?"

"Have you got it?"

Kristie had a scarf around her neck that she used to keep the sun off. She took this off and passed it over. Lily smoothed it out and placed it over Piers's face. He sighed, and lay still.

93

September 2043

Kristie died.

It was something she ate, something from the sea that wasn't as familiar as it looked. It was a common way to die on the rafts. She was thirty-eight. She had survived on the rafts two years since the sinking of the Ark.

Manco, orphaned at aged twelve, was inconsolable.

Kristie had kept her little pink kid's backpack from London, and Lily went through it. Inside there were a few cheap plastic accessories, Kristie's handheld computer, her ancient teddy. Lily decided to keep the handheld. She offered Manco the teddy, but it was too babyish for him. He kept a necklace of amberlike beads, however. He wore it wrapped around his wrist.

There had been no peace between Kristie and her aunt, even to the end. When she learned what had happened at Cripple Creek, Kristie hadn't been able to accept that Lily had wangled a place on Ark One, whatever it was, not for Manco, her own blood, but for Grace, a relic of her hostage days. It was no good for Lily to protest that they probably wouldn't have taken Manco anyhow, and that Nathan certainly wouldn't have supported him. Lily hadn't even *tried*, and that was enough of a betrayal for Kristie.

One way or another Lily's captivity had come between them most of Kristie's life, and now it pursued them to her death.

That night, when Manco was sleeping, Lily took a look at the handheld.

It had a calendar facility, but no satellite or radio link. And it had an extensive database that Kristie called her scrapbook. Lily remembered how she had started this thing on her mother's dining table in Fulham, with an observation of an old man who couldn't get to the football because of floods in Peterborough. That snippet was still here. She scanned through more items. They were selected judiciously, and written up with a hasty grace. Kristie could have been a writer of some kind, maybe a journalist, in a more forgiving age. In the last couple of years, after the Ark was gone and they were on the rafts, Kristie's access to global news had pretty much vanished, aside from scraps she heard over Nathan's clockwork radios. But her own world widened, oddly, as the raft communities crossing the world's oceans converged and dissipated, and bits of news were passed on among them, and she had recorded them on her handheld.

Curious, Lily scanned to the very last item Kristie had recorded. It was a bit of gossip, written up by Kristie a few weeks ago. The witness spoke of a time only a few months after Lily had deposited Grace in Colorado. She had been in the drifting communities in the ocean east of the Rockies. One night she had been sitting on her raft braiding her eldest daughter's hair, when a light sent shifting shadows across her lap. At first she thought it was a flare. She turned to see.

She made out a brilliant pinpoint of light that rose up into the western sky, trailing a column of smoke that was illuminated by the glow of that leading fire. As it rose it arced, tracing out a smooth curve across the face of the heavens. And then sound reached her, a soft rumble like a very distant storm. The spark of light receded in the sky.

Grace, Lily thought immediately. Grace. What else could it be?

Hastily she scanned the database. It was only a bit of gossip Kristie had picked up from somebody on another raft, who in turn had heard it from somebody else, who . . . And so on. It was unverifiable. The source didn't even have a name. Lily was never going to know if it was true. She read the entry over and over, trying to squeeze more information out of its few words, until Manco called for her in his sleep.

Later, spurred by curiosity, she looked up the second to last entry. It was a report out of what was left of America, relayed by radio, that the horse was believed to be extinct.

*   *   *

In the morning Lily prepared the body as best she could. She stuffed the teddy inside the backpack, and slung the pack around Kristie's neck.

Then she got help carrying Kristie's body to the edge of the raft. It was a big construct by now, nearly a hundred meters across, a floating village built on a substrate of Nathan's gen-enged seaweed algin products. Aside from her pack, Kristie was sent naked into the sea. They couldn't spare the clothes. At that they had to run a gauntlet of some of the raft crew, a younger set who didn't believe in sea burials. There was no cannibalism, but Kristie's body represented too valuable a resource to waste in the sea. That was their view, but Lily begged to differ, and as an elder from the Ark she wasn't impeded.

She didn't even have anything to weigh down the body. Kristie's grave would be the sharp teeth of the ocean.

So Lily and Manco were left alone together. They were from different worlds, strangers. They fought and cried.

94

When the moon went into totality, when the Earth's shadow crossed its face entirely and that compelling bloodred color bloomed, Lily could hear the gasp that went up across the community of rafts, a crowd's murmur of awe, children saying, "Look at that!" in a variety of languages. The orange light of the eclipsed moon washed down over Manco's upturned face, making it shine like a coin. As the sky was stripped of moonlight the other stars emerged, dominated by Jupiter, king of the planets.

Lily tried to imagine how it would be to look back from the moon itself, to see the breast of Earth's ocean glimmering in the tainted moonlight, unbounded from pole to pole save for the last scattering of mountaintop islands with its speckling of rafts and boats and islands of garbage, and the people turning up their faces to see the show in the sky. Lily felt like relaxing into the spectacle herself.

But she had work to do, information to drum into the thirteen-year-old head of Manco.

She shifted to get more comfortable beside Manco on the scrap of plastic tarp, salvaged from the Ark, that they spread out over the sticky seaweed-algin floor of their raft. "Now, Manco, you need particularly to watch out for the moments when the Earth's shadow touches the moon's limb, which is when the moon enters or leaves the cone of shadow. Because you can time those moments precisely, you see, within a second or so." She made an entry in Kristie's handheld, to make the point. "And then you note down the time, like this—"

"The light's funny," he said. "Not like moonlight at all."

"No. That's because it isn't normal moonlight. You get moonlight when the sun's light shines on the face of the moon. During an eclipse the only light the moon gets is refracted through the Earth's atmosphere. It comes around the edge of the Earth, and it's red. Like all the sunrises and sunsets in the world, all at once, falling on the moon . . ."

He wasn't interested.

And her voice was giving up on her. She was thirsty. God, she was sixty-eight years old, and for three years she had been living on a raft, and the plastic buckets had stood empty for long days. She had a right to a sore throat. You could always get a little moisture from the fish, from sucked-out eyeballs or spinal fluid, which kids like Manco seemed to have no problem with. But it always made Lily queasy, and left behind a salty, oily aftertaste that was almost worse than the thirst itself.

She tried to focus.

She was trying to drum into Manco's young head the method she had figured out for calculating longitude.

Because precise timekeeping was essential, figuring out longitude would be a challenge in the future when all the watches and clocks had stopped working. But she had her old astronomy almanac, a souvenir of the *New Jersey*, which had timing predictions of lunar eclipses as seen from Greenwich for every year until 2100. A lunar eclipse was an event visible from across one whole face of the planet. All you had to do was keep track of the date—she knew from Kristie's handheld that tonight was 13 March 2044—and if you spotted your moment of eclipse, and pinned it down to the right prediction in the almanac, you knew the precise Greenwich time at that moment. And knowing *that* you just had to look at the stars above you, and figure out how they compared to the position of the stars the almanac showed for that moment in the skies over London, and you could tell how far around the curve of the world you were . . .

Even to Lily it felt terribly complicated.

"I don't see what difference it makes," Manco said. "Longitude, yes, OK, how far we are from the equator—"

"Latitude," she said softly. "That's latitude. Longitude is—"

"Latitude's easy." He pointed at the pole star. "It just depends how high *that* is. And latitude's important." So it was. It was best to stay close to the equator, where the great hurricanes rarely roamed, but you would always venture north or south a little way, because where the hurricanes passed the water was stirred up, and the fishing was better. "But who cares about longitude? What difference does it make? It's all the same, it's just water, no matter how far east or west you go. I mean, where are we right now?"

"About seventy-five degrees east. Somewhere in the Indian Ocean."

"So what? Who cares? What's Indian?"

"India. It was called India. The point is—"

"Can I go see Ana? I'll tell her about the eclipse, and latitude and stuff."

"Longitude."

"Whatever."

And with that off he went, walking gracefully, wearing only a ragged pair of shorts. He padded over the raft's floor, thinking nothing of Nathan's marvelous substrate, an everyday, self-maintaining miracle that everybody took for granted, and most of the young didn't remotely understand, or even notice.

At the edge Manco slipped into the moonlit water and swam away.

She heard Nathan's cough long before he came looming out of the dark.

Nathan came up, hobbling; in the last few years he had become plagued with arthritis, blaming the damp of the sea. "Where the hell's Manco? I thought school was in."

Lily smoothed out a heap of blankets for him to sit on; he lowered himself painfully. "Oh, Nathan, you know how it is with these kids. You can't keep them still. Ana isn't a bad kid, anyhow. Have you met her parents? Russians, who made it to the western US after the flooding overwhelmed the mother country. Tough story. Ana doesn't remember any of it, of course."

"My perception is these kids just want to swim and screw all day. Some of them catch fish with their teeth, y'know. Hell of a sight."

"Well, maybe—"

"They got to be taught," he insisted, slapping his palm on the floor. "We can't let our kids turn into fucking seals. They got to learn their longitude. They got to learn to read and write and figure. They got to learn they live on a fucking ball in the sky. Because otherwise, in a generation's time, they won't be using your lunar eclipses to work out longitude. They'll be cowering from God's blinking eye."

"I know, know—"

"That damn kid Manco is worse since his mother died. Say what you like about Kristie, and she had plenty to say about me, she was a good mother, a tough one."

Lily flared. "Oh, you think I'm doing such a bad job? Christ, Nathan, I'm nearly seventy years old. If I could get his mother back I'd do it like a shot. It's not as if you did such a great job with Hammond."

As soon as he could after the sinking of the Ark, Hammond had commandeered a couple of the lifeboats and had headed off, making south, he said, hoping to find a foothold back in the Andes. His father hadn't wanted to release him. Their parting had been marked by a fistfight.

Now, though, Nathan didn't seem worried by the jibe. He leaned closer to Lily and whispered, though there was nobody around to hear, "Speaking of Hammond, got a message from him today." They had kept in touch via Nathan's wind-up and solar-powered radio gear. "Sent back some news about the Spot."

The Spot was an apparently permanent hypercane system that roamed around the Earth's tropics, feeding on the heat of the warming air, unimpeded by land as such storms had always been before. It was called the Spot because that was how it was thought it would look from space, if any satellites were still functioning, a permanent storm on Earth like the Great Red Spot of Jupiter. Nathan reeled off some coordinates. It paid to know where the Spot was, and its satellite storms, so you could avoid their destructiveness and yet plunder the mixed-up, nutrient-rich waters they left in their wake.

"And," Nathan said, "he got a message from Alma. Or rather he didn't get one."

"Alma, Colorado." The highest city in the US. "And now?"

"Glug, glug, glug," Nathan said.

"God." Lily tried to remember what smaller US cities had been like—the downtown, the out-of-town malls, the schoolhouses and gas stations and suburbs. Gone, all of them, erased more completely than any of the vanished empires of the past.

The endless litany of losses was increasingly unreal. The sea was so high now that even mountain cities in the Andes were being lost: Bogota, Quito, La Paz. And before that, Australia had gone, the first continent to vanish entirely from the face of the Earth. Lily had marked the day, following her scratch calendar, when she had calculated that the seas had at last closed over Mount Kosciuszko in New South Wales, two thousand, two hundred and twenty-eight meters high, the island continent's highest point. Lily had softly sung "Waltzing Matilda" as she bade it goodbye . . .

She wasn't listening to Nathan. As always she was drifting off into reverie. She tried again to focus.

Nathan, rocking gently, kept talking, the way he used to, as always setting out his vision of the future. "We got to keep these kids educated. They are the heirs to forty thousand years of culture. In the past the world humans made was all around you, the buildings and the books and the machines, and it shaped you. That's all gone now, erased, save for what's in here." He thumped his temple, but gently, favoring his arthritic wrist. "This isn't just a flood. It's a vast collective amnesia. Well, that can't be helped. They've got to learn. But they won't learn. They won't listen. They won't keep to the rotas we set for them . . ."

She had heard these arguments before, and not just from Nathan. More commonly people complained that the kids wouldn't pay any attention to the itinerant preachers and imams and rabbis who slowly worked their way around the raft communities. If the kids were rejecting Nathan's can-do vision of the world, they were also seeking their own gods, it seemed, somewhere in the endless water that dominated their world.

Nathan mumbled, "Anyhow the flood is just another climatic convulsion in a long line. Five million years ago there was a grand cooling in Africa, and the forest broke up. Our forefathers split off and started evolving adaptations for open country. The chimps stuck to the forest fragments, and you know what, they were still there when the fucking waters rose up to drown them. The Earth birthed us, and then shaped us with tough love. This new watery age, the

Hydrocene, is just another rough molding, and we'll come through it, smarter and stronger than ever. We are the children of the Hydrocene. Yes, I like that . . ." He looked around, as if seeking somebody to write the phrase down for him. "Damn chimps, I mean kids, they just swim . . ." His eyes were closing, as if he were falling asleep even while he was talking, and he rocked stiffly, seventy-three years old.

"Nathan, maybe you should go to bed."

"They just swim . . ."

A light flared in the sky. Lily glanced up, thinking it must be the end of totality, the bright sunlight splashing unimpeded once more on the moon's face. But the moon, still wholly eclipsed, was as round and brown as it had been before.

It was Jupiter. Jupiter was flaring, still a pinpoint of light, but much brighter, bright enough to cast sharp point-source shadows on the glistening weed of the raft substrate. But the light diminished, as if receding with distance. And soon Jupiter shone alone as it had before.

That was the Ark, she thought immediately. That was Grace. What else could it be?

Then a sliver of white appeared at the very rim of the moon, lunar mountains exploding into the sunlight. She was quickly dazzled, and Jupiter was lost. She was never going to know.

"I got you here, didn't I? I kept you alive."

"Yes, Nathan." She pulled a blanket around his shoulders as he rocked and mumbled about evolution and destiny and children, an old man bent over his arthritic pain. "Yes, you did that."

But if it had been Ark One, she thought, maybe the crew *planned* the timing of that strange departure, knowing that over much of the dark side of the Earth eyes would be drawn to the eclipse, the spectacle in the sky. It would be quite a stunt, one hell of a way to say goodbye.

"I kept you alive. We've got to adapt. The chimps, I mean the kids, they've got to learn . . ."

95

Gary Boyle came to visit Lily, on her slowly spinning raft. Lily went to the lip of the raft and watched the boat come in.

Gary rowed over with a younger man, the two of them pulling strongly on their oars. He came from what looked like a scattered archipelago of low, green-clad islands. These were actually the summits of the Collegiate Peaks, a chain in the Rockies, the highest in the US outside Alaska. Now those huge mountains hardly stuck out of the rising water.

Raft kids went swimming around Gary's boat, their little bodies like sea lions dipping and bobbing as they sang one of their endless nonsense chants: "I laugh you more my fun, you're my enjee, you're my tee-fee, I laugh you more my fun . . ." One of the kids was Boris, the son of Manco and Ana, not yet two years old, swimming as confidently as any of them. Ana stood by the water and clapped her hands to try to make him come in.

Gary and his partner pulled the boat in alongside the raft's ragged edge, and climbed stiffly out. Lily gave Gary a hand, more for affection's sake than for any practical use, and he folded her in a big hug.

He let her lead him across the raft. "Wow, what is this stuff, rubber? . . ." The slime-covered seaweed base of the raft, Nathan's last legacy, persevered three years after a lung infection had finally killed the man himself. "Gen-enged, really? Oh, I'm impressed."

They sat together in the little plastic-and-tarp shack Lily used, sharing sometimes with Manco or Boris but rarely with Ana, who preferred to stay with her own family. Lily gave Gary fresh water, and dried fish spiced with some of the precious pepper she had been able to buy from a big floating farm in the mid-Pacific. "You should see those farms, Gary. Hanging gardens and water fountains, wind turbines and solar cells, out in the middle of the ocean. They have chickens in coops bolted to the walls, and vegetables growing in old truck tires. Even Nathan would be impressed."

Gary, listening politely, was fifty-six. There were vestiges of the boy she had known in the old days, Lily thought. He had always kept fit, as a field scientist always outdoors, always on the move, and then as a refugee for so many years. Nothing much had changed about his life in that regard. He was well-dressed, comparatively. Where Lily wore the remnants of her AxysCorp overalls, repeatedly washed and mended, Gary was dressed in a shirt and slacks that looked barely faded, freshly plundered from some drowned American town. But his hair was drastically thinned and peppered with gray, and there was a kind of sad tiredness about his eyes. And there was a crease on his temple, the scar of a gunshot; he didn't talk about that.

Gary had spent decades in the Andes communities, where Walker City had finally ended its long trek. In the end, though, as the situation started to crumble there, he decided he wanted to end things at home, in whatever was left of the continental US, and after an oceanic odyssey of his own he had finished up in Colorado.

And now he was here. He leaned forward and took her hands. "God, it's good to see you, Lily, to hear you talk. It's good of you to come all this way, to have crossed the world."

So she had. The rafts were navigable, just, if you used rudders and caught the wind in your sails. After Nathan's death Lily had inherited his goods, including his precious radios. She'd used them to track down Gary when he moved back to North America. And when he had told her what a significant year was coming up she had felt compelled to come and seek him out. The others indulged her. They didn't much care where they were, it seemed to her, as long as the fishing was good.

He said, "You're living a life a lot more alien than anything I've gone through yet. What do you *do* all day?"

"We fish," Lily said. "We catch water. We tend to the rafts. We trade a bit. Mostly we swim and screw."

That made him laugh.

She said, "For me more of the former, none of the latter. They're having kids, you know, younger and younger. Manco and Ana, for instance, were only fifteen when little Boris came along. The mothers give birth in the water. Even Manco and Ana aren't much like you and me. And the new generation, the Borises, will have no contact with us. Nothing in common, no shared memories. That's my fear, anyhow. I tell them a lot of stories. Where they came from."

They spoke of other friends, of Thandie and Elena and the rest of the scattered community of scientists, still holding hearth-gatherings over their surviving radios, still trying to witness the vast transformation that was overcoming the world. They spoke of Nathan, who had died bereft of his son, and of their fellow hostages, of Piers and Helen and even of John Foreshaw, who had died in Barcelona and had known nothing of the flood.

And of Grace. Gary knew even less about Ark One than Lily did. Lily had long accepted she was never going to know what had become of Helen's daughter.

They spoke of the year coming up. "It is one for disaster connoisseurs," Gary said. "In the next twelve months or so we'll lose continents by the hatful. In January, Europe will finally go when Mount Elbrus in Russia is covered. In May it's Africa's turn, when Kilimanjaro drowns. By then the continental US will have gone too, save for a couple of mountains in Alaska. In the year after that South America, even the Andes, and there will be nothing left in the western hemisphere at all . . ."

She didn't like to admit that she wasn't sure when January was, what month it was now. You lost track out on the sea. "I wonder how we'll mark time when the land is gone. Maybe by the great events that we experience. I've heard Manco and Ana talking about 'the year of the big wave.'"

He leaned forward, interested. "What big wave?"

She described it, an immense pulse in the water that must have been a hundred meters high, spanning the ocean from horizon to horizon. It was disconcerting, terrifying. But the rafts had been in deep water at the time, and the wave hadn't broken over them. The rafts just rode up, and were lowered smoothly down the other side.

Gary nodded. "That sounds like a planetary wave. The

theory of ocean worlds anticipates such things. A wave-length on a global scale, a slosh that circles the world's unbroken seas over and over."

"Nothing to stop it."

"Right. Maybe it was started off by an underwater quake, or a landslide. The weight of the water settling on the land is still causing geological kickbacks. We see it in the seismic readings, but we can't usually tell what's going on. No way to get down there to see anymore, of course."

" 'Ocean worlds.' "

"Yeah. We even saw some in the sky, back in the day when we had planet-finder telescopes. When you think about it a world like Earth ought to be rare, a mix of oceans and rocky landscapes. Worlds that are all rock, like Venus or Mercury, or all water—like Titan, the ice moons, frozen oceans hundreds of kilometers deep over a rocky core—have to be a lot more common. Anyhow we're now seeing ocean-world features emerge here on Earth, like the planetary waves, and the perpetual hypercane-strength storms like the Spot, and a simpler global ocean circulation system."

"So what about life?"

He smiled. "Yes, what about it? Listen, I have my own theory about where we're heading. Don't quote me. Thandie would kill me if she could hear me."

"Jeez, I'm not reviewing an academic paper, just tell me."

"Actually there are precedents. In the days of Pangaea a couple of hundred million years ago, when all the continents were joined into one, you had a semi-global ocean that was an approximation of what we're facing now. Look, the flood has made a real mess of the biological cycling of carbon . . ."

Carbon was drawn down from the air into the vegetable matter of plants on land and in the sea by photosynthesis, and then released back into the air through the respiration of living things, and the decay of the dead.

"Before the flood this carbon cycle was dominated by terrestrial life, the green things on land, and we've lost that whole major land-based mechanism. And we pretty much lost a second mechanism too, which is the weathering of surface rock—the cee-oh-two is rained out dissolved in water, the acid rain etches the rocks, blah blah. That was only a thousandth the biological component, but on a longer timescale it's effective—or was.

"What's worse is that even in the seas the drawdown mechanisms are failing. The rising temperatures are reducing the efficiency of the phytoplankton. The increasing acidity of the oceans isn't helping either—carbon dioxide plus water makes carbonic acid. Also you don't get the cold polar currents descending under the warm low-latitude waters, taking oxygen and nutrients to lower layers. That's why you get algal blooms following storm systems; you get some mixing-up, temporary, localized."

"We know about that," Lily said. "We feed off it."

"We've lost all these drawdown mechanisms just at a time when we've had a massive one-off injection of carbon dioxide into the air from the fires, and the rotting of the vegetation cover of the drowned land. It's as if we made a bonfire of everything green on the planet.

"So things have to change. The Earth is a system of flows of matter and energy, of feedback."

Lily whispered, "Gaia."

"That's the idea. The biggest pressure on her has always been a slow heating-up of the sun—the energy the sun pours onto the Earth is up by about a third since life formed. Now, Gaia's systems adjust, unconsciously, to maintain an even temperature at the surface, a temperature at which life can survive, despite this heating up. In the early days methane was injected into the air, another greenhouse gas, to keep the temperatures *up*. Some time around two billion years ago the sun's output was optimal for life on Earth. Since then it's been getting too hot, Gaia needs to keep cool, and the main way she does this is by drawing down cee-oh-two from the air, and storing it in the rocks, fossil stores like oil, coal."

Lily nodded. "The less greenhouse gas there is, the less heat is trapped."

"That's it. But that mechanism is nearing the limit of its capability. The atmosphere's cee-oh-two tank is, *was*, pretty much empty. Gaia was already *old*, even before the flood, and the hot sun is pushing too hard.

"Some of us think that the glaciation, the Ice Ages, was a kind of experiment with a new stable state. The Ice Ages were tough for humans. But from Gaia's point of view, if you give up the higher latitudes to ice, you lose a percentage of your productive surface, but you reflect away a hell of a lot of sunlight. Meanwhile life can flourish in the cooled-down mid-latitudes, and indeed on the land surface exposed by the lower sea levels. And the oceans are more fecund when the water is cooler; Gaia likes it cool. So the mechanism worked. But it always looked like a last-gasp effort.

"And now suddenly Gaia is finding herself water-rich, very hot, with very high carbon dioxide levels. She's under stress again, a kind of stress possibly unprecedented in her history."

"That's what Thandie says. Stress—"

"Yes, but we know the Earth likes to settle in stable states, where all its geological, climatic and biological cycles work together. For the last couple of million years it's flickered between Ice Age and warm interglacial. Now I think Gaia is reaching for a new stasis, a new point of equilibrium, where we'll see a *much* higher level of carbon dioxide in the air, and a much higher global temperature. All that heat will generate storms and whip up the sea, promoting life there by stirring up the nutrients, and providing a drawdown mechanism for the carbon dioxide. So you'll get a stable state, though with a higher cee-oh-two level than before."

"I see. I think. No need for land at all?"

"No. A whole new stable equilibrium, on a hot, stormy, watery Earth. In a sense you could say this is *why* the deep subsurface reservoirs have opened up now, to release the water to make this new state possible; the old states, the glacial-interglacial, were on the point of failure. You know what? I did some calculations, just blue-sky stuff. I figure that with a configuration like that there could be *more* total biomass on the Earth than before. The planet will come out of this actually healthier."

"But without room for us," she said.

"Not necessarily. There'll be plenty of fish in the sea, if we've the wit to catch them. But this whole story has never been about *us*, has it? It's always been about the Earth, transforming herself as she has in the past. Even if we gave her the kick in the ass that induced her to start the process."

Lily looked at the children playing in the sea. "Our

civilization is gone. Everything we built. But look at those kids swimming. *They* don't care that the Smithsonian is drowned, or that we're all offline forever."

Gary murmured, "Yes. And even if we pass away, you know, it's a happy ending of a kind. 'One generation passeth away, and another generation cometh: but the Earth abideth for ever.' Ecclesiastes 1:4." He grinned. "It was Thandie got me looking up the Bible, but don't tell her that either."

"So what about you? When North America drowns, will you come with us?"

"I guess not," he said, as boyishly as if he was refusing nothing more than a second cup of water. "I think I'm done with traveling. And there are people back there I care about."

Lily smiled. "You always were a people person, in the end. If not for you, Grace couldn't have survived. But I can't see you quitting. You're only fifty-six. I'll give you some of Nathan's raft-seaweed to grow."

"Thanks." He seemed concerned. "But, Lily, look, the seaweed by itself isn't enough. Eventually you'll run out of other stuff. The plastic, nylon fishing lines, everything else."

"Oh, we know the rafts don't last forever. Every so often we get hit by a storm we can't avoid, and a few more are lost. And there are still pirates out there. It's a steady attrition."

"And doesn't that worry you?"

She shrugged. "What can we do about it?"

"It's a tragedy, you know," Gary said. "We just ran out of time." He looked up at the huge sky. "Another fifty years and we'd have had power stations in orbit, and mines on the asteroids and the moon, and we wouldn't need the damn continents. Well."

"Yes."

They stood, helping each other up. Arm in arm, they walked to the edge of the raft, where Gary's friend was waiting beside their rowboat. He was playing coin tricks for a shoal of children, some of them in the water, some out of it. They looked enchanted.

Gary said to Lily, "I know where you're heading next."

"You do, do you?"

"There's only one place to be, in the end, isn't there, one last sight to see? You've got time, a few years left yet." He hugged her once more, and clambered down into his boat. They pulled on their oars and the boat slid away. "You just know she's going to be there."

"Who?"

He had to call back from the boat. "The disaster tourist's disaster tourist. Thandie Jones! Give her my love when you see her."

The boat receded, heading back toward the near-submerged Rockies. The raft children splashed and played in its wake, begging for coins. Lily heard Ana's thin voice calling for little Boris to come in.

96

May 2052

Boris was six years old now. And he wasn't much interested in some lump of rock that stuck out of the ocean. You saw lumps like that all over, just sticking out. He'd never actually *been* on one. Why would you want to? It wasn't a raft, it didn't go anywhere, you couldn't eat it, what use was it? The only unusual thing about this one was the flag on its pole on the summit, bright red, with a cute little gold design in the corner. But even that wasn't *very* interesting.

But he had to show an interest, he was told by his father Manco, for Grannie Lily was interested in it. And, his father pointed, look, there were other people interested too. Other rafts had come to sail around the rock, a gathering on the sea, all of them strangers, approaching this place. If they were all coming here there must be something worth seeing, mustn't there?

Lily sat in her chair, under her blanket, seventy-six years old, an age she called "impossible." Mostly she slept. When she was awake she watched the rock approach, a dot of stern darkness against the sparkling ocean, and Boris listened dutifully as Grannie Lily told him about the strange days when the world had been all rock and hardly any sea, and nobody swam or ate fish, not unless they wanted to. In those days, she said, this particular rock had had various names, old ones like Chu-mu-lang-ma, and young names like Everest. And it was special because this would soon be the *only* rock left sticking out of the ocean, anywhere in the world.

That impressed Boris, just a flicker, but so what? Even when the rock was underwater you could always swim down to see it if you really wanted to. However he put up with being cuddled and patted and told he was a good boy in the hope of getting a treat, a bit of dried fish or a coin. And he liked old Lily too, he really did, and not just for the treats she gave him.

After a time she would fall asleep again, mumbling, drooling a bit, and Boris would stay with her, occasionally wiping the spittle from her mouth.

Another raft approached, bigger than theirs, buoyed up by fat black tires, a ragged sail fluttering.

The people on this raft were dressed in the same faded blue coveralls Grannie Lily always wore. But Boris was a lot more interested in the kids he saw playing on the other raft. They had a tire hung up on a rope; you could climb on this thing, and swing on it, or even climb *through* it and sort of swim in the air.

Some of the people hopped over from the other raft and came up to Lily. They bent over her, and smiled.

Lily stirred, and flinched from the circle of faces. *"¿Como se llama usted? ¿Me puede ayudar, por favor? Me llamo—"*

"Lily. Lily, it's OK. It's me."

Lily opened her eyes, squinting. "Thandie? Thandie Jones . . . And Elena, it's lovely to see you. I was always so glad you two found each other. Never easy to find somebody in this world of ours, I know. You come from that submarine?"

"The *New Jersey*? No, ma'am. We were evicted when factions from the federal government took it over, in the final evacuation. Congressmen with their wives, children and mistresses. Now we're rafting, as you are. And what became of the *New Jersey* I've no idea."

Thandie and Elena bent down to inspect Boris. Thandie was dark and tall, Elena shorter, blond. They were both old, though not so old as Lily, not so old they couldn't walk around anymore. Thandie ruffled his hair. "And you must be Boris. Ain't you the cutest button?"

Lily said, "He's half Russian, a quarter English, and a quarter Quechua—*if* you believe what Ollantay said about himself."

"I bet he'd be proud to see his grandson whatever he was."

"Have you any coins?" Boris asked. "Do you do tricks?"

"Don't pester, Boris," Lily said.

A man stepped forward. "Hello, Lily Brooke."

"Jang—Jang Bahadur, it's you, isn't it? Well, you could knock me down. Still a handsome devil, aren't you?"

"And you are the light of my eye, Lily Brooke."

"Liar."

"He's been working for us, Lily," Thandie said. "Him and his son, anyhow."

"As a sherpa? Never went back to the law, eh?"

"Nobody needs lawyers." He gestured at the rock. "But look at that! Just my luck, there goes the last mountain and nobody needs sherpas either. I am out of a job again."

"You'll survive, if you survived the stalag that Tibet became. I always knew you would. That's gone now, hasn't it? Gone with all the rest and good riddance. And you survived to see this, the waters covering the very roof of the world."

"I am blessed—"

Lily went white, and clutched her chest. Thandie looked concerned. Boris's mother Ana came to stand by Lily, as she did at such times, and stroked her gray hair.

"So many questions," Lily said, whispering.

"I know, Lily," Thandie said, kneeling before her and facing her. "Maybe you should try to rest."

A gong sounded somewhere, off on another raft, the sound pealing over the water. "It's time," people called, from raft to raft. "It's time!" Everybody on all the rafts turned to the rock in the ocean.

Boris looked too. He saw that the water had risen, even while Thandie had been talking to Grannie Lily. Already there really wasn't much left of the rock, just a few outcroppings with the sea lapping around them. It was just a *rock*, Boris thought, exasperated. But his mother held firmly on to his hand. He wished it would just go ahead and drown and get it over so he could swim.

"Questions," Lily said, her voice a gasp. She beckoned to Thandie. "Listen. I saw Gary. We met. This is years ago. He said I'd find you here today. He sent his love."

Thandie kissed her cheek. "Thanks."

"He has this theory. About life on an ocean world. Storms and stuff. A new equilibrium."

Thandie snorted. "Gary's full of shit. He hasn't done any real science for thirty years. I love him dearly."

"But do you think, you know, it might be possible? Is that the future? Is that what it's all been about? Earth finding a new way to sustain life?"

"I don't know," Thandie said. "None of us knows."

That great gong rang again, and even Boris turned to watch the rock.

"And," Lily said, plucking at Thandie's sleeve, "and this, this is a good one. It keeps me awake at night. Well, lots of things keep me awake at night. Thandie, I sailed on Ark Three, myself. And I saw Ark One fly off, or I believe I did. But—"

A gust of wind brought the waves crashing over the rock, and for an instant it was covered entirely by the water. Even the flag got a soaking. The wave washed away, and the rock rose in the air again, but it was wet now and it obviously wasn't going to show for much longer.

Another wave broke. The rock didn't reappear. A kind of ragged cheer broke out across the rafts.

The moment was over. The little band of rafts began to break up. Everybody started talking about real things like fishing, and if it would rain today, turning their backs on the rock. Boris gazed at that tire swing, longing to try it out. It was the most wonderful thing he had ever seen.

Grannie Lily still plucked at Thandie's sleeve. "But," she whispered, "but, Thandie—*what is Ark Two*?"

Afterword

As noted in chapter 34, the literature of global floods goes back to Noah and beyond, and has continued to the present, including such examples as H.G. Wells's *All Aboard for Ararat* (1940) and Garrett P. Serviss's *The Second Deluge* (1912). The flood is an ur-myth of our culture.

But there have been suggestions that humans really may have witnessed enormous floods in the past. For instance, when the ice caps receded twenty thousand years ago the rising ocean broke through a natural dam in the Bosporus Strait to fill the present Black Sea in just a few years (see *Noah's Flood* by William Ryan and Walter Pitman, Simon and Schuster, 1998). Perhaps our flood legends are relics of real traumas in the past.

Meanwhile there is some evidence that the mantle, the deep rock layers of Earth's structure, may indeed contain lodes of water that would dwarf the existing oceans (see A.B. Thompson, "Water in the Earth's Upper Mantle," *Nature* vol. 358, pp. 295–302, 1992). Recently two American scientists have claimed from the evidence of seismic waves to have discovered an ocean locked in the porous rocks deep beneath Beijing (*New Scientist*, 10 March 2007), while scientists from Tokyo have observed the dragging-down of water at subduction zones (*Science*, 8 June 2007). New theories showing how worlds even close to their parent stars could form with immense lodes of water were reported at the 37th Lunar and Planetary Science Conference held in Texas in March 2006.

James Lovelock, in his *Gaia: A New Look at Life on Earth* (OUP, 1979), put forward the idea that the Earth is best understood as a self-regulating system with physical, chemical and biological components, a system with several stable states. A new stable state of a hot stormy flooded world (chapter 95) is my speculation, however, though it is extrapolated from conditions on Earth at times when the planet was dominated by a single supercontinent and a world ocean (see *Supercontinent* by Ted Nield, Granta, 2007).

The vulnerability of the UK to flooding events has been explored in a report by the Foresight program, run by the government's Office of Science and Technology (*Future Flooding*, 2004, www.foresight.gov.uk). The depiction of the flooding of London given here is extrapolated very loosely from the events of January-February 1953, which led eventually to the construction of the Thames Barrier. The most recent "London Flood Response Strategic Plan" was issued by the London Resilience Partnership task force in March 2007 (www.londonprepared.gov.uk/downloads/flood_response_plan.pdf).

I'm very grateful to Malcolm Burke of Sharperton Systems (www.sharpertonsystems.com) for assistance with research, and with the basis of the maps included in this volume.

The biblical quotations are from the King James Bible.

Any errors or inaccuracies are my sole responsibility.

Stephen Baxter
Northumberland
January 2008

ALSO AVAILABLE

FROM

Stephen Baxter

ARK

It's the year 2030. The oceans have risen rapidly, and soon the entire planet will be submerged. But hope has arisen with the discovery of another life-sustaining planet light years away.

Only a small number will be able to make the journey there, and Holle Groundwater is one of the candidates. If she makes the cut, she will survive. If not, she will be left to face a watery doom.

In desperate circumstances, the competition for survival can kill human compassion. And as Holle prepares to endure life aboard the Ark, she comes to realize that her attempt at escape may be more dangerous than trying to stay afloat on a drowning planet…

"One of the most inventive writers that science fiction has ever produced."
—SF Site

THE *NEW YORK TIMES*
BESTSELLER

from

S. M. Stirling

The Sword of the Lady

Rudi Mackenzie has journeyed far across the land that
was once the United States of America, hoping to find
the source of The Change. His final destination is
Nantucket, an island overrun with forest, inhabited by
a mere two hundred people who claim to have been
transported there from out of time.

Only one odd stone house remains standing. Within
it, Rudi finds a beautifully made sword waiting for
him—and once he takes it up, nothing will ever be
the same...

**"NOBODY WRECKS A WORLD BETTER
THAN S. M. STIRLING."**
—*New York Times* bestselling author
Harry Turtledove

Available wherever books are sold or at
penguin.com

THE ULTIMATE IN
SCIENCE FICTION AND FANTASY!

From magical tales of distant worlds to stories of
technological advances beyond the grasp of man, Penguin has
everything you need to stretch your imagination to its limits.

penguin.com

ACE
Get the latest information on favorites like
William Gibson, T.A. Barron, Brian Jacques,
Ursula K. Le Guin, Sharon Shinn, Charlaine Harris,
Patricia Briggs, and Marjorie M. Liu,
as well as updates on the best new authors.

ROC
Escape with Jim Butcher, Harry Turtledove, Anne Bishop,
S.M. Stirling, Simon R. Green, E.E. Knight, Kat Richardson,
Rachel Caine, and many others—plus news on the
latest and hottest in science fiction and fantasy.

DAW
Patrick Rothfuss, Mercedes Lackey, Kristen Britain,
Tanya Huff, Tad Williams, C.J. Cherryh, and many more—
DAW has something to satisfy the cravings of any
science fiction and fantasy lover.
Also visit dawbooks.com.

*Get the best of science fiction and fantasy
at your fingertips!*